Praise for Lisa Armstrong

'Brilliantly funny' *Heat*

'Lisa Armstrong has a wry eye, and what she saw was the zeitgeist . . . a merrily entertaining novel with an eerie finger on the pulse of everything modern . . . irresistibly funny' Victoria Mather, *Daily Mail*

'Great escapism' *Woman's Own*

'Wickedly funny' *Heat*

'Intelligent, witty blockbuster . . . a fast and very funny novel – with substance' *The Big Issue*

'A witty read with plenty of glamour' *Woman's Weekly*

'Deliciously funny' *Good Housekeeping*

'Lisa Armstrong has a witty way with words and some intelligent side-swipes to make' Maeve Haran, *Express*

'Fab' *Elle*

Also by Lisa Armstrong

Front Row
Dead Stylish

About the author

Lisa Armstrong became a journalist after graduating from Bristol University. She has worked on newspapers and magazines, and was Fashion Features Director of *Vogue* before becoming Style Editor at *The Times*. She lives in North London with her husband and two daughters.

LISA ARMSTRONG

Bad Manors

CORONET BOOKS
Hodder & Stoughton

Copyright © 2003 by Lisa Armstrong

First published in Great Britain in 2003 by Hodder & Stoughton
A division of Hodder Headline

The right of Lisa Armstrong to be identified as the Author
of the Work has been asserted by her in accordance with the
Copyright, Designs and Patents Act 1988.

5 7 9 10 8 6 4

A CIP catalogue record for this title is available from the British Library

ISBN 0 340 83731 4

Typeset in Plantin Light by
Phoenix Typesetting, Auldgirth, Dumfriesshire

Printed and bound in Great Britain by
Mackays of Chatham Ltd, Chatham, Kent

Hodder Headline's policy is to use papers that are natural, renewable
and recyclable products and made from wood grown in sustainable
forests. The logging and manufacturing processes are expected to
conform to the environmental regulations of the country of origin.

Hodder & Stoughton
A division of Hodder Headline
338 Euston Road
London NW1 3BH

To Jackson

ACKNOWLEDGEMENTS

For their unending patience, understanding, advice and innate tact about deadlines, and the author's indecision, Carolyn Mays, Jonathan Lloyd, Alex Bonham and Paul Hadaway. For telling me about blood groups in words I could more or less understand, Jonathan Boulton. For telling me about Dorset's oil, my mother and for telling me like it is Harriet Gugenheim. For sporadic cups of tea and Simpson updates Kitty and Flora. Lastly, for the seed that grew into *Bad Manors*, that fateful raffle ticket that whisked me away to my very own Butely.

I

'Have you sacked him?'

'Who?' Cat looked up guiltily from Candida St John Green's latest 'Rural Idyll' column and asked the question casually. As if she had an army of people at her disposal instead of one slippery builder. As if it were normal to be taking life lessons from a ten-year-old.

'Ralph.'

'Why would I want to sack him?' She was stalling for time. The chapter on firing people in *Machiavellian Rules: How to be an Alpha in Business* by D.F. Finkelstein and A. Marzotti recommended telling them on a Friday afternoon and convincing them that a lifestyle change had been their idea all along.

'Because it's been seven months and he still hasn't found where the damp in the kitchen's coming from. Jess thinks he's probably doing secret government work on the side.' Lily's crooked eyebrows corkscrewed up her forehead.

'And what would that be?'

'Collecting benefits. That's what Jess calls it. She also called Ralph a useless shi—'

'All right, Lily.' Three grand a term, thought Cat, and her daughter still couldn't tell the difference between useless shits and utter morons, which was what Ralph was.

'Well, have you?'

'No, Lily. I have not sacked Ralph.'

'Why?'

'Are you trying to humiliate me?'

'No. I—' Lily paused. She chose her next words carefully.

'He seems to make you quite angry, that's all.'

Pecked by remorse, Cat shifted in the dilapidated armchair to make room for her daughter and discovered Lily's electric tooth-brush, which had been missing for days down one of the sides. She started to giggle. Reassured, Lily returned to her original line of questioning.

'Is it just a phase, do you think? Or will you always be like this?'

'Like what?' Cat stroked her daughter's wild curls.

'Anti-men.'

'I am not anti-men.'

'You never have boyfriends.'

'You're meant to be pleased about that.'

'Are you?'

'I don't think about it.' It was almost true.

'Ralph would be your boyfriend if you wanted him to be.'

Cat looked at her daughter with a growing sense of foreboding.

'It's true. He's always staring at you. Especially when you wear that halter neck. It would mean you didn't have to pay him.'

'Lily! Look, the point is, Ralph's not really . . . my type. And in case you hadn't noticed, he's going out with Jess.'

'I'd hardly call it going out.' She stared at her mother search-ingly. 'The problem is, no one's your type. You hate my dad, you hate your dad—'

'I don't hate your father. And I never knew my father. You know that, Lily. If I had things might have been different.'

'How would they have been different?'

Cat looked at her daughter warily. Why was it that every conver-sation with Lily ended up going round in circles? She wanted to tell her that if she'd met her father at least she could have detested him from a position of knowledge. Instead she asked Lily whether she'd finished her homework and Lily said she would have finished it if only Ralph had got round to putting up the shelves in her bedroom.

How likely was Cat McGinty to succeed in life?

Cat leaned back in her not very comfortable swivel chair in her small but perfectly appointed glass cubicle on the Thrusting Young

Executives floor of Simms House and surveyed the open file on her screen. Cat liked – needed – files that organized her life. She'd compiled dozens over the years, constructed on the Simms' model. It made her feel in control. She looked at her sub-heading. It wasn't a McGinty classic. But it was okay.

All she had to do was answer it. She might as well. She'd received an e-mail an hour earlier requesting that she be on stand-by for an early evening meeting with the vice-presidents of Simms. This had not been accompanied by anything as specific as a precise time. So now she was killing time.

She got up to coax a coffee out of Simms' health-and-safety-standards-defying machine and tried not to look at the TV sets that were permanently switched to the world's news channels. She wasn't in the mood for Kirsty Young crinkling her large blue eyes in telegenic concern and crossing live to Washington from her sofa.

'Would you agree, Minister' – Kirsty's eyes crinkled telegenically – 'that the entire culture in which we raise our children needs a radical rethink if we are to avoid a generation of traumatised and unhappy teenagers . . . ?' She smiled and daintily rearranged her position. 'And would you say, Minister, that in most cases the parents are to blame?'

Cat tossed Kirsty an unhappy look – she was part of a growing army of women Cat found threateningly well groomed – and returned with half a cup of coffee to her exquisitely contoured desk, where she resumed typing.

Cat McGinty was this likely to succeed:

1. In four years she'd worked her way up from being a secretary to being a management consultant. A good one. When she'd arrived, Simms hadn't really had any clients in the media. While there was still a long way to go before the London office came close to the reputation the Simms media division had in New York, thanks to some work Cat had done on the Frupps empire they were starting to generate some buzz as an original, no-nonsense voice in that field.

2. She worked a sixty-hour week. Minimum. More if you counted the analysis done in her sleep. If this was France they'd

have had her up in the European Court for breaching her own human rights.

3.   She had never used the internal e-mail to a) get rid of unwanted tickets, b) tell a lame joke, c) ask whether anyone had found her keys.

4.   She had been informed at the last office party by one of the seven vice-presidents in London that she was tipped for the top. Actually he had said she was so rational he sometimes forgot she wasn't a man.

5.   She always cleared her desk by the end of the week.

6.   She never cried in the office, even when she'd missed Lily's sports day. Not *in* the office. Not at her desk. In fact, not complaining was one of Cat's defining traits (*Machiavellian Rules* was very unambiguous on the need to develop defining traits).

On the downside – in the interests of completing a professional case study of herself, Cat had decided to include a debit column – she wasn't seeing an awful lot of Lily. Strictly speaking, she only managed to clear her desk every Friday by taking most of it home with her for the weekend. She rang Lily every night at bedtime to touch base, which was modern if you like that sort of thing. Lily unfortunately didn't. Even Cat could see there was a certain physical dimension lacking in the transaction.

Also in the debit column, she didn't have much of a social life. But as recommended in *Machiavellian Rules*, she never whinged, not even about her salary, even though every man at her level was on twenty per cent more.

She stretched and glanced at the clock on the wall: 6.20 p.m. Just time to collate some more analysis on the Cat McGinty project. She wrote down *Sex*, underlined it and looked at the clock again: 6.20, still. Time for another coffee.

Cat couldn't remember the last time she'd had sex. But then technically speaking she couldn't remember ever having had the great I'm-leaving-you conversation either, even though it had made a pretty big impact on everything that had happened since. Technically speaking, Ben had just been going to Malaysia for a few months to 'y'know, take syncopated jazz to the world'. At the time of his departure Cat assumed it was a fairly harmless late-youth crisis which, being Ben's late-youth crisis, inevitably entailed going somewhere hot with his mates.

When it became clear he probably wasn't coming back, she'd wondered whether it was divine retribution for the times she'd acci-dentally on purpose forgotten to renew the Amnesty standing order she'd been shamed into filling in outside the Piccadilly branch of Tower Records. She hadn't told Ben about that. She knew he'd never understand how anyone could refuse to support oppressed minorities when they'd just squandered £13.99 on Simply Red. She didn't even like Mick Hucknall, but the more Ben disapproved the bigger the urge to buy *A New Flame*.

Later – about four years later – she realised that Ben's walking out was the best thing that ever happened to her and Lily. At least it had forced her to take her career more seriously. Before Ben left her, she'd coasted along on a series of desultory jobs – editorial assistant in a publishing company (shocking pay); coordinator of a charitable foundation that rented out listed buildings to rich visiting Americans, mainly from East Coast college towns (pay slightly better until the visiting Americans discovered Prague). Nothing that had overly taxed her, but with Ben and a baby to look after, she'd reasoned, she had enough on her plate.

If you love someone, let them go, Sting said. So she had and they'd gone. Sting hadn't had a riposte for that. Not even a chorus. So perhaps Ben had been right about him all along.

The console on her desk lit up like a fruit machine. Cat sighed. She'd been avoiding the call all day but only with the wearying knowledge that she'd have to take it eventually. Yesterday her mother's counsel on being foxy had been more explicit than usual – normally she tried to slip advice about Kegel exercises and control tights in between bouts of feminist solidarity. Cat braced herself for the next round and picked up line one.

'Hello, Mommie Dearest.'

'Ha ha. Very droll. Have you sent it, then?'

'Not yet.' Cat squinted at Kirsty Young's half-fringe and

wondered whether she should get one. 'I'm still refining one or two details.'

'What details?'

'My life. I'm reassessing it.'

There was a heartbroken sigh in Manhattan, which was over-doing it in Cat's view. Her life wasn't that much of a disaster. But then Suzette thought that Jessica Lange, holed up with Sam Shepard, was a tragic recluse. 'Cat, it's been six months. At this rate they're never going to take you seriously. You have to put your feelings about the place in writing. Make it official. And if that doesn't work then go somewhere they do appreciate you. Your pay packet's a joke.'

Cat sipped some lukewarm coffee. She was wounded by her mother's disparaging reference to her salary, which in the grand scheme of things wasn't that bad. Not wishing to find herself in the somewhat irrational position of arguing against her own rise, however, she resisted any form of direct response.

'The publishing deal's gone brilliantly. Herr Frupps wrote me a letter himself. He said without me they'd never have got round that indecency charge.' He'd also said that if she were a man she'd have been a junior vice-president by now. 'So someone appreciates me, thank God.'

'I wouldn't waste your time thanking God,' retorted Suzette. 'Unlike you, He still gets a bit of credit for what he does. You must be very proud of your work in the pornography industry,' she continued, unaware of causing any offence. 'Did you go to Syrie's, by the way? Oh, hang on, I've got a line thingie waiting. Call you in the morning.'

As far as Cat could make out, her mother's position as Style Director of the *New York Clarion*, where she wrote a column called 'In touch with Fashion', mostly entailed getting completely out of touch with reality. By Cat's reckoning, Suzette hadn't paid for an item of clothing since 1976. To be fair, she was generous with her freebies. The (American) size-four sample dresses went straight into Lily's dressing-up box. The shoes, which according to Suzette's columns were foxy in the extreme, sat in Cat's wardrobe like little phallic sculptures – poignant statues commemorating her non-existent social life. Or they had done in Ben's day. Now she wore them all the time – the more inappropriately the better – as an ironic nod to her inner fox, should she ever turn out to have one. They certainly spiced up the suits she wore. Cat always wore a suit to work. Simms valued a sense of corporate unity in its nine thousand employees. Suzette said she was in danger of looking like an extra from *LA Law*.

But that didn't stop the flow of freebies. Which is how Cat had found herself at Syrie's, waxer to the stars.

Syrie Kuchinsky had a gleaming 'studio' off Knightsbridge and the kind of plumped-up, lineless skin Cat had only hitherto encountered on overcooked rice. Suzette had told Cat that Syrie was in need of some business advice about expanding her personal beauty system to the stars into a chain for the plebs. She'd also said that in order to understand what was so special about Syrie's beauty system, Cat needed to try it out for herself. Later, of course, Cat realised it was just another of Suzette's ruses to keep her in shape for any putative men that might stray into her life.

'Playboy, Brazilian or Thong?' demanded Syrie from behind a white surgical mask.

Cat had come to Syrie's partly to escape having to make decisions for an hour. She wondered what a Playboy looked like. Syrie's eyes acquired a hard glint.

'Do you want a landing strip, internal works or the whole lot?'

If Cat had had any idea quite how agonising any of the options were, she would never have agreed to visit Syrie's in the first place.

Syrie began obsessively combing and trimming. She called it erotic topiary. Cat thought it was more like My Little Pony for adults.

The waxing proper passed in a daze of acute pain. 'Why don't you supply epidurals?' Cat moaned at one point.

Syrie smiled behind the mask. At least, from the smudge of cranberry lipstick that appeared on the inside of the gauze, Cat assumed it was a smile. She looked down at her blotchy skin, once discreetly veiled behind a sweet little thatch. Talk about an *anus horribile*.

'Don't worry, it's worth it,' said Syrie. 'All my clients tell me how much their men love it afterwards.' She slapped some cold cream on to the rash, which had turned a spectacular shade of purple. 'Of course, the Playboy's best. But Brazilian's okay too. At the very least you'll get a diamond ring out of it.'

Cat sat up in outraged indignation. Not that it was easy to tell, but Syrie was probably about the same age as her mother and Germaine Greer. What a betrayal of the sisterhood. 'I buy my own jewellery,' she said disdainfully.

Syrie cast a look at Cat's ringless fingers and tossed her a pitying smile. 'So you do, dear.'

That was absolutely the last time Cat followed one of Suzette's business leads. Not that Suzette didn't have a sound commercial head when it suited her. For reasons Cat had never been able to fathom, 'In Touch with Fashion' had been clasped to America's bosom, syndicated across the nation and reheated in a series of fabulously successful books with names like *Dress for Success*, *Dress to Impress*, *Dress for Less*, each title carefully selected to fit the pre-occupations of the moment. All of them had sat on the *New York Times* best-seller list for months. And then, two years ago, she'd outsold the lot with a hardbound glossy load of rubbish entitled *Emotionally Intelligent Dressing*. Success had come far too easily to Suzette.

It was 7 p.m. Cat scrolled down her screen, bypassing the *Sex* heading and making a new one: *Mitigating Circumstances*.

At half past seven there was a persistent strobing on line two. It was Wilhelm Frupps – Kaiser Vill to his enemies, who were numerous – calling to thank her for the latest work she'd done on the ad campaign for a new fortnightly magazine he was publishing. Strictly speaking, copywriting was way beyond Cat's brief, but the tag lines the ad agency had come up with had been so feeble that Cat hadn't been able to resist improving them.

In the end she'd rewritten the whole ad. It was easy, really, given that the entire magazine had been her concept in the first place. Kaiser Vill had been looking to expand into what he called the highbrow end of the market for some time, having happily made a fortune out of the pornographic end of it. The history of the world seemed an obvious – indeed blameless – choice to Cat. Kaiser Vill thought she was a genius. Her ads – classy black-and-white montages of racially diverse children, athletes, twinkly old people and down-and-outs, all discovering the joy of knowledge through Villi's magazine serialisations (parts one to three came with a free DIY family tree CD-ROM, which Cat supposed the homeless could always use as a frisbee to amuse their dogs) hit the mark. She'd even come up with some copy lines, among which 'It Makes You Think' had almost brought on one of his asthma attacks.

'I am so thrilled with everything you have been doing,' he wheezed over the phone. 'I want you to know that any time you want to come and work in Hamburg there is an in-house job waiting for you.' There was a pause while Cat searched for a suitably diplomatic response. 'And a company BMW,' he added. 'Conwertible. Three series.'

'That's very kind, Herr Frupps—'

'Villie, please.'

'But I have family commitments here and—' She'd told him she had a sick mother, which wasn't technically a lie.

From the other end of the line in Hamburg came the distinct sound of a brow being mopped. 'I understand,' he said hurriedly. 'But I think you should know, Cat, that you are wasted at Simms. They are not a company that supports women. And if, *Gott in Himmel* forbid, you ever had a child, you would be *kaput*. Promise me you'll think about the BMW . . .'

He trailed off. Cat needed to bring the conversation to a close. She was never going to get home before bedtime – Lily's or her own – at this rate.

'Cat?' He was off again. 'I know that we've never met but you have a marvellous woice, you know. Wery warm. I have this strongest feeling that we would really be getting on if we were meeting.'

Even surveying the desolate desert that was her romantic life, Cat couldn't summon up enthusiasm for a liaison with Kaiser Vill. Especially not with Mrs Kaiser Vill still such a prominent part of his landscape. Fortunately, like a gift from heaven, a message flashed up on her screen summoning her to the eleventh floor of Simms House. Immediately.

No one was ever summoned to the eleventh floor unless it was to be fired – or promoted. The upper echelons at Simms managed by evasion. Irksome e-mails – including any from Cat outlining why she was worth a rise and a car – were routinely ignored until the sender gave up.

So Cat's relief at escaping Kaiser Vill's clutches was short lived. Screwing her courage to the sticking place and violently yanking her skirt round so that the zip wasn't running down the front of her crotch, she took half her tights, which were caught in the zip, with it. Damn, now she'd have to face the Vices with bare legs that sported so much undergrowth there was a real danger Sting might start campaigning for their preservation – in the unlikely event that he ever stumbled over them.

She went to the loo for a quick outfit rethink. Unhappy and trau-matised teenagers were obviously the hot issue of the day. Up on the screens that flanked the mirrors, they were still being discussed on the eight o'clock news bulletins. Cat tried not to listen. It wasn't as if she hadn't tried to get a proper nanny. But on her wages it was never going to happen. The Angels of Mercy Agency in Knightsbridge had been quite frank when Cat had rung looking for help. 'To be honest, I don't think you're quite ready for a nanny,' the MD had told her. 'Where did you say you lived?'

'West Kilburn,' said Cat, feeling more miserable by the moment. 'K.I.—'

'Which part of the country is that?' The deliberate obtuseness was starting to grate on Cat.

'London. NW10,' she said politely.

There was an epoch-defining silence while the woman grappled with disbelief that such a postal code existed. 'Ah, well, that's it, then,' she said conclusively. 'Ours are strictly number-one girls, you see. That's W1, SW1 and, at a pinch, N1, but only since Tony and Cherie.'

For celestial beings, the Angels of Mercy turned out to be remarkably dependent on being given their own cars to drive – 'automatic, preferably of the German variety' – and a net income that would have left Cat with about ten pence a week to live on, after she'd finished haemorrhaging money into the house.

Then, in her darkest hour, Jessamy Hutton had turned up, not so much an Angel of Mercy as a Sister of Satan. Her Goth period had been in its first flush then. Armed with three duffel bags, a highly suspicious-looking visa and a map someone back in Melbourne had drawn purportedly showing where Robbie Williams's house was, she wasn't exactly Norland nanny material. But she was, just about, in Cat's league.

At one point – when Jess had crashed Cat's ancient Polo and admitted that she didn't, as such, have a driving licence because she hadn't, as such, taken a test – Cat didn't think it was going to work out at all. She'd resolved to replace Jess and her customised ripped T-shirts with Come and Get Me unevenly felt-tipped across her ample breasts, just as soon as she could afford to get a proper Angel of Mercy.

But as the years rolled on, Jess and her mysteriously 'open-ended' visa had become seemingly immovable fixtures. Lily for one was thrilled. And if Lily was happy, then so, more or less, was Cat.

She took off her tights. In her experience men – i.e. Ben – never noticed hairy legs, focusing instead on what they called the Bigger Picture. As an afterthought she stuffed the tights in her bra in the hope that it would improve her Bigger Picture. Or at least just make it bigger.

The lift whooshed up to the eleventh floor in less time than it took Cat to open the temperamental front door at home. She stepped out on to miles of monogrammed charcoal stone, her eyes adjusting to the low lighting, her ears to the very expensive hum of almost but not quite silent air conditioning, and headed for Room 7b.

She rarely got this far up Simms House, but when she did she was always struck by the boy-racer luxury of it all. Not that the rest of Simms House was a slum, but it hadn't been designed with the bespoke attention to detail, harmony and ayurverdic flow that the penthouse floor had been. Tugging her jacket down, she knocked on the double doors of 7b nervously, attempted another CNN smile and decided not to wait for a 'Come in'.

The door opened from the inside just as she was pressing against it, and she found herself stumbling into a tiny rock pool of Salvadorean pebbles from which flowed a tiny but perceptible trickle of purified water.

The rest of the room was pared down, or pitifully bare, depending on your taste. A bronze statue of a dolphin, erected in all the Vices' offices by Simms's feng shui consultants, held court over a leather Eames chair (the size of a small van) and a desk. At least, Cat assumed, from its position in the centre, that it was a desk. What it looked like was a sheet of Sellotape hanging from the ceiling on some metal wire. On it was etched, in customised emerald ink, an enormous dollar bill. This was the interior decorator's proudest flourish. Each Vice had a different currency. The Vices themselves were nowhere to be seen. Instead, a complete stranger leaned back in the Eames, as if trying it on for size.

'Hi.'

'Hi.' Cat hauled her skirt round again, taking in the slim black utilitarian chic suit and dazzling smile. She smiled back uncertainly as he approached.

'Toby Marks.' He took her hand firmly in both of his and looked her candidly up and down before marching towards the floating Sellotape, on top of which sat a bottle of Krug in a titanium ice bucket.

'Cat McGinty,' she said, racking her memory bank. She'd heard of Toby Marks. He was something of a legend at Simms, having been packed off to the States a couple of years earlier, just before Cat had been relocated to the Thrusting Young Executives floor. She knew the type – grating, bumptious. Probably thought he was a master of the universe just because he'd had a good run in New York. She felt the tights scratching her nipples.

He settled back into the Eames chair again and gestured at her to sit down. Primly she perched on the concrete ledge that clung to three of the walls and wondered whether her legs would look marginally less hairy crossed or uncrossed.

'Perry asked me to apologise on behalf of all the Vices.' His eyes continued to rake her up and down. So, not only was he about to edge in on the patch she'd carved out for herself – a pleasant spot where she'd more or less been left to her own devices – he was going to sexually harass her. 'They all suddenly got called away. Urgent troubleshooting at the Hornlake Hotel consortium. Apparently the kitchen staff are revolting.'

Was this a joke? If so was a full-throated guffaw required? Or would a smile do the trick? Humour was not a noticeable part of daily dialogue at Simms. Cat cast a sideways glance to check out his expression. About six feet one. Way taller than Ben. Curly black hair that just brushed the collar of his fashionably colourful shirt. Expensive suit. No tie, which made him a rebel by Simms standards. Tall, dark and a handful, then.

Cat tried to maintain a killer composure while he poured some Krug into a couple of glasses and handed her one. 'I jest. It doesn't take three Vices to improve a hotel chain. Three of them have had to go to a meeting in Paris. Air France,' he added conspiratorially. Cat nodded knowingly, although she didn't have a clue whether he was referring to their mode of transport or a potentially huge new account. 'The others are in a video conference with LA. Steven Spielberg's thinking of merging with Disney. So I'm office-squatting. And very nice it is too, I must say.' He nodded towards the views across Regent's Park. 'Love the shoes, by the way. Manolos, are they?'

Cat nodded dismissively. Toby Marks looked impressed.

'They're very sorry to miss you. They all wanted to congratulate you in person on your brilliant coup with the Frupps ads and –' He paused, looking at her uncertainly. '– to introduce us.'

Embarrassed by the twinkling intensity of his gaze, Cat took a gulp of champagne and tried to work out what tactic to adopt. She settled for silent inscrutability.

Toby Marks's scorching grin shrank marginally. 'I've been hearing a lot about you. You're seen as a bit of a hotshot—'

Cat blushed, suddenly feeling part of a wonderful world where Tube delays and relying on her mother to plug up the holes in her constantly leaking bank account were distant memories. A world in which blasted concrete and water features that didn't consist of rising damp were part of her working environment.

'Which is why I'm so flattered that they want us to work on Frupps together from now on.'

Alarm bells began ringing so loudly in Cat's head she thought he was bound to hear. 'What do you mean?' She gulped some more Krug. Frupps was her baby, a project that had started out small and become an increasingly significant slice of Simms's domestic turnover the longer she'd worked on it. Not that she'd got much credit from the Vices. Now they clearly thought she needed help, which must mean her P45 was only a matter of time.

Toby Marks tapped the tip of the dollar sign. 'Those slogans you came up with – genius. Especially "It Makes You Think".' Cat flushed. Why was she the only one who thought they were weren't remotely genius? Or perhaps she wasn't. Perhaps Toby Marks was already plotting her downfall.

'Thanks to you,' he continued, 'Frupps is about to make a long-term commitment to Simms. We're going to need a much bigger team.' He paused again. 'Headed by you and me.' He picked up the bottle of Krug and poured another glass. 'Any problems with staying on a bit later tonight?'

Cat wanted to tell the devastating – if conventionally – good-looking stranger in front of her that of course there was bloody well a problem. Numero uno being that she'd already put in a ten-hour day. Numero two, she wasn't accustomed to being passed over in favour of smooth, too-handsome-by-far career bastards who clearly just wanted to pick her brains. Numero three, she had a child to nurture, educate and set a rounded example to. She wanted to tell Toby all this. But catching the overwhelming wattage of his smile – and feeling the hand of fear grip her stomach – she had another idea.

'That'll be fine.' She smiled weakly. 'I'll just need to make a quick call.'

'Let me guess. You're going to be really, *really* late.'

'Come on, Jess, don't give me a hard time.'

There was a punishing silence.

'Lily was really looking forward to watching *Animal Rescue*,' said Jess eventually.

'I know,' said Cat quietly. *Animal Rescue* was an integral part of the fantasy she and Lily shared about moving to the country. 'But things are going to change. I promise.'

'Followed by *Dinner in Devon* and *The River Cottage Year*.'

'I know, I know,' said Cat.

'Have you finished your case study yet?'

'Not you as well.' She might as well move in with Claire Rayner.

'It's for your own good.' There was a moment or two's stand-off at the end of which Jess caved in. 'I'll go and get Lily.'

Cat reached for her glass of Krug. She could hear Jess's bondage boots stomping upstairs. Eventually Lily came on the line.

'Hi, Mum.'

'Hi, Lil. Are you ready for your story?'

'It's okay, don't worry. You sound tired. It's probably better if you spend the time working so you can get home sooner. It's not as if I can't read myself anyway.'

'I know. It's just that I know you like being read to. And I like reading to you,' she added.

'It's okay, honestly. I'd prefer it if you weren't always coming home in the dark. It's dangerous.'

'Okay. If you're sure. But I'm not going to be back until really late. You might be asleep.'

'That's okay. And Mum?'

'Yes?'

'Promise me you'll take a taxi.'

It was her ten-year-old daughter's stoicism which broke Cat's heart every time. When it came down to it, it wasn't the juggling till your hands bled which was the downside in all this. The downside was hoping you were a good mother and then settling for not actively being a terrible one.

Two hours, one champagne bottle and thirteen buff files of Frupps facts and figures later, the lift swooped Cat and Toby down to the underground car park, stopping only briefly on the sixth floor for Cat to pick up her documents case and coat. She felt light headed. It was such a novelty to work with someone who seemed to be on exactly the same wavelength, albeit several miles farther along it. She was so exhilarated she'd forgotten that she didn't even have a company car, until Toby offered to walk her to it.

'We'll have to see what we can do about that,' he said, stepping to one side so she could exit the lift in front of him. Ben would have managed to bash into her with a cello or at the very least a triangle. And then jam the lift doors. 'It's the very least a woman of your talents should expect from her package.'

Cat wondered exactly what Toby had in his. A platinum American Express card at the very least, to judge by his suit and the Louis Vuitton briefcase.

'And in the meantime, I'll run you home.'

'Don't be silly, it's miles out of your way,' said Cat weakly, wishing she hadn't established that Toby lived in Hoxton because then she could have accepted his offer without a twinge. 'I'll get a taxi.'

'Like hell you will. At nine o'clock during late-night shopping on Oxford Street!'

As they walked to his car, a shiny navy blue Porsche – quite a big package, then – Cat felt a little stab of envy. And something else which may or may not have been anticipated pleasure. It was so long since she'd had any she couldn't be sure. The really enjoyable aspect of the next twenty minutes was that Toby Marks was so clearly not her type she could sit back and enjoy a little sophisticated, adult, urban banter with the clearest of consciences.

'Glad you've seen sense,' said Toby, walking over to her side and opening the door for her. 'About the lift, I mean. It gives us that bit more time to discuss Frupps's top-shelf magazines. Where do you stand on *Big Girls Do It Better*, by the way?'

2

'Did you really come up with the slogans on your own?

Cat fiddled nervously with the glove compartment as the Porsche growled towards 15 Makesbury Road, praying that for once the grease-sozzled fish-and-chip wrappers from In Cod We Trust, the local chippie, hadn't draped themselves round the lamp-post in front of her house.

She nodded. Toby eyed her admiringly. 'Genius.' There had been remarkably little traffic. That combined with Toby's encyclo-pedic knowledge of back routes and the very expensive-sounding speakers inserted into every inch of spare surface of his car meant the journey from Oxford Street to Kensal Rise was over far too quickly.

He certainly knew his stuff. It turned out that while he'd been making waves on the second-largest media takeover deal in US history for Simms he'd also done some work on a foundering wholefood business in New York. In less than eighteen months he'd helped turn it into America's third-largest fast food chain – while also finding time to keep up with all the most depressing art house movies and impossible-to-get-to theatre productions.

Cat's last trip to the cinema had been to see *Ice Age* for Lily's birthday, which reminded her that Lily's next birthday was imminent. She sank into the buttery leather interior, allowed herself to be enveloped in the soaring surge of Wagner – Toby liked his music amazingly loud – and tried to think of something nice to do for Lily's party that would meet her friends' exacting standards without necessitating a loan from the IMF. Against the clash of cymbals, Toby moved from a Polish film about Solidarity he'd recently seen to the subject of pulses, air – especially air – and soya compounds. More extraordinarily still, he made it all sound fascinating.

'The big mistake people make in business these days is giving the consumer sodding great portions. There's too much of everything. It's overwhelming.'

She sneaked a surreptitious look to check whether he was teasing her again.

'They're obsessed with bunging in more and more and selling it for less when really the secret is to put less and less in and charge more.'

'And how do you do that?'

'Okay. Take portions –' A tramp weaved drunkenly out on to a zebra crossing in front of them. Toby honked his horn loudly, startling the tramp almost into sobriety, and put his foot down. 'At the fast food chain we halved their sizes, called them Diet Zone and put the price up by fifty per cent.'

'Commendable.' She threw in a worldly laugh.

'You don't believe me, do you?'

She experimented with an enigmatic smile. Telling him he sounded like an amoral shit seemed terribly provincial somehow.

'It's business. Look, ingredients, especially in food, are dirt cheap in the twenty-first century. And with good reason. For the most part they're crap. So you're not doing the customer any big favour by just giving them more and more.' He tapped his forehead. 'It's the thought that goes into it that costs now. We did a soya spread that had three times the amount of air in it compared with all the others on the market. We called it Pure and made it fifty per cent more expensive than its nearest competitor – we sold the same number, for three hundred and fifty times more profit.'

'Was it GM'd?'

'I bloody hope so.' He chuckled. 'Organic. Purity. Authenticity – they're meaningless buzz words for the middle classes, Cat. Everyone else wants cheap, fast and filling. We have a moral duty to give people a choice and not get caught up in snobbish, *Guardian*-type values. It's all about having a Defining Trait. Makes the product stand out. It's good to have one at work too.'

'What's yours, then?' asked Cat, intrigued.

He pressed his foot down and smiled. 'Smooth bastard. What's yours?'

Cat panicked. Was it really possible to be someone with absolutely no Defining Trait? Even her cat Seamus had one. Bloody Expensive. Fortunately they were coming into Kensal Rise – or Kensal Sinking, as Cat liked to think of it – and she had to give directions.

By the time they'd crossed the Harrow Road, Cat had decided Toby was the most amoral man she'd ever met. She just hoped she managed to remember everything he'd said until after she'd got inside, given Lily a goodnight kiss, listened to Jess's Byzantine account of the day, and got to her Palm Pilot.

As they purred into Makesbury Road she offered a silent prayer of thanks that it was dark. Preston, the estate agent at Fiend and Duffer's, had sold her the house when she was eight months pregnant on the grounds that it was deceptively spacious. But despite Preston's many predictions about the area being an up-and-coming hot spot, Makesbury Road had stubbornly refused to rise. Fortunately the streetlights were on the blink again and the entire road was shrouded in faltering chiaroscuro. Number 15 was a pretty enough terraced house, oozing what estate agents carefully referred to as idiosyncratic charm. But the road in general was sadly let down by what the interior magazines referred to as unsuccessful window treatments. She looked up to see whether the manic depressive in number 11 was home and whether he was on a high. You could generally tell because he switched on all his flashing Christmas lights, even in July. This time of year, however, it was harder to judge. Year-round illuminations were, she supposed, along with his liberal views on personal hygiene, his chief Defining Trait. Just as the pungent aroma hanging heavily outside number 19 was the Defining Trait of Makesbury Road's resident pot-heads.

'Here was are,' she announced with as much nonchalance as she could muster. Cat had had great plans for number 15 in the beginning. On the strength of Candida St John Green's 'Rural Idyll' column in the *Sunday Telegraph*, which Cat secretly devoured, she had planted enough foxglove, hellebore, borage and pansy seeds to recreate Sissinghurst. The only cultivation that really seemed to thrive there, however, were endless butt-ends and slips of Cellophane that got drunkenly tossed over the patchy hedge. Chatsworth it was not. Even though Ralph had been lurking around intermittently for two years, the place was still what the more charitable glossies might call a work in progress; though there wasn't much work happening on it and what little there was could hardly be defined as progress. Occasionally, after a marathon session with the Sunday supplements, she longed for plumped-up cushions and rooms painted with colours that had names like Old Wainscotting. Tonight she would simply have settled for Not Peeling.

The black rain hurled from the skies in horizontal sheets, possibly lending the street, thought Cat in a moment of wild optimism, a sort of bohemian appeal. In the meantime, to invite Toby in or not. That really was one hell of a question.

From a professional point of view she should at least make the gesture. On the other hand, assuming that Ralph hadn't pulled a miracle that day and actually done something, such as nailing down the stair runner, or that four years of slipshod housework hadn't rearranged themselves into a semblance of domestic order in the last eight hours, it would be an unnecessarily foolhardy move. There was also the not irrelevant matter of Lily. If Cat invited Toby in, in addition to explaining why there was a child's bike in the hall, she would have to explain why there was also a child. A child whom she had so far failed to allude to at all – which would, she supposed, make her defining trait forgetfulness . . . No, all things considered, inviting Toby in was a non-starter. He parked the car and switched off the engine expectantly. But perhaps it was just so that he could get out and open the passenger door for her. No one had ever done that for Cat before, Ben's passenger door not actually functioning as a door, as such.

'Looks like you've got visitors.' He nodded towards the porch, where Lily's bobble hat was outlined against the glass window of the door, next to Jess's doom-laden figure and an outline of Seamus.

Cat scrambled out of the car, dodging the carpet-bombing of pigeon droppings on the pavement. As if the turmoil caused by not knowing how to deal with the Toby question wasn't enough, she was now in a complete panic over Lily. Why wasn't she in bed? And why was she wearing her bobble hat? The central heating must have broken down again. And how was she going to instruct Lily to pretend to be her niece without Toby hearing? Heart pounding, she raced up the front path and almost tripped over Seamus, who, startled by her rapid approach, had leapt out of Lily's arms and was now bolting towards the dope dealers' house.

'Mum, look what you've done,' said Lily accusingly. Cat coughed loudly and tried to signal to Lily not to repeat the M word.

'We were just on our way to the vet's,' said Jess, her wonky black eyeliner making her look even more mournful than usual.

'At half past nine at night?' Cat couldn't keep the bitterness out of her voice. Seamus ran up more medical bills than Elizabeth Taylor.

'Now we won't see him for hours,' said Lily, her voice wobbling dangerously.

'He's been throwing up all day,' said Jess balefully.

'Is this what you're looking for?' Toby dived into the under-growth of number 19's unruly privet and emerged with Seamus's eerily compliant body stretched out in his arms. He looked un-cannily like Burt Lancaster surging through the surf with Deborah Kerr.

'He seems a bit disoriented, or is he always like that?' To give him credit he sounded genuinely interested. He knelt down beside Lily, who hugged Seamus as if he'd just returned from an expedition to Antarctica.

'We think he's got flu,' offered Lily.

'Or cancer,' added Jess.

Imaginary vet's bills circled in front of Cat like carrion. She caught sight of Lily's small anxious face and immediately felt guilty. Her daughter nearly always had a concerned expression on her face these days.

'How awful for the poor old chap,' said Toby. Cat looked at him suspiciously. Not entirely heartless, then.

'We've probably missed the night bus now,' said Jess.

Cat rolled her eyes in the darkness. Why, all of a sudden, had Jess lost her capacity to drive the Polo?

'Well, we can't have that, can we?' said Toby, standing up. 'Allow me.' He held out his arm to Lily and lead her towards his car. 'Toby Marks at your service.'

Cat stared at his receding back in awe. Since when had knights on platinum charge accounts existed? And since when did Lily waltz off with the first good-looking man who roared up in a Porsche? She would have to have words with her daughter. In about thirty years.

Since Seamus certainly hadn't looked his best in the strip lighting of the vet's surgery, it was safe to assume she looked a sight as well. To add insult to multitudinous injuries, Cat was forced to acknowledge that Seamus's eyelid did indeed appear to be twitching ominously.

The new vet in the West Kilburn Domestic Pet Practice was, it seemed to Cat, absurdly young, absurdly cheerful and much given to trying out alternative treatments on his largely uncomplaining patients. It took him forty-five minutes to work his way through two rabbits and a three-legged Jack Russell who seemed to be suffering from a sexual disorder.

Eventually he got to Seamus, no thanks to an old lady who'd queue-barged in front of them with an off-colour goldfish and an affronted-looking woman in a Boden moleskin jacket that Cat had repeatedly imagined herself wearing in her other, Rural Idyll, life, who kept telling everyone she really ought to be halfway to Norfolk by now. She was the owner of the sexually deviant Jack Russell, which had had a complete turn just as she was trying to load the family into the car for the weekend trip to their country house. 'As if I didn't have enough to do.' She scowled at Cat in accusation.

'He hasn't been the same since *Big Brother 3* finished,' the old lady with the goldfish said to Toby sadly.

Seamus, needless to say, didn't have flu or cancer, but was merely, in Mr Harrison's view, under the weather. Cat would give him under the weather. Mr Harrison, meanwhile, gave Seamus a cranial massage and, while he was lulled into a full sense of security, a flu injection. He prescribed some herbal drops, two sacks of Hills science food and asked Cat for £120. Then they all wedged into the Porsche again and whizzed back through the streets of West Kilburn.

On reflection, Cat was relieved that Toby had zoomed off into the night almost immediately upon delivering them all safely back to number 15. Especially when she opened the door and swung into a basket of washing that Jess had been in the middle of doing something with when Seamus's eye had swollen up. Not even clean washing, noticed Cat, reaching for the roll of deodorant she had left by the phone in the hall that morning and stuffing it into her briefcase along with the newspaper she'd been meaning to read all day. It was fair to say that the only way Cat held it all so admirably together at work was by allowing it to fall completely apart at home.

'Stir-fry?' Jess bustled past her into the kitchen. 'I've been experimenting with sunflower seeds. They're very good in the fight against heart disease.'

Cat pulled out her copy of the *Guardian*, inside which was an article entitled 'Au Pairs: The New Slavery'? She stuffed it back in her briefcase, though a much safer place would have been the oven, now that Jess had taken to frying everything to a pulp rather than incinerating it.

She sighed. Much as Cat loved the idea of cooking, in practice her domestic deification was confined to the copy of Nigel Slater's *Appetite* she kept by her bed under the pile of old Candida St John Greens. Even on a good day, she was mostly too tired to read all the way to the end of a single recipe, though she dearly wanted to be the kind of woman who could oversee an international merger by day and nurture her family with wholesome, nourishing 'social' glue. It was left to Jess to provide number 15's social glue. And glue was what it resembled – on days when it didn't look like *Lord of the Rings* special effects. These were more and more frequent now that Jess had joined the enterprise culture and was supplementing the salary Cat paid her by working shifts in the vegan café at the Karma Factory, the local yoga centre. And so Cat and Lily pretended to eat what Jess put in front of them while secretly living off a supply of Sainsbury's Blue Parrot Café ready-meals that were kept in an old freezer in the shed at the bottom of the garden.

Exhausted, she watched Jess clattering among a forest of saucepan handles that jutted out lethally from the oven hob like Spitfire propellers, each one transmitting volcanic degrees of heat, and wondered when she'd get a chance to nip down to the shed. Fortunately the phone rang. Jess darted into the hall. Reflecting that she might as well be a primitive yurt dweller, condemned to forage for eternity, for all the quiet moments of luxury her supposedly high-powered job afforded her, Cat waited a few respectful seconds, before nipping out of the kitchen door for a quick ciggie in the shed. She was too tired and too champagned up to eat, but even getting hold of an ordinary PG Tips tea bag required a deviant imagination now that Jess had outlawed them. She looked up at the starless sky and breathed in the aroma from In Cod We Trust.

'It's for you.' Jess poked her head round the back door. 'Persia's mother wants to discuss something important. And put that bloody fag out.'

'It's half past eleven, for God's sake.'

'I wouldn't put this one off, if I were you.'

Fifteen minutes later Cat returned with a thunderous expression on her face.

'Did you know that Lily's been e-mailing all her friends the answers to their homework in return for two pounds a subject?'

Jess looked at her self-righteously. 'I told you you weren't spending enough time with her.'

*

'I don't know why you're getting so aerated,' said Suzette, who was somewhat flustered herself at being disturbed at a time when she usually counted on her daughter being in bed. 'I would have thought Lily was merely embracing the kind of enterprise culture you so clearly value yourself.'

'Oh, for God's sake. It's obvious she's getting her warped materialism from Lady Eleanor's.' Cat blamed everything on Lady Eleanor's, the school Suzette had insisted on sending Lily to after Makesbury Primary and Junior had been officially classified a sink school by Ofsted four years ago. Suzette supposed it made her feel less guilty about sending Lily there.

Reluctantly Suzette wriggled out from underneath Eduardo. Having been a child of the Free Love revolution of the sixties, she prided herself on not needing men. But being licked all over by a bronzed Brazilian was no longer such an everyday event in Suzette's life that she could afford to be dismissive.

'What's the matter? Isn't Lily happy there any more?'

'It's not that. It's the one-upmanship. It's having a very detrimental influence on her. You should see the way the mothers and nannies slam their multi-storey Mercedes Jeeps over kerbs, flower beds and small animals in a race to get their darlings into early club first. And just so that they can hot-foot it to John Frieda and Pilates. Last week Persia's mother almost got into a fight with Henrietta's nanny over the last remaining double-parked car space.'

'Who won?' Eduardo was nibbling Suzette's toes.

'Henrietta's nanny. Blessed with the considerable advantage of knowing that any damage would not ultimately be paid for by her, she rammed her Jeep into a full-grown oak that was presented to the school last year by Xanthe's parents. She wrapped the accompanying cedar bench round her fender.'

Suzette chuckled and contemplated running her fingers through Eduardo's cappuccino-coloured hair before deciding against in case it came away in her hands.

'So what are you doing for Lily's birthday this year?'

'That's another thing. Henrietta's tenth birthday was in the ballroom of Claridge's. It's impossible to compete.'

'How about if I pay?'

'That's not the point,' said Cat hastily. 'Anyway, it's all sorted. We're doing a swimming party.'

'Well, what is the point?' Eduardo began to moan softly.

On second thoughts, Suzette decided, contemplating Eduardo's hirsute back again, the hairdo might be genuine. Ideally she would have preferred someone less densely forested. Still, Eduardo was funny, urbane and the world's leading ears, nose and throat man. That was ears as in cutting little slits around them and hoiking up the surrounding physiognomy; nose as in giving everyone an Audrey Hepburn; and throat as in plenty of collagen. But Suzette preferred not to think of it in those terms because officially, and in at least two dozen of her columns, she was opposed to plastic surgery.

'The point is –' Cat had no idea what the point was. Suzette's views had become so woolly headed over the years Cat found it impossible to conduct a consistent argument with her. 'The point is it's so narrow. When the headmistress talks about widening the social mix at Lady Eleanor's she means introducing the girls to minor foreign royalty as well as the Windsors.'

'Well, if you want to find another school for her, I'll back you all the way. If anyone should know about educational establishments, it's you.'

'Oh, that's right. Duck responsibility.'

Getting expelled from six schools – two of them Rudolph Steiners – had required a considerable energy, not to mention inge-nuity, on Cat's part. It would have been seven but the Garden never expelled anyone as a matter of smug pride. So she'd had to run away, which had involved several days of lying low in a rancid squat with some very boring drug addicts whom she had cultivated with the sole intention of horrifying her mother. If Suzette hadn't by then become so middle class, she'd have been taken into care. As it was, she'd been taken in for one last, fruitless term at Bedales.

'Don't be so priggish.' Suzette plucked at the tufts of hair that sprung between Eduardo's shoulder blades like delicate heads of broccoli. It was a bit like starring in a film about Diane Fossey.

'You're just upset because you feel guilty that you're not there like the other mothers to fetch and collect their little darlings from school every day. And you're taking that frustration out via a mis-directed sense of anger at the school's privileged pupils. Though God knows why. Being there is a very over rated maternal virtue, if you ask me.'

Cat didn't. Not least because the other frustrating aspect of these never-ending phone calls which had become a constant soundtrack to her life was the number of times her mother proved to be right.

Notwithstanding her constant tiredness, early mornings were the best part of the day for Cat. Sometimes she felt guilty about waking Lily an hour before she needed to. But it was the only way she could rely on spending any time with her. Every morning she dragged herself out of bed and crept across the landing into Lily's bedroom, ignoring the Very Private Indeed sign with its three exclamation marks. A small foot dangled like fruit from beneath a duvet. Taking it in her hands, Cat kissed it gently, until her daughter finally woke up.

Those sixty minutes on their own, with nothing more pressing than having to tip some Sheba into Seamus's bowl before his whingeing drove them both mad while Lily recited her square roots, were precious to both of them. Cat deliberately told Jess to lie in, so that they could be alone. And she made sure that they had a leisurely breakfast while Lily ran through the previous day's events at school.

Nothing was permitted to shatter the peace, until 7.30, when Jess appeared in the kitchen. On Tuesdays and Thursdays she switched on Kiss FM. The rota had been Cat's idea. On Mondays, Wednesdays and Fridays they listened to the Today programme. Jess had made a small objection to Cat's getting the lion's share of options and suggested they work a fourteen-day rota. Cat had replied that it was her radio and her house. Jess was still thinking of a comeback.

3

Four minutes and twenty-seven seconds. That was how long the Tube had been sitting between Warwick Avenue and Paddington. Rank steam visibly rose off its damply resigned passengers. It was the third delay that week. At least Cat had a seat. Actually she always had a seat, because she'd worked out that the 8.13 was generally only two-thirds full while the 8.16 was a bubonic pustule of seething, chaotic, overflowing, stuck-in-the-doors humanity.

This exercise in precision was what her mother called Manifestations of Cat's Disturbing Behaviour. Another manifestation was her ability to worry about everything. But someone had to. Take the Toby situation. Why had he been put on her case? On the plus side, since he'd arrived Cat had found work even more stimulating. There was nothing Toby didn't know about re-orienting perceptions of under-performing products in the newspaper and broadband media segment. And he was generous enough to share it with her. But – and it was a big but – why did the Vices think she needed him?

She returned to her calculations. Two hundred and sixty-seven seconds times three was eight hundred and one. Multiply that by fifty-two weeks in a year – forty-one thousand, six hundred and fifty-two – and then by the two million people who used the Bakerloo Line every year, and by Cat's jerky estimate United Kingdom Inc. was losing eighty-three billion – or was it trillion? – seconds every year. No wonder the country's economy was going to the dogs. She made a note to write an official letter of complaint on Simms embossed paper to London Transport, the *Evening Standard* and the Minister for Transport. She made another note to book Lily's swimming party. Then she made another note to find out who the Minister for Transport was.

'Have you seen Ralph lately?' asked Cat over the din of Kiss FM. She could have sworn Jess blushed – or at least turned a dangerous shade of beige – but it was hard to tell because she just bent lower over Lily's head, mowing her hair with an electric nit comb.

'He's obviously been, because the note I left on the table for him has disappeared. But there doesn't appear to be much danger of any work actually having been completed.'

'Must have been while I was out. Shouldn't you have left hours ago?'

'Toby and I have a meeting with Herr Frupps at ten at the Heathrow Hilton. He's coming by at nine to pick me up.'

'You're cutting it a bit tight, aren't you? Could be very congested this time in the morning.'

A series of high-pitched ululations were followed by the faint but unmistakable buzzing sound of small creatures being electrocuted.

'Murderer!' Lily turned accusing eyes on Jess.

'Oh, for heaven's sake, it's got to be done. Your hair's positively feral.'

'Does it have to be so barbaric?' yelled Lily.

'What do you want me to do? Cook them a stir-fry?'

'Yeah, that should do the trick.'

'What do you mean?'

'How did he get in, then?' intercepted Cat, more in an attempt to divert the Third World War than any profound sense of curiosity. She had a horrible feeling that years ago, in a misplaced sense of trust and affection, she had given Ralph a set of keys.

Jess turned up the radio. Upstairs there was a distinct creaking of floorboards.

'Did you have a guest last night?' Cat enquired cautiously.

'Certainly not,' said Jess.

Cat opened the fridge and groped among the thickets of decaying tofu, bean sprouts and sunflower seeds for some jam.

Nothing. There never was, at least nothing nice. Just unidentifiable health foods that no one wanted to eat – Cat lived in fear that Lily would eventually succumb to scurvy.

She automatically removed a small canvas wallet from the egg tray, too injured to Jess's idiosyncratic housekeeping to remark on it, and turned round to come face to face with Ralph in a pair of Rip Curl shorts.

'Whoops, girls. Ralph's blown it again.' Having sauntered halfway across the kitchen before he'd spotted Cat, Ralph was now grinning with the laid-back confidence of one who repeatedly surfed through life on a wave of so-called charm. Jess silently handed him a pair of trousers, which had been drying on the radiator – Cat hadn't even noticed. She had forgotten, too, how good looking he was and how soothing – misleadingly, as it turned out – his Aussie twang could be.

'Sorry, Cat,' he drawled. 'Timing never was my forte. Still, now I'm here I'll get that carpet nailed down and I'll put Lily's shelves up.'

'Don't strain yourself,' she said. She had never forgiven him for informing her – with all the insouciance of someone used to sponging off others – that what she really needed to do with Makesbury Road was spend £100,000 on it. Or sell.

'Oh, now don't go and spoil it all, Cat.' He sat down opposite her, blissfully unselfconscious in his shorts. 'That's just your problem, you know.'

'What's my problem, Ralph?' The gall of people who constantly projected their own shortcomings on to her was starting to wear very thin.

'You're too uptight.' He winked at Lily. 'You keep getting all mistress of the universe on us all. Gotta kebab that aggression and work on your instinct instead. You need the yogic breath.'

'And what exactly would that be?' asked Cat acidly.

He placed his right thumb on his right nostril and inhaled deeply, closing his eyes in the irritating manner of the truly smug. And then he breathed out of his left. 'See. It's simple.' He inhaled nosily through his left nostril now. 'You wanna try it. You'll never get the best results with all that bollock-shrivelling stuff – 'scusing my French, little Lily – but you certainly shrivel mine, Cat.'

'I doubt that,' said Cat.

'What French?' asked Lily.

'What you need to work on is your people skills,' continued Ralph. 'You may be a ball-breaker at work, but you need a different approach at home.'

'And what approach would that be?'

'Learning to wait for the Seventh Wave.'

'Oh, and where did you glean that particular philosophical gem – the Koran, the Torah or *The Little Book of Crap*?'

He held his palms up in mock self-defence. 'Whoa. Don't take it amiss, Cat. It's just some of Ralph's harmless lore.'

'You're right. Sorry. Listen, how about I make you a proper breakfast. Fry-up? Continental? Egg-white-only omelette?' continued Cat with what she hoped was exquisite sarcasm.

'Nah,' said Ralph, stretching his bronzed legs in front of him. 'You're all right with a bit of toast and Vegemite. Although if you're making some I'll have a slurp of fresh coffee. With boiled milk, if you don't mind.'

In his deeply insensitive way, Ralph had a point, thought Cat, stooping to pick up an empty cigarette packet on the garden path and put it in the bin as she waited for Toby by the gate. She did need to lighten up. And she should start by refusing to feel threatened and confused by Toby's arrival. After all, hadn't the seventh Vice e-mailed her pointing out that with Toby's knowledge of grass-roots business and her personal experience of Frupps they would make an unbeatable team and that an entire department of Simms devoted to media was a logical next step? And hadn't he also thanked her for helping to ease Toby back into the London office? Surely a rise and a car that didn't look like a motorised dustbin were now merely a formality.

Far from resenting the fact that Toby had installed himself in a large glass office that spanned three windows just across the floor from her own workstation, she should look and learn. Besides, he had suggested that Cat might like to move in with him. But Petula, Toby's lithesome PA, who had followed him to New York and, like a faithful dog, back again, looked so put out that Cat had muttered something about needing her own space. Lack of space would have been more accurate. But it was done now. At least Toby's presence had coincided with the arrival, at last, of a huge chrome espresso maker crenellated with knobs and switches.

Even better, she had begun to really love her job. Before, it had been challenging and – for great big chunks of the time – profoundly stressful. But Toby made all the gristly little moral issues she had at Simms seem like academic irrelevancies. Even more revelatory, he managed to be utterly professional and still have time for a social life. At least, judging by the number of personal phone calls Petula juggled on his behalf he did.

He never seemed to get bogged down in his clients' personal lives the way Cat did. It must be a male thing, she thought. It allowed them to be more productive in less time. She had noticed, however, that Toby got regular calls from someone called Cynthia. And that he seemed to spend quite a few weekends down in Dorset, which was odd for someone who professed to hate the countryside.

A throaty growl and a blast of Queen announced the arrival of the Porsche. Toby got out to let her in and grinned – he really was remarkably good looking. Thank God he wasn't her type.

'Morning, McGinty. Almost didn't get here, fucking awful jams all the way. Love the stockings.'

Cat flushed. How did he know they weren't tights? She slipped in next to him. 'God this country's a mess.' He edged the Porsche back out into the traffic, nudging a few cones out of the way to skip the lights. 'I mean, no offence, but what they need is to bulldoze West London and start again.'

Cat grinned. He was looking particularly dashing today, in a black suit and a turquoise shirt that matched his eyes. She, on the other hand, was having severe difficulties with an old Joseph suit. Her shirt appeared to be attempting devolution from her skirt; her cuffs were engaged in skirmishes with her jacket sleeves. It was civil war.

'Surely you're not including Makesbury Road along with Chiswick, Barnes and Buck House?'

'Well, maybe I'd make an exception for Kensal Rise. But someone ought to nuke Buck House. Bloody monstrosity. Why can't we have a proper palace? Get bloody Disney to do it. Couldn't make a worse balls-up.'

'Not enough money, I suppose.'

'Not you as well, Cat. Money, money, money. That's all anyone thinks about in this country. No one ever does anything beautiful 'cos it's all about how many kidney machines you could spend the money on instead.'

Cat sank into the leather seats and let 'Bohemian Rhapsody' swoop her up. Toby certainly had Catholic tastes. Ben had been a musical fascist who had operated a police state over their CD collection, systematically sidelining Cat's shelf. He said that anyone who liked musicals or cried all the way through the Oscars every year and didn't have the excuse of being gay deserved to be shot. She would always remember to reserve a little well of scepticism somewhere in her soul for Toby, but that didn't mean she couldn't enjoy his company and his cheesy music. Unfortunately, as they reached the M4, his mobile went off and for a good twenty minutes he was otherwise engaged.

'Yes, fine,' he said as the conversation finally drew to a conclusion. 'Don't worry, darling, I'll be there. Must dash. In the middle of a meeting.'

For some reason she couldn't acknowledge, hearing Toby call someone darling proved very disconcerting.

Once they were back in the office, Toby suggested a late lunch at the Ivy to celebrate a fruitful meeting with Herr Frupps. 'I don't know if I'll have time,' said Cat doubtfully. She had to e-mail all Lily's invitations between writing up an urgent report on Frupps's latest results, and a proposal for some new business.

'Come on. All work and no play—'

'Makes Jill an obsessive compulsive?' suggested Petula helpfully as she tottered over with a mug of coffee for Toby.

Cat watched Petula drape herself on a desk as she handed Toby his coffee. Her long auburn hair fell either side of her perfect eyebrows, just like spaniel's ears, decided Cat. Where did people get eyebrows like that? She almost wished she knew. The phone went in Toby's office. Petula glided over to pick it up.

'Daniel Wiley for you, Toby,' she cooed. Toby sauntered casually over to his desk and Cat heard him pick up the receiver.

'Hello. Yes. Well, it's not really up for discussion any more, you know. It's yes or no and fifty k per month, basic package.' After some further brief, unemotional exchanges about money, he concluded with the words, 'Delighted to work with you too, Daniel. We'll be sending the contracts over later today, okay?'

Now that, thought Cat, was how you conducted a business conversation. No heart-rending agonising about what was fair; no sleepless nights wondering how to tell clients that they couldn't afford you. No soul-searching about whether you should be touching their filthy businesses. And still time to take in something really depressing at the Donmar.

Walking into the Ivy with Toby was a bit, Cat imagined, like walking into the *Vanity Fair* Oscar Party with Tom Cruise. All the waiters seemed to know him. He stopped at three tables to say hello to people, so whatever else he'd been doing in New York, he clearly hadn't lost contact with his network of glamorous friends back in the little old UK.

'So, how d'you think it's all going?' Toby spread his arms expansively along the top of a plush leather banquette. 'You and me, I mean. As a team to take on the world?'

Cat pretended to find something utterly absorbing on the menu. She had decided that the best way to deal with Toby was to engage in knockabout banter. But the more time she spent with him the more unsettling she found him and the harder it was to be knockabout. He was so . . . inscrutably flirtatious. He gave off waves of charm – great tsunamis of beguilingness. But he gave them off to everyone. Petula was constantly emerging from his office in fits of giggles, blushing over something he'd said to her. And he was always buying her little gifts. Cat was sure he didn't mean anything by it. Petula was engaged and Toby had even arranged for Petula and her fiancé Alan to have a weekend away in some luxury hotel on his air miles. Charm, Cat had decided, was simply the oil that lubricated Toby's devastating axles. He was the kind of man who would pause momentarily to flirt with the photocopier if he thought it might make it more efficient.

'I think,' she said, savouring the vodka tonic that Toby had ordered for her, 'that it's going reasonably well in the circumstances.'

'What circumstances would those be?' A waiter appeared and looked expectantly at Cat.

According to the *Evening Standard*, everyone who was anyone always ordered bangers and mash at the Ivy, which made Cat want to order roast swan and floating islands. 'Sausages, please. And mashed potato.'

'Same here,' said Toby, snapping the menu closed. 'I love the bangers here.' He assumed an art-critic voice. 'So ironic, don't you think?'

'A veritable satire on postmodern society.' Cat tipped back her vodka and wondered whether Toby's Porsche was ironic. 'It certainly beats lunch with the Kaiser.'

He knitted his eyebrows together disapprovingly. 'I hope you're not casting slurs on our patron.'

Cat scanned his chiselled features for clues. She could never quite work out when he was being sincere.

'He's a bit lecherous.'

'Not that old sexual harassment charge again? Honestly, McGinty, that's all in the past. Kaiser Villie is our ticket to fame and fortune at Simms. He loves us. Ergo they do. Anyway, you were saying –' He reached for the water, brushing her hand lightly. '– something about us being good *in the circumstances*.'

'Yeah, well.' Cat relaxed more with each sip of vodka and craned her neck to see whether Nicole Kidman or the Beckhams were in. 'Working with you is okay, I suppose.' She stressed the *with*. 'But I think the real test will come when Simms finally put their money where their mouth is and devote a department to media clients.'

'And place us in charge?' There was a slight catch in his voice. Was he teasing her again?

'You don't think it's going to happen?' she asked, as nonchalantly as she could.

'I didn't say that. I think they'd be insane not to do it, to be honest. And equally crazy not to give you a key role. I've told them as much, in fact.'

So it was Toby's recommendation which had prompted that congratulatory e-mail from the seventh Vice. She might have known. It was gratifying to know he at least appreciated her – but she wished the Vices would recognise her contribution without being prodded by Toby.

The waiter returned with their food and Toby lent over to tuck Cat's napkin into the collar of her blouse. 'Can't have you messing up that fetching little shirt, can we?' He ploughed his knife into the caramelised skin of a perfect, slightly pink sausage and let the sizzling juices explode over his knife. Cat was mesmerised. There was something lusty about his enjoyment of food. It was almost Elizabethan.

'And it's particularly fetching, not to say downright distracting, with that middle button missing,' Toby continued. Cat turned scarlet. She'd had no idea she'd been gaping all morning.

'What I'm getting at,' she said, trying to ignore the magnetic pull from Toby's direction and the way his lips slipped round the creamy mashed potato, 'is that it would be really helpful if my role at Simms were more clearly defined . . .' She trailed off.

'Are you going to eat any of that, McGinty?' His eyes creased slightly.

'I mean, since I've been with the company, I've worked my way up sort of from nothing. It's not that I'm hung up on titles or anything, but I'd just like to know whether anyone there rates me.'

'My God, McGinty – do you mean to tell me that the bouquets haven't been arriving?'

'Oh, shut up, Marks. You know what I mean.' She wasn't

playing this right. She shouldn't leave all the driving to him, even if he was the closest she'd come to having an ally there.

'Yes. You just want someone there to tell you they love you.'

'A bonus would do.'

'I see. Money talks.'

'Well, no one else there does. For a bunch who make their living telling people what to do, they're crap at communicating.'

'Yes, and that's why I've been drafted back from New York.' He put on a hammy American accent. 'To improve core inter-departmental relationships. I thought I'd been doing rather well. Petula loves me—'

'Petula loves herself – and you happen to look a bit like her.'

'You woundeth me verily, Mistress Catherine.' He shot her a teasing glance that made her heart lurch.

'Is the money very important?' he asked, waving a forkful of sausage.

She thought of her spiralling overdraft and the sleepless nights. 'Yes,' was all she said.

'I see,' said Toby. 'Look, I'll do my best to bring the Vices round to your way of thinking. It shouldn't be a problem, especially if things continue to rocket with the Frupps account.' He looked at her pensively. 'Don't you ever find it hard juggling motherhood and work?'

Cat dropped her fork. This was the first time Toby had alluded to her ambivalent status at Simms. Not that he didn't enquire about Lily's welfare all the time – and Seamus's, come to that. But somehow, without her ever having to ask him, he had the tact not to mention Lily in front of anyone else at Simms. It was probably the thing she most liked him for.

'Is this the part where I get a lecture about my responsibilities?'

'Hey. I wasn't lecturing.' His tone grew gentler. 'I take my hat off to you. It can't be easy. Simms are hardly known for their enlightened attitudes to working mothers.'

'What do you mean?' Cat felt anxious again.

'Look at their record. How many mothers do you see with real responsibility there? I think it's terrific the way you're prepared to break through all those preconceptions.'

The way he put it made it seem as though she were trying to achieve the impossible. 'Sounds painful,' she said, trying to sound flippant.

'It could be – but I'm sure if anyone can hack it you can.'

It wasn't quite the ringing endorsement she'd been hoping for, but perhaps she was being oversensitive. 'All I'm saying is that I think it's time my position was officialised.' *Officialised?*

'Officialised?' snorted Toby.' I like it, McGinty. Any more like that and they'll have you on the *Today* programme for crimes against plain English. Seriously, the long-term aim at Simms is to create fewer hierarchical layers. Not more. But I take your point.' He extracted a Palm from the emerald lining of his cashmere jacket and began making notes. Cat leaned across the table and saw that he'd written MORE DOSH FOR CAT.

'Why do you do it?' He fixed her with his vivid blue eyes. Was this a trick question?

'Money. Why do you?'

He leant back in the banquette and considered for a few moments.

'For the challenge of getting people to do things I wouldn't ever do myself.'

Cat looked at him. Was he serious?

'It isn't only the money, you know,' she said later as the waiter returned with the menu. 'I'll have cheesecake with double cream, please.' She smiled sweetly at the waiter.

'Go for it, McGinty. I like a woman with an appetite. Now where were we? Oh yes, your position—'

'I just feel—'

'That clarification is called for. And you're right. That's the problem with somewhere where you work your way up from the bottom. They never appreciate you as much as if they'd wooed you for some obscene amount from outside.' He accidentally brushed her hand again and stared into her eyes. 'I'll do my best, I promise.'

The waiter brought coffee and the bill and Toby plopped his platinum company Amex on the table with the assurance of a man who'd never had to worry about his endowment mortgage. He certainly talked the talk of one who could get her salary raised, thought Cat. Time would tell whether he delivered. They taxied back to the office together – casually sauntering across the soaring atrium at ten past three. She'd have to pay for the long lunch by staying late. There was a message from Ariadne's mother responding to the party with a definite maybe – and a comment about what a novelty it was not to receive handmade invitations. It was then that Cat realised she hadn't actually consulted Lily about her party.

4

'What do you mean there's no record of the booking?' Cat's entrails began to wither. She could see from the heavily perspiring face of the girl behind the counter that she would need to draw on all Ralph's people skills for this one.

'It's not here.' The girl, who according to her name badge was blessed with the staggeringly inappropriate name of Hope, stared bleakly at a chaotic chart.

'I booked three weeks ago and have been ringing weekly to confirm numbers and discuss menus. We've got the frankfurter and fries package . . .' She began to repeat herself in the hope that something she said might jog someone's memory. 'Where's Jed?' she said inspirationally. 'Jed's the person I last spoke to.'

The girl's eyes all but disappeared in a frown of concentration. 'Anyone here heard of a Jed?' Cat glanced behind her shoulder at the fascinated expressions on the sixteen Lady Eleanor girls behind her. 'Is it always this slow in public swimming baths?' asked Xanthe loudly. Cat looked at Lily, who smiled back nervously.

'He's gone on leave,' said another voice from behind the counter. Cat tried again. 'Shall I have a look at the chart?' She willed her voice to stay calm. 'Sometimes it helps to have a fresh eye.' She peered at Jed's clearly deranged scrawlings with a mounting sense of hysteria. 'There we go,' she almost shrieked. 'McGinty. Ten-forty-five.'

Hope looked at the chart impassively. 'It's been crossed out,' she said with, Cat thought, an unhelpful note of triumph.

'I think you'll find it's the name next to it that's been crossed out,' she said in her most Ralph-like voice.

Ten metres away, by the door to the changing rooms, a woman

wrapped in Cat's favourite aubergine-coloured Toast sarong and fifteen small boys who'd been gorging themselves on chocolate was going into meltdown. 'Don't you bloody contradict me. I definitely booked the ball pool at ten-forty-five and I've got the frigging receipt somewhere to prove it.' By the end of her last sentence she was almost screaming. All eyes in the sports centre were upon her, apart from Lily's, which were now fixed on the floor.

Encouraged by the way the woman in Toast had lost it so completely, Cat strolled over, marshalling every trick she'd ever learned for dealing with difficult clients.

'What a nightmare. We seem to be double non-booked.'

'You're bloody telling me.' The woman turned on her in accusation.

'How about sharing? There's two of us and one slot. So let's make the best of things.'

'Are you joking?' The woman gazed adoringly at the biggest boy in the group, who was clutching his stomach and making loud gagging sounds. 'Harry hates to share. Anyway, I've paid for my own slot.'

'So have I.' Cat waved her arm proprietorially towards the pupils of Lady Eleanor's sixth year, who were gazing with awe at the screechy woman's boys, who were literally attempting to climb the walls. 'But the alternative is that neither of us gets anything.'

'I want to see the superintendent.' The woman's voice had risen dangerously and her face was now the same colour as her sarong.

'Jed?' said Cat.

The woman fished a bright blue party file out of her bag and scowled at it. 'That's right.'

'AWOL,' said Cat. 'Come on, let's get on with it before we miss our slot altogether.'

'And let these incompetent bastards get off scot-free?'

The woman clearly had no people skills whatsoever. Cat breathed deeply and swept past a small boy attempting to crack his head open on the swing doors that led to the changing rooms. 'Follow me, girls. Jess, you bring up the rear. A prize for the first one in the pool.'

Twenty minutes later she saw the Toast woman still waving her fists at the hapless Hope while 6b frolicked with the wave machine. 'It's great, Mum,' said Lily, swimming up to the surface suddenly through Cat's legs. 'You did brilliantly not to lose your rag like that other mother.'

'It's all about being calm but firm,' said Cat, feeling virtuous for once. Suzette was right. Working mothers probably kept things in perspective more than those whose lives revolved round the next carol concert. She wouldn't have been able to deal with Jed and Hope so calmly without her Simms experience. She swam into a tidal wave of small girls surfing on Lilos and decided that Toby's confidence must be contagious. She hadn't even brought her laptop home this weekend.

She was only ten hours into her new programme, but already cutting the strings of the workplace was proving incredibly liberating. Except that she'd forgotten to turn the mobile off. They were slicing the cake when it bleeped. She only registered Lily's wince after she had taken the call.

'Who's that?'

'Cat McGinty. Who's that?' Cat sighed. As if she needed to ask.

'Ah, Cat. It's Villie. Who else is calling you on weekends? Cat, you are being my one respite from Frau Frupps. Frankly I don't know if I can take much more.'

Judging by Villie's latest proposal for slashing production costs at his printing plant, Cat doubted that.

'When I think what I could do for you in Hamburg, I could weep,' he continued. 'Not that anyone else at Simms takes care of you. All they think about is profit, profit, profit.'

Cat's temple throbbed. She knew this was his cue to wax rhapsodic for the next half-hour about the good old days when he and Frau Frupps had manned the sex chat-lines in Hamburg all by themselves.

'Now I'm not saying that she vas right about everything.' He sighed. 'But she had very high standards. She was an inspiration to us all. And what a beauty. *Mein Gott.* Before the steroids you wouldn't believe what she was looking like—'

Jess glowered at Cat. 'Not that bloody lech. I thought you were leaving your mobile switched off at weekends.'

Cat looked at Lily apologetically. 'Won't be long,' she mouthed unconvincingly.

'Ja, right,' said Jess in disgust.

'The thing is, Herr Frupps—' Cat braced herself to break the news that she didn't actually work on weekends when a bleep told her there was another call waiting. Grasping at straws, she took it. Even Suzette was preferable to listening to Villie on the subject of Frau Frupps's haemorrhoids.

It was Toby. 'Hello, Marks.' Lily and Jess exchanged knowing glances.

Is there someone else on the line?' asked Toby casually.

'Just Kaiser Vill. Hang on.' She flicked back to Villie, who was still reminiscing about his wife's eighteen-inch waist.

'Never ate. Lived off cigarettes and gin. Such wonderful discipline . . .'

'Herr Frupps—'

'I blame the doctors, of course,' declaimed Villie. 'They should never have agreed to the third liposuction.'

'I'll call you on Monday,' said Cat firmly, leaving Villie suspended in disbelief.

'Don't tell me he stalks you on weekends as well?' said Toby incredulously.

'Not *every* weekend. He's just a bit overwrought at the moment and I can't help feeling sorry for him.'

'Well, it's quite apt, as it turns out. He's stayed on in town with Mrs Frupps. At a loose end. Which is where you step in, I hope, fair Cat.'

Cat looked across at Jess and Lily, who were pretending to re-count the slices they'd divided the cake into.

'Anyway, it just so happens that my Aunt Hermione is chairing a charity dinner this evening. I bought a table ages ago, and what with all the changes recently, I clean forgot about it. She reminded me a couple of days ago – no getting out of things with Aunt

Hermione, I'm afraid. Anyway, I've invited the Frupps, but omitted to ask you. I know it's unforgivably late notice but—'

He paused just long enough for Cat to try to get her heartbeat under control. 'I'm afraid I dangled you as an incentive to Villie. He's completely besotted with you, in case you hadn't noticed. Mrs Villie didn't need any encouragement. I just had to mention that Freddie Windsor and Jude Law might be there.'

Cat mentally raked over her wardrobe. There was a torn Victorian nightie from Ben that Seamus had slept on and half a dozen size-four slip dresses from Suzette. She had nothing to wear, which was the best excuse ever to go shopping. After all, work was work.

'Look, you two,' she said as she twirled for the umpteenth time outside the changing room in Selfridges, 'Toby Marks's interest in me is purely professional.'

'Yeah, and I'm a flying possum,' said Jess.

'He's got a girlfriend anyway.' Cat's heart dipped as she spoke. In the excitement of being asked out, she'd forgotten all about Darling. A ray of hope struck her. Where was Darling and why wasn't she going out tonight with Toby? She caught sight of a tall, narrow, sequinned figure with a hint of pot belly in the mirror and realised it was herself. She was twinkling so much she looked like a badly constructed landing strip. Darling was probably on a shoot somewhere for *Harper's Bazaar*.

'I'm going to get the suit,' she said decisively. 'At least then I can wear it to work later.'

'That figures'. Lily rolled her eyes in a gesture of withering contempt. 'The suit's minging. You should get the vintage black halter neck. It's much more dramatic.'

'Do you really think so?' Cat fingered the fine black jersey on the halter neck longingly and then slapped the undercarriage of her arms and watched it wobble slightly. 'I don't think so. I'm not even sure it fits properly.' She slipped into it again and zipped it up, feeling the black jersey skim over her hips.

'Like a glove,' pronounced Lily. 'It would look beautiful with the silver Manolos Sukes sent you and some make-up. You'll have to get your hair done, of course.'

'Yippee,' said Cat. Having spent her life trying to escape one fashion editor, she had apparently fallen into the clutches of Diana Vreeland. On the way back to the car they passed a display of luxurious long suede sheepskin coats in the window of Joseph. 'Oh my God. Cop the red one. It would look amazing with your hair,' said Lily, pressing her nose up against the plate glass.

'So would a new bathroom, which is what you could buy for the same money,' said Cat wistfully. It was a beautiful coat.

'Don't exaggerate. Anyway, you haven't bought yourself a new coat for years,' Lily pointed out.

Getting ready later at home, Cat had to concede that Lily had been right about the dress. It looked just right – especially after Lily had selected a big marquisette flower-shaped brooch for it. She peered at her dark hair, examining it for rogue grey strands. That would be the last straw. Fortunately, in the light of the bedroom, she couldn't make out any, and decided that at this point there was nothing to be gained from scrutinising it under harsher conditions. If she could just get her hair to stay where it was, grazing her collar bones and from certain angles giving her impressive cheekbones, she might even make it through the night looking sleek.

She surveyed her white skin in the bedroom mirror. She hadn't properly looked at her breasts since about 1997, and was appalled to see that they had never quite returned to their neat, manageable pre-pregnancy size. Nor had her stomach. Ben had always said how much he loved her little pot belly. He'd even composed a song about it – shortly before he'd left her. She looked in the mirror once more. She could never again allow a man to see her body naked.

'I thought he wasn't your type,' said Jess, bustling in with a tube of Veet.

Cat was appalled. Why was she even thinking about men seeing her naked? Toby was an outrageous flirt, but no one could possibly take him seriously.

'If you're referring to my client Herr Frupps, I can assure you he's not.' On the other hand, there was no reason she shouldn't flirt back. At some stage she was going to have to have sex with someone, if only to avoid becoming the sort of person the rest of the office joked about.

'I'm referring to 007. Your boss.'

'He's not my boss. And not my type.' It was true. Years ago, Cat had created a file on her computer called Ideal Men. It was mainly for Lily's benefit – a father figure wouldn't have gone amiss in her life – and mainly empty. But under Desirable Qualities she'd listed shyness (with hidden depths), dependability and solid family values – the very traits she'd once thought Ben possessed. At least she was wise enough now to know that they didn't exactly fit Toby.

'Are you insane?' Jess deposited Seamus, who had been scratching at Cat's door, on the rug. 'He's gorgeous. Almost too gorgeous. I never trust men that gorgeous. Unless they happen also to be considerate and rich.'

Cat examined Jess's face for signs of sarcasm. Toby was every-thing Jess disapproved of. On the other hand, Cat had become accustomed to Jess's leaps of logic. 'I told you, he's taken,' said Cat, piling her hair on top of her head and then brushing it down again. 'Oh, sod these frigging shoes. They keep slipping off.'

'Superglue them to your heels. By the way . . .' Jess paused by the door and looked pointedly at Cat's little belly. 'Have you thought about doing any more yoga?'

'I take it that wasn't a serious question?' said Cat. The one time Jess had persuaded Cat to join her at the Karma Factory had ended in a humiliating rejection. Far from finding the atmosphere relaxing, Cat had been exasperated by the heavy nostril-breathing of the person to the left of her, appalled by the feet of the person in front of her and explosive when the teacher insisted their beads of sweat were God's flowers. Then, in order to maximise the space in the studio – and to stop herself punching someone – she'd persuaded everyone within a three-mat radius to shuffle around. After sixty-five minutes the teacher had come over to correct her Standing Tree, whispered that she was upsetting the karmic energy of the room and asked her to leave.

*

Cat was so nervous about inviting Toby in, especially after finding a tube of spermicide pointedly left by the front door by Jess, that she decided to brave the unseasonal sub-zero temperature. As she waited for him by the gate, the wind whipping her hair across her face like a frayed blanket, she cursed Jess's puerile sense of humour and made a mental note to tackle it at some point.

Fortunately Toby was as punctual as ever and she barely had time to clear the path of some sodden fish batter that had somehow ground its way into the cement before she heard the unmistakable growl of his Porsche.

'Mmm, you smell delicious. Agent Provocateur?' He pecked her lightly on the cheek.

Toby's all-encompassing knowledge of fashion amused and fascinated her. She buckled her seat belt and allowed U2 to wash over her. How many other men would be able to identify a perfume? Ben wouldn't have registered if she'd turned up in a gorilla suit. Even when she'd had all her hair cut off in a fit of post-natal depression it had taken him four days to notice anything different – and then he'd spoiled it by asking if she'd finally taken Suzette's advice and bleached her moustache.

The only other man with such an abiding interest in fashion was her hairdresser, who was gay. That would certainly explain some things. The non-appearance of Darling, for instance. She looked at Toby as he negotiated the Hammersmith roundabout and wondered whether he also stayed up every year to watch the Oscars live in their entirety.

Toby had insisted on taking her for a quick cocktail at the Windows of the World bar on top of the hotel, where the diamonds on the guests almost out-twinkled the headlamps of the traffic streaming past below. Cat felt unbelievably glamorous, especially when Toby asked whether her dress was Halston.

'I'm not sure. Lily chose it from the vintage section at Selfridges. Here . . .' She yanked at the halter ties. 'What does the label say?'

'Knew it.' He thrust his hands deep into his trouser pockets. 'Circa seventy-eight, I'd say.'

By the time the lift flew them twenty-eight floors back down to earth again, Cat was almost completely relaxed, though whether it was down to Toby's easy banter or the two martinis she had consumed, she couldn't say.

By the time they arrived at the Grosvenor House hotel the ball was in full swing. Cat paused briefly at the top of the sweeping double staircase that straddled the vast room below like a can-can dancer's legs. Beneath the twinkling chandeliers she vaguely recognised a glamorous figure with legs like pipe cleaners, heading towards them.

'Hi, Toby. You're looking well.' The girl patted his cheek and winked. Cat smiled across at her nervously. The girl looked at her blankly and with a sinking heart Cat realised she'd just been snubbed by Tara Palmer-Tompkinson. Not that she was convinced being embraced by Tara P-T, as Toby appeared to have been done, was much of an accomplishment either. Toby took her hand and surfed nonchalantly towards the bar, through a crowd that seemed to Cat as though it could have stepped straight from the pages of *Hello!*, though being far too busy to read *Hello!* except occasionally when it fell into her lap at the hairdresser's, she couldn't be sure. It might have been Yasmin Le Bon, gorgeous in a white goddess dress, chatting to someone who looked like Nicky Haslam. Patsy Kensit could have been gliding down the curved staircase with Elizabeth Hurley's double, both dressed in matching pearl-grey marabou that floated out behind them like a giant halo.

'Rent a bloody crowd's in, I see,' muttered Toby out of the side of his mouth. 'Still, Kaiser Villie will love it. Oh, look, Liz Hurley's being interviewed by *Hello!*'

'I don't get out much these days,' Liz was telling the *Hello!* reporter. 'I find I prefer to stay at home with my son in front of—'

'– the paparazzi,' muttered Toby in Cat's ear.

'Toby, how nice of you to pop by.' A voice dripping with sarcasm boomed from a tiny crêpey figure that had wedged itself between them.

'Aunt Hermione. How lovely to see you.' Toby stooped down to kiss a pair of heavily rouged cheeks.

Aunt Hermione snorted. 'Unfortunately for you, Toby, I'm afraid you've only managed to miss half the evening.'

'Darling Aunt Hermione. You look amazing, as ever.' Toby's eyes swept over his aunt's one-sleeved black sequinned dress. It was at least thirty years too young for her. 'Allow me to introduce you to my colleague, Cat McGinty.'

Hermione hurled a haughty smile in the direction of Cat and reached up to pluck an imaginary speck off Toby's jacket. A flurry of trumpets signalled that they were about to be graced by minor royalty. Patting her chignon with a tiny, liver-spot-speckled claw, Hermione scuttled off.

'Cat, I don't believe you've met Mrs Frupps,' said Toby, guiding her past Tracy Emin, whose breasts strained against a lilac Vivienne Westwood bustier like two overcharged torpedoes.

Having polished off most of the vol-au-vents, Mrs Frupps radiated intense gloom. 'You look divine, Frau Frupps,' said Toby. 'What a heavenly dress. Salmon pink, isn't it? Frau Frupps attempted a smile. 'Radioactive,' whispered Toby to Cat as he pulled out a chair next to Kaiser Vill for her.

'Marvellous to meet you face to face at last.' Herr Frupps pulled a vast spotted silk handkerchief from his pocket and began dabbing at his immense forehead. 'You are looking vonderful, my dear.'

Cat weighed up her options and decided dishonesty was the best policy. 'So are you. Have you had a pleasant stay in London?'

'Not really,' he said mournfully. 'Lotte has set her heart on a manor in the Royal Berkshire. We have been looking at country estates all day.' He squinted at Cat's cleavage through a cloud of cigar smoke. 'The countryside is full of physical activities I hate it, don't you?'

'I haven't really thought about it,' lied Cat. Candida St John Green's last 'Rural Idyll' column had been all about the joys of fox-hunting.

'Are you doing much physical activities, Cat?'

'Er, I don't really have time.' Even as she said it she was aware of sounding like a freak with no life outside her job.

'Well then, I am doubly admiring you.' He dragged his gaze reluctantly from her breasts and looked on her with renewed respect. 'You must be extremely dedicated to your work.' A waiter rushed past with a tray and the Kaiser's eyes lit up as he scooped half a dozen canapés from it.

Across the table, Cat heard Mrs Frupps ask Toby whether he was knowing the Lady Victoria Hervey. Cat was about to ask her husband some searching questions about his other publishing interests when Hermione scuttled back with a tray of raffle tickets. 'All in a good cause,' she said in a voice that could flay flint. She rattled the tray pointedly under Cat's nose.

'Let me see,' said Cat, scrabbling in her bag for some money. 'I'll take ten.'

'That's the spirit,' exclaimed Aunt Hermione. For a moment she appeared to deliberate over which tickets to give Cat. 'That will be a thousand pounds.' She clawed the perforations gleefully. 'We are doing well this evening.'

Cat turned as white as Aunt Hermione's hair and prayed for a natural disaster to take place at God's earliest convenience.

'Good God, Hermione, you're not serious!' Toby leant across Mrs Frupps's canapé-spattered décolletage. Cat's heart almost stopped in embarrassment.

'I most certainly am,' exclaimed Hermione, drawing herself up to her full five feet. 'There are some simply marvellous prizes. Beginning with a week at Butely health farm.'

'And what's the booby prize?' asked Toby, extracting his wallet from inside his dinner jacket. 'Two weeks?'

'Don't be tiresome, Toby. Apparently Butely is wonderful for detoxifying.' She glowered at his glass of champagne.

'Oh well, in that case I want these,' he said, refusing to be riled by Hermione. He snatched the tickets playfully from Cat and waved a Coutts card at Hermione. How many accounts did he have? wondered Cat.

'Don't worry about her,' he muttered later to Cat behind the generous expanse of Mrs Frupps's sun-blasted back. 'I've always thought Hermione must have got her warmth and gaiety from Stalin. By the way, McGinty, did I tell you how amazing you look?'

'Several times. Would that be amazing as in Hermione amazing?'

'Certainly not. She's amazingly terrifying. You're just amazing. Chic but sexy at the same time.'

The last time she'd been told she looked sexy had been at least ten years ago, and didn't count because she'd been walking past a building site. She felt herself blushing again. Fortunately Mrs Frupps decided she'd had enough pavlova and leant back, blotting out Toby and, for that matter, the rest of the room.

'Tell me, my dear,' resumed Kaiser Vill in a low voice, 'would you be happening to know where the best lap-dancing clubs are in London?'

Cat froze. She felt sure this was some kind of test. 'I just love this song, don't you?'

'The best,' said Kaiser Vill, mopping his forehead again. He leapt to his feet with surprising lightness, shaking a few beads of sweat over Cat's shoulders like an eager gun dog. Taking her hand with the kind of proprietorial force with which Germany had annexed Austria, he led her firmly into the fray and proceeded to karaoke in her ear along to 'I will survive'.

Three songs later, the next six months of Frupps business was clearly in the bag. And to cap it all, they were playing 'How Deep Is Your Love' on the dance floor. It was one of her favourite songs – although she'd always pretended she thought it was kitsch rubbish whenever Ben had caught her singing along to it.

She looked wistfully across the dance floor at Toby, who was clasped against Mrs Frupps's capacious bosom. He winked at her and steered Mrs Frupps across the room, where he made her evening by introducing her to Lady Victoria Hervey, who had draped herself across the minor royal. He made his way over to Cat. 'Here's your raffle ticket. Your commission for helping to make the evening such a success. Hermione selected it herself, so blame her if you don't win anything.'

Overcome by the stirring harmonies of the Gibb brothers, Cat had a flash of inspiration. 'I couldn't possibly accept. Unless you dance with me to my favourite song.'

The evening seemed to have gone okay, Cat thought later, as she peeled her hand from Kaiser Vill's lips and Toby waved a relieved farewell to Mrs Frupps. They had secured another tranche of business from the Frupps and Toby had danced with her. True, she had asked him, but nothing could detract from the moment when she had finally let her head sink against his jacket. She breathed in the sharp lemony tang of his aftershave and let herself be expertly steered around the room. And then she'd heard her name being called over the loudspeakers. For the first time in her life she'd won a prize in a raffle. So of course they'd had to have another dance to celebrate. He was an excellent dancer. As she pressed against his chest, feeling the sinews of his thighs press against hers, the rest of the room disappeared – literally. They were the last people to leave.

'One last nightcap,' Toby pleaded, before whisking her upstairs to the all-night bar.

In the corner a piano was tinkling more Bee Gees, which Cat took to be some sort of sign – she'd work out what later. She settled into a leather armchair as deep as Lake Tahoe. Toby ordered a bottle of champagne and Cat found herself rearranging her dress to allow for maximum leg exposure and silently thanking Jess for the Veet.

'Bloody good team work, McGinty,' said Toby, placing a stuffed olive on his tongue. 'As a business team, I'd say we had the force of Tate and Lyle, Rolls and Royce or—'

Richard and Judy?' offered Cat, feeling an overwhelming need to deflect Toby's gaze from her face, which was presumably the colour of her last bank statement.

'Kaiser Vill couldn't stop singing your praises while you and Frau Frupps disappeared to the loos. What took you so long, by the way? I was beginning to worry you'd got lost between her chins.'

'She was wanting to know about the British public school system for her grandchildren. She has eighteen of them.' She could have sex with him, she supposed. As long as she remembered to treat it as an entirely meaningless exercise. It might even do her good.

'Well, I'm certainly going to make sure the Vices hear about your contribution to the evening.' His jacket fell open and the Pure Wool emblem on its lining blurred into triple vision. A wolf in sheep's clothing.

He stopped twizzling his champagne and gazed at her intently. His eyes were an extraordinary bluish green.

'I've never had anyone in my team like you,' he continued. 'You really go the extra mile. I mean, look – Saturday night, when you could be relaxing . . .'

'I thought you said we were partners,' said Cat, suddenly feeling clearer headed.

'Of course we are – in practice. It's just that I'm perfectly aware of the iniquity in our pay packets.'

Gay or not gay? Spoken for or not spoken for? She needed to know for Petula's sake. The poor girl obviously had an enormous crush on him.

'That's what partners do, isn't it?' She stretched her leg out where Toby wouldn't fail to see it. 'Go the extra mile.'

'You certainly went the extra mile with Kaiser Vill. Excellent plan to get him talking about the rest of his publishing empire. Practically had him eating out of you. Great tits, by the way, McGinty. Really impressive.'

'Are you sexually harassing me, Marks?' God, she loved champagne. It meant you could flirt with impunity and deny everything the following day.

'I certainly hope so.'

Skewered by the unabashed fashion in which Toby was scrutinising her, she fumbled in her bag. 'You're forgetting why else I'm brilliant.'

'Which is?' said Toby, pouring her yet another glass of champagne.

'I win raffles.'

'Wrong, you won one raffle. For the first time in your life. You said so yourself.'

It was true. She'd never won anything before.

'And as you also said, you hate health farms.'

'Well, strictly speaking I haven't actually been to one,' said Cat, leaning forward to give Toby vantage over her breasts. Somebody might as well appreciate them. 'There was a time when I think I'd probably have relished spending all day being pampered.'

'Well, I wouldn't start with Butely.' Toby smirked.

'How come you know so much about health farms?' asked Cat. She was starting to feel nauseous.

'It's near my mother's place in Dorset. Lower Nettlescombe, on the River Piddle.'

'You are joking. The River Piddle?'

'Are you casting aspersions on Dorset's ancient nomenclature? Beautiful scenery, I'll give it that. And gorgeous Restoration house. Parts of it are even medieval – notably the plumbing parts. I'm amazed it hasn't had a demolition order slapped on it.'

Cat felt a little stab of disappointment, In her heart of hearts she'd often fantasised about having the time to go to a health farm – if only so that she could sleep uninterrupted for a week. Just her luck that Butely was in danger of imminent collapse.

Standing up unsteadily, she became aware that she too was in danger of falling apart. She sat down again. She'd have to wait until the floor stopped buckling. She asked Toby a bit more about his mother, who, it transpired, was on her own, like Suzette. And when she'd listened for a while, she found herself telling him about her own lack of family. She even heard herself talking about the devastating effect not having a father had had on her. How all her life she had felt something was missing – as if a part of her were emotionally cauterised.

'Did you never even visit his grave?' asked Toby gently.

'That's just it.' Cat lurched for the bottle of champagne. 'There isn't one. Or at least, my mother won't tell me where it is. She refuses to talk about him. It's sick – and ironic considering how indiscreet she is about everything else.'

'And you – have you ever had any counselling?' asked Toby, sounding suddenly very caring indeed.

'Only from my mother. Usually about which handbag's in.' The walls stopped moving. She could even see the clock – a quarter past two. He accompanied her to the revolving doors – she managed to stumble just the once – and flagged a taxi down for her. 'Sorry, I don't think I'm in any fit state to drive either of us,' he said, leaning in to peck her on the cheek. 'Are you sure you'll be all right getting home?'

'Perfectly.' A slug of cold air hit her. She instinctively reached for the strap next to her ear and almost toppled off the seat. What did she do now? Eight years out of the dating game meant she had no perception of what was or wasn't appropriate. For all she knew no one actually bothered with beds any more. The bits she picked up from the tabloids seemed to involve quickies up against walls. Or maybe that was just the name of a cocktail. She vaguely remembered Jess reporting back from a party where all the drinks had been named after lewd sexual acts. Or had that been Lily?

'I'm fine.' Had she already said this?

'McGinty, if you don't mind my saying, all of a sudden you look bloody awful. Green's definitely not your colour.' He jumped in beside her. The intoxicating tang of whisky and cigarette smoke clinging to his clothes stung her nostrils. She felt hot, cold and queasy all at the same time. Not because she was under the slightest illusion regarding Toby's intentions but because she remembered that Jess's tube of spermicide was still by the front door.

5

'I suppose the sixty-four-thousand-dollar question is did you shag him?'

Cat flinched. Whenever she felt homesick Suzette turned to what she fondly imagined was modern vernacular English. Cat felt herself losing the will to live – and she'd only been awake a few minutes. It was a fair question, though. Had she?

If she had it was the worst of all possible worlds – guilt without pleasure, or at least without any pleasurable memories. She squinted at the photograph of Ben that she'd never got round to clearing from her bedside table. He was holding Lily, who would have been about eight months old. They were in Salcombe – their one and only holiday as a family. Ben, wearing the Calvin Klein sunglasses that Suzette had sent him, stared out, uncharacteristically urbane. They both looked like people from a Boden catalogue – a mass of cherubic blond curls and dimples. She could just imagine the captions: Ben – jazz musician and pot-head; Lily – crooked accountant. She kept it only because, despite Ben's manifest failings, she was determined Lily should grow up more aware of who her father was than Cat had ever been.

'Well?' Suzette's question mark hovered over the Atlantic like a neutron bomb. Cat stuffed her head under the pillow, where her abused, reddened eyeballs encountered the tube of spermicide and a crumpled-up version of the elegant black halter neck she'd worn the night before. Mounting panic competed with waves of nausea. Gingerly she reached across the bed to check for another sentient being.

'No, I did not.' It was a bit too muffled to have quite the Lady Bracknellish quality Cat would have liked, but it packed a certain emphatic level of outrage. Apart from the potential humiliation, Cat didn't want to sleep with Toby. Yet. She had a feeling that the frisson in their relationship, the spark that fuelled their crackling conversations, partly depended on their not sleeping together. Or was that just another excuse to keep a man – all men – at arm's length?

'Don't sound so aghast. You must be getting a bit rusty down there. It's not good for you to be so emotionally pent up.'

For the millionth time Cat wished her mother modelled herself on Julie Andrews rather than Hugh Hefner.

She put the phone down.

The house was as silent as a village church – or almost. Screwing her eyes up against the shafts of sun, she reached for her bedside clock. Ten o'clock. Jess and Lily must have gone for breakfast at the Karma Factory. A siren began wailing down the street. Thieves must have broken into In Cod We Trust again. It was such a regular occurrence the police no longer bothered to hurry.

There was no point attempting to go back to sleep. Cat groped her way to the bathroom, where bottle after bottle of Suzette's hi-tech freebies stood sentinel along the cracked surfaces of Ralph's slapdash tiling. She squinted at the mirror; her eyes were so blood-shot she could barely make out the timing instructions on any of the bottles, let alone the ingredients.

The good thing about Toby, decided Cat, slathering on a salmon-and-caviar oxygenated multi-vitamin power recovery masque (ten minutes), was that his Porsche, Rolex and complete lack of self-doubt probably made him precisely the kind of man her mother would most disapprove of. Swampy was probably Suzette's preferred line in sons-in-law, though second-guessing Suzette was an inexact science, as Cat had learned through bitter experience. She combed some ginkgo biloba extract through her hair, tried to imagine Toby in an Animal Lib balaclava and gave up. The only march he was likely to have been on was one to the cash dispenser in Portman Square. Then again he probably sent Petula to do that sort of thing.

The bad thing about Toby – the truly shameful, utterly humiliating, never to be rectified thing – was that he had almost seen her throw up. She slapped some anti-cellulite Exfoliante Energisante on her thighs and began rubbing it around rigorously (minimum thirty minutes).

Oh, and she may have slept with him.

She scraped some Spa Strength foam over her hands and thrust them into a pair of pale rubber gloves (twenty minutes). Then she took a large tub of Cellulux – whatever that was – downstairs and placed it in the oven to warm gently as instructed for ten minutes before application. After that she went round the house looking for stray alarm clocks, which she arranged round her bed, set to ring at ten- and twenty-minute intervals, and promptly passed out.

Propped against a mountain of plump pillows, Suzette decided she must be missing Eduardo, who had had to nip back to Rio. At any rate, she couldn't sleep, which was a bloody nuisance as she was due on *Good Morning America* the next day to plug *Dressing for Two*, and if she didn't get her eight hours there was a serious risk she'd look like Helen Mirren, who, in Suzette's view, had let herself go round the eye area. She contemplated counting sheep. Stupid idea. Counting tax returns used to work but at the moment the whole fiscal issue was a bit fraught. She thought about Cat's love life again. That shouldn't take long. And then the phone rang. 'I was just thinking about you,' she said drowsily. 'Look, it's not as if a one-night stand has to be a life commitment. At least, it didn't in my day.'

'More's the pity.' A thin voice quivered down the line from what sounded like a million miles away. A voice from another life. 'Rodney, is that you?' she asked, hoping against hope it wasn't. The voice, though frail, still had the power to stop her in her tracks. Even thirty-four years after she'd heard it for the very first time.

'How gratifying that you still remember something about me,' he said, before going on to tell her that he needed to see her as a matter of urgency. 'It's important. But I'm afraid I can't make it to New York . . . I was hoping you might agree to meet here. I assume you come back to England quite often.'

'It's a bit difficult at the moment. I'm immensely tied up at work. Can't really get away, and then there's a rather important interview I've got to do in Paris, so you can see life's a bit busy.'

'Paris, then?' he suggested in a voice that was strangely hard to contradict. There was a pause while she weighed up her options. She could simply hang up. Leave the answerphone on for the next six weeks until he gave up. On the other hand it was true he had never once, in sixteen years, reneged on their agreement. On that point at least he had been entirely honourable.

'Rodney, you know I'd love to see you, but I really am on a very tight deadline over the next few weeks.'

'And I'm dying. The doctors give me three months max. So you could say I'm on one too.'

Trust Rodney to have the best bloody lines.

That one little phone call wrecked her beauty sleep for the rest of Sunday, and several days to come. But that was Rodney Dowell for you. Trouble from the moment she'd laid eyes on him.

The last time she'd heard from him had been sixteen years earlier, shortly after her first book had stormed the best-seller list and sat there for fifteen months. Desperate to repeat the success, but terrified it was a one-off fluke, she'd persuaded Cat to take part in 'Relative Values' in the *Sunday Times* and had set about frantically rearranging her life for public consumption. In Suzette's case that meant spin-doctoring at Olympic levels and skirting round one or two omissions, Cat's father being one of them.

'*I was a bit shocked to read of my death, frankly,*' he'd written to her after the article appeared. '*And possibly even more shocked to discover I had a daughter. But I know you must have your reasons for keeping us both in the dark.*'

'*How can you be so sure that Cat is yours,*' she had scrawled back on her best Smythson, '*when I'm not even certain myself? Cat's father could,*' she added gratuitously, '*have been one of half a dozen.*'

He had persisted. '*Cat is so uncannily similar to me in looks,*' he wrote, '*that I can't believe she's not my flesh and blood. The dates make perfect sense. My dear Suzette, I have treasured the memory of our one night together even if you have not. I understand that your feelings for me may be such that you would prefer not to have me in your life. But if there is any way in which I can make amends to my daughter, via financial arrangements or—'*

There was not, she wrote back crisply, and with no small sense of satisfaction. They were just dandy without the intervention of any men. Nor was there the remotest possibility of him meeting his daughter. Cat thought he was dead. Any evidence that he was not would traumatise her.

To her astonishment he had acquiesced. All he had asked was that Suzette occasionally update him on Cat's welfare. Then he had left them both alone, having made it clear that if either of them ever required any help, they had only to get in touch. With Rodney so clearly occupying the moral high ground, Suzette was left with no real choice but to write him long, rambling letters about Cat, accompanied by the odd photograph of them both, strictly edited, of course, so that Suzette never looked less than ten years younger than her real age. In keeping with the agreement, he had never replied. She knew nothing more about Rodney Dowell than she had in 1969.

And now, out of the blue, he'd called to tell her he was dying . . .

Sir Rodney Dowell, to be precise. CBE. Erstwhile industrialist, one-time medical officer in the British Army and the biggest blot on Suzette's formerly impeccably anti-Establishment credentials.

In some ways they were the ideal sixties couple. He was a bourgeois entrepreneur with several million in the bank. She was a working-class rebel with fantastic legs. He'd risen rapidly and seamlessly through the ranks of a pharmaceutical conglomerate. She'd risen somewhat bloodily up the masthead of *Fair Sex*, a daringly outspoken magazine that was considered enough of a hotbed of radical feminist thinking to be quoted in a speech in the House of Commons. He was rumoured to have his sights on a safe political seat. She secretly hankered after a chair in the *Daily Mail*'s well-paid fashion department. It was odds on as to who would get what they wanted first.

Suzette McGinty hadn't got what she wanted by dithering. And what she wanted most was to escape from the grimy back-to-back where she grew up in Liverpool with a sadistic grandmother who had taken over when Suzette's single mother had bunked off to Canada with a teddy-boy mechanic called Tonto.

At sixteen but claiming to be eighteen, Suzette had arrived outside the offices of *Fair Sex* with one small suitcase and a very bad copy of a Mary Quant miniskirt. She was young, gorgeous and bolshy. The four other women running *Fair Sex* were only marginally less young and gorgeous and even more bolshy. Recognising a kindred spirit in Suzette, they signed her up immediately to make the tea and open the post, even though there was meant to be no hierarchy on the magazine and they were all supposed to take their turn washing out the mugs.

It sort of worked. Within six months she had become agony aunt, answering fraught enquiries from girls desperate to find out whether they could get pregnant from swallowing their boyfriend's semen. Eighteen months later she was promoted to fashion editor.

Actually, in the *Fair Sex* scheme of things, fashion editor could hardly be seen to be a step-up from anywhere, being the ultimate folly of global greed. But the famous five, as they'd become known in the press, were realists. A bare-breasted model in a tutu shifted far more copies than a picture of Desmond Tutu. Plus it meant Suzette got to go to Paris four times a year with David Bailey, Terence Donovan and a dazzling array of degenerate young actors and consume wildly inappropriate amounts of illegal substances.

And so she embarked on a heady period. Life was wild. She became a political firebrand, waving placards against American troops in Vietnam, male oppression and the Bomb, and standing shoulder to shoulder with Julie Christie and half the Redgrave clan. Her social life as she was fond of telling everyone, was in every sense a riot. And then she'd met Rodney Dowell. Strictly speaking they were never formally introduced, police cells not being bastions of genteel etiquette.

Rodney Dowell was exactly the kind of hate-figure the staff of *Fair Sex* loved best: rich, Establishment and suavely good looking.

According to the editor, he was also the thing that dared not speak its name. 'A homosexual?' Suzette had asked, her eyes round with excitement. 'No,' said her editor. 'A Tory.' He was also vocally in favour of a controversial new children's vaccine for whooping cough.

Naturally, when Rodney Dowell had gone to address the students' union at the LSE on behalf of the pharmaceutical industry, Suzette had taken along all the rotten eggs she could cram into her YSL suede patchwork shoulder bag. Plus several dog turds, although they could have been the work of cats – she didn't linger long enough to corroborate their provenance. Whatever, it was the turds which got her arrested. On their own, the policeman who slipped the handcuffs round her wrists informed her, the eggs might have been overlooked. In the same way presumably that he was looking over her miniskirt. But a turd was a turd and as such constituted a breach of the peace.

Swinging her legs jauntily backwards and forwards as she sat on the bench in her cell in Paddington police station, and reading the copy of *Spare Rib* she had stuffed under her poncho, Suzette had felt strangely jubilant. At last, after countless marches, she was finally causing ructions. And then bloody Rodney Dowell – he hadn't been Sir in those days – had tipped up at the police station, polluting her cell with his exploitative handmade shoes and his excessively conventional Savile Row suit. He came bearing mercy and flashing a patrician smile – not to mention a few bottles of Pouilly-Fuissé for the arresting officer – and charmed everyone by gallantly dropping all the charges against Suzette. And like the amoral global industrialist he was, he'd smarmed his way into taking her out to dinner. She only agreed because it had seemed like the perfect opportunity to subvert from within. Which in his case, once he'd got her into bed, technically speaking, it had been.

Even now it made her blush to think quite how subversive he'd been. He may even have shared a joint with her in the huge bed they'd ended up in at Claridge's. He must have been at least twenty-five years older than she was. It was disgusting really. And very enjoyable, at the time. And even more so when a long-stemmed rose had arrived at the *Fair Sex* offices with a ruby and diamond bracelet coiled round its stem.

After Cat was born, motherhood had completely consumed Suzette for almost two years. She read Dr Spock, gave up smoking and breast-fed her daughter in the American embassy, making the front pages of the *Evening Standard*.

In the spirit of the times she never, ever revealed the identity of Cat's father. She didn't need a man. After the labour she'd been through, she didn't much want one either. By now, she'd moved to the *Daily Mail*, in return for a huge salary and jettisoning all her left-wing principles. Needs must, she always said. And no one had the heart to argue. After all, she was going to raise her daughter herself. Which, to give her credit, she did – with a bit of strategic input from some of the country's leading boarding schools.

All in all, things had worked out brilliantly. No small thanks to herself. And now, after Rodney's bombshell, her shipshape little boat, her cosy, highly enjoyable life, her personal solar system (in which all planets revolved conveniently around her) had been rocked in the most shocking way. With a heavy sense of foreboding, she called Cat.

'I can't believe the communications in that bloody country of yours,' began Suzette, conveniently forgetting it was also still her country. 'You'd think Tony Blair could at least sort that out.' Cat let Suzette rant on, graciously omitting to point out that Suzette had been one of Tony's greatest fans. Ever since the arrival of Anita Roddick, another phenomenally successful career woman with left-wing credentials, Suzette had described herself as a Caring Capitalist, which as far as Cat could see meant Not Voting Tory and then emigrating when the whole of the country went on strike under Labour. But now was not the time to vent her views on this. Not least because she didn't want to crack her face mask.

'Anyway, I was really calling to see if you and Lily would have supper with me on Tuesday at the Ritz.'

Cat was dumbfounded. Her mother hadn't been to London for two years, partly, Cat suspected, because she owed Her Majesty's

Inspectors a wodge of money. And why was her mother staying at the Ritz? What was wrong with Makesbury Road?

And what was wrong with her face mask, which was starting to tug violently at her cheek muscles? Surely it wasn't meant to feel quite like that. She wondered how long she'd been comatose on the bed.

'I meant the Ritz in Paris.' Suzette gave the tinkly little laugh that always signalled guilt on her part. 'The publishers are insisting I stay somewhere that will impress Karl – he's agreed to write the foreword to *Dressing for Two* on condition that I personally come and take dictation from him. I thought the four of us could have dinner. I know Lily would love Karl.'

'Out of the question, I'm afraid. I couldn't possibly get time off.'

'Sorry. Forgot the country would grind to a halt without the next instalment of the Frupps history of the world.'

Feeling her mask cracking like Arctic ice, Cat groped for a reply that didn't contain too many vowels. A bleep announced that someone was on the other line.

'Jstasc.'

It was Toby, crooning 'How Deep Is Your Hangover?'

'Actually I'm feeling remarkably chipper,' lied Cat. There was an audible rip as the mask split from ear to ear. 'I may have the body of a weak and feeble woman but I've got the stomach of a . . . er, king, to quote Boadicea.'

'I think you'll find it was Elizabeth I. She also said she was a virgin. A pathological liar, clearly.'

'Well, I feel great,' she persisted, cursing her sketchy education. At least her feet had stopped throbbing.

'That's good,' said Toby smoothly. 'Because Kaiser Vill called first thing this morning. He's got another proposition for us. Apparently it can't wait till tomorrow. A cable network's suddenly come up for sale in Poland and he wants us to put a feasibility plan together by Wednesday at the latest. I know it's a lot to ask – but you couldn't make it into the office later on today, could you?'

She racked through what was left of her recent memory for any evidence that she might have promised to do something special with Lily today.

'I know it's tough on Lily, but I wouldn't ask if I didn't think it was really important. I can dig up a lot of the stuff on eastern Europe, but no one's got such a deep inside track on Frupps as you—'

'I'll see you in one hour,' she croaked, which was ambitious considering that the silver stilettos she'd superglued on last night were still stubbornly attached to her heels.

Four days later, Suzette sank back into the deep leather armchair of the Ritz Bar and surveyed the gaunt figure opposite her. In an eerie way, he hadn't changed at all. Stooped, thin and white. But still with those arresting blue eyes. And still not her type. It was like discovering your worst fashion mistake at the back of the wardrobe, trying it on in a fit of nostalgic sentimentality, only to find it looked just as terrible thirty years later. A round mahogany table loomed between them like a vast lake, laden with vessels on which were heaped shiny fat coral-coloured prawns that had been dipped in breadcrumbs and perfect circles of bread, barely bigger than a euro and embellished with translucent slivers of smoked salmon. Suzette pushed the plates away in disgust. Hadn't the French heard of wheat intolerance? 'Waiter, take this away, please, we won't be eating any of it.'

The waiter behind the bar shot her a disdainful look and carried on polishing his cocktail shaker.

Rodney had kept his body trim, she'd give him that. And so, she thought, admiring her own neatly crossed legs, had she. Not that she was looking her absolute best. She hadn't slept properly since he'd phoned four days earlier, what with the jet lag and being riddled with worry about what he could be up to. At the very least he would presumably ask her to arrange for him to meet Cat. She'd have to say no, of course, but given that he was dying it would be a harrowing night. She would just have to avoid looking at those frail, sunken cheeks. Otherwise she didn't know whether she trusted herself to take a firm line.

It would kill Cat if she agreed to the meeting. Or rather it would kill Cat's affection for her. She decided to stall. She summoned the waiter and ordered a magnum of iced champagne. With any luck, she thought, pouring them both a glass, she could keep him talking here in the Ritz until he kicked the ice bucket or cirrhosis of the liver finished him off.

'I have to say, Rodney, for a man at death's door, you look remarkably fit.' She rearranged her legs to offer maximum exposure of her trim calves. Assuming he could still see properly.

'You look splendid too, Suzette.' He coughed and adjusted his silk cravat. 'New York obviously agrees with you.'

It certainly agreed that she looked splendid, she thought contentedly. *New York* magazine had just voted her number three in its Fit and Fifty list. 'I could hardly go around looking like a wreck in view of what I do for a living, could I?'

'You have to admit there's a rather satisfying irony in the way our lives have mapped out,' he said, before embarking on what she considered a rather ostentatious coughing fit.

'But Rodney,' she said coolly when the coughing had more or less subsided, 'I haven't the faintest idea how your life has mapped out. Thirty years ago you were busy trying to inoculate most of the Third World against diseases they were very unlikely to ever come across. That's when you weren't trying to dismember small animals.'

He looked at her in amusement, momentarily considered entering into a debate, for old times' sake, then thought better of it.

'Let's just say I had a change of heart,' he said softly, turning to the waiter and ordering a bottle of still mineral water. 'Actually I had a brush with death – the cancer that's come back to haunt me. I first got it shortly after you and I met. It made me take stock. Faced with a three-month death sentence you either carry on drinking two bottles of claret a day, or set yourself the challenge of beating the odds.'

'You're not telling me you're TT?'

'And vegan.' He sloshed the water round his mouth as if it were chateau vintage. 'I was sent to an alternative cancer clinic that saved my life. No alcohol, no meat, no dairy—'

'Yes, I do know what a vegan is, Rodney.' Suzette looked appalled. How could he have taken the moral high ground when it came to food as well as everything else? 'You're going to tell me you didn't stay in politics either.'

'I'm afraid I am – unless you count keeping the peace between chiropractors and osteopaths. They're very competitive.' He smiled and then began coughing again. Suzette looked perplexed. 'I opened a naturopathic retreat instead – to try and spread the message I learned in the cancer clinic. It was quite ground breaking in its day. That's why I was knighted.'

'Nothing to do with politics, then?' She popped a prawn in her mouth in disbelief.

'No. I didn't stay in politica long. I was knighted for alternative therapies. In Dorset. It's been terribly rewarding. Perhaps you've heard of it? It's called Butely.'

'I'm afraid not, Rodney. You know how it is in New York – Britain seems so very far away and . . . small.'

He floated serenely above her put-down. 'Yes, well, it's had quite an impact one way and another. I like to think we were part of that movement that pioneered the whole holistic approach to health.' He coughed again.

'Of course, in the seventies,' Suzette couldn't resist saying, 'all you had to do was cut down slightly on the Benson and Hedges and limit yourself to one fry-up a day to be considered far-out in medical terms.'

'Quite. I don't suppose it matters if word of our little enterprise never crossed the ocean.' It had, though. The last she'd heard – from a colleague on *Vogue* who'd stayed at Butely in 1994 – the place was a shambles. How strange that she'd never made the connection between the father of her child and the mother of all wacko health farms – but then Rodney had never given interviews, preferring the place to speak for itself.

'Well, well, well,' was all she could think of saying. She bit into a smoked salmon blini. And then, 'well, well,' again.

'You seem shocked.' He flashed her one of his scorching smiles, though thirty-four intervening years of gravity had robbed it of some of its force.

'It is a little surprising. From mass animal torturer to vegan is quite a big step, you must admit.'

'I was never a vivisector, you know,' he said. As he poured another glass of Evian, Suzette couldn't help noticing how violently his hand shook. Their drinks were going to be shaken rather than stirred. Fortunately a waiter bounded over to the table and finished the task before half the bottle ended up in her lap.

'I believed in a lot of things I now oppose,' he continued, 'but vivisection was never one of them. I never knew how that rumour started. Some misinformed journalist, no doubt. Sorry,' he said, interrupting her on what was remarkably close to a guilt trip. 'No offence meant. I've met some very fine members of the press over the years.'

She let it pass. She was hardly in a position to do otherwise. She scanned the conversational horizon for a lifeline that would steer them into less choppy waters.

'How's it all going?' She could have kicked herself. Considering he had less than three months to live, clearly it wasn't going brilliantly.

He smiled again, more weakly this time. 'It's been better. Butely's a bit expensive to run. The old place could do with a lick of paint. But you should see it, Suzette.' His eyes twinkled in the gloom of the bar. 'It's part fourteenth-century, nestling between two valleys and the sea.' He began to mist over. 'Damp or no damp, it's the most ravishing place on earth. Which is why I asked you to meet me.'

Suzette fiddled with her Cartier Tank nervously. She sincerely hoped he wasn't planning to leave it to Cat. How would she explain the sudden – and from the sounds of it dubious – windfall of a medieval millstone to Cat?

'I want to leave it to Cat.'

Suzette looked at him aghast.

'I realise it's a bit of a poisoned chalice.' Sir Rodney sounded distinctly nervous now. 'But I think it could be turned around with some youthful energy and fresh ideas.' Suzette turned the full blast of her still babyish round eyes on him in stunned horror. 'Cat's a talented businesswoman,' he forged on. 'You said so yourself. And it's a wonderful place to bring up children.'

So was boarding school, thought Suzette.

'The thing is, she won't have to carry it on her own. My lawyers have worked out a solution to Butely's, er, problems. It entails me leaving the land to my son, Jake – he's not a businessman really, but he does love the place. This way they both get something, but neither can sell without the other's agreement. In which instance, both would have to sell together. So Butely and its land will remain forever intact and—'

'What son?'

'Ah, have I never mentioned Jake?' He tapped his knee with a liver-spotted hand that almost melted her with its translucent fragility.

'Not since the beginning of this conversation, no. Not ever, actually, Rodney. And the last conversation we had, you begged me to allow you to see our daughter, whom you said meant more to you than anything—'

'And so she does,' said Sir Rodney, throwing longing looks at the peanuts. 'But you made it clear that you would be very unhappy if I were to establish a relationship with Cat, and so I didn't.'

'Look, Rodney, you've already got a son, for God's sake. Cat's all I've ever had.'

'I can see I've made you cross. Do you think those peanuts are very salty? Only I'm starting to think at my point in life it might not matter.'

'Oh, for heaven's sake, Rodney. Have the whole bloody bowl, and chuck back some of this Krug while you're at it. Look, when did you have this son?'

'During my marriage to Cynthia Radlett,' he said, looking hurt.

'Cynthia?' echoed Suzette. She sounded so affronted an onlooker would have assumed that Sir Rodney had jilted her at the altar, leaving her with unborn triplets and a father standing at the ready with a cat-o'-nine-tails.

'You didn't give me a lot of time to explain the one night we were together,' he reminded her gently. 'Don't worry. I wasn't committing adultery. Cynthia and I were already divorced by then. Let me think . . . Jake would have been about three at the time you and I met. He came along rather late in my marriage to Cynthia. Sadly we were separated shortly after his second birthday . . . and you're quite right to think me very fortunate in having two families, though I was a little devastated that in the end I didn't get to play much of a role in either of them.'

He stared morosely into the peanuts and for one awful moment Suzette thought he was going to weep.

'It was having Jake grow up near by that made me realise it would be unfair to insist that you let me see Cat. But now – well, I hope you understand the situation is entirely different.'

Suzette turned as pale as her cashmere sweater. She understood perfectly that the situation was different in that for once he had the upper hand. Even she could hardly refuse a dying man his last wish.

'Don't worry,' he said, anticipating her objections. 'She wouldn't have to know who I am.'

'What do you mean?' Suzette was willing to grasp at any straw, however flimsy. She looked directly at him again. This time her eyes were pleading.

'I hope you don't mind but I've already enlisted the help of an old friend of mine, Hermione Ffoulkes-Haddingham. She was on the committee of that ball, you see. I got her to put some pressure on Toby to attend – he was just going to send in some money. I knew he'd want to bring Cat. And then Hermione arranged for Cat to win that raffle ticket. I dare say Cat mentioned it to you.'

Suzette found herself plunging into the peanut bowl too. Anything to distract her from the fact that Cat hadn't told her about any raffle ticket.

'Yes.' Sir Rodney's cough erupted again, almost drowning out the cocktail mixer which was being flung around behind the bar like a matador on a losing streak. 'By the funniest coincidence, Toby, Hermione's great-nephew, is my ex-stepson.'

'Hilarious,' said Suzette uncertainly. Who the hell was Toby?

'To be perfectly honest with you' – he glanced round the bar before lowering his voice – 'I'm not sure that Toby is quite right for Cat. I feel disloyal saying this. Since he got back from New York he's been very solicitous. He's been to visit me several times. Always makes a point of telephoning regularly too – to ask how I am. It's kind of him, I suppose . . .'

Suzette wondered whether there was a not so subtle recrimination embedded in this, but decided to ignore it.

'And he seems very concerned about the future of Butely, which is why I've made him executor of my will as well as a trustee of Butely. I'm sure he'll be extremely effective in both roles.'

'Why don't you leave the place to him, then?' blurted Suzette.

Rodney looked at her uncomprehendingly. 'He's not my son, Suzette. And even if he were my son, there's something slightly quixotic about Toby. I won't put it more strongly than that. He's an excellent operator, I won't deny that. But I'm not sure he altogether approves of Butely. I do hope Cat's not getting too serious about him. I'm not sure he's the type one ought to get serious about.'

Suzette turned over the conversation she'd had with Cat a few days earlier. It had been mystifyingly inconclusive. Had Cat slept with whoever it was she was likely to have been sleeping with? And was his name Toby? For the first time in her life she saw with sickening clarity how little she really knew about her daughter.

'The point is' – Sir Rodney's eyes watered slightly, and the veins on his neck throbbed painfully – 'that I want you to help me see my daughter. I promise I won't tell her who I am. I just want to see her. I've supplied the means. Cat's won her week's stay at Butely but from what I understand, she's not the alternative medicine type.'

'So you want me to convince her to come?'

'Sixteen years ago you denied me any contact with my daughter. I acquiesced because, as you rightly point out, I had a son already, and it didn't seem fair on you. But now I wonder if it was fair on Cat . . .'

'And coming into her life now when you've only three months to live is fair?'

'Calm down, Suzette. As I said, I don't want to make things difficult for you. But I will if you don't help me. I've stayed out of your life so far, and I will continue to do so. But I must see my daughter. Just for a week. Just to get to know her a little. To hear her voice, to see the way she walks. Find out what makes her laugh. Look—' He pulled a battered leather wallet from inside his jacket. Inside were fifteen small transparent folders, each containing a photograph of Cat. 'These are all I have of my daughter. The photos you sent me every year on her birthday, just as I asked you to sixteen years ago.'

Suzette looked at him mutely, torn between remorse and wanting to hit him with his walking stick. 'What makes you think I have any influence over Cat?' she said bitterly.

'If you have a conscience – and I strongly believe you do – you'll make sure she comes.'

She drained the remains of the champagne and leant back in her chair. 'Very well, Rodney,' she said evenly. 'You win. But please, I beg of you, don't saddle her with Butely's problems. Flog the place. Burn it down and collect some insurance and leave that to her – anything but load more responsibilities on Cat's plate.'

He looked at her sorrowfully. 'I didn't realise it would be such an unwelcome burden.'

'Well, it is,' said Suzette, feeling slightly churlish. But as Cat's mother she really felt she knew a great deal more than Rodney what was good for her. And she was determined to protect her, come what may.

6

Cat loved it when her mother invited herself to stay. Almost as much as she loved the inevitable eleventh-hour cancellation. That way they both got to bask in the glow of mother–daughter closeness without having to experience it. So when Suzette called to ask whether she could drop in on her way back from Paris, Cat calmly said of course she could.

'Of course, the house is still a bit rough around the edges,' she said, considerately supplying her mother with an excuse for calling back in a few hours to postpone the visit. Gales of charcoal-coloured smoke began to emanate from one of Jess's saucepans.

Suzette sank back into the foam and flicked the Jacuzzi in the Ritz to pulsate, oblivious to the mayhem unfolding in the kitchen of Makesbury Road. Jess switched the radio from the *Today* programme to Kiss FM.

'Is there anything I can bring from Paris?' Suzette asked, reaching for her loofah. 'What is that horrendous noise, by the way?'

'Nothing. We'll see you on Friday, then?'

A flurry of mixed emotions settled on Cat like snowflakes, cloaking her in confusion. Despite everything, she found her mother a reassuring presence – in minuscule doses. But the house – she cast a despairing look round the kitchen, which looked like a post-apocalyptic scene from a Ridley Scott film – was hardly an advertisement for how well she was coping with single motherhood. She was going to have to get things under control in case Suzette really did turn up. She began by marching over to the radio and wrenching the dial back to John Humphrys. It came away in her hands as the tuner hovered over Radio 2.

'Now look what you've done.' Jess looked at her in disbelief.

'Radio Two's very cool these days. They've got Jonathan Ross and—' Cat broke off as the unmistakably brassy sounds of Terry Wogan singing along to the Grimethorpe Colliery Band competed with the noise of drilling outside.

'School coffee morning on Thursday,' Jess reminded her spitefully. Lily's dark-fringed eyes looked at her pleadingly. Cat knew she'd be letting her down if she were the only mother not to turn up.

'Thirty-one shopping days to ye olde Christmas,' crooned Terry Wogan. Cat's mouth went dry. What if Suzette really did come and decided to stay until the end of the year? What if she decided to move back to England? Their relationship was just about sustainable long distance. But it would never survive a week if they actually had to see each other.

Suzette called twice more to confirm she was on her way. Both times she tried her utmost to convey the impression that this time her intentions were serious and both times she sensed Cat's rising panic. That was all to the good, she supposed, if it meant that Cat might actually take up the offer to go and stay at Butely. But the dawning realisation that the only way to get her daughter to move out temporarily was to threaten to move in and behave like something out of *Absolutely Fabulous* was enough to deflate even Suzette's normally irrepressible optimism.

Yet even though she knew the visit was bound to end in a quarrel – it had to, and fast, because she had only two weeks before her next book manuscript was due – she couldn't help being excited about seeing Cat and Lily. Not even the memories of her daughter's neighbours and that horrible cat could take that away from her.

Cat would rather have stepped in front of a bus than face the next forty minutes, but for Lily's sake it was something that had to be endured. The cranberry-coloured door of the Lindens swung back to reveal Persia's mother, flanked by two Filipino maids in black uniform. Cat shook her umbrella on to the bullrush mat and leant it against the door to dry. Persia's mother winced. 'Umbrella, Delphine.' Delphine immediately removed the offending item. 'Sorry.' Persia's mother turned daintily to address Cat. 'We've just had everything painted again. Nantucket Sky.'

Cat resigned herself to a hideous eternity of maternity. Persia's mother beckoned Cat down a glass spiral staircase into a vast industrial space. Judging by the coffee cups set out on one of the surfaces, it was the kitchen.

'Quentin, our architect, doesn't believe in ceilings,' said Persia's mother, following Cat's upward gaze. 'Ever since we had the place redone it feels so much airier.'

'Quentin's a genius,' said a blonde cocktail stick with a mobile wedged permanently between shoulder and ear. Beneath the hair, Cat vaguely recognised her as Xanthe's mother. 'He's doing our next house. Got to strip everything out. Kensington and Chelsea Council are being so petty about it all. Honestly, you'd think a Grade Two listing was one of the Ten Commandments.'

'And who follows those?' said a wafer-thin brunette in a Marc Jacobs dress.

'He's such a refreshing antidote to traditional thinking, don't you think?' continued Persia's mother, eyeing the enormous, pristine espresso-maker in her kitchen as if she were seeing it for the first time. 'Jug, Delphine.' Delphine extracted a spindly fuchsia plastic stepladder from another cupboard and wobbled alarmingly up it as she reached for the collection of jugs.

They were just settling into position on Quentin's amusing collection of inflatable furniture when Fortress Lindens was buzzed again and a few moments later a man with a nose that spread halfway across his face and Arthur Scargill hair shuffled in. It was Gavin, Lady Eleanor's token single father. Who Worked from Home.

'Gavin, how super you managed to make it,' gushed Persia's mother.

The other mothers clucked round him as if he were George Clooney and Dr Spock rolled into one irresistible package instead of a rather unattractive man who consistently turned up late at all school events. Cat took a cup of coffee from Delphine, trying not to spill its contents on the white latex floor, and helped herself to a croissant. None of the others touched any of the food.

'Love to,' said the brunette in Marc Jacobs, 'but my nutritionist says the gluten would kill me.'

'Absolute bloody poison,' agreed Xanthe's mum. 'No one eats that stuff any more. It's just there for ambience.'

'Now,' said Persia's mother, her charm bracelets crashing like a waterfall of loose change, 'I hereby call this meeting to order.'

'Robbie did what?' Xanthe's mother cackled into her phone.

Persia's mother looked at her with distaste. 'I'm sorry to have to tell you that last year 6b came seventh in the fund-raising competition.' She shot them all an accusing look. 'So after a great deal of heart-searching, the fund-raising subcommittee and myself decided that bring-and-buy stalls and those piffling little raffles we did last time are a complete waste of time. They just don't raise enough dosh. Instead we've been canvassing our contacts. So far we have a weekend in Venice and a trip to New York on Concorde. Oh, and Ophelia's daddy has kindly offered to fix it so that one of the winners can appear as an extra in the new play he's producing in the West End.' She paused triumphantly.

There was a cowed silence. Cat raised her hand.

'Would you mind telling us what the money will go to?'

'I think most of us all already know,' said Persia's mother. 'Those of us who come regularly to the coffee mornings, that is.'

'I meant which charities?' persisted Cat.

'Lady Eleanor's is a charity, you know,' pointed out Persia's mother. 'It was given charitable status in 1926. So most of the money will be used to make sure that our less well-off students don't miss out on important cultural experiences. It's so vital the girls get acquainted with Florence and Venice at an early age, don't you think?'

There was general nodding round the room. 'Any leftovers will go to St Mungo's orphanage.'

'Fuck me,' spluttered Xanthe's mother into her phone. 'Is that actually *legal*?'

*

The following Tuesday, Cat popped into Marks and Spencer to pick up some supper, just in case Suzette didn't share Cat's own enthusiasm for Sainsbury's Blue Parrot Café ready meals. Suzette had been with them for four days and she couldn't inflict Jess's cooking on her yet. Far better to hold it in reserve for the end of the week, by which time Suzette would have irrefutably outstayed her welcome.

The moment she stepped in the front door and put her foot down on the freshly vacuumed carpet, Cat sensed something was amiss. There wasn't a stray piece of underwear or pile of old newspapers in sight. She looked round the hall, suspiciously. She could swear someone had been using beeswax and furniture polish. Or at least a room spray that smelt like beeswax and furniture polish. Suzette appeared at the top of the staircase in a black trouser suit. Cat had to concede, she was remarkably good looking; the sleepy eyes still luminous in their cavernous sockets, the cheekbones as angular as Sydney Opera House.

'I hope you don't mind but I got Jess to do a bit of tidying up. She's been doing some ironing for me too. She seems to have quite enjoyed the novelty factor.' There was a crashing of pans from the kitchen. The door slammed open. Jess stormed past Cat with a mound of Suzette's ironed clothes and pounded up the stairs. Her mascara had been so emphatically mashed into her face she looked like a newspaper that had been left out in the rain.

'Is she always that temperamental?' asked Suzette. 'Really, Cat, if you'd told me how dire the staff situation was in London I could have found you a Guatemalan. You should have seen the food she served up for Lily this evening. I'm not sure it was completely dead.'

'She's a vegan.'

'I might have known from the horrible clothes. I caught that boyfriend of hers lurking in front of the television. Quite good looking, amazingly.'

Cat's spirits lifted marginally. If Ralph was back *in situ* the chances were that Jess wouldn't be leaving just yet.

'I got him to put some shelves up in the bathroom and he's offered to do something about those appalling kitchen cupboards.'

Cat brandished her M & S carrier bag, determined to look in control of domestic events. 'I've brought some supper home,' she announced proudly.

'Don't bother on my account. I'd forgotten how exhausting British facials are. I completely collapsed in the taxi back from Space NK. I must say, their rose cocoon is rather good.' She raked her eyes over Cat's rain-sodden coat. 'You should try one.'

'I'll bear that in mind the next time I can't think of anything whatsoever to do.' Cat marched into the kitchen, where Lily was embellishing one of Suzette's old Fendi bags with Power Puff girl stickers, and kissed the top of her daughter's head.

'Sukes says finding the right bag is like a lesson on life,' explained Lily, hardly pausing to look up. 'She gave me this so I'm customising it. She says that's the key to personal style.'

'Lil, what did you have for supper tonight?'

'Boiled tofu. And leaves from the garden,' said Lily.

'You mean lettuce?'

'No, leaves. Ralph brought them in. He said they looked nutritious.'

'I thought we agreed that while Sukes was here we wouldn't let her see any of Jess's cooking?'

'Why not? We have to. And eat it.'

There was a brief silence while they both grappled with this sad truth. Upstairs Cat heard her mother squeaking away on her ab-roller.

'You know what Sukes is like,' she resumed briskly. 'She'll worry and then the next think we know she'll be saying we can't cope on our own and try to get us to move to New York again.'

Lily narrowed her eyes thoughtfully. The one time she'd been to New York Suzette had taken her to FAO Schwartz and she'd emerged with a PlayStation, an iBook, her doll's house and two robot dogs, even though they'd only gone in for a set of felt-tips. Sensing she was on dangerous territory, Cat switched subjects.

'What a deliciously *Blue Peter*-ish vision!' Suzette burst into the kitchen with her laptop and several miles of flex trailing in her wake and swept her eyes over Lily's creative endeavours. 'I thought we could have a lovely cosy family chat down here,' she said, plugging in her computer.

'Round a roaring iMac, you mean?' said Cat. Her mother's distended view of cosy family life was already riling her. 'I thought you were exhausted by the travails of your facial.'

'It's a bit chilly upstairs,' continued Suzette, settling down with a copy of *Hello!* 'I revived. Now come and sit on my lap, Lily, and explain who all these people are before I get on with this article.'

'Have you done your homework?' asked Cat, aware of sounding priggish.

'Take a look at that face-lift.' Suzette pointed at a group in tiaras. 'And look at that. A hundred years ago that family weren't even royal!'

The phone emitted a baleful ring. Suzette ignored it.

'So how did they get to be queens and stuff?' said Lily admiringly.

'Pushy,' said Cat. 'Lily – homework?'

The phone continued ringing.

'Cat, darling,' began Suzette, looking at her daughter thoughtfully. 'Did you read that article on kick boxing I sent you. It's meant to be really good for out-of-condition biceps. Kate Moss and John Galliano swear by it, apparently. You never know, you might meet some interesting creative types there.'

The phone stopped ringing. Cat looked at her mother warily. 'Don't you have *any* regrets? About your old life, I mean.'

Suzette looked at her daughter for a few moments. 'Only that I didn't sleep with Warren Beatty when I had the chance—'

'What's wrong with my biceps?' said Cat hastily.

Fortunately the phone started ringing again. Suzette spent the rest of the night on the phone to New York, Paris, Milan and Hong Kong, collecting and trading gossip for her column, in between doing facial exercises. At nine o'clock Cat marched Lily to bed. At twelve she packed herself off, leaving her mother shouting down the line to Sydney.

★

KIXXX met every Thursday evening in a disused garage on the Harrow Road. Cat hadn't been inside a gym since . . . well she hadn't been inside a gym, preferring to spend most of her PE lessons behind the bike sheds with the other Player's No.6 aficionados. But six days into her mother's visit she was at her wits' end trying to find activities that would keep her out of the house, now that Toby had instigated a new regime of leaving the office by 7 p.m.

Feeling self-conscious in her tracksuit, she scanned the garage, with its breeze-block walls, dangly leather sausages and dumb-bells, searching desperately for someone who might be a soulmate. The article Suzette had sent from *Harpers & Queen* had waxed at some length about Kate Moss and John Galliano but had failed to mention the distinctive aroma – two parts sweat and old diesel to three parts decomposing jockstrap.

But it was too late now. They – that is to say Cat and eleven people who looked as though they could happily go ten rounds with Lennox Lewis – were holding hands in a circle round Benson, the massive genetic distortion of muscles that had grunted to her at the garage door.

'Whadda we want?' Benson was saying.

Kate Moss's figure, thought Cat.

'Power!' came the ringing response from the other eleven.

'When do we want it?'

'Now.'

'How do we get it?'

'By knocking the shit out of those who try to knock it out of us.'

'That's right. We are the powerfuckers of the universe.' Benson seemed to be directing his sing-song voice expressly at Cat. The others all put their hands together. The evening was starting to feel like a prayer meeting. 'Our Father,' began Benson. Cat tried not to stare at his thighs. *Harpers* hadn't said anything about boxing leading to massive thighs.

'So, fellow motherfuckers,' said Benson, 'we have a new member tonight. I'd like to introduce you all to Cat.'

Cat smiled wanly. Now she came to look, there were quite a lot of big thighs pulsing on the Harrow Road that night.

'Okay, Cat,' Benson began, 'What you got to realise is that boxing's as much a mental thing as a physical thing, right?'

Cat nodded.

'You got to be in the right place emotionally,' continued Benson. The others looked at her expectantly.

'And a lot of that comes with motivation, Cat. Right?'

She nodded again.

'So what we gonna do, Cat, right, is go round the circle and find what motivation brought us here. Let's start with Stan.'

Stan, a wiry, muscular figure with luminous white skin and Ingerland tattooed in Gothic script across his shoulder blades, stepped forward. 'It's about self-respect, innit?' He sniffed. 'And finding yourself when you get out of the nick.'

'Good, Stan. Right. Ella, what about you?'

'Anger management.' Ella glowered at them all in a manner that suggested she hadn't quite conquered that particular problem yet.

The circle continued to list the woes that had led them to KIXXX. Mac, a Glaswegian, had Gulf War syndrome and two missing fingers, though it was hard to tell under the gloves. Someone whose name appeared to be Fridge was a fire-fighter looking for what he called his extreme edge. By this time Cat had given up the idea of meeting any soulmates. Next to Fridge was Vivien, a small, tanned figure with a gold tooth and a spear-shaped quiff, who'd just done eighteen months for forgery – but that, as he pointed out, was because the police had got hold of some of his early stuff. His most recent work, he told the room, was indistinguishable from the real thing.

As Benson edged towards Cat she decided that the first of the two options she had considered – inventing a trauma so harrowing that even Benson would be stilled in his tracks – required an imagination greater than her own.

'So, Cat, where did you get the calling?' said Benson. She felt time slowing down as the rest of the room stared at her. What she should have said, she realised later, was that she got the calling while her boyfriend was beating her up for her social. It wasn't particularly original but it was better than what she did come up with.

'*Harpers and Queen.*' No amount of self-deprecating grimacing seemed to help. Even laughing to indicate her highly developed sense of irony and self-awareness didn't do the trick. Benson paired her off with Stan, who told her he hated women and repeatedly punched her in the stomach while the others called her Kate Moss all night.

'Christ, Cat, you look terrible. Are you all right?' said Petula at lunchtime the day after the KIXXX débâcle. She was waltzing past Cat's workstation on her way to meet her fiancé Alan for a trawl through Liberty's wedding department. 'Only you look as though you're about to outsource your breakfast.'

Cat looked blankly at Petula's black patent knee boots.

'Throw up,' Petula explained.

'Yes, I know what outsourcing is, thank you. And I'm fine.'

'And a bit waxy. Round the pores. Have you tried strips?' As Petula bounced out the door, her miniskirt a tiny receding speck, Cat wondered – not for the first time – whether she'd ever get her own PA. While she recognised that she had only been at Simms four years and Toby had been there at least fifty per cent longer and was a cert to become a Vice himself in the next twelve months, she suspected that it would take her twice as long and three times the effort to get half the recognition – or perks – that he did. She'd have to talk to him about it at some point.

By day seven, even Lily was hollow eyed from lack of sleep. And Suzette was desperate. Any leeway she still had with her publishers was about to run out. She had to get Cat out of the house and into Butely within the next five days.

It was an uphill struggle. Cat was determined not to let Suzette rile her. Even when Suzette, catching sight of the winning raffle ticket flapping on the noticeboard, asked her why she hadn't been to Butely.

'I hardly think I could get the time off work so close to Christmas.'

'But you said yourself you were feeling tired all the time. Butely might do you the world of good, make you more efficient. It's not one of those silly indulgent places. It's very serious.'

Cat quite fancied the idea of some unadulterated indulgence and longed to lie around having her toenails painted, her face buffed and her body massaged – it was so long since she had been touched by anyone other than Lily that she almost ached for physical contact.

'I don't know quite what you imagine I do all day long,' she began, slamming the shutters down on the fantasy, 'but even if I could get the time off, it's not practical. I couldn't leave Lily with Jess. Not the way things are at present.'

'Well, what about leaving her with me?'

'That's very kind, but have you thought it through?'

'I did raise you, you know.'

There was a diplomatic pause.

'It's meant to be marvellous,' continued Suzette. 'No frivolous treatments.' She glanced slyly in Cat's direction. 'Only those with medical integrity. And none of those ghastly celebrities you get at other health farms. Just really intelligent ones. I expect Cherie Blair goes there. I wouldn't be surprised if you found yourself swapping herbal remedies with Kate Winslet or Jude Law.'

In an attempt to avoid murdering her mother, Cat began ignoring Toby's edict on working late, until Toby, taking pity on her one night, insisted on whisking her out for dinner, promising to drive her home afterwards.

'You seem a bit fraught', he said as he opened the door to the Porsche for her. 'Is your mother still with you?'

She nodded morosely. 'I can't help wondering what's happened to her. She used to be really interested in politics and the big issues,' she said as he darted through the traffic along Park Lane.

'Middle age,' he said in the darkness. 'I think you'll find it affects most of us that way.' Cat sank back into the heated cream leather. She'd come to expect sharpness and acumen from him, but emotional insight on top of everything else made him almost too perfect. Even with Destiny's Child pounding through the speakers, she found herself dreading the moment when she'd have to get out.

'Don't you think you might be underestimating your mother a bit?' Toby interrupted her reverie. 'I've been looking her up on the Internet. Her columns are syndicated to more than five hundred publications in the States, you know. *And* there're the books.'

'From picket lines to hem lines. O! what a fall was there. *Julius Caesar*, act three,' she added glumly.

'*Love Story*, the bit just before she snuffs it,' said Toby.

Cat stared at him in delighted disbelief. No one else she knew would have got the reference. Ben had banned *Love Story* from the video shelf.

'I love that film,' she said. 'I used to watch it till it gave me migraines from crying.'

'Fabulous clothes. Specially the kilt scene.' Cat pulled a face. 'Come on, McGinty, clothes matter too,' retorted Toby. 'It's a six-billion-pound industry in Britain alone.'

Cat peered at him. Was there anything he didn't know?

'She used to go on hunger strike to free radicals, for God's sake. Now she just wants to zap them with her anti-oxidants.'

'Best thing to do with radicals, if you ask me,' said Toby, swerving suddenly and hooting at the squeegee merchants on the Embankment. 'Bloody parasites. You'd think they'd have worked out something more profitable to do.'

Cat looked at the twinkling lights along the Thames and for the first time in years felt that an affair with another human, as opposed to her work, might be quite a rewarding experience. It would certainly prove that a single working mother could have it all.

'She's obviously a bright woman—' he began again.

'In her business, just getting through the whole of *Harry Potter* makes you an intellectual colossus.'

'Would it help dilute her a little if we all went out for dinner one night?'

Cat pretended to give the matter serious thought. The last time she'd gone out for dinner with her mother and a boyfriend – Ben – he had waxed lyrical about Suzette for months.

'Oh, I nearly forgot,' said Toby, reaching into the glove compartment and pulling out a beautifully store-wrapped present. 'I bought you this.'

Cat unwrapped it nervously, hoping it wasn't anything too personal or something she hated. She wasn't good at receiving presents. It was the Bee Gees' *Greatest Hits*. Small – and all the more perfectly formed for being their private joke.

'The Brothers Grim,' said Toby. 'You do have the most appalling taste in music, McGinty. It's the one flaw I've found so far.'

Feeling her stomach pleat, she slipped the disc into his CD player and closed her eyes as Maurice, Robin and Barry scaled fool-hardy heights with their voices. They pulled up outside Makesbury Road just as 'How Deep Is Your Love' struck up.

'Now this one does have a certain cheap potency, I'll give you that,' said Toby, switching off the engine.

Now what? Cat's heart pounded. What did parking mean in modern dating terms? For once she wished she had devoted less time to 'Rural Idyll' and more to Jess's back copies of *marie claire*.

'Cheap potency? That's rich coming from someone who thinks Destiny's Child are musical prodigies. But don't let me subject you to this torture any longer.' She reached towards the eject button.

Suddenly he caught her wrist and took her hand in his. Her heart began to thud as he drew her towards him and she gave in to the dangerous whiffs she'd been resisting for weeks. Before she could remind herself of the mechanics of kissing, his lips were on hers and his tongue was making preliminary investigations in her mouth. And then suddenly she began kissing him as hungrily as he was kissing her. She could feel the hardness of his arms around her and the slight roughness of his skin. It was so long since a man had held her she'd forgotten how good it felt. It was almost a relief to discover she could still respond to instinctive desires like this. His hand began to inch along her body, settling confidently on her right breast. A coil of desire slithered through her as he fondled her through the thin layer of shirt. As long as she remembered not to get too emotionally involved, this had to be a good idea. She grabbed his hand and placed it inside her bra, where it began expertly to massage her right nipple.

From an upstairs window, Suzette blinked into the intermittently fizzing light. Below, she could just make out Cat in an expensive-looking car, shaped like a toad. She was with a man. About time too. The street lamp died.

She hoped he was nice, whoever he was. And if it was Toby, she hoped Rodney was wrong about him. He was probably concerned that having once been his stepson, Toby was a bit too closely related to Cat for comfort. How typically bourgeois. Cat deserved some happiness. The street lamp spluttered into life again and Suzette caught sight of their silhouettes outlined in an embrace. Instinctively she turned away from the window, about to go to bed, when she remembered that she had come to London on a mission. Torn between the desire to leave Cat in peace and the obligation she had to Sir Rodney, she went down to the kitchen, filled two mugs with tap-water and padded out of the house towards the Porsche.

Blissfully cocooned in wraparound Bee Gees and both of Toby's arms, which had somehow pulled her on top of him *and* moved the cream-coloured leather into a horizontal position, Cat was giving herself up to the moment, while simultaneously fretting that after almost four years of celibacy she ought to be doing this somewhere more dignified. Just as she was about to dispense with dignity altogether and guide Toby's hands into the confusing tangle of her tights, she became increasingly aware of a persistent tapping on the passenger window.

'Cat.' Her mother tried to rub a porthole but was having no effect on the heavy condensation that lay on the inside of the electrically operated tinted glass. 'Would you and your young man like a cup of dandelion and horsetail extract?'

★

It was, reflected Cat later, lying in bed, just about the most humiliating thing that had ever happened to her, excluding the time Suzette had pitched up at the Garden to give a careers lecture to the sixth form and ended up dispensing advice on free love, complete with graphic displays of her favourite positions.

But perhaps it was just as well. She had got a bit carried away back there in the Porsche. She needed to take this slowly. Maybe she should take advantage of her mother's presence and go to Butely after all. It would be nice for Lily to spend some quality time with her grandmother. It would probably do Lily and her good to spend a week apart as well. And it would certainly wake her mother up to have some real responsibility, as opposed to the kind that could be instantly made to disappear at the flourish of a cheque book. The phone next to her bed bleeped gently. It was Toby.

'Missing you,' he said softly. Just the sound of his voice made her nipples stand to attention all over again. 'And I wanted you to know I think your mother's a hoot. Great looking, too. Like her daughter,' he added quickly. 'Fab haircut. Very modern. Touch of the Didos.'

Dido? That was the famous face she'd been groping for. Unfortunately Cat didn't want Dido's older sister for a mother. She wanted someone – anyone – with more gravitas. Someone who looked like a bloody mother. It wasn't much to ask. She wasn't going to risk any more meetings between Suzette and Toby. Butely it was.

'Night-night, Toby,' she murmured. She sank back into the pillows, and thought how nice it must be to have the kind of balanced life that made time for exercise and healthy eating. This was her chance. She could test out all the treatments she'd read about over the years, from Balinese massage to sacred mountain springs. Who knows, she might even be persuaded into trying some yoga again? She drifted into a dream-speckled sleep in which she was tended by armies of solicitous therapists, each one desperate to fulfil her every desire, massage rose-scented oils into her skin, paint her toenails and relieve her of her pot belly.

7

Cat's sense of direction wasn't brilliant. Ben's had been even worse. Additionally he'd developed a handy allergy to *A–Zs* that conveniently left him free to strum his instruments while Cat juggled with articulated lorries, petrol caps and seventy-four pages of the enlarged, wipe-down road map of Britain he had thoughtfully given her one birthday. Cat had duly learned to plan her journeys several days in advance with meticulous attention, plotting pit stops at service stations known to have drinkable coffee and circling potentially hazardous junctions with one of her marker pens.

What with the tearful leave-taking of Seamus, who drooped mournfully by his untouched Hills diet food, and Lily, who had insisted on repacking Cat's suitcase with several changes of evening wear in case she met someone famous, Cat was an hour late setting off. Night had fallen by the time the endless suburbs began to give way to what might be fields but to Cat's decidedly urban eyes looked like terrifying black swamps of nothingness. To take her mind off things she went back over everything she had managed to glean about Butely from the faded brochure that had been dispatched with her booking reservation.

It sounded a bit more serious than she'd initially imagined – and a lot less glamorous – with more emphasis on Scottish douches than seemed ideal, lots of brisk constitutionals and Butely's giant compost heap (the fount of its wonderful organic vegetables, apparently). There was no mention at all of lying around in rose cocoons chatting to Kate Winslet and Jude Law. But she couldn't help being excited. Just the thought of rest exhilarated her, especially as Toby had announced he wasn't even going to be in

London, thanks to an unmissable meeting he had in Glasgow with some mystery client.

Naturally she'd fretted about absenting herself from work – and just as things were getting really interesting. Just as she'd worried about leaving Lily with Suzette and Jess. But Lily had begged her to go, and Toby had pointed out that she was still owed a week's holiday and since she wouldn't be able to carry the days over to the following year she might as well take them now. Besides, he reassured her, nothing much was going to happen with any of their clients so soon before Christmas.

In that remote region of her imagination marked Not in a Million Years, Cat was constantly communing with nature. Her daydreams always placed her and Lily fairly and squarely in Candida St John Green territory. The format never varied: Cat, in a Cath Kidston pinny, industriously dabbling at an easel in front of a thatched cottage; Lily skipping through meadows of towering poppies (at least, Cat thought they were poppies; she wasn't very good on flowers) and the pair of them dressed like something out of a 1970s flake advertisement. It was odd because she hadn't been in proper countryside for years – not since the Devon débâcle when Ben had been stung by a jellyfish, the first case on Slapton Sands in forty years, according to the local hospital. In her fantasies the countryside was a place to which she yearned to retreat. In reality it scared the living daylights out of her.

It was the silence which really freaked her. Not that it was very quiet in the Little Chef where she made her first pit stop of the evening. But she needed a fag. Then she found there were three in the packet and it seemed silly to waste them. She was left with such a foul taste in her mouth that she had to eat something. She scanned the Little Chef menu for something light but sustaining.

One shrivelled chicken in a basket later, and armed with a box of Celebrations for the journey, she was back on the road making quite good progress until she discovered she was halfway to Swansea. This necessitated another stop.

Back behind the wheel of the Polo she shivered, listening to the engine splutter and regretting bringing only fingerless gloves and just three ciggies. Ralph had said the Polo was suffering from the equivalent of reverse thrust, whatever that was. Bollocks probably. It had begun to snow lightly and it looked as though it would settle. She rubbed vigorously at the condensation on the windscreen, only to discover it was on the outside. It was going to be a long, long night. Half an hour later she passed Swindon for the second time, but from a different direction. It wasn't quite the pastoral paradise she'd envisaged, but things were definitely getting more rural. Glittering scarps of land rolled gently down to six lanes of traffic cones, and fields of snowcapped crops were punctuated by the occasional car park, petrol station, Aqua-World and Travelodge.

You could tell you were in proper countryside, she decided an hour later as she passed an old-fashioned dark green sign saying 'Dorset', because the air felt colder, purer. God's compensation, she supposed, for sluggish property prices. She grinned. That was just the kind of thing Toby would say – jokingly, she presumed, though she was never *quite* sure. It was snowing quite hard now.

At around half past midnight the Polo experienced a near-terminal crashing of gears as Cat reversed it back up a tiny twisted lane to an even more twisted pair of rusting gates with the initials BM entwined in their spikes. One had almost come off its hinges. But if the entrance to Butely Manor was surprisingly humble, the driveway that wound its way for about five minutes through what looked like several hillsides was unforgettable. As were the bats that circled the Polo like persistent groupies. It was darker than Hades, with only one yellowish light on in the hallway. Cat was so frightened she didn't dare get out of the Polo at first. When she finally pressed the doorbell – a nice old-fashioned brass one set into the stone wall like a jewelled belly button – it gave out a reassuringly deep ring. It seemed an eternity before it was answered by Will Carling's double – a solid-looking girl with a cleft chin and enormous bosoms that made her look top heavy, like a squeezed tube of toothpaste.

'I'm so sorry I'm late,' said Cat, ducking slightly in case any bats were still hovering. The girl shrugged and picked up Cat's suitcase as if it were a discarded newspaper. Cat followed her through the massive arched doorway and across several hectares of flagstone. She was too tired to take much in but her overall impression was of a very beautiful hall and a carved staircase that rapidly gave way to miles of bulging walls. Will Carling trudged on in silence.

She barely had the energy to unpack her electric toothbrush – an exercise that ended in futility as it had spent the journey pressed against the spare wheel in the boot of the Polo with its button accidentally pressed on and was now out of power. Since the only wall plugs Cat managed to locate were of the ancient round-pin variety, she gave up and crawled into bed with a file of Frupps reports as her bedtime reading. It was only when she had finally turned out the light thirty minutes later and tugged the grey sheets and mustard-yellow blankets up to her chin that Cat realised Will Carling hadn't actually checked her in. How quaint.

How terrifying. Cat sat bolt upright. How many other guests had been let in as casually? she wondered. And how many of them were weirdos and wackos? She got out of bed and fished in her wardrobe for the bobble hat and matching socks Lily had given her for her birthday. Whatever else was active in Butely at this ungodly hour, it certainly wasn't the central heating.

'Splendid, splendid,' spluttered Dr Anjit, fondling his stethoscope. 'You have a fascinating left kidney.' His eyes wandered off towards Cat's notes, to which his contribution had thus far been several magnificent blue blotches courtesy of a leaking Biro so that they now resembled a map of the Lake District.

'Your spleen is completely at sixes and sevens, however,' he continued jubilantly.

Cat watched his breath make charming puffy white patterns between them.

'Bloat,' Dr Anjit explained. 'It's the curse of the twenty-first century.' He patted her hand. 'It's nothing that a five-day fast shouldn't go a great deal towards improving, though I don't know if it would be entirely wise ever to go back on the wheat.'

Cat's eyes, which had been glazing over thanks to the hypnotic effects of Dr Anjit's frost patterns, snapped open. Nowhere in any of the literature about Butely had anyone said anything about fasts. Wonderful, *plentiful* organic vegetables, yes. Starvation, no.

'What, no pasta?' she asked, aghast.

'Don't worry. On the third day we'll add some bark.'

Cat began to feel mildly hysterical. Breakfast had consisted of some dried hay and rice milk, and she hadn't even been on the fast then. The thought of five days of boiled water with bits of twig floating in it was unbearable.

'But I've got low blood pressure,' she protested meekly.

Dr Anjit examined her notes again. 'You can drink as much fennel tea as you like. We'll probably prescribe sterol extras and some yucca root as well. You won't go short. But remember, no yeast, no dairy, no wheat. Ever. They're modern poison.' Where had Cat heard that before? Xanthe's bloody mother. 'Now,' continued Dr Anjit, 'if you run along to the Circular Bedchamber you'll find the Isadora Duncan expressionist movement session is about to start with Miss Lezzard. And in the afternoon you're down for a wax job.'

Cat's spirits lifted marginally. Despite her vow never to place her follicles in the hands of someone like Syrie again, she couldn't help thinking a little grooming wouldn't go amiss now that there was a distinct possibility she might – God willing – be sleeping with someone soon. She made her way out of the Long Building, a hideous fifties monstrosity that housed Butely's consultation and treatment rooms, and followed a series of flapping home-made signs to the Circular Bedchamber. It wasn't easy. Butely seemed to be a model of crazy geometry, bursting with treacherous floorboards and twisting staircases that seemed to lead nowhere in particular.

The Isadora Duncan class had just begun. 'Excuse me,' whispered Cat, squeezing into a gap next to a tiny lollypop figure in a lilac towelling tracksuit and matching eyeshadow.

'Silence, please,' a voice echoed from the far side of the bedchamber. Miss Lezzard, the teacher, Cat presumed. 'I must have absolute peace. Isadora is among us.' Cat's eyes swivelled around the room towards the teacher. Unless Isadora had taken to wearing billowing floor-length kaftans with red Virgin Atlantic socks, she wasn't there in bodily form.

'It is always preferable to be absolutely on time for your daily movement.' The teacher gazed at Cat over a neckful of huge African-looking beads. 'And to remove all headwear,' she added pointedly. Cat removed her bobble hat. 'Otherwise it is so hard to get the flow.' The teacher reached out her arms in front of her then swung them to the side as if she were demonstrating the doors-to-manual procedure on an aircraft.

Cat looked at the quivering line of violet-veined throats turned towards the ceiling and tried to concentrate on her flow. The sum total of everyone's age in the room must, she estimated, come to about fourteen hundred and twenty, which by coincidence appeared to be the last time the Circular Bedchamber had been spring-cleaned.

If scale wasn't a problem at Butely, decor certainly was. Even *The World of Interiors* would have been hard pushed to describe the shabby curtains as chic. Countless centuries of paint buckled away from the woodwork and mounds of dust clotted the corners of the mantelpiece. Still, it was a beautiful room, flanked at either end by two vast fireplaces and four immense bookcases.

'Stroke your abdomen, everybody, *please*, and do remember to open your buttocks to the sky. Imagine you are daughters of the winds and the waves.'

Cat turned to her neighbour for enlightenment.

'Sssshhh!' Miss Lezzard pressed a long bony finger to her bright purple lips. 'Rise like Aphrodite, liberate your body from its shackles and free your anal energy.' She began to sway between two enormous rocks of crystal that had evidently been transported up to the Circular Bedchamber with the aid of a Spar trolley that was wedged in the corner between the complete works of George Eliot and a giant rococo urn.

'It is essential that you maximise your spirits,' continued Miss Lezzard.

It was almost a relief when they moved on to mat work. But there was to be no rest.

'Imagine your legs as hollow bamboos tossed by the elements. The wind is your hair. The roots are your feet . . .' droned Miss Lezzard, her wrists flip-flopping like seals. She appeared to be entering an enraptured state. 'Feel the personal energy.'

'Sylvia's very big on elemental forces,' muttered Cat's neighbour. Her large eyes, made even more striking by two vast orbits of mauve kohl, flashed mischievously.

Cat spent the remainder of the class waving her legs like storm-tossed bamboo until she thought she was going to be sick. This wasn't how she'd envisioned her first exercise class at Butely at all. She was so worn out by the end that she barely registered Miss Lezzard crashing her tiny pair of cymbals to mark the departure of Isadora. Then Miss Lezzard tried to flog them a copy of The Magic of Gong Therapy, her latest cassette.

'Is it always that demanding?' Cat asked casually over elevenses – a cup of hot water containing what looked suspiciously like hay again and some organic honey with half the hive still attached. Her neighbour from the Isadorables, who turned out to be Daphne Lightbridge, one-time Bluebell dancer and faithful Butely client, had been so kind, helping Cat out of the class, that Cat didn't want to seem churlish by appearing to criticise anything about the place.

'The woman's a sadist,' said Daphne. 'More fennel tea?' Cat nodded gratefully. It was amazing how tasty fennel seemed when you were starving and your left temple was throbbing violently.

'Nicotine withdrawal, is it?' asked Daphne sympathetically, returning from the urn and setting the teacups – antique Meissen, from the looks of them – down on the table.

'I don't smoke,' said Cat, clutching the sides of her armchair.

'I see,' said Daphne. 'Where was I? Oh, yes. The problem with Sylvia Lezzard—'

Here, let me help you.' Cat jumped up.

'Now you just relax,' said Daphne in a quavery voice. 'I'd get some Nicorette patches if I were you. Until the acupuncture kicks in. I know he doesn't look it but Dr Anjit's really awfully good.' She disappeared into a vast faded floral armchair opposite Cat. 'As for Sylvia Lezzard . . . well, it's obvious what the problem is, isn't it?'

She leaned forward conspiratorially. 'She's a lesbian who never came out. Hence the Isadora fixation. You know her father attempted to escape the law by dressing up as a woman? Isadora's, I mean. Though I wouldn't put it past Sylvia's either.'

'Don't they have any Iyengar here or Ashtanga?' asked Cat, eager to appear knowledgeable. She'd been looking forward to showing off some asanas to Jess.

'Not for years.'

'There's an awful lot of portraits of yogis around the place for somewhere that doesn't practise any yoga.'

'Butely used to have a marvellous teacher but he got eaten by sharks.'

Cat waited for further enlightenment. But none was forthcoming. 'So now we're stuck with Sylvia,' continued Daphne. 'Her Greek dancing's completely inauthentic, as you probably spotted. I doubt if she's ever been farther east than Frinton. The trouble is the young, fashionable teachers won't do it for the money that poor darling Butely pays these days. It's all terribly sad.'

'Never mind. Those yogis in the waiting room are enough to put you off for life. One of them looks pregnant – so much for toning.'

'The sad truth is you're not seeing Butely at its best.'

'No?'

'Surely you must have noticed the state of everything?'

'It does seem a bit . . .' Cat grappled for the *mot juste*. '. . . dusty.'

'Dusty?' Daphne dragged a tiny gnarled finger through a fine film on the table in front of her. 'That'd be Mrs Faggot. You can't really blame her. The place is a wreck. And so are most of its clients.'

'Isn't that the point?' said Cat. 'Judging from the testimonials I've been reading in the visitors' books, Butely has a long tradition of treating wrecks.'

Daphne looked at her thoughtfully. 'You must be the youngest person to cross Butely's poor benighted threshold by about four decades. Are you sure you're at the right place?'

Cat's right temple had started stabbing away in percussive competition with her left. Of all the health spas in all the world, she had to win a trip here. But she was rapidly warming to Daphne, who clucked around her and told her to drink her tea. 'It's so important to keep hydrated,' she said. 'Simply zaps cellulite.'

It was pretty important to keep moving too. Butely's erratic heating meant that there wasn't a significant difference between external and indoor temperatures.

'Freezing, isn't it? Does mean you lose weight, though. Whistling winds burn through those calories. Do you fancy a tour?'

They began with Butely's famous kitchen garden, where someone had evidently been fighting a losing battle against nature. A few desultory cabbages, dark green kale and the occasional mulchy carrot peeked through the soil beneath a thin cloak of frost, and a knot garden of sage and bay gave off an enticing aroma when Cat brushed against them. But every so often there were little patches of tangled weeds where neatness yielded to anarchy.

'Poor Mimms does his best,' said Daphne sadly, 'but he must be at least eighty.' She lifted the rusty latch on the creaking gate and led Cat through an ancient archway away from the vegetables round to the back of the house. 'It's such a shame, because Butely's combination of diet and treatments really does work. In its day it was such a pioneer.'

'How long have you been coming?'

'Since the start. You should have seen it back then – completely wild. Sir Rodney was a great one for nudity. I think that was half the attraction for some of the guests. Omar Sharif swore by the place. Used to run his bridges syndicates from the steam room. And the parties. It must have worked, though. Guess how old I am, for instance.'

Long experience with Suzette had taught Cat that this line of questioning nearly always ended in tears. In the cruel light of a sunny winter's day Daphne looked about a thousand.

'Seventy-five,' crowed Daphne. 'And it's all down to this place. I met the last two Mr Lightbridges here, you know.'

'How many Mr Lightbridges have there been?' They approached a ha-ha that gave on to the surrounding countryside.

Everywhere she looked there was a ravishing vista – of woods, gently rolling fields dotted with fat, beige-coloured sheep and, in the very far distance, the foamy white crests of the sea. It was a spectacularly perfect setting.

'Exquisite, isn't it? The gardens are Capability Brown. The National Trust own zillions of acres round here and they're desperate to get hold of Butely. Before you know it the place will be wall-to-wall Laura Ashley and toasted teacakes.'

She shuddered. 'I've had four husbands, my dear. Five, if you count the Austrian, which I prefer not to. They weren't all Mr Lightbridges, obviously. Only the first, but after a while it's easier to stick with just the one name. Cuts down on the paperwork. And you know what crooks lawyers are when it comes to paperwork.'

They strolled on companionably. The throbbing was definitely abating and Cat didn't feel quite as desperate for a ciggie as she had halfway through Miss Lezzard's class.

'This is my favourite aspect.' Daphne sighed as she threaded her arm back through Cat's and marched her gently across lawns pock-marked with molehills.

'It's vast,' exclaimed Cat, surveying the meadows that undulated away from Butely all the way towards the sea.

'Most of it's leased out to Guy Fulton, who farms it. Now there's a wild one. Once rode one of his Arabs up the staircase during one of Butely's parties. Stark naked too. Those were the days . . .' She trailed off wistfully.

'You were saying,' prompted Cat, determined not to be side-tracked by more scandals. 'About the farming?'

'Oh, yes. Guy looks after all of it. Biggest farmer for miles around. Very successful. That's why the fields look tidier than the house – though I wouldn't be surprised if he diddles Rodney too. Nearly everyone does now.'

The two of them gazed back at Butely's south-western façade, which was indeed an exquisite example of some of the finest Restoration architecture in the country. The odd wispy trail of smoke fluttered into the neon sky from one or two of its vast, imposing chimneys, and rows of mullioned windows looked down inscrutably upon Cat and Daphne, much as they had done for the past three hundred years.

'The best thing,' said Daphne, stepping nimbly along the edge of the ha-ha, 'is the history. The Butely family was here from the time of James I. Lady Butely went insane designing the place with the architect. You can see why. Sir Rodney bought it in the sixties.'

'It's a pity about the Long Building,' said Cat, her eye once again assaulted by its ugliness.

'More a case of the Wrong Building,' agreed Daphne. 'God knows how they got planning consent. But Rodney liked it because he could fit most of his antique car collection in there.'

'Car collection?' Cat began to feel the hunger pangs gnawing at her intestines. Her personal energy seemed to have been thwarted by the bodily equivalent of reverse thrust. 'Isn't that a little at odds with his other interests?'

'That's what's so wonderful about Butely.' Daphne dragged Cat back through the main door. 'It was always such a broad church. Rodney was determined not to turn anyone away. You'd get people from the East End here, mingling with the Rolling Stones. I once shared a mud bath with three members of the Saudi royal family. It's not really the same any more. The 1924 Bugatti went first. I told him he'd regret it. Followed by lorries full of antiques. But he was determined to keep the fees down.'

'It does seem a little quiet—' Cat followed Daphne across an expanse of flagstone so chilling they could have filmed *Shackleton* on it.

As they headed back in the direction of the library a piercing screech shot through the still air. Cat turned round to see Will Carling behind them, blowing her whistle.

'Luncheon is served – and with Samantha's usual finesse, I see,' said Daphne, leading Cat past Samantha, who in broad daylight looked less like squeezed toothpaste and more like Desperate Dan. 'Though heaven knows poor Micky tries. He learned to cook in the Navy. I don't think they believe in vegetables. Consequently he's never quite got his head round the Butely vegan philosophy.'

Lunch indeed beggared belief, reflected Cat later, although even beggars would have turned their noses up at the paltry sustenance Samantha had seen fit to provide her with.

'Fasters shouldn't really be in here,' Samantha thundered, looking at the instructions Dr Anjit had handed her and slapping a beaker of what looked like pulped grass in front of Cat. 'Only ends in tears.'

Cat's heart sank. She'd forgotten she was meant to be fasting.

'Never mind, dear,' said Daphne, squeezing her hand, 'at least you got to see the dining room. It's an architectural gem.' It was indeed, with three pairs of enormous French windows that looked out on to the lawns and enough stucco on the ceilings to reclad Bath. 'Grinling Gibbons,' said Daphne, tucking into a mountain of kale curry. 'The Nicky Haslam of his day. Shame about Samantha's table decor.'

She nodded to where Samantha dolloped out kale curry behind a once proud example of exquisite William and Mary marquetry now covered with a plastic tablecloth and crowned with a smudged sign saying 'Wait Here to Be Ignored'.

Even so, Daphne was right. The dining room was an architectural wonder. Cat perused the towelling-clad human hillocks clustering round the tables, and felt that at that moment she would happily have swapped it for a Little Chef. She slunk off miserably to her bedroom and waited for her afternoon therapies to begin.

'Works wonders on arthritis, that does.' An unbelievably ancient and gnarled figure called Bill interrupted Cat's daydreams in sing-song West Country tones that were as soothing as the wax he was pouring over her feet. 'Though why a young girl like you should be suffering from something as pernicious as bone-rot beats me.' With surprising gentleness, he placed her feet in a bowl that had clearly been a chamber pot in another life.

Cat wasn't suffering from anything more pernicious than a stomach that had gone into famine mode, a pounding skull and a tongue that was starting to develop a mink coat. Still, even if it wasn't quite the wax job she'd imagined, it was strangely relaxing watching the paraffin slowly solidify round her feet in the chamber pot.

'What's a spritely young filly like you doing here?' enquired a rich, chewy voice opposite her.

'Now Hector, don't start all that nonsense,' interrupted Daphne. 'Remember what it does to your pacemaker.'

'Can't blame a chap for trying.' Hector looked at Cat ruefully and twiddled with his hearing aid. 'Been on a tight leash ever since I remarried. Haven't so much as tipped my hat at a woman under seventy-five for two years.'

'Serves you right,' chided Bill. 'The way you used to carry on.'

'I don't think it was strictly illegal,' said a middle-aged woman sporting a tight leopard-print négligé and a tangerine tan. Apart from the glistening fuchsia toenails she reminded Cat of an overweight Airedale. 'Can't somebody do something about the heating?'

'At the prices you pay, Veronica, you shouldn't even think of complaining.' Hector let his bathrobe slip open unnecessarily wide over his knobbly knees. 'Though I must say it is a bit chilly.'

'What I want to know is why Sir Rodney didn't snap up that facial analyst who helped Kate Winslet lose four stone,' said Veronica, changing the subject. 'I would have thought that was right up his street.' She pulled her négligé tighter round her shoulders.

'Veronica's right,' said Hector. 'Can't you turn the Primus up? It's freezing in here.'

'Try covering yourself up a bit more, Hector dear,' suggested Daphne.

'I hear they've got age management programmes at Cal-à-Vie,' said Veronica.

'Load of twaddle,' muttered Bill. 'Butely has always been concerned with health treatments. Not fripperies. And you know very well how many people it's helped over the years.'

'There you go again, banging on about arthritis and all that dreary stuff. What's the point? You can take drugs for all that now. What thirty-somethings get traumatised about these days are early wrinkles.'

'Of course, some fifty-somethings simply blitz them.' Hector stared pointedly at Veronica's forehead.

'You have to look at it from the point of view of the workplace.' Veronica was now addressing herself to Cat. 'I mean, there's a hell of a lot of age-related prejudice. Anyone who looks over thirty-five is just sidelined.'

'Is that why you started working from home?' asked Hector innocently.

'Oh, pipe down, do,' said Bill. His ruddy face clouded over. 'Don't s'pose any of you are paying what you ought to. That's half the problem. Sir Rodney's too generous by half.'

'What problem?' Veronica tossed back her magnificent marmalade hair, which fell in stiff waves halfway down her back.

'You must have noticed Sir Rodney's not looking his usual self,' said Bill, blowing on one of the Primus rings, which threatened to sputter out.

'Haven't noticed the old chap at all,' said Hector. 'I thought he must have done what any sensible chap would do this time of year and scarpered off to Barbados.'

'Chance would be a fine thing. The poor man's fair riddled with worry,' said Bill. 'Don't think he can support this place much longer. Doesn't even wash its own face any more.' He slapped the wax against the sides of his saucepan mournfully. 'Still, mustn't complain.'

'Can't say I'm surprised.' Veronica picked idly on a tiny chip in her pink nail polish. 'Butely's fallen so behind the times it's practically a museum piece. I mean, where's the Botox and the lasers? Or the electromagno therapy? They've got a gemstone transducer at Champney's that did wonders for my insomnia last summer. But when I mentioned it to Sir Rodney he looked at me as if I was completely mad.'

'Bloody gimmicks,' chided Bill. 'What's a gemstone transducer when it's at home?'

'Bloody good income generator,' said Veronica. 'Look, it's all very well being holier than thou, but the young generation demand these sorts of facilities. Butely hasn't even got a pool, for Christ's sake.'

The others ruminated this sad truth.

'What is it you do for a living, my dear?' Hector asked Cat after a while.

'I'm a librarian.' She'd decided before arriving that it was probably not in her best interests to reveal that she worked for a company that went around turning places like Butely into multi-storey car parks.

'In that case you've probably never come across Veronica's books. They're not really of library quality.'

'They analyse you with lights to see which stones would be most appropriate,' said Veronica, ignoring him. 'Mine were diamonds,' she added happily.

'I had a La stone massage in Spain,' said Hector, his competitive hackles rising. 'And a Sacred Sound Journey.'

'Ought to be ashamed of yourselves, the pair of you,' grumbled Bill. 'Taking your custom to Butely's rivals. When I think of all the people Butely's helped over the years, none of them on full rates. We've cured rheumatism, cancer, eating disorders. And what about your ague, Hector, and your puffy ankles, Veronica? You could barely walk the last time you came.'

'Spare us the roll-call of distressed gentlefolk.' Veronica yawned. She only came to Butely because its absurdly cheap rates meant she could stay there for weeks on end writing her bonkbusters with her two accomplices. 'All I'm saying is that the world's changing.'

'Now for God's sake,' said Daphne, as much to deflect them from Butely's addled state as anything, 'don't anyone light a match.'

They fell into a sleepy silence while the wax solidified round their extremities, miraculously soothing their muscles. Cat pondered the text message that had arrived on her mobile from Lily that morning, *Met N E 1 famous yet? Luv Lil*, and gazed at Hector's bunions, which looked a bit like icebergs under the coat of paraffin.

'If you don't mind my saying,' said Bill as, ten minutes later, he carefully peeled long curls of wax from Veronica's feet and hands, 'yours is the kind of attitude that's been our ruin.' He shook his grizzled head sadly. 'When Butely used to pioneer it was proper stuff. But now it's here today, gone this afternoon.' He shuffled over to Cat and began removing the dried paraffin from her feet, which emerged from their waxy carapace as soft and plump as a banker's wallet. 'Magnet therapy! No wonder we can't keep up. You must have seen how the staff've been cut back to the bone. Wouldn't be surprised if we was about to go down like the *Mary Celeste.*'

'But that's terrible,' blurted Cat. And with her feet feeling strangely rejuvenated and cared for, she meant it. If she, who was relatively fit and healthy, was starting to feel the benefits of Butely already, it must be a life-saver for people really in need. She hoped her next treatment, whatever it was, was equally soothing.

She was still reflecting on this in the waiting area – a rather odd collection of plastic stackable chairs with the odd Chippendale and Parker Knoll thrown in, gathered around an electric fire that from the looks of things hadn't seen active service since the days of Procul Harum. On the wall was a gilt-framed portrait of an Indian guru carrying a begging bowl and a very large-looking stomach bearing the legend 'Feed the flow and the flow will feed you.' Next to him was another fat guru in the lotus position. Cat focused on her next treatment, a massage – the wild optimist in her hoped it might in some way resemble Suzette's rose cocoon – and tried to blot out the gurus' pot bellies. In marketing terms they were a disaster.

'Next,' came a familiar bark as a domineering figure, its face still pink from the exertions of lunchtime, darkened one of the door-ways leading off the waiting area. 'Come along,' said Samantha, beckoning to Cat, 'time for your Scottish douche.'

8

There was no denying that Samantha had a firm touch when it came to administering the dandelion and kale scrub that was meant to be the pay-off for the Scottish douche. She was also a dab hand with the hose, which was, Cat saw out of the corner of her eye, as Samantha aimed it at her back, a genuine piece of the common or garden variety. She was an unexpectedly gifted masseuse, with firm but sensitive hands. Also, unlike the only other time Cat had ever had a massage, there was no Enya music or whales honking eerily in the background, which had to be a major plus. The only sound was of Samantha's grunting, and Cat found that oddly comforting.

'Not local, then?' she asked, as Samantha pummelled her back and thighs.

'Welsh born and bred,' came the surprisingly lilting reply. 'I'm from Mumbles. Like Catherine Zeta-Jones. Sometimes I get taken for her double.'

Cat smiled, encouraged by this evidence of a satirical turn of mind. 'Kale seems to be very versatile,' she ventured as Samantha worked her way down the backs of her legs. 'I noticed you used it in the curry today.'

'That was because we didn't have any pak-choi,' said Samantha, panting from the exertion of scrubbing Cat down. 'And the reason it's in this scrub here is because we don't have any Japanese kelp. We don't have asparagus either. So it'll be in the vegan soup tomorrow.'

'Like the rest of you.' Samantha turned the water back to freezing. 'Doubling up, I mean. Do you all have more than one job here?'

'Some of us have six. Minimum's three. Dr Anjit does all our

Eastern treatments. You're down for acupuncture at five, by the way. He's bloody brilliant with needles. I've seen him bring back the near-dead, though he's never managed to breathe any life into those bonkbusters Veronica's lot writes. And we all have to take it in turns to do the cleaning with Mrs Faggot. You'll meet me taking the aerobics class later.'

Cat tried – and failed – to imagine aerobics with Sam, who was possibly the same height but certainly not the same width as Catherine Zeta-Jones, even when the latter was pregnant.

'And you'll see Bill giving this evening's talk on managing your waste.' Sam handed Cat a towel that in colour, texture and dimensions could easily have been mistaken for a Post-it. Then she wrapped her in about twenty miles of tatty bandages that would have been soaked in mint, if Butely had managed to grow enough, but had instead been dipped in Micky's old cabbage water. Cat wrinkled her nose. 'It's decongesting,' Samantha said. 'And a very challenging experience. Now I'll let the treatment take its course.' What this meant, as Cat knew full well, was that she was popping out for a fag. She could hear her lighting up even before she'd left the building.

While she lay stewing, Cat tried to clear her mind and visualise all the toxins, free radicals and evil fat cells being drummed out of her body, never to return. Instead she kept thinking how Butely would be transformed if they started offering Brazilians and oxygen facials. Every so often, she experienced a mild spasm of anxiety about what was happening at Simms in her absence. Toby had been very supportive when she'd told him she was thinking of going to Butely. But that didn't mean she was entirely relaxed about leaving the office right now. There was masses to do on Frupps's new Polish account, not to mention Petula, who had doubtless leaped at the opportunity to undermine Cat while she was away.

She could hear Samantha hacking away outside. She banished her doubts to the back of her mind. She had to learn to trust people more. Granted, most of humanity didn't give her much to go on, but if she didn't open up a bit she'd end up as shrivelled as her bandages, which had cooled to the point where she felt like an

Arctic explorer with wet knickers. And the thing about Toby was that beneath all his cynical braggadocio he showed every sign of being a softie. She closed her eyes and allowed herself to wallow in a brief fantasy sex scene with him. After twenty minutes she felt the bandage experience had gone on long enough. After thirty minutes Sam reappeared and unravelled them. 'That's worked nice, that has,' she wheezed. 'Got rid of some of the sag. That's caused by toxins, that is.'

'I thought Butely didn't believe in beauty treatments.'

'We don't, not really. This one's actually for your digestive system. I just throw in the bit about the sag for city types.'

Cat let this pass. She would quite liked to have inspected her thighs, just in case anything had improved, but there was no mirror in the room. She would have quite liked a shower too, but Sam insisted she keep away from water for the next twenty-four hours in order to allow the cabbage residue to work the rest of its miracle cure.

'Don't forget Bill's lecture, will you?' she said, scraping away some greenish residue from Cat's ankles. 'Next time we'll try the wet suit on top of the bandages. He likes a full house, Bill does. You wouldn't think it to look at him but he's quite a raconteur. And afterwards, in the games room, Sylvia Lezzard's lecturing on the history of chrysanthemums.'

Cat could hardly wait – if only so that she could recount the whole quaint experience to Toby. She knew he'd find it every bit as endearing as she did. But it was not to be. After afternoon fennel tea back in the library she slipped back to her room for a short nap and slept right through until morning. The good news, according to Samantha, whom she ran into in the corridor dragging a reeking wheelie bin of compost behind her, was that her urine test from the day before had shown that by Wednesday she would probably be ready for a new infusion. Beetroot.

'It's brilliant for the digestive tract,' said Samantha firmly.

Cat rolled her eyes in a meekly rebellious gesture. At this stage even the promise of her least favourite root vegetable was like being offered a plate of foie gras.

'Only problem is that we haven't got any,' continued Sam. 'The slugs got to them. So you'll have to make do with kale.'

The next forty-eight hours passed in a surprisingly pleasant blur. Remarkably the timetable of acupuncture, gentle aerobics, wax applications and fasting did seem to be working wonders. She almost believed Sam when she told her that the wet-suit treatment had made a noticeable impact on the dimples in her buttocks. And Hector, undeterred by his lack of success to date with Cat – she barely seemed to notice that he'd tried to flash her during the first paraffin wax session – remarked that her skin looked as clear as a nun's conscience. Then he spoilt it by commenting on the peculiar odour of cabbage that seemed to be wafting around the place.

'Your young man will be delighted,' he said slyly. 'Another librarian, did you say?'

'No, I didn't. I don't actually have a young man, per se, Hector.'

'Any room for an old one, then?' He looked at her hopefully.

'Oh, for heaven's sake, Hector, stop sexually harassing Cat,' said Daphne. 'You're enough to drive her back on to the cigarettes.'

'What would I do without you?' said Cat, after Daphne had snatched her from the jaws of nicotine defeat for the umpteenth time by roping her into *The Times* crossword. They were in the library, another paradigm of serene proportions, Gibbons wood panelling and copious but ultimately futile clingfilm that stretched the length of its vast windows and was about as effective against the chill winds as a scrap of Versace chiffon in a Siberian snowstorm.

Daphne looked up from the crossword. 'Instinctive reply, 3,4.'

'Fuck off.' A voice floated over to them from a faded chintz armchair in the corner.

'That's 4,3, Veronica,' said Daphne crossly.

'It's a tricky one, isn't it?' Cat gazed out of the window ruminatively, trying to organise her thoughts about Toby into something vaguely coherent. Some moments she thought of him as an amusing diversion – her passport back to the land of the living; other moments, when she was being more honest, she thought she might be falling for him hard.

'You know what they say. A crossword a day keeps senility away,' said Daphne.

'Well, the staff round here should live until about 2350 in that case,' grumbled Veronica, tugging at the leopard-skin négligé that clung to her ample bronzed curves like Sherpa Tensing halfway up Everest. Her tan, a miracle of sunbed technology and St Tropez, glowed with a toxic luminosity. 'They do nothing but engage in cross words. I do think Samantha's manners are getting worse. As for Micky's cooking . . . Still, one can't exactly say standards have fallen because that would imply there were some in the first place.'

'What does she expect?' muttered Daphne indignantly. 'Marco Pierre White?'

Privately Cat thought Veronica might have a point.

'Considering he trained in the Navy I think Micky's very imaginative,' said Daphne defensively.

'His descriptions certainly are. Guess what crunchy tabbouleh and lightly sautéd vegetable pavé is?' Veronica raked her heavily mascara-ed eyes over Cat. 'Millet and boiled kale.'

'Which are free of gluten, wheat and dairy,' said Daphne staunchly.

'And taste,' added Veronica, whipping out a nail file.

'Personally I really admire what Micky does with millet,' said Daphne.

'That's because you eat like a bird.' Veronica yawned. 'Weezie, Josie and I are doing the Zone diet this time. As advocated by Jennifer and Brad. A thousand cals a day. They're Fed-Exing it to us every two days from LA. Costs a bomb but Josie told them she's writing it up for the *Sunday Times* Style section. You should try it, Daphne. Might put some weight on you.'

Veronica stretched out her legs on the low carved table in front of her to admire her marabou mules and pulled out a packet of Hobnobs from behind a cushion.

'Is that safe with your cholesterol levels, Veronica, dear?' asked Daphne.

'Well, hello, Veronica.' Hector hobbled into the room, wheezing. 'Don't see you in the library often. Too busy writing those bonkbusters of yours, I suppose. Where are your lovely colleagues?' He sat down opposite Veronica, coughing violently. Crossly, she stuffed the Hobnobs back into the armchair's recesses.

'Veronica comes as part of a package, not that you ever see the others.' Daphne put down her pen. 'And lovely is certainly stretching it a bit. Once every two years she and her fellow Fleet Street hackettes come to Butely to churn out six hundred pages of utter drivel. They lock themselves away for weeks in the dorm, where they proceed to contravene every one of the Butely philosophies.'

'Why do they come?' asked Cat.

'Because it's far cheaper than taking a suite in a hotel. Louisa and Josephine not with you?' Daphne asked Veronica sweetly.

'Josie's in bed.' Veronica flipped open a jewel-encrusted compact and applied another slick of lip-liner until her mouth looked as though it had been shot in double vision. 'We snuck out last night and got back rather late. Had a few bottles of bubbly – just as well judging by the bloody heating. Then we tossed to see whose go it was to write the next chapter. Weezie got the short straw. She's up there calling on the muse as we speak.'

'That'll be a first, then,' muttered Daphne. 'If you're that concerned about the state of Butely, Veronica, there's an extraordinary meeting in the billiards room tonight for Friends to discuss the dire situation.'

It was the first Cat had heard of any meeting. 'Extraordinary in that I've just thought of it,' said Daphne under her breath. 'Might as well get those dreadful hacks drumming up some publicity for the place. It's quite clear something very urgent needs to be done.'

The problem, thought Cat later on, as she surrendered her increasingly malleable muscles to Miss Lezzard's African drumming and movement class, was knowing where to start. It was obvious Butely couldn't begin to compete with the glamorous spas she had been reading about on the Internet. Not in terms of facilities. Or food. Or treatments. Or clientele.

What was laughingly called a gym was a motley collection of old machines that made Heath Robinson look like the last word in space-age technology. When Cat had tried out the bike, she had discovered that the speed had jammed at two miles an hour. It was the same with the step machine. In fact everything seemed to have been set on a maximum speed that was somewhere between a crawl and a stagger.

Butely's brochure, which, Cat was starting to realise, was so out of date it read like a work of fiction, had referred to the shop. But it was less like the proud commercial heart of a country estate and more like the Oxfam branch on an inner-city one. Desolate recipe books from the palaeolithic era flapped dejectedly from their stands and a motley selection of homoeopathic remedies gathered dust.

'Good grief. How did you find your way in there?' demanded Daphne when Cat quizzed her about it. 'Nobody's been there for years. Not even the staff.'

'What's on the top floor?' asked Cat, who had noticed some attic windows under the roof.

'It's where the dormies are.'

'Dormies?'

'There are two, each sleeping six. They're for people who can't afford their own room. They have some of the best views. And of course nowadays bookings are so sparse people know they can virtually guarantee having one to themselves.'

'Not very efficient, business-wise.'

'Not a lot about Butely is. But Sir Rodney was always adamant that Butely should be accessible to everyone. Now you are coming to the SOB – Save Our Butely – meeting later, aren't you?'

Cat didn't need to be asked twice. Even though she was beginning to feel more relaxed than she had in years, she had been unable to switch off completely. Popping her dressing gown over her tracksuit, a coat over that, and donning a woolly hat, she decided to make another external tour of the house and grounds.

It was a spectacularly clear day. Butely's gently undulating meadows and ancient apple trees spread out before her, twinkling like sequins in the brilliant frosty sunlight. In the distance the sea glittered like pale steel as Cat crunched along the gravel paths, past the mellowed balustrades and the fountain, with its four battered stone lions. A pair of glossy blackbirds competed for a worm on a stretch of verdant green grass.

She followed the terrace, which wound round the house, taking in the alarming crevices and cracks that splintered its perfect symmetry. Poor old Butely. It had a chronic case of broken veins. In the unforgiving light, she could also make out some ominous-looking damp patches where the russet brickwork turned to a deep murky charcoal – the architectural equivalent, she supposed, of uneven skin pigmentation. Yet for all its scars and blemishes, Butely was undeniably a ravishing beauty of the first order – a breathtaking masterpiece of refined yet simple craftsmanship. She opened her notebook and wrote *Exterior*. Walking backwards for a better view, she was listing the more alarming of Butely's external shortcomings when she reversed into a tweedy figure carrying a dowsing stick.

'I'm terribly sorry,' he said, the breeze mussing the white fluffy crest of hair on his head and making his startling blue eyes water.

She eyed his dowsing stick with curiosity. He looked an unlikely advocate for New Age Therapy of any kind. 'Oh, that,' he said, following her gaze. 'It's an energy channeller. For locating poisons and blockages in the body, really, but I thought I might be able to use it to weed out a few blockages in the grounds. They're a little bit swampy just here, have you noticed?'

Cat shook her head. He held out a little handful of crushed white petals that gave off a pungent, bitter-sweet smell.

'Wild garlic,' he said. 'Who would imagine that such a pretty-looking weed could harbour the secret to healthy blood?'

Cat nodded politely. Not her, for a start. She'd assumed they were dandelions. 'It's unseasonably early,' he said sadly. 'Out of their time. They probably won't survive much longer—' He broke off and gazed mistily at Butely. 'The poor old place is in desperate need of a bit of a face-lift, isn't it?'

'Perhaps a few nips and tucks would do the trick.' Cat smiled. 'The funny thing is, I rather like it like this.'

He peered intently at her with his shrewd blue eyes. 'Do you really?'

'Well, I can see it's hopeless financially. Actually I'm just making a few notes for tonight's meeting. But the wonky bits are what give Butely her character. If she were perfect she might be a bit forbidding, and that's the last thing any of us would want. It's so important that Butely should be allowed to continue its good works – especially with people who wouldn't want to or couldn't afford to go to a fancier, more modern place.'

This outburst surprised Cat as much as it did Sir Rodney. Until a day or so ago the strongest emotion she'd felt about Butely was acute disappointment that she hadn't won a week in Champney's. But something had got into her in the past twenty-four hours, something that felt remarkably like contentment.

'I certainly do, Miss, er—'

'Cat. Cat McGinty.' She thrust out her hand, and Sir Rodney felt his eyes grow moist. He had been observing Cat from a discreet distance for four days – nearly always through the window of his little study – until he could no longer contain his curiosity. Noticing that she'd fallen into the habit of exploring the grounds in the afternoon, he'd been lurking in the gardens for an hour until he'd almost given up hope. But his fortitude had been more than amply rewarded. After a few short minutes Cat had fulfilled his wildest dreams. His daughter was clearly a soulmate. Offering her a frail arm, he escorted her back to the terrace.

After lunch Cat went back to her room to work on some proposals for Wilhelm Frupps's onslaught on Polish television. As usual Toby's chiselled dark features intruded on her good intentions and every so often she lost herself in the knee-buckling charm of his twisted, mischievous smile. She felt her hands running through his curly hair, across the sharp planes of his face and down his taut body. Trying to banish the disturbing sensation of Toby's hard muscles pressing into her body and the minty taste of his tongue flicking expertly in and out of her mouth, it struck her that her nicotine addiction had been replaced by another, potentially equally pernicious one. She imagined herself slowly being undressed – and undressing him. Slowly, she glided his hands between her legs – and consoled herself that lust wasn't the same as love. If lust was all it was. She sighed. Ralph was right, though it pained her to admit it. Somewhere along the way she had lost touch completely with her instincts. When? Probably about the time she'd joined Simms and picked up *Machiavellian Rules*.

She was roused from her reverie by a loud pounding on her door. Mrs Faggot was outside, straining beneath an enormous bunch of lilies.

'Arrived for you this afternoon when you was having your acupuncture.' She thrust the flowers into Cat's arms. 'From your boyfriend, are they? Whoever they are must be a bit flash.'

Cat's heart leapt. Sure enough the attached card was from Toby. '*Only sixty-seven hours and thirty-two minutes to go. Longing to test-drive the new improved you.*'

'I'd best be off finding a bucket, then.' Mrs Faggot hobbled back down the corridor, trailing a cloud of asthma-inducing detergents behind her. Cat splashed some of the water from the jug by her bedside on to her throbbing temple. She couldn't remember ever having received flowers from a man before. The best Ben had ever come up was a few weeds, of the smokable variety.

At seven she padded back across Butely's magnificent hall, where she ran into Daphne, standing next to a striking portrait of an exceptionally hideous woman in a startlingly low-cut taffeta dress and what looked like two large black puddings on either side of her head. 'The third Countess of Butely,' said Daphne. 'One's tempted to say she's no oil painting, but that would clearly be untrue.'

'She's very strong looking, isn't she?' said Cat diplomatically. 'Good grief, who's this?' she asked, gazing at the bulbous assets of a scrofulous-looking gargoyle in silk breeches and shiny black boots.

'The sixth Earl,' said Daphne. 'Used to get his wife to pleasure him in the stables while he was still wearing his boots in case he couldn't keep it up by the time he got to the bedroom. Poor thing. Still, when you look at her you begin to see she might have been grateful for any displays of affection, however brief.' She nodded towards an imposing gilt frame farther up the stairs which contained a woman of such uncommon hirsuteness that Cat wondered whether the sixth Countess might not be the missing link.

'They are a bit homely, aren't they?' she swept her eyes over the other Butely ancestors.

'Hideous. It's hard to know who was more pissed in their conception – God, or the poor buggers who had to paint them.'

Cat scanned the others. 'Things improve in modern times,' she said, allowing her eyes to rest on a lovely-looking woman with an intelligent, angular face, piercing blue eyes and a strikingly elegant off-the-shoulder grey silk dress.

'Oh, that's not a Butely,' said Daphne. 'She's got a chin, for one thing. That's Evelyn Dowell, Sir Rodney's mother. She was quite something in her day.'

'Beautiful face,' said Cat.

'Nice jewels too,' said Daphne, flicking a finger at the ruby and diamond bracelet round Evelyn Dowell's wrist. 'Rodney sold them off, of course, to pay for this place. The ones that Cynthia Dowell didn't run off with that is. Come along.' She looped an arm through Cat's. 'Our audience awaits.'

There were seventeen people in attendance, including two who were snoring. Samantha, Bill and Dr Anjit were part of the group, as was a small, athletic figure sporting a carving knife and an apron that was spattered with remnants of kale. Micky the chef, Cat presumed.

'It will not have escaped your attention,' began Daphne importantly, 'that the situation at Butely has become very grave since we were all last here. There is even speculation' – she looked pointedly at Samantha – 'that plans are afoot to redevelop the place.'

'Steady on, old girl,' blustered Hector, who was still bristling from not having thought of calling the summit himself. 'Don't you think you might be allowing your imagination to run away with you?'

'At her age it's about the only thing that will run away with her,' sniggered Weezie to the coven of hackettes.

'Daphne's right,' said Veronica. 'The place has gone completely downhill in the last few years. When I was at Shrubland Hall last spring—'

'I thought it was just the one time at Champney's that you betrayed us,' said Bill accusingly.

Veronica ignored him. '– I realised that it is perfectly possible to maintain the integrity of a beautiful old building and have thoroughly up-to-date facilities. Butely needs to get real.'

'I think we're all missing the point,' said Sylvia Lezzard.

'And what is that?' asked Hector, his eyes out on stalks at the sight of Sylvia's heaving cleavage.

'Oh, for God's sake, someone free the Butely Two, and put us all out of our misery,' hissed Veronica to the hackettes.

'The point,' replied Sylvia grandly, 'is that, be they ever so humble, the facilities of Butely should not detract from the core teaching, which is second to none.'

'Thank you, Sylvia,' said Daphne. She paused. 'Now does anyone have any suggestions to take us forward? We need a list of proposals to put to Sir Rodney. It's quite clear the poor man can no longer cope.'

'A bulldozer?' sniggered Weezie.

'I meant constructive proposals,' said Daphne sternly.

'That is constructive. The Long Building is an eyesore – and completely unnecessary. It must be very expensive to run.'

'Frankly I wouldn't be surprised if Rodney was deliberately running the place into the ground so he had an excuse to sell it,' said Veronica, fishing in her make-up bag for some lip gloss.

'How can you say such a thing?' stormed Bill. 'Sir Rodney's the most honourable man I know. When I think of the sacrifices he's made to keep this place going . . .'

'All right, don't get your long johns in a twist. All I'm saying is that Butely's worth a hell of a lot more to a bunch of asset-strippers than it is as a naturopathic clinic.'

'Well, you'd know all about strippers, wouldn't you?' said Daphne sweetly.

'Frankly,' continued Veronica unabashed, 'some of it looks as solid as the sets on that funny little production you toured the provinces in, Daphne – what was it called now?'

'*South Pacific*,' said Daphne haughtily. 'And the sets were highly original. If you must know the art director won the *Evening Standard*'s design award for 1967. He made them all out of Japanese rice paper and cardboard.'

'That figures,' drawled Veronica, 'given the amount they wobbled when anyone spoke.'

'Well, I don't know how you'd know,' retorted Daphne. 'According to that snippet you did in *OK!* you would only have been three.'

'Girls, girls,' said Hector, seizing his chance to take over the proceedings from Daphne. He beamed beneficiently at the room. 'I think the point is that deterioration has accelerated of late and as loyal Friends of Butely we all urgently need to think of a rescue plan. Even if we have to raise the money ourselves,' he added rashly. 'Now,' he continued, seeing Cat's raised hand, 'our librarian friend no doubt has some very learned suggestions. Over to you, Cat, my lovely.'

Cat was about to unleash a torrent of radical ideas when she caught sight of Sir Rodney through the half-open door. She couldn't tell whether he just happened to be passing, or whether he'd been trying to eavesdrop, but to judge from his face, which was ashen, he had heard the entire exchange.

'I just wanted to say,' said Cat, 'that I think I can smell burning.' With that she darted out of the door after Sir Rodney, who was hobbling down the corridor. Making painfully slow progress in the opposite direction was Mimms, the gardener. Poor old thing, thought Cat. By the time he made it to the meeting to throw in his pennyworth, Butely would have been sold off for millions and turned into retirement homes. She heard Micky stomp out of the room to check his curry for the next day and Veronica cackling that if the place burned down at least they'd finally get a decent fire going.

She eventually caught up with Sir Rodney at the foot of the staircase.

'They all have Butely's best interests at heart,' she began softly.

'I know.' He sounded worn out. 'You must think us a hopelessly sentimental bunch.'

'Not at all,' retorted Cat. 'Butely's very special. Even I can see that and I've only been here a few days.'

He looked at her for a few moments. 'Would you like to see all of it – the bit where I live, I mean? The Cottage is the oldest part of the house and quite unspoilt by fire doors and other planning vandalism.'

He led her along a narrow wood-panelled corridor to a heavy gnarled oak door covered with a handsome tapestry, behind which lay a cluster of cosy rooms with mullioned windows. Attached to the main house, the Cottage was at the end of the east wing and felt completely different in scale – less grand than Butely, but much more homely. Through the gloaming Cat spied layers of rugs, tartan blankets and more books than she had ever seen. They spilled off shelves and lay in precarious-looking piles about the place. Books on eighteen-century French poetry. Books on meditation. Books on philosophy.

Sir Rodney followed her gaze. 'I'm afraid Butely's library is sadly depleted. The fifth Earl burnt a lot of books for heating. There's not much from before 1802.'

On top of a yellowing mound of newspapers she saw a copy of *The Prophet*, one of Ben's favourites. He'd copied out one of its poems in the letter he'd sent from Jakarta to help explain why he had to leave her.

In the hearth a small fire sputtered, staunchly trying to counter the ferocious cold. Sir Rodney beckoned to Cat to sit down in a deeply worn leather armchair on one side of it and, pouring her a glass of water, sat down opposite.

'How long have you lived here?' asked Cat.

'Almost since you were born,' replied Sir Rodney, looking at Cat again in that odd, intense way she'd noticed earlier. 'I had rather grander quarters then – in the days when I was married with a family. I don't need so much space now. My son Jake's in New Zealand. And my wife is now my ex-wife.' He cast an indulgent look round the room. 'It's a bit of a mess, I'm afraid. Mrs Faggot's knees aren't what they were. Still, I'm inordinately fond of the old place.'

'It's lovely.' Cat settled back into the armchair and swept her eyes round the cosy room. 'And you've got my favourite view of all – the one where the sea looks like a grey squirrel hibernating between two giant mounds of leaves.'

'Those would be the Butely tussocks.' Sir Rodney's eyes lit up. 'Do you really like it here?'

'Who wouldn't? It's magical.'

'We're not as luxurious or modern in our facilities as some other places,' he said.

'No, but you're unique. I can see the treatments work.'

'Can you?'

'Very much. I was horrified when Dr Anjit put me on that fast. But I feel so much better. Famished, but a lot more relaxed and positive.' It was true. She'd even decided she might give the wheat-free, dairy-free regime a go when she got back.

He ground his trembling hand into the handle of his walking cane.

Cat pulled a tartan throw over her knees. Despite the fire it was just as chilly in Sir Rodney's private quarters as in the rest of the house. 'Daphne Lightbridge tells me Butely's saved lots of people from near-death.'

'Dear Daphne. So loyal. You know she more or less lives here all the time in return for drumming up bookings.'

Sir Rodney ought to ask for Daphne's room back in that case, thought Cat. But it certainly explained how Daphne could afford to spend so much time at Butely.

'Not that what she says about us saving lots of people isn't absolutely true,' he continued vehemently. 'We still do. I know people think things like gyms are terribly important. But you can get just as much benefit pounding up these hills.' He looked across to the tussocks. 'Probably more. It's not about one week of clean living, it's about changing your whole approach.'

'I agree,' said Cat warmly. 'As a matter of fact,' she continued.

'I was wondering if I might be able to help in a professional capacity. With some advice. I'm a management consultant for Simms. I've told the others I'm a librarian because I thought they might not approve of the kind of clients I have.'

An eyebrow shot up into his corrugated forehead.

'Are Simms so very wicked?'

'Depends on your moral standpoint,' conceded Cat. 'But they pay the bills. Well, almost. I've got a small daughter – Lily – you see. And London's not exactly cheap. You're not too disappointed, are you?' She looked across at him.

'Disappointed? I think it's wonderful that you've got a sound business mind. Not Jake's strong point, I'm afraid. You remind me of myself, you know. Only I was far, far more wicked.'

'Really?' Cat sounded incredulous. She couldn't imagine the beatific figure opposite her doing anything more evil than putting too much salt on his steamed kale.

'I used to put far too much faith in science,' he continued dreamily. 'It was my god. I thought that because it was so rational, so transparent, it was the answer to everything, when of course sometimes you just have to have faith in the inexplicable.'

'I see,' said Cat, taken aback.

'I was a politician briefly,' he continued wistfully. 'And so strong was my belief in scientific medicine that I pushed through legislation to get every single man, woman and child in the country inoculated against whooping cough.'

'What's so terrible about that?' Cat asked.

'My dear child, surely you've seen in your short time at Butely that protecting the body artificially isn't the answer. You have to educate its own antibodies—'

'Do you think I shouldn't have had Lily inoculated?'

'I'm sure you did what you thought best and that she'll be fine. Injections are probably a necessary evil for some diseases,' he added. 'But not in every case.'

Cat gazed into the fire.

'Where's Lily's father?' asked Sir Rodney gently.

'Last heard of at Kuala Lumpur airport. Then I think his phone gave out.'

'You're very brave.' Sir Rodney glanced at her again. 'It must be lonely bringing up a child on your own.'

'Sometimes. For four years I hardly had a social life at all,' said Cat, eyeing a tower of medical journals on the floor next to Sir Rodney's books. 'It's picked up a bit lately, though.'

'You've met someone?'

Cat shook her head. 'Not really. Well, yes. In a way. He's not my type at all but that's what's so good about it. Neither of us is taking it seriously. It'll be a bit of fun. I'm sure he's not in it for the long term.'

'Then he's a fool – or a saint.' Something in Sir Rodney's tone of voice made Cat wonder whether he was teasing her. She thought of Toby's driving, of his ruthless business tactics, his extraordinarily agile tongue and the equally extraordinary effect it had had on her nipples. 'No, I can safely say Toby's not a saint.'

'Toby?' said Sir Rodney, trying to sound as casual as possible.

'Toby Marks.' She looked flushed, as if the mere act of slipping his name into the conversation still gave her a thrill. 'His family lives locally. Do you know him?'

The fire crackled momentarily into life, flushing Sir Rodney's chalky face with colour. He looked so pale and frail Cat feared he might crumble into dust. Eventually he spoke.

'You could say so. He's my stepson.'

9

'Is that a Butely folder I can see there?' A small blowzy woman with a tight, mottled perm peered over the counter of the most dispiriting Spar-cum-village post office that Cat had ever been in and eyed Cat's basket suspiciously. Two Counties Radio blared away on an ancient-looking wireless that was turned up full blast. Cat blinked guiltily at the booty of salamis, cheeses, crisps and Garibaldi biscuits spread out in front of her and reflected that the last few days at Butely had flown past. Not that she hadn't missed Lily or thought from time to time about Toby, but she had to admit her stay had passed in an almost trance-like serenity.

'Only we're under the strictest instructions not to break the Butely code,' continued the woman loudly. She tapped out some numbers on the till with painstaking slowness.

'Is that the time?' Cat stared at the old station clock above the perm. There was no answer.

'I had that woman with the orange skin in here yesterday trying to buy a job lot of Jaffa cakes,' continued the woman, directing her comments at Cat's feet. 'And after all Sir Rodney's pioneering work there. I told her straight. That's not going to do your thyroid problem any good at all, is it, now, I said. "Oh, but Mrs Potts," she says, "I need it for my insular levels." ' Mrs Potts rolled her eyes to show Cat that she might be old and selectively deaf but she knew what worked for insular levels. 'I mean, what's the point of putting yourself through all that if you're only going to sneak in here and undo the good work?' She pummelled away on the till, which was decked with some singularly dusty strands of tinsel. 'Not that I ever get ill. But some people won't be told.'

'Actually this food's for my daughter,' explained Cat, wondering why she was apologising to Mrs Potts for buying something from her mange-ridden shop. Mrs Potts looked unimpressed. 'I'm on my way home to her in London now. The treatment's finished,' Cat added pointedly.

'You don't ought to be giving her that stuff.'

Exasperated, Cat returned the biscuits and the crisps. While she was searching for the right shelf, something small and rodent-like shot over her foot. She let out a scream that would have bayoneted most ears, but not Mrs Potts'.

'There you are, Cilla. Come here, darling. Did the lady from London scare you?' With infinite slowness, Mrs Potts staggered to her knees, scooped up the ferret and placed her on the counter next to the salami. 'Now where's Des?'

'Des?' Cat watched Cilla curl up next to Mrs Potts' knitting by the till in stunned disbelief.

'Yes, Des,' said Mrs Potts with barely veiled contempt. 'O'Connor. Television's greatest entertainer. I suppose you're too young to know anything about that. Now where was I?' She dragged herself back to her feet and cast a disparaging eye over Cat's shopping. 'Packed with additives. Now I know this is going to seem a bit radical to your generation. But have you ever considered fruit?'

Cat looked at the shrivelled apples by the door and retrieved the biscuits and crisps.

'I know, I know.' said Mrs Potts sadly. 'More chemicals than BP. But it's ever so hard getting hold of the good stuff – all goes to London 'cos the farmers know they can get better prices for it. 'Course, in the good old days Butely grew beautiful stuff. Used to sell its surplus to the villagers. But the whole place has gone to rack and ruin from what I hear. Only a matter of time before it gets bulldozed and they put up a bunch of executive homes . . .'

So it was true, thought Cat on the drive back to Kensal Rise. Butely really must be in danger if the entire village was speculating about it. She wished she'd been more use at the extraordinary meeting. That she could have been of more comfort to Sir Rodney, with whom she'd ended up spending quite a lot of her remaining time at Butely. Somehow she'd kept running into him. But it was hard to find much hope of salvation in the way things were currently run there.

As Cat's Polo bounced over the potholes of Makesbury Road, past the anorexic trees with their light blossom of Sainsbury's carrier bags, Toby's plane soared over the chequered lowlands of Scotland. He was disappointed not to be in London to meet Cat on her return, but – he smiled absent-mindedly at the blonde flight attendant – business was business.

'Can I get you anything else, sir?' The attendant leant over his tray,' her frosted pink nails fluttered a white napkin over his lap like a flag of surrender. He felt the synthetic silk of her shirt brush against his hand. Everything about her was uniformly ordered. Even her vanilla-coloured hair stood to attention in meringue-like peaks above her forehead. Presumably she'd be equally efficient in bed.

'What do you suggest?' His aquiline nose flared teasingly. The attendant bent down and busied herself with her trolley. 'Let me see.' She emerged with another packet of peanuts. 'On a short journey like this it's hard to offer the full range of in-flight services . . .' She trailed off. Toby looked up from a file of figures and sighed inwardly. He really didn't have time for this. He would shortly experience the toughest meeting of his career. He wanted to be prepared for the worst. She stood up and slipped a card with her telephone number under his tomato juice.

He eyed it warily. 'I think you dropped this by mistake,' he said, handing her back the card. Her honeydew foundation turned a furious shade of cantaloupe. 'In that case you probably won't be needing these.' She snatched back the peanuts with as much dignity as she could and slammed the trolley into the seat in front of Toby. He smiled and returned to his figures. Cat must be getting to him.

In reality there wasn't much to smile about in the rows and columns in front of him. Felix Hark, the notoriously ruthless MD of Golden Fields PLC, and unofficially Toby's biggest client, would not be impressed. This unsalutary thought was enough to make a man of even Toby's confidence feel shaken.

Something had fostered within Felix Hark a misanthropy so deep that nothing – not even kippering everyone who got in his way – could abate it. The business pages of the newspapers had dubbed him the Shark, and not without reason. In less than ten years his company had gone from a slow burn to an inferno that demanded quite a lot in the way of human sacrifice. Felix was constantly gobbling up smaller businesses, stripping them of their assets, squeezing the workforce and tossing what was left on to the flames of Golden Fields. In the process he'd built a corporation that had made him four hundred million in a succession of audacious and not entirely transparent deals. This latest one would double that sum. At least, that was the idea. Nervously Toby ploughed on. But things only seemed to get worse. Whichever way he tackled the numbers they added up to a worrying deficit. He tried to order another Bloody Mary but Vanilla Peaks ignored him.

The plane began its approach to Glasgow airport, lights piercing the frosty night sky like the candles on a chocolate cake. Vanilla Peaks sauntered over to Toby, adjusted his seat belt violently and spilt the dregs of a Bloody Mary on his black suit.

'Sorry, *sir*.' She dabbed his jacket with a cloth she'd just used to mop up some sick. Harnessing all his patience, he calmly handed her his boarding-ticket stub.

'Be a good girl and fetch that for me, would you?' She stomped off, returning with his coat, which she promptly dropped on the floor and trod on. 'Whoops,' she said sweetly. 'I seem to have put my heel through it. You will send the invoice for repairs in, won't you?'

Silently Toby counted to ten.

'The service in business class has really gone downhill,' said his neighbour sympathetically. 'Never been the same since the government got rid of BOAC.'

Clutching his ripped coat, Toby slid across the back seat of the waiting limo. Looking on the bright side, being insulted was good practice for what was about to be unleashed on him once he got to Golden Fields' HQ.

★

'But you must have met *somebody* famous,' Lily insisted.

'Nope.' Cat slipped into her bathrobe – somehow nothing else seemed comfortable any more – and jumped on to her bed next to her. 'Unless you count an ex-Bluebell dancer.'

'Blue? You mean pole dancers?' Jess asked hopefully.

'I'm not entirely sure what Daphne danced round. Rich men mainly.' Cat stroked Lily's hair with one hand and massaged Seamus's neck with the other. She was not going to give in to panic, even though Toby hadn't returned her last call.

Lily looked at her quizzically. 'You look nice anyway. Sort of younger.'

'Oh, I've missed you,' Cat hugged her and bathed in a rare surge of warmth from number 15's radiators.

'And we've missed you.' Lily nuzzled Cat's neck, which smelt vaguely vegetal but nice, like a warm, wholesome soup. 'It's been really quiet without you and Sukes.'

'Where is she?' said Cat, sitting up suddenly. It was true her mother hadn't been home when Cat had arrived but Cat had assumed she was out shopping.

'She had to flee,' said Jess. She began humming the theme tune from *Prisoner Cell Block H*.

Cat looked mystified.

'What Jess's trying to say,' said Lily, 'is that Sukes is wanted by the law. She got a nasty letter. They're trying to take all her money so she's gone home.'

Jess tried to change the subject. 'Would you like some stir-fry pancakes?'

Cat arranged her features into a paradigm of disappointment. 'I'd love some. But I've given up wheat.'

Jess snorted. 'You of all people! Hey, Lily, it just means there's more to go round for you and me.' She drifted out of Cat's bedroom. Cat kissed the top of Lily's head.

'Can I give up wheat and dairy too?' Lily wiggled out of Cat's arms. 'I'm begging you. Jess discovered how to make pancakes on Wednesday and she's been force-feeding us tossed puke ever since.'

Cat grimaced and reached under the duvet for the packet of salami she'd managed to get past Mrs Potts.

'So did you at least lose some weight?' Suzette asked on the phone that night.

'Four pounds. And I'm definitely less bloated.'

'How's Toby?' continued Suzette.

Cat looked at the damp patch on the ceiling above her head – a mere speck compared with poor old Butely's acres of wet and dry rot. 'Who?'

'Don't be tiresome, Cat. I'm in a delicate condition as it is.'

'You mean you've paid some tax.'

Suzette glanced in the miniature silver Tiffany mirror on her desk. 'You won't forget to take Lily to her riding lesson on Saturday, will you? I booked her a course while you were away. I was thinking of getting her a pony for her next birthday.'

'That's nice. And where do you suggest stabling it? Number nineteen's spliff patch?'

'Anyone would think you'd never heard of livery,' said Suzette. Or handsome, strapping stable lads, she thought, although these days there seemed to be more strapping stable girls. It was a pity Rodney hadn't been keen on Toby. He'd looked all right to Suzette: a bit ostentatiously handsome, like his car, but nothing a few weeks of Jess's cooking couldn't cure. Still, Rodney had seemed adamant, so it was up to Suzette to entice Cat away from Toby, into the arms of an honest horny-handed toiler of the soil, and introduce Lily to the delights of rural life. She'd paid her tax bill, she thought grimly. She might as well settle her debt to Sir Rodney bloody Dowell.

'And what the fuck is this contemptible piece of fucking shite?' roared Felix Hark across the Siberian expanse of his office. The force of his anger was such that the pale gingery hairs in his nostrils were quivering like a storm-tossed field of barley. In the lobby outside his three secretaries exchanged knowing glances and continued juggling his diary. A row on this scale always involved complex rescheduling.

Inside the office, Toby visibly relaxed as much as Felix's tortuous neo-baronial furniture allowed.

'They're the figures for next year, which I've amended on the basis of this year's performance,' said Toby. He fiddled with a silver cufflink.

'*Lamentable* performance,' corrected Felix, his staccato Glaswegian consonants sounding like machine-gun fire. Having removed his jacket to reveal scarlet braces and a two-tone shirt that accentuated his paunch, he looked like a prize wrestler. 'And how can I be sure they're not a towering work of fiction, like the last lot you bastards presented me with?'

Toby released one of his deadly, lopsided grins. 'Because, Felix, I give you my word that I worked on them myself this time, *by* myself. Since your last, er, purge, there's no one else left, as you know. And in defence of the dearly departed I should say that no one could have foreseen the extraordinary events of the past year. It's just one of those unpredictable things.'

'Yes, well, I fucking pay you to fucking predict the unpredictable. That's why I don't haggle over your fucking extortionate bills. Or did you think I signed the cheques purely for the pleasure of your much-touted fucking charm?'

Felix placed a stubby finger inside his collar and yanked it away from his neck, which had turned into a throbbing purple monster. Behind him on the wall a pair of antlers projected from the top of his head like giant devil's horns. Toby brushed a fleck of dust from his trousers.

'I promise you won't be disappointed,' Toby said smoothly. He plucked a silver Mont Blanc pen from his breast pocket and handed it to Felix. 'If you just sign there I'll get out of your hair and get on with things.'

Glowering, Felix snatched the pen. 'Well, I admire your cool, I must say. Quite impressive for an Englishman.' He scrawled his signature on the document in front of him. 'Most people fucking collapse at this point. It's pathetic.'

The worst was definitely over. 'There is one other thing, Felix.' Toby tried to sound nonchalant.

Felix's coppery eyebrows met across his puce brow. 'Is there, now?'

'It's this business with the share prices.'

'And what business would that be?' Felix's breathing had turned into an exasperated rasp.

'It's just that when things looked a bit dodgy for Golden Fields last summer, the share price didn't drop at all. If anything' – Toby scanned his notes – 'it went up.'

'And?' Felix's eyes glinted malevolently.

'Well, it's a bit odd. Even you must concede.'

'I've got a lot of financial journalists as friends, that's all. They gave Golden Fields an easy ride when things were a bit shaky,' said Felix, suddenly urbane. 'An expensive lunch at the Savoy here, a case of vintage wine there. Even a family holiday once. I've carefully cultivated the fuckers over many years. And if you've any sense, you'll do the same.'

Toby looked evenly at Felix across the reproduction mahogany desk.

'You do want to be rich, don't you, Toby?'

'Not if it means breaking the law, Felix.' Toby fixed Felix with one of his burnished-to-perfection stares. In return, Felix unleashed the full horror of his reddened eyeballs on him. There was an ominous silence. Then Felix threw back his head and chuckled. 'What a load of fucking shite.'

He stood up and showed Toby to the door. 'I'll see you in a fortnight. *Here* – in Glasgow. I won't be coming to fucking London for ages.' He chuckled again. 'Have a nice day.'

On cue, Felix's three personal assistants, who'd been listening in rapt attention to the proceedings in Felix's inner sanctum, began pounding their keyboards, casting sidelong glances as the dashing visitor in the dark suit and eau-de-Nil shirt sailed past. Toby tossed the prettiest one a demi-lopsided grin. Just to keep in practice.

'Can we move to the country?' asked Lily.

You could always tell the festive season was upon you, reflected Cat, because the supermarkets played wall-to-wall Slade, the central heating unfailingly broke down and Lily's questions acquired an urgent edge. She wondered when Toby would be back in the office. She'd been shocked at the little stab of disappointment that had lodged itself in her breast all morning after Petula had announced triumphantly that he'd been called away on urgent business. And even more shocked to discover how much she wanted to call him.

'I think it would be good for all of us.' Lily crunched through some of Jess's home-made grey muesli. 'You'd be much less stressed, Jess wouldn't keep imagining the police were about to deport her and I'd be less precocious.'

'I hate the country,' said Jess, packing some tofu burgers into Lily's rucksack. 'It's primitive and unhealthy. And the food's disgusting.'

Only a few months earlier, Jess, in one of her bids to reduce Cat's stress levels, had been leaving estate agent's details of thatched cottages by her bed. But as far as she was concerned, home was now where Ralph was.

'London's more dangerous than New York,' persisted Lily. 'Xanthe's nanny was car-jacked last week.'

'Oh my God, where?'

'Outside the school.'

'It was nothing really,' said Jess. 'Better than dying of boredom.'

'I bet you learned lots of interesting things to do at Butely,' said Lily.

'I certainly learned how to be an Isadorable,' said Cat. 'Not that I was very good at it. The country is lovely, Lily. But not very practical. There's the issue of how you make a living, for starters. How did the car-jacking happen?'

'Henrietta's mother says it's vulgar to work these days. It deprives those who really need a job.'

'Like me.' Cat kissed the tip of Lily's nose. 'I really need a job, and if I don't rush now I'll be looking for another.'

'Toby in today?' she asked Petula as casually as she could when she arrived at the office. She couldn't help herself. She was mystified by his absence and a little hurt. What was he working on that she didn't know about?

Petula perched daintily on the edge of Cat's workstation and glanced proprietorially at the watch Toby had given her last Christmas. 'Should be landing any moment now.'

Cat pretended to find the winking lights on her console massively interesting. Six new messages since last night.

'Four of them are from that Frau Fruppenführer,' said Petula, flicking the tamed mane that she had painstakingly straightened at the hairdresser every other day. 'I heard her leave three of them this morning before you got in. She wants to know where she can be finding the person who makes Princess Michael of Kent's suits.'

'Oh,' said Cat bleakly. There was an e-mail from Herr Frupps asking her what she thought about targeting the under-twelves with a new line of body jewellery called Coollerie. Her heart sank.

'If you ask me you want to think about rationalising Frau Frupps into a negative equity situation.'

Cat narrowed her eyes in an attempt to frame Petula's neat little derrière in widescreen. Toby must have left a message.

'De-hire her. Make her walk the golden plank. Eliminate her from the picture,' explained Petula imperiously. 'It's obvious Villie Frupps has got a thing for you. If I were you I'd snap him up. He's loaded, isn't he? Could be your best bet in the long run.'

Cat felt her newly charged batteries running down. Even though Petula's opinion on anything other than tweezers was clearly worthless, her blithe dismissal of Cat's career prospects snagged on her nerves. She began composing a diplomatic response to the Coollerie idea, gave up and instead ploughed through the rest of the e-mails, which weren't much more comforting. Four were from her e-bank informing her she was dangerously overdrawn; one from Persia's mother informing her that she was down to man the sushi stall at Lady Eleanor's next fund-raiser; and one from Daphne telling her that the situation at Butely had deteriorated dramatically since she'd left and suggesting that if by any chance Cat did come up with any novel fund-raising ideas for Butely, could she kindly forward them to her and not Hector. There was also a deceptively innocuous-looking e-mail from the seven Vices' office informing her that she had been selected to 'look into' a potential new tobacco client which wanted to reposition itself in the teenage market. And every so often an image of Xanthe being held at gunpoint against a Mercedes Jeep floated across her thoughts.

'What do you know about White Stick Tobacco?' Cat marched across to Toby's glass empire, where Petula was opening his post, having arranged a large, mysterious bunch of flowers on his desk.

'Not much. My cleaning lady smokes them. Lousy packaging. Ripe for rebranding, I'd say. Why?'

'I think they could be our new client,' said Cat. 'Toby's and mine,' she added. 'Though where we'll find time . . .'

'*Your* new client, possibly.' Petula pursed her inflatable lips. 'There's absolutely no way Toby's got a spare second. Not with all the work he's been doing on Frupps. The data he's analysed on that place are phenomenal.'

It was not in Cat's nature to be resentful, but she couldn't help wishing that Petula would give her a little more credit for all the work she'd done on Frupps. Why did she keep being handed more work that took her away from her media expertise?

'Anyway, it's much more your thing. Toby doesn't smoke.'

'Nor do I now,' retorted Cat. 'Not that I ever did.'

Petula shot her a pitying smirk. Cat returned to her desk and spent an uncomfortable hour or so scanning the Internet for information on cigarette advertising and jewellery-buying habits among the under-twelves.

Bang on 10.30, Toby strode into the office bearing a wraparound smile and a bunch of peonies for Cat to welcome her back. Every time Petula was on an errand, Toby called Cat from the phone on his desk and whispered innuendoes down the line. By lunchtime he'd succeeded in distracting her from her tobacco research six times. By mid-afternoon he'd invited her for dinner at his flat.

'Or we can go out, if you'd prefer,' he said gently. Through the glass wall of his office she could see him leaning back pensively in his swivel leather chair. 'But I thought it might be nice to be somewhere a bit intimate for a change.'

'Dinner in would be lovely.' She wouldn't ask him why he hadn't called once during the two days since she'd got back from Butely. Dinner must mean something. Even Petula hadn't made it through the hallowed portals of Toby's stunningly appointed penthouse loft for dinner, although, as she told Cat, she had been there on business several times, having done everything bar the actual conveyancing to facilitate his purchase of it.

'What time?'

'I'll drive you from work.'

In some ways the situation wasn't entirely ideal, decided Cat as the Porsche glided through the wet streets towards Hoxton. Going straight to Toby's from work meant she hadn't been able to spend four hours making herself look as though she hadn't spent any time getting ready. At least her suit didn't look too bad, especially as she'd accessorised it that morning with a pair of slightly kinky Jimmy Choos.

'I have to hand it to you, McGinty, Butely's done wonders. You're glowing.'

'Must be all the lead in Butely's rusting pipes. Does wonders for a girl's complexion.'

'Clearly. And full marks for lasting the course. I know it's not exactly the Ritz.'

'No. But wonderful in its way. Your stepfather's quite something.'

There was a moment's pause. '*Ex*-stepfather. He and my mother divorced years ago.'

'Why didn't you tell me about your connection with Butely?'

'There isn't really one,' he said airily. 'I'm afraid my mother doesn't go in for amicable divorces. I haven't seen too much of Rodney lately. I'm fond of the old fellow, though. But I didn't want you to think I was putting pressure on you to go. To be honest I was dreading not seeing you for a whole week.'

Cat was flattered, but not easily appeased. 'And you never mentioned that you had a half-brother either.'

'Jake?'

'Are there any others?'

'None that I'm aware of.' He put his foot down. 'We're not close. I don't think Jake approves of me.'

'I don't approve of you either.' Cat grinned. 'Particularly when you put your hand there while you're driving.' She dropped her gaze to his left hand, which had worked its way up her thigh and was now exploring her underwear. She placed it back on the gear lever. 'One thing at a time, please, Marks.'

They pulled up in the underground car park of a raw-looking warehouse. A huge, rackety industrial lift chugged them slowly up to the top floor and then Toby led her into an open-plan area so vast she couldn't actually see an end to it. He must need to pack supplies every time he crossed the living room.

'Oh,' was all she managed, before the views from the windows that ran the entire length of one wall and looked out over the Thames magnetically drew her towards them. 'Couldn't you find somewhere more spacious, Marks?'

'Good, isn't it?' He whipped her coat from her shoulders.

'Amazing.'

And it was. Toby's unabashed adoration of all things material tickled her. At any rate it was a lot more honest than Ben's sanctimonious blasts against all forms of consumerism apart from his own. She paused before venturing any farther into the flat, which she could now see was divided into interesting architectural spaces by a series of interconnecting sunken floors that appeared to have been wrestled out of the inside of a washing machine. A constellation of blue and white sunken stars washed the room in ghostly halogen.

'Drink?' He headed towards a door. It was a bit like watching Captain Scott set off across Antarctica, except that eventually Toby did return – with a hollowed-out orb of frozen vodka and tomato juice. Everywhere she looked she saw what were clearly some very adventurous textures. But apart from a concrete coffee table resting on four old railway sleepers and a vast leather-and-steel sofa there wasn't much in the way of furniture. And no decoration, unless you counted the log fire winking in the gloaming of a raw brick wall and several hundred books neatly arranged on a line of industrial-looking shelves.

'It's very—'

'Pretentious?'

'I was going to say impressive.'

'You're very diplomatic. The view are breathtaking. That's what sold me in the first place. But the rest . . .' He glanced at the rubber bean bags, made from reclaimed tyres – Cat had seen them in Suzette's *World of Interiors*. They cost a bomb. 'That's what you get when you leave your domestic arrangements to your PA and Precious O'Dowd, leading light of the BritGrit brigade and the most pretentious architect in Europe.'

'That's not a real name?' Cat giggled.

' 'Fraid so.' He sidled up to her. She could see the skin pulsing on his neck. 'They worked very hard, I'll give them that. No disused factory was left unraided. They ripped the floor from an old car plant in Walsall. It's recycled zinc, I'll have you know.'

'Well, it must be wonderful having all this space.' She hiked across to the bookshelves, where she pretended to examine one of about three dozen arcane law books.

'Now, McGinty.' Toby flicked a switch and suddenly the room was flooded with the soundtrack of *The Mission*. 'Make yourself as comfortable as is possible in this pitiful monument to BritGrit and I'll order in.'

While Toby was busy in the kitchen – ordering takeout from the local restaurant – Cat perused the rest of Toby's bookcases, a fest of weighty law texts, Booker contenders, exotic travel books, philosophical tomes and coffee-table bricks. He certainly had eclectic tastes, thought Cat, wondering where he found the time. She flopped on to the sofa, or tried to. Precious O'Dowd clearly didn't believe in comfort. The sofa was as hard as the single cracked rock that presided over the concrete coffee table. 'I take it these nodules are meant to massage you?' said Cat, trying to make herself cosy on its hostile expanse. 'It's quite clever really.'

'It would be if it worked. Instead it just looks as though it's got a bad case of acne,' he called from the kitchen.

Within thirty minutes they were seated across the stuccoed aluminium kitchen table, tucking into a flawless filet mignon and salad drizzled in the most perfect dressing Cat had ever tasted.

'It's delicious.' She licked some juice from the corner of her mouth.

'Profiteroles?' he asked. 'With crème anglaise?'

'I think I'd better walk this off.'

Cat felt the heat rise off her body like swamp steam. She walked over to the windows, only to find that Toby had followed her. She leant her face against the plate glass, praying for the burning sensation to wear off. When she looked up, Toby's face was even closer. 'I'm sorry I didn't call,' he said softly. 'Things got a bit hairy up there. Forgive me?' He cupped her face in his hands and pressed his cool lips against hers. And then, quite suddenly, she relaxed and let events take their course.

Or rather her body did, because what happened next was more to do with its needs than what Petula might call logical brain deployment. Cat found herself returning his kisses with equal hunger. With infinite lightness and considerable efficiency he slid his hands down her back, caressing her skin through the wool suit, and when that became frustrating slipping them beneath her shirt until his hands had worked their way inside her bra.

Feeling giddy with rapture, Cat found herself tearing at his clothes and edging back towards Precious O'Dowd's sofa. 'Not that bloody rack,' Toby moaned, steering her towards his bedroom. 'It's even more uncomfortable than the sodding floor. I keep meaning to replace it.'

Her knees buckled as his handsome cheekbones projected towards her like the wings of an aeroplane. Encircling her with his arms, he kissed her again. She felt her thighs melt and her stomach somersault. In the distance a siren sounded.

'It's for you,' said Toby hoarsely, fetching her her mobile, which had fallen out of her discarded jacket's pocket on to Precious O'Dowd's sea of zinc.

*

She felt like a naughty schoolgirl in the taxi back to Makesbury Road, although if anyone should be feeling ashamed it was Ralph for blowing up the oven in the first place.

'What the hell were you fiddling with it for anyway? You're a builder, not a bloody electrician,' said Cat when she got back.

'He was only trying to help,' said Jess.

Cat peered at the blackened hole where the oven had been. Just when the kitchen had started to look habitable again. 'What's this?' She pointed to an incinerated heap of plastic.

'God knows.' Ralph frowned in concentration. 'One of Jess's specials maybe.'

Jess scowled. 'I never use the oven. Probably one of Cat's three-hundred-calorie ready meals she thinks I don't know about.'

Cat prodded the ashes and suddenly remembered the tub of Cellulux she'd put in there weeks ago. It must have exploded. Still, the first of the Machiavellian rules was Never Complain, Never Explain. 'I thought something really bad must have happened,' she said, her voice softening a little.

Ralph brushed his hand through his unruly hair and looked marginally sheepish. Not for the first time Cat reflected how attractive he was. 'Tell you what. Why don't I go and get a new one tomorrow and install it myself – no charge?'

Even Cat's finances weren't that bad. 'No, you're all right, Ralph. Save your energy for the kitchen. I'll sort something out, don't worry.'

'Right you are. Tell you what. Why don't I throw in some shelves in your bedroom for free? You could do with some more storage space. In return for wrecking the oven.'

He high-fived her and padded back upstairs with Jess. Cat smiled. Learning how to deal with her builder was surely conclusive proof that she was finally getting her life under control.

'Is he being nice to you?' Suzette was finding it hard to get the tone of this conversation right. She didn't want to drive Cat back into the not so splendid isolation of her recent non-existent social life.

But she couldn't help being concerned about Rodney's opinion of Toby. What did he mean when he said Toby wasn't the type to get serious about? Or was it just sour grapes? Toby was Rodney's *ex*-stepson, after all. And how dare he have a son, an *ex*-stepson and a daughter? It wasn't fair. She wished she could reach him to clarify things, but his phone seemed permanently engaged.

'Okay.' Cat thought of the okay meal he had brought from the Ivy to Makesbury Road three days earlier; of the okay single white rose tied with an okay amethyst necklace that had arrived the following evening; and of the okay La Perla bra and knickers she had found in her drawer at work. No one had ever bought her underwear before. Ben paying for her J-cloth knickers at the hospital where Lily was born didn't count because she'd ordered them. She was like a hyacinth that had been underground far too long and had finally seen the light. She wasn't in love, of course, but whatever she was in was a good substitute.

'What did you say he does for a living again?'

'The same as me.'

'But he drives a Porsche.'

'He's been working for them in New York. It tends to inflate salaries.'

'Cat?'

'Yes?'

'Would you say Toby's a good person?'

It was a fair question and one she sometimes asked herself. But she was not prepared to discuss it with Suzette. 'If you're asking whether he's ever done VSO, given up both his kidneys or chained himself to the railings outside Ten Downing Street, then no. But—' Cat paused, remembering the four Tintin books he'd bought Lily to complete her collection. She didn't want to talk about it, for fear of jinxing it, whatever it was. 'Whatever he's like is beside the point because he's not my type.'

'What do you mean?' Suzette did her best not to sound jubilant.

'He's a man.' Cat turned out the light. 'Night-night.' She rolled over, and closed her eyes.

*

The next week passed in a blissful blur of stolen lunches and romantic evenings. Better still, according to Toby the Vices had agreed she was hugely undervalued. A rise was just a formality now. She wanted to hear that they'd taken her off the White Stick account so that she could concentrate on building up their media division too. But one thing at a time.

When Toby was called away unexpectedly on business again she felt twisted with disappointment. She thought about him constantly for the three days he was gone, existing in a hyper state of excitement between his phone calls and watching *Ready Steady Cook* and *Casualty* in an attempt to keep herself on an even keel. Even being without Toby was more enjoyable than her old life, she decided. If only the cigarette project would disappear and Herr Frupps would stop pestering her about his wretched Coollerie everything would be perfect. Still, almost perfect was good enough for her. Anything more would have been worrying.

On the fourth morning of Toby's absence, she was woken at 6 a.m. At first she thought it was the car alarm that had been intermittently wailing all night but as she surfaced from her sleep she realised it was the front doorbell. Instinctively she looked around the room – in her sleep she had taken the phone off the hook, presumably imagining it had been the source of all that noise. Fearing something had happened to Lily, she flew down the stairs. Toby was on the doorstep, looking unusually agitated. His eyes were bloodshot and he was unshaven. Cat thought it made him look even sexier. He leant against the door frame.

'Can I come in?' He sounded tired. She led him into the kitchen, praying he wouldn't notice the little heap of washing up in the bowl. At least it looked more normal since Ralph had been doing his improvements.

'To what do I owe the pleasure?' she asked lightly.

'To the fact that your bloody phone doesn't seem to be working. I've been trying to get hold of you since last night.' He walked over to the table and sat down.

She wanted to snuggle up to him but the physical distance between them suddenly seemed unbreachable. 'What's up?' She ran some warm water over the dishes, willing herself to stop panicking. She had never heard Toby sound like this, cold and slightly distant.

'Rodney Dowell's dead. He died the day before yesterday.'

'Oh, Toby, I'm so sorry.' To her shame, relief flooded through her like warm milk. She had thought Toby was about to tell her he had a wife and four kids in New York.

'It was hardly a shock,' said Toby, standing up again. 'He's been ill for ages.'

Cat felt a strange prickling sensation at the base of her neck and realised this must be what people meant when they talked about their hair standing on end. There was something in Toby's tone that jarred – the barest hint of annoyance that only people who knew him well would have spotted.

'The thing is, Cat, I'm the executor of his will. That's where I was yesterday.'

She watched the bubbles form clusters on the plates. She wished he would come over and slide his arms round her. 'Poor Sir Rodney,' she said. 'And poor you. You must be devastated. Obviously I didn't know him very well, but he seemed such a wonderful man.'

'Clearly the feeling was mutual,' said Toby. He paused. Cat stopped wiping the dishes. 'You must have made a very big impression on him, Cat. Because he's left the whole place to you.'

10

'You didn't tell us you'd inherited a stately,' whistled Jess in awe.

'Not a stately,' said Cat, hastily tidying away the aerial photographs and maps that the solicitors had given her of Butely. 'Just a state. A shocking one.'

'I think it looks gorgeous,' said Lily dreamily. 'I'd love to live somewhere like that, with real grass and no crisp packets.'

Cat looked at her daughter. Nothing in her face suggested that she had spent days working out what would make Cat feel most guilty about turning her back on rural life. She hardened her heart. There was no way they were moving to Butely, where, as the solicitor had put it, she would be responsible for stopping the place from collapsing.

Whichever way you looked at it, Butely wasn't remotely viable in its present state. Strictly speaking, it wasn't even wholly hers either. As the solicitors had explained, Sir Rodney had left the land to his son Jake, who, according to Toby, was practically a communist who believed all property was theft. 'Perhaps he won't mind giving it all to me, then,' Cat had joked. Toby couldn't seem to see the funny side.

Then there was the slightly alarming news that Butely had closed for business immediately after Sir Rodney's death. And the even more alarming news that Samantha, Micky, Mrs Faggot and Dr Anjit still remained on the payroll. Bill, as Samantha had written to tell her, had finally kicked the great paraffin bucket in the sky. Thinking of him faithfully shuffling off this mortal coil so soon after Sir Rodney filled Cat with melancholy. Still, as Toby so rightly pointed out, it was one less salary they had to fork out for.

The next night Lily woke up screaming about car-jackings and burglaries. It turned out that despite having the same alarm system as the Pentagon, the Lindens had been broken into the day before and was now minus its industrial espresso machine.

Jess poked her moon face round the bedroom door as Cat cradled Lily and smoothed her sweat-soaked hair. 'They say you're six times more likely to get mugged in London than in New York,' she said helpfully.

'That's just propaganda,' said Cat. 'I thought you hated the countryside.'

'I've changed my mind. What about the pollution in London? It can't be good for Lily.'

'The rate of asthma is far higher in some rural areas than it is in cities.' Cat snuggled into bed next to Lily. 'Some scientists believe a little pollution is good for you.'

'Would you say Butely was bigger than Persia's house?' said Lily. 'You can't always tell from pictures.'

'She'd be able to keep a pony,' said Jess.

'What about Ralph?'

'He's going back to Australia after Christmas. His visa's up.'

'I didn't think you lot believed in visas.'

'I can't talk about it.' Jess's voice trembled ominously. 'Let's just say I'm very disappointed in Ralph's lack of moral fibre. Men are bastards, Lily.'

'Not you as well.'

'Goodnight,' said Cat. In the dark, narrow bed, she stroked her daughter's long, curly hair until she dozed off. But Cat couldn't get back to sleep. Her mind was too full of possibilities.

'All I'm saying,' said Jess the next day, 'is that you should seriously think about this opportunity. Maybe Sir Rodney was trying to tell you something about your life. Perhaps this is a sign that it's time to change.'

'*Five days until ye olde Christmas*,' crowed Terry Wogan.

'It's out of the question. I couldn't possibly take it on. It would be a full-time job—'

'Healthier than the one you've got at the moment. Don't tell me you're happy about that new tobacco account because not even you could fail to see that for what it is—'

'– and one that's bound to end in tears. How did you know about White Stick?'

'It's not my fault if you keep leaving your papers lying around.' Jess squirted some Mr Sheen at a pile of Ben's old CDs that were stacked against a wall.

'It hasn't been finalised yet. Anyway, I think I'm sufficiently established at Simms to be able to turn away an account if I'm not morally comfortable with it.'

Jess gave Cat one of her looks.

'What?' asked Cat innocently.

'That company wouldn't let you get away with not giving Hitler a blowjob if it didn't suit them.'

Later that night, curled up in bed with a pile of old 'Rural Idyl' columns, Cat allowed herself a brief wallow in her rustic fantasy.

> As I look out on the meadow, two jackdaws skim the wintry sky like Nureyev and Fonteyn, dipping and diving for worms. In the fields beyond, the grass is topped with icy crystals, like sparkling champagne flutes. Christmas will soon be here and excited children will gather round our inglenook to toast home-made marshmallows and oatcakes before setting off on the village carol-go-round . . .

Cat sighed. In the unlikely event that she and Lily and Jess ever went carol singing in Makesbury Road they'd probably get mugged. She turned out the light and gave in to the flake ad tableau, which she had been resisting all day. This time Toby was there, holding her paint palette for her. Lily was trotting on the back of a perfect Thelwellian piebald pony. And she herself had turned into the kind of person who knew the difference between jackdaws and blackbirds.

She rolled over and put her head under the pillow, trying to blot out the orange-blue light from the street lamp. Toby had been right all along. Butely was a hopeless case. He hadn't even had to say anything when they'd been at the solicitor's. The figures spoke for themselves. Even before he'd looked at her with that mixture of sympathy and concern, she knew the best thing she could do was let him help her and the mysterious Jake offload it for the best price as soon as possible.

Anyway, the timing was hopeless – it would be idiotic to chuck everything in just as her social life was finally picking up and she had a new champion at Simms. Jess was right. The country was stultifyingly boring. She seriously doubted whether the whole of Dorset could provide the kind of sparky, thought-provoking conversations she had with Toby. Not that she was going to let that cloud her judgement. The point was Lily would end up at an even more narrow-minded school, and what would they live on? She could hardly commute to Simms. She tossed and turned until, finally, sleep rescued her. And then a car siren went off.

Toby's reaction to Sir Rodney's will, which Cat had originally interpreted as acute disappointment at not being left anything, but later decided was shock at his death, seemed to change again after his next trip to Scotland. It was then that he'd asked her if she had thought through her decision to sell it.

'I don't have to.' She looked at him in surprise. They were perched on the edge of Precious O'Dowd's buttock-flayer. 'It's so obviously a non-starter. You said as much yourself at Great-Aunt Hermione's ball.'

'I said it was run down and out of touch with modern tastes,' said Toby, fiddling with her bra strap. 'Have you changed your body lotion, McGinty? I'm catching top notes of frangipan.' She wriggled against his chest and began to undo his shirt.

'Seriously,' continued Toby, unzipping her skirt, 'I've been thinking things over while I've been in Glasgow – you won't believe how boring that bloody Scottish project is – and I'm starting to think Butely might have real potential.'

'Why don't you tell me about the Scottish project? A problem shared and all that.'

'Love to, but it's like the Scottish play. Can't be mentioned by name.' He pulled Cat gently towards him and began kissing her, but for once she couldn't concentrate. He unbuttoned her shirt.

'Shit.' Cat had caught sight of the illuminated clock on a distant wall. 'I promised I'd get back early. Jess's got a ten o'clock yoga class. She's in a slump since Ralph decided to go back to Melbourne.' She hastily did up her clothes. She had to hand it to Toby; he hid his disappointment well. He even drove her home. 'You don't really think Butely could be a goer?' she asked, getting out of the car.

'Absolutely. And I'll prove it.' He roared off, leaving Cat in a cloud of warm air from the exhaust.

Steering the Porsche down the M3 with his right hand on the wheel and his left massaging Cat's knee, Toby seemed like a restored man. Any chill in his manner towards her had been replaced by a new affection. He still bantered and flirted outrageously – thank God – but nowadays Cat caught wind of something else, a tenderness that made her think he might really care for her.

On they thundered over frosty hill and dale, leaving most of the traffic standing. As a vast turreted Victorian mansion shimmered on the horizon, he put his foot down to the floor and turned the volume up on Beethoven's Fifth.

'What's that amazing building?' asked Cat, taking in the glories of the Dorset countryside.

'The East Scraggerton School for Young Offenders,' he replied against a rolling of orchestral drums. 'And yonder is the second-ugliest housing estate in South-West England. And just over that tor is an old tractor factory . . .'

'All right, I get the message.' Cat giggled. 'You're not a natural lover of the countryside.'

'*Au contraire*. Who could resist the haunting tang of silage? Or the melancholy call of an authentic village karaoke night? I love it all. True, the inconvenience of not being able to nip out for some pesto at eleven p.m. can be a little trying. And not being able to buy a fresh lettuce can wreak havoc on your salads. And then there's all those animals that insist on blending with your bumper.

But on the whole, no one could be more rurally minded than me.'

She gave him a sidelong look. The emergency meeting he'd had to attend in Scotland had worked wonders. It was amazing how he appeared to thrive on pressure, although Cat couldn't help feeling a tweak of disappointment that, so far at any rate, he hadn't confided in her about the project he was working on up there. Especially after she'd been so open about sharing every last bit of her research on the Frupps empire. At least any vestigial disappointment about Sir Rodney's death – and the will – seemed to have evaporated. She stroked his hand, twisting her fingers through his. She would always be grateful for his rational advice in this turbulent time.

She was probably still in shock about it even now. The inheritance had thrown her completely off balance. After her initial reaction, which was to offload Butely on Herr Frupps as the perfect English estate, she had been assailed by conflicting emotions. Not the least of which was an overwhelming sense of duty to Sir Rodney.

'It feels a bit like playing truant,' she said, as they left East Scraggerton School for Young Offenders behind them.

'Honestly, McGinty, for the child of a renegade you make a lousy rebel.' The Porsche hit a hundred and twenty miles an hour and he turned the heating down a smidgen. 'You're a nervous wreck. Anyone would think this wasn't a genuine business opportunity we're investigating.'

'I suppose so. It's just so glorious to be out of the big smoke that it feels like a holiday. Just look how clear the sky is. It's like neon silk. And the grass is like—'

'Radioactive swamp?' suggested Toby. 'It's probably smothered in chemicals. Shit. Look at that bloody queue. Some moron's probably fallen asleep and wrapped his Ford Mondeo round a bloody cow. That's the problem with the countryside – fuck all to do and you still get traffic jams.'

'Very Keats.'

' 'Course, what this county really needs is a state-of-the-art sixteen-lane motorway.'

'What an idyllic thought.' She ran her eyes over his chiselled profile. She still couldn't be sure how much of his bluster was put on.

'I'm serious. The countryside has brought untold misery to millions. Famine. Potatoes. The Wurzels. Name me one good thing to come out of it.' He grinned and pressed her hand to his lips. Then his mobile rang.

'Where the fuck are you?' A terse Scottish voice rang through the car speaker, mingling with the Beethoven. Cat looked out of the window again and pretended not to listen.

'Felix, how delightful to hear from you.' Toby flicked the speaker off and plugged in his earpiece.

Cat stared out rapturously at fields of fawn-coloured sheep and little clusters of newborn lambs and tried not to listen to what Toby was saying.

'Hard to say. I'm having to go softly, softly—' He looked over at Cat and blew her a kiss. 'Quite so,' he said into the mouthpiece. Cat could hear a string of loud expletives coming out of the phone. Concerned, she tore her eyes from the rural idyll outside and looked at Toby. A small vein throbbed on his forehead. She leant across and kissed it. 'Are you all right?' she whispered.

'Fine.' He smiled at her.

'What's that?' she heard the voice on the other end of the phone shout.

'I said it will all be fine. Trust me. I'll have it in the bag in the next twenty-four hours. You have my word. Toodle-pip.'

'Are you sure your mother doesn't mind us descending on her?' asked Cat, nervously.

'She'd be mortally offended if we didn't. She and Butely are next-door neighbours – if somewhere with two hundred and fifty acres can be said to have neighbours. Anyway,' he added slyly, 'she's dying to meet you.'

Cat, on the other hand, was just dying. She'd never been introduced to anyone's mother before. Ben had always been vague on the precise whereabouts of his and her nerves were jangling. 'Does she have a lot of visitors?' she asked casually. She was still hoping against hope that Toby's mother would turn out to be an apple-cheeked picture of rural cosiness, the way she used to envision Candida St John Green before she began banging on about her passion for fox-hunting.

'She used to be quite a grand hostess in her day.' Cat's heart sank. 'But she's much more down to earth now,' he continued. 'She's very modern in that way.' She could hear a trace of pride in his voice, which she took to be a good sign. A man who loved his mother was a man who loved women. 'Don't worry, you'll like her. And she'll like you. You look gorgeous, by the way.' Cat smiled weakly. Her purple Gina boots had seemed like a witty touch when she'd put them on this morning in Makesbury Road, but now they just looked trashy.

'Relax,' said Toby. 'That's an order, by the way. It's all very casual at Ashdown House. No standing on ceremony.'

Just a lot of sitting on exquisite Hepplewhite furniture. Cat's stomach lurched as the Porsche swept through a pair of immaculate filigree gates, up a creamy gravel drive that looked as though it had been freshly vacuumed. In front of them stood a perfect specimen of Regency elegance.

'Welcome, Mr Toby,' said a black-and-white figure standing to attention by the door.

'Morning, Harbury. How's the back?'

'Much improved, sir,' replied Harbury, ushering them past a tastefully decorated Christmas tree and up a wide oak staircase that smelt of beeswax and lavender polish. 'Pleasant journey?'

'Most bracing,' said Toby, placing a hand lightly on Cat's elbow. 'Didn't leave London till ten – had a few things to sort out in the office first. We've made excellent time, considering.'

'Quite so,' said Harbury in tones that left Cat in no doubt as to his views on fast cars and ostentatious workloads. 'Lady Cynthia's waiting for you in the long gallery, sir.'

'*Darling!*'

Cat had never seen so many shades of cream coalesce in one place. Like the room, Lady Cynthia was swathed in it.

'Hello, gorgeous.' Toby swept his mother up in a bear hug and then pulled away to examine her. 'Wonderful as ever. New hair?'

'Trust you to notice. So adorable of Nicky to fit me in at such short notice. I slipped up to London last week – not that you were there.' She pulled a disappointed face.

'I've been away rather a lot on business lately. Sorry about that.'

'Well, it suits you, you look wonderful.' Cynthia stared at her son appreciatively. Cat might as well have been a crumb on the Aubusson. Although had she been she would have been nuked instantly. Lady Cynthia looked like the kind of person who operated zero tolerance on bacteria.

'But then success always did make you even more handsome. And no one deserves it more than you. Still, after all that time in New York I was looking forward to seeing a bit more of you.'

'Darling, you know I'd love nothing better. So next time give me a little warning at least.'

'It's all in the hands of Nicky. And now' – she patted the vacant silk next to her, indicating that Toby should occupy it – 'your friend must think us very rude. Do at least introduce us, darling.'

She held out a silky manicured hand and Cat caught a whiff of Calèche. For a moment she thought she was expected to curtsy. Instead she squatted awkwardly on the edge of a cream Hepplewhite sofa. Lady Cynthia's furniture seemed to have achieved the impossible by being even more uncomfortable than her son's.

'Toby tells me your mother's made quite a success of her life. Didn't you say she was a fashion editor or something?' drawled Lady Cynthia.

Toby tells me you've done fuck all with your life, Cat was tempted to say. Instead she explained about *Fair Sex* and watched the sun dapple through the mullioned windows, highlighting Lady Cynthia's charmingly retroussé nose. 'It was quite radical in its day,' added Cat. 'It used to campaign a lot.'

'Really. What for, hot pants?' There was a momentary lull in the conversation.

'Have you been on a diet again? You look fantastic,' Toby said. Lady Cynthia folded her hands on her emaciated knees. 'It's

Harbury. He's got me on a jogging regime.' Presumably her trainers were being aired on shoe trees at this very moment, thought Cat.

'Good old Harbury,' said Toby.

'Yes,' mused Cynthia. 'He really is my rock.'

So, thought Cat, as well as merrily stoking her son's Oedipal complex, she was happily chugging along in her very own Princess Diana one.

'Do you exercise, er . . . ?'

'Cat,' said Toby.

Cat considered telling Lady C about her one encounter with Benson and the motherfuckers.

'Too busy, I suppose. Pity.' Lady Cynthia raked her up and down and turned to her son. 'Did Toby tell you what a marvellous athlete he is?'

Cat looked expectantly at Toby.

'Downhill skiing,' he explained. 'But only because I can't get a tan any other way. I get a heat rash.'

'What did you say Cat's mother was called?' said Lady Cynthia, addressing herself exclusively to her son.

'Suzette, darling. Suzette McGinty.'

'Ah, yes.' She began pouring tea from a silver teapot. 'I think I once saw her on an infomercial when I was staying with Toby in New York. Does she have her own range of mothballs?'

'Handmade cedar,' said Cat. 'They're part of a wardrobe storage system she helped design.'

'Really? I wouldn't know. Ashdown House came complete with its own neo-classical wardrobe system, fortunately.'

'Cat's mother is a bit of a fashion phenomenon,' Toby leapt in chivalrously. 'I'm longing to meet her properly—'

'I rebelled against my mother too, 'said Lady Cynthia sweetly, focusing on Cat's curling lapels. She sighed. 'I suppose it's inevitable.' She brightened momentarily as a thought struck her. 'Does she write for *Harper's*?'

'Newspapers mainly,' said Cat. 'She's syndicated all over the world—'

Lady Cynthia's eyes flickered with minimal interest. 'Heavens, is that the time already? Whatever are they up to downstairs? Lunch must be ready by now.'

Over lightly steamed vegetables and heavily polished silver, Lady Cynthia chatted away graciously, leaning forward in rapt attention every time Toby said anything. When he popped out to get something from the car, she fixed Cat with her icy blue eyes and asked her how she found working for Toby.

'We're partners, actually,' said Cat, wondering how quickly they could evacuate Ashdown House for Butely.

'I suppose Simms have had to go in for a lot of that ridiculous positive discrimination?' said Lady Cynthia thoughtfully. 'Have you ever been to Nicky Clarke's, dear? He's so good with thin hair.'

There was an awkward pause while both of them fervently willed Toby to reappear as quickly as possible.

'Who's the photograph of?' Cat pointed beyond Lady Cynthia's right shoulder to a table on which a black-and-white picture nestled among a cluster of larger ones, mainly featuring Lady Cynthia, Lady Cynthia and Princess Margaret and Lady Cynthia, Princess Margaret and Toby.

'Viscount Linley, do you mean?' Although she couldn't quite summon the energy to turn round, the smack of satisfaction in Lady Cynthia's voice was unmistakable. 'Charming boy. Hero-worshipped Toby, of course.'

'I don't think it's Viscount Linley,' began Cat uncertainly. 'He's got fair tufty hair. And he looks as though he's holding a spanner.'

'That would be Jake,' said Lady Cynthia crisply. 'My other son.'

'He looks very nice.' Cat wandered across to look more closely. 'He has beautiful eyes.'

'I believe Toby took that photograph. He's a very good lensman.'

'A very good what?' asked Toby, bustling back into the room with two large gift-wrapped packages, one of which he placed in front of his mother, giving the other to Cat. 'Please don't let me interrupt you while you're paying homage. And in the meantime, I think both of you could do with these.'

'Darling, you spoil me,' purred Lady Cynthia, skilfully untying the ribbon and pulling away the layers of tissue paper to reveal a lush cream sheepskin coat, just like the one Cat had admired in Joseph's shop window with Lily.

'Now don't tell me you've already got one.'

'Of course not, darling.' She slipped it on. 'How do I look?'

'Elegancé personified. I know you've been missing your old furs—'

'Quite right. But people get so hot under the collar about all that sort of thing these days. Even down here. You'd think they'd be grateful to find a use for a few smelly old mink . . .'

'Aren't you going to open yours?' Toby asked Cat.

'Of course.' She fumbled with the wrapping paper. Inside was the crimson version of the coat he had just given Lady Cynthia. The same one Lily had urged her to buy all those weeks ago. She looked across at him, feeling slightly odd.

He studied her intently. 'To the two most gorgeous women I know.' He raised a glass of wine while the two most gorgeous women he knew smiled wanly.

'I hope you don't mind,' he muttered softly as they followed Lady Cynthia into the drawing room where Harbury was serving yet more tea. 'Lily told me how much you liked it. And you're going to need it tramping around Butely.'

'Ah, yes, Butely,' said Lady Cynthia – there was clearly nothing wrong with her hearing, even if some of her facial muscles had been culled. She gestured for Cat to sit opposite her and Toby again. 'How long did you say you knew my late husband?'

'I didn't. It's all a bit embarrassing really. I hardly knew him at all. But on another level I think there was probably a deep connection between us. At the time I wondered whether I was imagining it. But I suppose he must have felt it too . . .'

'He always was eccentric,' said Lady Cynthia. 'At least, I can only assume that's why he left all the land to Jake, who isn't even here. And nothing to Toby – the only real businessman in the family.'

'Come on, darling.' Toby took his mother's hand. 'Jake was hardly to know his father was about to die. And you know how passionate he is about that solar-powered heating he's working on. Anyway, I think it's wonderful about Cat.' He flashed Cat one of his dazzlers. 'I'm trying to persuade her not to sell it.'

'Whatever for?' said Lady Cynthia abruptly. 'What on earth would anyone want with that crumbling shambles?'

'It doesn't have to be a shambles. I think I could raise enough investment among my contacts to turn Butely into a thoroughly modern sort of enterprise.'

'Not more wrinklies in British Home Store dressing gowns?' said Lady Cynthia, aghast.

'Hardly,' said Toby. 'What I've got in mind is a very upmarket weekend retreat for stressed-out city slickers. It'll have all the mod cons of the office with state-of-the-art spa facilities. So you can go straight from having your bikini line ripped out to ripping off your next client. Babbington House with knobs on.' He winked at Cat.

Lady Cynthia looked at her son with something not far from adulation on her face. Cat simply looked mystified. There had been no previous conversations about office technology and bikini waxing. In fact there had been no previous conversation about anything, other than Cat's overwhelming desire to find a sympathetic new owner for Butely. She felt his foot caress her thigh under the table. 'I meant to tell you all this on the way down,' he whispered. 'We'll discuss it all later.'

Now that there was a distinct prospect of having the mediacracy frolicking on the lawns of Butely instead of a bunch of clapped-out OAPs, Lady Cynthia's spirits were rapidly rising. Especially as it seemed that her clever son had carved out a serious role for himself in the project. 'Do you know Babbington House?' she asked Cat with exquisite condescension. 'Guy and Madonna used to stay there, before they bought in Wiltshire.'

Just when Cat had despaired of ever escaping the cloying cocoon of Ashdown House, Toby announced firmly that he and Cat had to go and see Butely. 'Do give my regards to the grandchildren,' said Toby to Harbury as they walked towards the car. 'How old is Simon junior now?'

'How is it you manage to remember everyone's names?' asked

Cat, as they scrunched across the gravel towards the road. He tapped his Palm Pilot. 'It's all in here. Including your dress size. You don't mind do you? Only I'm looking forward to lavishing you with more of the same.'

'You spoil me.' Her voice sounded acidic but Toby didn't seem to notice.

'Someone has to.'

Butely was barely six minutes from Ashdown House by Porsche and most of those were taken up with its magnificent oak-lined drive. Cat felt a familiar tingle as they approached its winking chestnut façade, standing proud and gracious against a shiny azure sky. From three minutes away, you couldn't actually see its many defects, just its perfect, serene symmetry.

They spent at least an hour walking round its strangely empty grounds, their boots etching prints in the frosty grass and echoing round the deserted rooms. There must be so many ghosts here, thought Cat, sliding her hand down the oak banisters, and wishing the ancestors hanging on the walls could talk.

'It is utterly beguiling.' She sighed as they walked through the Gothic arch. She turned round to look at it one last time before the sun finally set.

'And that's exactly why you shouldn't sell it,' said Toby, wrapping his arm round her. 'I've never seen anyone in love with a place as you are. It's a one-in-a-million chance. You could really do something with it—'

'How? By remote control?' Her voice grew cold again. 'I can't just up and leave everything in London.'

'Leave what exactly?'

'Work, for one thing—' And you. Not that Toby seemed despondent at the thought of her departure, she thought forlornly.

'Cat – admit it. Your heart's not really in it . . .'

'What do you mean?' She pulled the collar of her new coat round her for warmth.

'Do you really think you've got the killer instinct to stay the course at Simms?'

'I haven't done badly so far.'

'No. . . but you're not exactly racing to do the White Stick commission.'

'No, but once we get started properly on setting up the media division . . .'

'I've noticed a distinct lack of enthusiasm, and to be honest so has everyone else.'

'Is that why I haven't had my pay rise?' She looked at him in disbelief.

'Cat!' He grasped her shoulders. 'It's not about you. You know how the economy's been – it's hardly been a record year for Simms.'

'It has with the accounts I've worked on,' she said. She had put her heart and soul into every project Simms had shoved her way.

For once he couldn't meet her gaze. 'Look, it's not the end of the world.'

'Not to you maybe,' she said bitterly.

'So make a new future. It's here on a plate – the chance most people dream of. Christ, how much more satisfying to make a new life here than slave away at Simms for the next twenty years. Do you really want to become like one of those dried-up old Vices?'

'You do.'

'I used to.'

She looked at him sharply. The wind rippled through the overhead branches. He shrugged helplessly and looked at her, almost mournfully. 'You must know how I feel about you.'

Her heart surged. It began to rain, large, fat drops spattering her brand-new coat. Toby pulled her beneath one of the huge, spreading cedars that dotted Butely's lawns, and wrapped her in his coat. 'Look.' He pointed her towards a pale disc. They watched it glide between two hills, wrapping them in a milky embrace. Suddenly the whole landscape was enveloped in a primeval darkness.

'You're right. It is incredibly beautiful.' He nuzzled her hair and slipped his hands beneath her coat until they found their way inside her shirt. 'This could be a whole new start for you. For us,' he added, kissing her urgently. 'I want to help you, Cat. I want . . . to be here with you. Give me another year at Simms, just long enough to finish that Scottish job—' He broke off. He seemed on the verge of telling her about it.

'Can't you discuss it with me, just a bit?' she coaxed.

He studied her for a moment. 'Not yet, darling. But it could be quite lucrative – enough for me to give up the rat race and come and help you here. If that's what you'd like.'

She looked at him in astonishment. Did he mean what his eyes seemed to imply? Her stomach cartwheeled. Much as she had primed herself to fall for Toby, it seemed a bit early to be rushing into anything too serious.

'We could turn this place around,' he continued, excitedly. 'Think what a great life it could be for Lily. The village school is marvellous,' he added slyly. 'Think how nice it would be to have Lily somewhere local and unpretentious.'

'Somewhere the rural underclass dump their children with teachers who couldn't cut it in the city, you mean.' She said it more to deflate the moment, which was in danger of turning into something out of *Brief Encounter*, than out of any real fear.

'Not Lower Nettlescombe Primary.' Toby snorted. 'Jesus Cat, most people would give their right arm for a chance to start again with a clean slate.'

Uprooting to the country was what she and Lily had always dreamed off, and now they had the opportunity she was terrified.

'You can do it. *We* can do it,' he added gently. 'I know you think I hate the countryside but it's in my soul. I was born here. It's always been my dream to come back one day. And it would show those bastards at Simms a thing or two.'

'Er, can I get back to you when I've thought about it – in a year or three?'

'What's to think about?'

'It's a little bit more complicated than deciding to buy a new dress, Marks! It's probably one of the biggest decisions I'll ever make.'

He shrugged and grinned. 'Looks like a no-brainer to me.'

They drove back to London in a state somewhere between

euphoria and shock, which in Cat's case was complicated with an additional fury at Simms's idiotic refusal to recognise her true worth. But maybe it was a sign. Toby was right. This was the opportunity of a lifetime. And it wasn't as if off loading Butely was a genuine option anyway, unless Jake agreed to sell the land. And Jake, as Toby's delectable mater had only half got round to pointing out, had gone AWOL.

Christmas came and went with considerably more panache than it had in previous years, thanks to Toby, who arrived on their doorstep on Christmas Eve bearing gifts that made the Three Wise Men look cheap. There was a gorgeous bracelet for Cat wrapped in a devastatingly impractical black lace nightie the size of a handkerchief, some Christy Turlington yoga clothes for Jess and half of Hamley's for Lily.

It hadn't been without its stressful moments, however. What had seemed a straightforward entry on her List of Things to Do – Get Rid of Butely, and straight in at number one as well – now had her wavering constantly.

She had anticipated that Toby probably wouldn't stint on their gifts and was at a loss as to what to buy him. In the end she'd opted for a year's subscription to *Vogue* and a whoopee cushion for the Precious O'Dowd sofa, which were intended to reflect the jokey intimacy that existed between them. Cat hoped that what they lacked in monetary value they made up for in thoughtfulness. Then she got cold feet and bought him a beautiful cashmere blanket for his sofa which she'd be paying off for months. At least he'd seemed delighted with all the presents. She was certainly pleased with hers, even if they were a bit overwhelming.

Cat had worked out that if she asked Toby over for 3.45 p.m. – sundown – he wouldn't actually see number 15 in daylight at all (he had to spend Christmas Day itself with his mother). She spent most of the preceding hours desperately trying to inject her home with the faded Library Chic that *Homes and Gardens* had displayed to great effect in its December issue. And when that didn't work she scurried off in a panic to Habitat to buy some throws and cushions to drape over everything. When that still didn't work she considered pretending they'd had a power cut and bribing the rest of the street to turn off their lights. In the end she sent Jess off to buy some very low-wattage bulbs while she rearranged the throws in the sitting room for the fifth time.

By 3.45 number 15 had almost acquired the requisite distressed casual chic air – or at least it had to Cat, who had consumed three glasses of champagne from the Christmas hamper Herr Frupps had sent. She decided to greet Toby at the door with a goblet of champagne and try to get him drunk before he reached the kitchen.

It didn't quite work. But even though he was still sober by the time they sat down to eat, in the fug of steam the kitchen looked quite cosy. Thanks to Herr Frupps's beneficence and the foresight of Fortnum and Mason practically everything in the hamper was pre-prepared and idiot-proof and they had – as far as Cat, who was now completely drunk on nerves and champagne, was concerned – a delicious meal.

'Fantastic tucker, McGinty,' said Toby, eyeing her appreciatively as they dried some pans later. 'Is there anything you can't do?' He took another slug of champagne.

Have sex with you, thought Cat. Not with Lady Cynthia demanding his immediate presence at Ashdown House.

Cat made gallons of strong black coffee and reluctantly he set off at midnight. She had settled in front of the television to wrap her presents when it struck her that she might actually see more of Toby if they moved to the country. The next few days were restorative. She hung out with Lily, reacquainted herself with 15 Makesbury Road and decided she liked her life in London after all. On 28 December she arrived at her desk in Simms House to find a letter confirming that regretfully the Vices would not be able to comply with any of her requests for an improvement to her package.

11

You can't keep everything,' said Jess, snatching *Machiavellian Rules* and dropping it in the buffalo-hide litter bin that Ben had brought back from a Royal School of Music-sponsored trip to Senegal.

'What about this?' Cat pulled out one of Lily's earliest attempts at abstract expressionism and retrieved *Machiavellian Rules*.

'Very Jackson Pollock.' Jess took the potato-cut print from her. 'Like the other thirty-two you've already put in the folder. And what's this?'

'A receipt from the first date Ben took me on. Bowling.'

'Feral!'

Cat grabbed the potato print back from Jess. 'To remind me never to fall for someone like him again. Sorry, Lil,' she added automatically. 'Daddy is a lovely daddy but he wasn't a very good husband.'

'He's a crap father,' said Lily. 'I'm crossing him off my birthday card list.' She picked up a handful of Ben's overdraft statements and let them fall into the waste bin.

'Well, I think we can safely say that Toby is nothing like Ben,' said Jess.

Cat looked piqued. The fact that Jess had never actually met Ben hadn't prevented her from formulating strong opinions on his shortcomings. Was she now going to start pontificating about Toby?

And would it matter if she did? Surely Cat ought to know her own mind by now without seeking approval from Jess. But that was just the problem. She did need approval. She was attracted to Toby. She was intrigued by Toby. But surely it didn't amount to love? She sighed so loudly Lily and Jess both stopped what they were doing to look at her, but she was too lost in her thoughts to notice. Ever since she'd made the decision to move to Butely and sell Makesbury Road – one she had convinced herself was based on sound financial and lifestyle considerations rather than some fantasy constructed around her and Toby being together – she'd been a bundle of nerves. And now that they were finally clearing out the house she'd bought with Ben she was overwhelmed by how emotional she felt.

Or rather the home she'd bought without Ben, since the grand total of his contribution to the overall purchase price had been £3 – and that had been the cost of their Tube journey to Fiend & Duffer, the estate agents who had first told them what an up-and-coming area Kensal Rise was.

'Lily, I don't think it's wise to be making any rash decisions concerning your father,' Cat heard herself saying. Sometimes her wisdom astounded her. Jess scooped up an armful of yellowing music manuscripts and dumped them in an empty black bin liner. Cat winced.

'Why not? He can't even remember Christmas. Birthdays I can forgive. But Christmas.'

'He's living in a predominantly Muslim country . . .' began Cat, wondering why she bothered to defend him. She was furious with Ben for forgetting even to send Lily a Christmas card. Not a phone call. Nothing.

'Dr Livingstone's, I presume?' she asked, holding up a pair of what looked remarkably like Ralph's unbleached eco-cotton boxer shorts.

'I'll take those,' said Jess with as much dignity as she could muster in the circumstances. She dropped them in the bin liner. Cat looked on admiringly. Ever since the split, Jess had been amazingly stoical about Ralph. The phone rang. It was Preston from Fiend & Duffer, returning her call from the night before.

'Hi, Cat. How you doing?' He coughed nervously.

'Fine, thank you, Preston.' Cat wished Preston weren't so unfailingly polite. It was hard to be a terrifying bitch in the fact of such relentless niceness. 'Any news from the Ropers?' she asked crisply.

Preston drummed on his desk manically.

'Ah, yes, the Ropers.'

'It can't still be the price, surely?' said Cat. 'Not after we just dropped it again. Because as I told you, the leak in the bathroom's been fixed.' Cat crossed her fingers and hoped that Ralph had broken the habit of a lifetime by doing a decent job.

'I'll give them another ring. I'm sure everything's just tickety-boo.' Cat always felt doomed whenever Preston attempted heartiness.

'You mean they haven't called you?'

'Been engaged all morning.'

'I thought you said it was a quiet time of year,' said Cat.

'It is. At other agencies. But at Fiend and Duffer we never stop working on your behalf.'

'But it isn't working, is it, Preston?'

'What do you mean?'

'The policy you suggested at the beginning. The policy of playing it straight and reflecting the slightly lived-in qualities, as you put it, of Makesbury Road in the knock-down price. As a result of which, and I quote, 'we will probably end up having to fight off buyers in a bidding war.'

'It's still early days,' said Preston. 'Or you might consider renting it out.'

Cat sighed. They'd been down this road before. According to Preston, they were crying out for rentals at Fiend & Duffer. But she had made it plain she needed a large cash sum.

'It just needs one buyer to fall in love with it,' he continued, 'and I think that could be any minute now, what with the weather turning and everything—'

Turning arctic, thought Cat, marvelling at Preston's almost insanely heroic optimism.

'Once they see the crocuses in the front garden – and what with the price drop—'

'The two price drops. And those aren't crocuses, Preston.

They're crisp packets. This is Kensal Rise, not Sandringham.'
There was an audible wince at the other end of the line.

'Kensal Village, Cat. Kensal Village. Oooh, sorry, urgent buyer
on line six. Now if you'll just bear with me—'

Cat didn't bear with Preston because she knew he was about to
do what he always did when she got testy, and accidentally on
purpose cut her off.

Despite Preston's saintly fortitude, the weather deteriorated to the
point where it could have got a job in Alaska. The crocuses did not
blossom outside number 15 and nor did a Sold sign. However, to
the intense relief of Cat, Lily, Jess and all at Fiend & Duffer, a rental
prospect finally turned up in the form of Demelza de Villeneuve,
one of the eternally optimistic presenters on BBC Choice's
Hurricane House, a makeover DIY programme. Demelza declared
herself absolutely smitten with number 15's potential – and Fiend
& Duffer were even more delighted when Cat, weary from the
effort of keeping the place tidy for yet more prospective vendors,
had agreed to all her redecorating schemes.

Wrapping her in his arms, Toby had told her she was doing
absolutely the right thing. As usual, she had felt all her doubts
dissolve in the face of his overwhelming certainties. She certainly
enjoyed handing in her notice, though she had a moment's pang
when she saw the shock and even distress in the expressions of the
seven Vices. But this was more than compensated for when she
handed in Lily's notice at Lady Eleanor's and informed Persia's
mother that she would be unable to help out on the sushi stall
after all.

Even so, it was with a heavy heart that she handed the keys of
number 15 over to Demelza, who couldn't wait to begin cladding
the kitchen cabinets with multi-coloured Fablon and constructing
interesting ornaments for the front garden out of bubble wrap. Hair
streaking across their reddened cheeks in the force-seven gale, and
tears pricking their eyes, Jess and Cat tied the final rope round the
roof rack, which was buckling so pathetically that the Polo looked
more like a dustbin than ever. It was just as well, thought Cat,

wiping her nose with the back of a pair of Ben's old fingerless gloves, that Toby had been called away to Scotland again and wasn't here to see them off.

'Okay,' said Jess, looking up from the map in the passenger seat, 'let's go, for God's sake. Before it gets dark.'

Not even the Bee Gees at full volume and the Tupperware container full of Demelza's home-made shortbread could entirely alleviate the melancholy timbre of their journey. In all Cat's rural fantasies and Candida St John Green's columns, neither of them had ever fully taken on board the true bleakness of the English countryside in February. London was dismal enough in the cold, grey rain, but the waterlogged fields and the lowering sky, so heavy it seemed to be bearing down on the Polo with even more force than the three over-stuffed Globetrotters on the roof rack, were enough to instil feelings of suicide.

By the time the Polo spluttered into the final furlong, dusk had fallen, Cat's eyes were misty with tears, and the windscreen so mottled with condensation that she couldn't see very much at all.

It was the gut-wrenching sound of imploding metal which first alerted her to the fact that all was not entirely well with the Polo's fender. Peering through the small heart-shaped patch of clear windscreen that Jess had marked out for her during their most recent pit stop, she stared into the dark with a mounting sense of panic. She wound down the window and was immediately assaulted by an artillery fire of hailstones. Around them the wind whipped with the intensity of a tornado. Any minute now, she thought, the Polo was going to be lifted off its axles – whatever they were – and whirl them, Dorothy-like, into Oz. Or knowing the Polo's track record on unreliability, it wouldn't and they'd be left here, having to face the consequences of Cat's first incidence of roadkill.

'Don't wait up. I may be some time.' Bracing herself for a potentially harrowing scene, she stepped out of the car to investigate. A rustling of leaves in the ditch that separated Butely's crumbling walls from the lane made her jump. From within the relatively safe confines of the passenger seat, Jess let out a piercing scream.

'It's only an animal,' shouted Cat through the whistling wind. 'A fox or . . . something.' She trailed off, her knowledge of native wildlife as yet being limited.

'For Christ's sake, what do you think you were playing at?' A tall, shambolic figure emerged from the ditch and wobbled towards her, brushing a wheelbarrow's worth of leaves from a disreputably old-looking tweed coat. Fearing that he was some crazed tramp, Cat backed away towards the Polo and almost tripped over the tortured front wheel of a bicycle, trapped beneath its tyres.

'Oh my God,' she exclaimed as the tweedy figure took a shaky step towards what remained of his bike. Bracing herself for a nasty lawsuit, she felt her fists go rigid. Once they got to court, she would have to home in heavily on the lack of lighting, both in Lower Nettlescombe Lane and on the stranger's bike. In the meantime she should be sure to show due concern for his well-being. 'I'm so sorry. Are you all right?' she said.

The stranger butted his head with the palm of his hand. 'That remains to be seen.' He bent down unsteadily, unlaced a shoe, turned it upside down and watched as a slurry of mud slid into the ditch. 'Your car looks terrible.'

'It was like that already,' Cat said, then cursed herself. This wouldn't advance her court case at all. 'Please say your bike resembled something post-apocalyptic and arty before this encounter.' He followed her gaze to the mangled wreckage impaled beneath the Polo's front bumper.

'Actually it was brand new.' It was obviously his pride and joy. He ran a muddy hand through his spiky hair. She tried to unclamp her right fist. It appeared to be in the early stages of rigor mortis.

'If it's any consolation, I think Tate Modern would probably give you a lot for it now.'

'It isn't,' he said tersely.

The man clearly had no sense of humour. Cat stood there sinking up to her calves in mud. As charm offensives went, this one didn't. 'Can I at least give you a lift?' she said, staring at his mud-caked face. He looked vaguely familiar.

'I doubt it. At least not until I've disentangled my bike from your front wheels. I don't suppose you have anything useful in there, like a toolbox.'

'Of course we do.'

There was no need to be quite so hostile, thought Cat. It was only a bike. It took them twenty minutes to locate the toolbox, between two plastic carrier bags containing Jess's make-up and the wok, which Cat could have sworn she'd unpacked twice in an attempt to leave it with Demelza. Lily's teeth began to chatter.

'Perhaps you two should walk to the house, before Lily freezes to death,' she suggested. Jess looked at the black overgrown drive and gazed back at the stranger incredulously. 'Is that Pommie irony? It's as dark as a nun's underskirts up there.'

'How are you getting on?' Cat asked brightly, as the stranger attempted to disentangle his pride and joy from the Polo.

'I'll say this for you, you're very thorough.' His face was now coated in a light film of grease, with the odd fleck of tar mixed in with the mud.

'Please let me drive you home,' said Cat. She looked at his sodden clothes. 'Or perhaps you'd like to come back with us and dry off first.'

'If you don't mind I think I'll quit while I'm ahead.'

'I insist. Look, you're starting to shiver.' He was obviously going into shock. The last thing she needed on the eve of her new life was to be landed with a writ for inducing hypothermia. 'Please let me make you a cup of tea.'

'I suppose you could give me a lift to the house and I could make a phone call.' He sounded doubtful.

Lily rolled her eyes as the dripping figure folded himself into the back seat next to Seamus, who refused to travel in a basket. The Polo lurched into a crater and a spray of mud spattered the windscreen. The car snagged what was left of its paintwork on the gnarled gates. Seamus hurled himself into the front, landing with claws fully extended on Jess's fishnets. Cat slammed on the brakes, wondering how many millions it would cost to restore the battered track into something resembling a driveway.

'Now look what you've done!' shouted Lily in accusation. 'We'll never calm him down.'

'Here, here, old boy.' Reaching forward, the stranger scooped Seamus up from the front, where he was spitting at them all, hackles raised. Gently he nestled the cat between his knees and massaged the rolls of fur round his neck until the animal gradually relaxed his muscles. 'I think he's okay now,' he said after a few moments.

'How did you do that?' asked Lily, suddenly impressed. 'We always have to leave him alone when he has one of his freak-outs.'

'There,' said the stranger, pointing to one of the bands of fat round Seamus's neck. 'If you rub this between your thumb and finger, it usually does the trick. At least, it always did with my cat.'

'Here we are,' said Cat brightly as they stalled in front of the fountain. She had wanted Jess and Lily to see Butely in all its glory. Unfortunately, in the current climatic conditions, it was hard to see anything. Of Samantha, with whom Cat had been in more or less constant contact over the past few weeks, there was no sign. Cat tried not to feel disappointed. Samantha was hardly the type to string up bunting.

The key to Sir Rodney's Cottage was indeed under the loose brick to the left of the path, as Samantha had promised. Unfortunately Cat hadn't reckoned on how many loose bricks to the left of the path there would be. While Jess made heavy work of untying the suitcases from the roof rack, Cat crawled around the little Gothic porch at doorstep level, pushing her fingers into numerous cavities of varying texture. Finally through the murk – Sir Rodney clearly hadn't believed in exterior lighting – she saw something glistening in a small gap by the door. She plunged her hand in with relief, only for her fingers to meet something squashy and disgusting. Almost hyperventilating with horror, she pulled it out to discover a grotesque beast impaled on the end of her first finger. She waved her hand around frantically, trying to dislodge it, and when it finally took the hint began stamping on it.

'What is it? Are you okay?' screamed Jess.

'Snail,' said Cat sheepishly, wiping her finger on a sodden leaf.

'City folk, are you?' asked the gloomy stranger.

His irony sailed over Jess. 'How did you guess?' she asked, dragging four duffel bags and Seamus's basket up the pathway.

Eventually Cat located an enormous rusty key that looked like an arthritic finger. The door creaked open and she stepped into the freezing, dark hall. With a pang she realised her new home was so unfamiliar to her she didn't even know where the light switch was.

'By the grandfather clock,' mumbled the stranger, arranging their belongings in a neat pile at the foot of the stairs. 'Look, would you mind? I think I do need to sit down.' He half fell into a chair near the door. Cat reached for the light switch. Nothing happened.

'Don't worry, we'll have everything fixed in next to no time,' she said brightly, more for Lily's sake than anything else. 'In the meantime, Jess, torch.'

'Search me.' Jess shrugged. 'I didn't pack it.'

Cat thought she heard a snort emanate from their guest. She was beginning to go off him in a major way, but determined to remain blameless and calm, in a Ralph-like sort of way. The stranger pulled a bicycle lamp out of his pocket. Cat resisted asking why he hadn't thought to rig it up on his bike. 'Thanks so much,' she said sweetly. 'Oh, look, Lily and Jess, come into the kitchen. There's an Aga. And it doesn't need electricity. Tea anyone?'

Needless to say, there was more chance of locating the Koh-i-noor in their luggage than anything resembling tea bags, though they did manage to find more of Demelza's shortbread, a pork pie and half a jar of her home-made pesto. The other half seemed to have emptied itself into the toolbox. Fortunately Jess tracked down an antique-looking caddy of tea leaves in a drawer marked Boot Polish and managed to rustle up a barely drinkable brew.

The stranger didn't seem to notice the peculiar taste. Slowly the blood seeped back into his face. After twenty minutes or so, he stood up. 'I'll be off, then,' he said stiffly.

'Do you know anything about fuses?' called Jess innocently from behind a load of boxes she was carrying into the hall.

'I'm sure we can sort it out ourselves,' said Cat hastily. The last thing she wanted was for this stranger to think she couldn't even change a plug. Somewhere in the house there had to be a number for South-West Electricity.

'I'd better have a look,' he said gracelessly.

'I suppose you think that's clever?' hissed Cat after he'd hobbled out of the room.

'What?' asked Jess, looking the picture of injured innocence.

'Making us beholden to Squire Goodwill.'

'Well, it's better than freezing to death.' There was a loud juddering and the lights came on.

'Thanks,' said Cat, trying to ignore the fact that his limp appeared to be getting worse. 'Now you really must let me run you home.'

'Thanks, but I'd quite like to end the day with one leg intact.'

At least he hadn't so far asked for her name or the details of her insurance company. Things were looking up. Or he was concussed.

'Well, very nice to meet you anyway, er—'

'Jake.' He hobbled past her into the darkness outside. 'Jake Dowell.'

Things could have got off to a worse start, decided Cat later that night. But she was buggered if she could think how. Despite Jake's best efforts with the electricity, it took ages for the Cottage to heat up. And even longer to unpack. Partly because most of the cupboards were already stuffed to the gunwales with Sir Rodney's clutter.

'He must have been very absent-minded,' remarked Lily as she pulled a tin opener out of the fridge. Eventually they managed to rustle up a warmish supper of Demelza's leftovers. They were bracing themselves for one of Jess's puddings, which she'd thoughtfully prepared in London, when they heard a car pull up outside. A few moments later a pair of mauve ringed eyes appeared round the kitchen door.

'Cat, I don't suppose you've got any cash on you? Only the wretched taxi driver won't take cheques.'

'Daphne!' exclaimed Cat. 'How nice to see you. I thought Butely was closed.'

'I could hardly let you turn up to an empty house, could I? I would have been here hours ago if it weren't for leaves on the track. Anyway, I assumed you'd want to get the place open again as soon as possible. Don't tell me you didn't get any of my e-mails.' She perched on a chair by the table, oblivious to the fascinated stares of Lily and Jess. 'Now let me guess. You must be Jess and you must be Lily. Gosh, you look worn out, poor darlings. Was the journey very bad?'

'The traffic was very bad,' lied Cat.

'And we ran somebody over,' added Lily.

'Anyone nice?'

'Abso-bloody-lutely not!' said Jess.

'His name's Jake Dowell,' said Lily helpfully.

'Tea, Daphne?' asked Cat quickly.

'I'd prefer some of Rodney's Chateau Lafitte. I think you'll find it under the stairs, by the greenfly spray. I'm afraid he didn't keep things very tidy towards the end. Mrs Faggot did her best, but it wasn't always easy. Jake Dowell, did you say? What have you done to the poor darling, Cat?'

'Caught him off colour for one thing,' said Cat, trying to recollect anything darling about Jake. She went to find some wine – anything rather than explain to Daphne about the crippling.

'Mum ran him over. It was his fault, though,' said Lily loyally. 'He wasn't wearing any lights.'

'He's a bit forgetful, sometimes,' said Daphne, taking the Chateau Lafitte from Cat and opening it with ruthless efficiency. 'But only when he's really involved in something. He's been fiddling around in the Jericho all day. It's his pride and joy.' They looked at her blankly. 'It's an old name for an earth closet – an outside loo. There's a late-sixteenth-century one round the back of the stable block that the local council are very keen to slap a preservation order on. Gives them a sense of purpose. Jake was sent to authenticate it and he's become quite obsessed.'

'How long has he been sniffing around toilets, then?' asked Jess, her interest in Jake rocketing.

Daphne considered. 'Hard to say really. He only got back a few days ago. I spoke to him this afternoon just before I left Chalfont St Giles. I thought I might get hold of you but he was here instead, tinkering around. His mother seemed to think he'd emigrated to New Zealand for good. Not that you'd expect Cynthia to know much about her son. She makes Colonel Gaddafi look maternal.'

'She seems very fond of Toby,' said Cat, not altogether surprised that a mother might want to disown someone as curmudgeonly as Jake. And what exactly did Daphne mean by tinkering? Having offloaded Ralph, the last thing she needed was another odd-jobber who let themselves in and out of her house as they pleased.

'I don't think her feelings for Toby have anything to do with motherly love.' She raised her mug. 'It's so lovely to have you here at last. Chin-chin.'

'They don't look like brothers,' remarked Jess.

'Half-brothers. But even that's incredible. Jake's salt-of-the-earth. And Toby, well, Toby's terribly charming, isn't he? Always good on big gestures. I hope you don't mind, Cat, but Mrs Faggot told me about the flowers he sent you. I always think he could repackage acne and sell it back to teenagers. They're chalk and cheese. Toby looks like one of those handsome men in the tooth-paste ads. And Jake—'

'– looks like Wurzel Gummidge?' suggested Lily.

'He certainly doesn't suffer from charm,' said Cat, stung by Daphne's aspersions about Toby.

'He's been working with solar-power heating,' continued Daphne, pouring them some more wine.

'We could do with some of that,' said Jess. 'Lily's almost blue.'

'Once the Aga's truly up and running you'll be as warm as teacakes. After poor Rodney died Mrs Faggot rather neglected it. I think that's why Jake was here so long. He said something on the phone about wanting to clean it up and get it lit again. He's terribly practical.'

Cat felt another little pang.

'Which bit of him did you run over?' asked Daphne.

'All of him,' said Lily.

'And his bike,' added Jess.

'Not the mountain one from New Zealand? He brought it all the way back. Apparently they cost four thousand pounds here.'

Cat took a gulp of wine.

'Damn cyclists,' said Lily.

'They're saving the planet.' Daphne sounded shocked. 'We should all cycle.'

'At least he doesn't have far go to if he's lodging at Ashdown House,' said Cat.

'Oh, he isn't staying with Lady Cynthia,' exclaimed Daphne. 'I think she's got the builders in or something. So Jake's renting a little cottage in the high street.'

'But that's at least a mile away,' exclaimed Cat, guilt stricken. She couldn't imagine what, in Lady Cynthia's immaculate domain, needed building work, unless she was putting an extension on to her neo-classical wardrobes.

'You know these strapping country lads. Now I suppose you've got lots of exciting plans for Butely. Are those the files there?' Daphne eyed a pile of grey folders on the kitchen table.

Cat nodded and did her best to outline some of her ideas, which didn't necessarily coincide with all of Toby's. Jess disappeared upstairs with Lily to unpack and dredge what hot water there was in the system into a bath.

'Would you like me to show you around a bit?' asked Daphne. Cat realised that she hadn't even seen the upstairs of her new home. 'And I could show you how to light the fire in the drawing room before I go. There's a bit of a knack.'

Cat followed Daphne across the hall into a charming beamed room, one side of which was lined with small mullioned windows that gave out on to moon-flooded lawns. A heap of logs crackled away in the inglenook fireplace. 'I told you Jake was a good boy.' She smiled indulgently. 'Rather attractive too, don't you think?' she added slyly.

'Hard to tell, under all that mud.'

Cat followed Daphne upstairs, where she counted four bedrooms filled with rugs, yet more piles of books and more antiques than were to be found at Sotheby's. The rooms themselves were charmingly decorated with pretty floral curtains and iron fireplaces. Filtering through the lead windows, the moonlight bathed the rooms in a ghostly, fractured light which for the moment looked very romantic. God knew what it would look like in the morning.

'Practically everything's listed,' explained Daphne, weaving erratically across the uneven oak floors. 'Listing as well. Quite badly in the case of the old Jericho. I suppose your house in London was minimalist?' She led them back into the sitting room, where they sank into Sir Rodney's vast sofas.

'Not exactly.' They watched the golden flames dance in the hearth for a few moments.

'It's very important that you and Jake become allies,' said Daphne suddenly.

Cat's heart sank. She was hoping that Jake would be called back to New Zealand as soon as possible. 'Perhaps I should offer to show him the files on Butely?' she said, unconvinced. 'Make him feel included.' And try to reclaim any sets of keys he might have.

'Figures aren't really Jake's thing. He knows all about Jerichoes but finances are a mystery.'

'Surely he'll mind what we do?'

'Well, of course, he'd hate it if you messed about with the look of the place – but he won't think you look like the kind of person who would do that.'

Cat doubted that.

'Not that you'd be allowed to anyway,' continued Daphne. 'Anyway, he's not the possessive type. He'll just want the best for Butely.'

They finished another glass of wine each and then Cat walked Daphne to the door of the main house.

'Damn,' said Cat when they got there. 'I forgot to lock the Cottage.'

'Don't worry about that,' said Daphne. 'The last major theft round here involved two Jack Russells and the winning entry at the village cake fayre. Goodnight, dear.'

Just as it had on her first trip there, the silence struck Cat with a ghostly force. She watched a flock of sleepless birds, black as bats against the night sky, swoop between the ancient oaks. This was what she had come for. This is what would make the upheaval all worthwhile. This was her gift to Lily.

Or perhaps they *were* bats. She quickened her pace and then her mobile rang.

'Toby!' she exclaimed, glad that she had forgotten to turn it off.

'Cat? Is that you?'

She was tempted to deny it, but as ever her work ethic got the better of her.

'Yes, Herr Frupps, it's me.'

'Villie, please. Have you heard what those bastards have done now?' he wheezed.

'Which bastards?' asked Cat.

'The Poles. Toby told me not to trust them.' His voice was dangerously close to breaking. Cat waited patiently, watching the leaves dance against the sky. 'They've used my bid to up their value and gone and sold the whole lot to a bunch of Swedes.'

'Maybe it's all for the best.' It was amazing how irrelevant the Frupps empire seemed to her now. 'You said yourself it was a very volatile market.'

'But the betrayal, Cat. It will be wall-to-wall porn by next Christmas, you mark my words. The Swedes don't know the meaning of quality programming.'

This was a bit rich coming from Villie. He rasped loudly at the other end.

'Herr . . . Villie, are you smoking?' asked Cat sternly.

'Don't lecture me, Cat. I've got enough to cope with without the tobacco Gestapo on my back.'

'What about the Coollerie idea?' she suggested. 'You've said yourself you were very interested in the man-made gemstones area.'

'Where would I find the expertise for that market?' he asked slyly.

'Would you like me to ask Toby if he could find you someone?'

'Oh, Cat, dear, you couldn't set something up, could you?' he wheedled.

She pulled open the front door of the Cottage, breathing in the reassuring aroma of crackling logs. 'Actually, Herr Frupps, I'm afraid I couldn't. You see, when I said that I was leaving Simms, I meant it. Today is the first day of my new life.'

'Not that decrepit old health farm?' said Villie in tones of no uncertain outrage.

'No.' Cat smiled. 'That decrepit old clinic. Perhaps you'll come and visit us one day. In the meantime, goodnight. Oh, and good luck.'

She turned off the phone, padded upstairs to where Lily lay sleeping and gave her a kiss. The moon had slipped out from behind the clouds again. It was almost too beautiful to sleep. As if in a dream, she floated into another bedroom and knelt on the low stone window sill, scanning the silver-tipped lawns dreamily. *Her* lawns – or at least Jake's lawns and her stone window sills. She fiddled with the latch of the mullioned window, feeling like Cathy in *Wuthering Heights*, and flung it open. To her horror, the casing dropped clean away from the wall and fell with a spectacular crashing of glass and splintering of seventeenth-century metal on to the gravel path below. She held her breath and prepared herself for all hell to break loose. Not a thing stirred. Giggling, she climbed into bed, still with two jumpers on and tried not to think of Jake Dowell's limp. Instead she focused on how ridiculously muddy his face had been. It was hard to be intimidated by someone who looked quite that much of a shambles. She closed her eyes, blissfully unaware of the smuts and smears besmirching her own face.

12

Despite promising Lily – and herself – that she'd slow down in their new life, Cat threw herself into Butely's rescue with the force of a 747. Fortunately Lily was too delighted with her idyllic surroundings and starting a new school to notice, and Jess was too busy exploring every facet of Lower Nettlescombe's social calendar.

A week after they moved in, at the start of March, Butely reopened with the minimum of fanfare – and the minimum of guests. Just a few of the old faithfuls. Cat set up office in Sir Rodney's old study. It was a far cry from her work station at Simms, although Sir Rodney seemed to have as much clutter as she did. The only difference was that his was antique.

There was masses to do – starting with showing Mrs Faggot where the Hoover was kept. Then she would refresh some of the shabbier rooms in the main house, getting rid of the hideous carpet upstairs, replacing the gruesome fire doors with more sympathetic ones, overhauling the heating and plumbing, gluing some of the windows back in – or whatever one did to keep windows dropping off their hinges – finding a new cook, enticing a young gardener – or at least one under seventy – to help Mimms, and luring a yoga teacher down to Butely. The list ran on – installing a proper computerised booking system, finding more patients. And on – discovering a bit more about Dr Anjit and the other remaining staff. And on – deciding on menus, tracking down builders. And on – pulling down the hideous Long Building. And on. Thank God. Cat had a nasty feeling she'd suffer from some kind of post-traumatic disorder if she actually had to slow down rather than just talk about slowing down. She wouldn't go so far as to say she missed London. But the countryside was ominously quiet and eerily devoid of litter.

At least she had Toby to look forward to at weekends. She got into a routine of watching TV or listening to music with Lily until 9.30 on a Friday night and then taking a scented bath so she was ready for him when the Porsche roared up the drive like clockwork at around ten.

The first weekend she'd put him in the guest room – for Lily's sake more than anything – and waited in bed for him to come and exploit her in the manner she longed for, but he'd chastely remained in his room all night. She began to wonder whether beneath that jocular, cynical exterior there didn't beat a deeply sincere, old-fashioned heart. Perhaps he was a born-again Christian.

Tactfully she'd tried to broach the subject the following day, but he'd seemed embarrassed and then he'd got a call from his Scottish client. And then he'd had to go to bed with a headache. It was the closest she'd ever seen him to stressed. A huge bunch of flowers had arrived at Monday lunchtime, with some cashmere socks.

Halfway through the week it occurred to her that she ought to buy some condoms, just in case Toby didn't keep a permanent supply in his Vuitton briefcase. It would be richly ironic if, when she finally did get him into bed, neither of them was adequately prepared. Not wanting to make this purchase in the village Spar, she'd driven into Dorchester, but in the afternoon Toby had called her to say he had to go to Glasgow at the weekend on more business. At least he'd sounded bitterly disappointed.

On the plus side, there hadn't been a squeak from Jake Dowell and Cat began to hope the ditch incident and any subsequent writ might be quietly forgotten. Meanwhile there was a whole new routine to be devised. It was just as well a stray cockerel woke her at six every morning, because by the time she'd grappled with the lack of hot water, made Lily breakfast, walked her to school and dropped into the Spar-cum-post office as part of her charm offensive, it was 9.30.

It would be quicker if she didn't walk back through the fields, but part of the new routine she'd drawn up on the Mac was a subsection entitled Developing an Appreciation of Nature. Theoretically the walk was meant to set her up for the rest of the day. She was certainly sleeping much better since moving to Butely, though that may have been from sheer exhaustion. Life had hardly become less pressurised. But nothing, she decided, sweeping her eyes over the carpet of daffodils and puddles of crocuses on the walk back from Lily's school, seemed insurmountable. Not even Micky and Samantha, who had made it abundantly clear that they weren't about to surrender their iron grip on the place without a struggle. That was understandable. In the last years of his life Sir Rodney had handed over more and more of the day-to-day running of Butely to them. Cat knew she couldn't expect them to fall in with her new plans in the first few weeks.

Those plans, she was happy to say, were in their own modest way quite radical. She sat down at the computer and wrote out an ad to put in the *Sunday Telegraph*, emphasising the unique character-building qualities of Butely and injecting a scintilla of – she hoped – self-deprecating wit.

'Beautiful old pile seeks companions for fun, frolics and fasting. Unforgettable experience guaranteed,' it began. 'We will shortly be having a holistic face-lift to gear us up for the twenty-first century. In the meantime we are still open. If you like magnificent architecture, breathtaking countryside and are ready for a retreat like no other, call us.'

There. No one could accuse her of over-selling the place, but in her experience a little humour went a long way.

'So what exactly are you intending to do about the menus?' Samantha loomed in the doorway to her study while Cat was admiring her latest draft.

She had prepared for this, realising on her first day in control that deploying the deadly efficient manner she'd acquired at Simms would not be well received by Micky and Samantha. Since then she had adopted more of a laid-back approach, more – though she would never have admitted it – of a Ralph-like take on life.

'Only Micky's feeling very vulnerable at the moment.' Through the window Cat watched as Mrs Faggot squirted one of her lethal furniture glazings in the vague direction of the flagstones in the porch outside. 'What with all the upheaval.'

Since the only changes Cat had so far managed to instigate had been getting Samantha to log future reservations on to the new computer system, rather than attempting to memorise them, and planting the seed of a thought in Micky's head about one day possibly trying an alternative source of fibre to millet, she didn't feel their outrage was entirely justified. She gazed across the lawns to where Seamus was licking himself next to a stone lion. Talk about delusions of grandeur.

'Nothing very drastic.' She fiddled apprehensively with one of the dozen Meissen shepherdesses lining the dusty shelf next to her bureau and resolved to buy Mrs Faggot a new set of dusters. Now probably wasn't the best moment to mention that Micky was going to have to clean up his act too, starting with his fingernails, which looked like the hoofs of a Mongolian goat. She took a deep breath.

'I've been thinking we could broaden our appeal by focusing on a less dogmatic philosophy. Instead of limiting ourselves to vegan fare, it might be better to concentrate on doing simple but delicious all-round menus, with the emphasis on seasonal organic produce.'

Samantha looked at her as if she were insane. 'And how much is that going to cost?' she demanded.

Cat had prepared for this too. She'd been videoing Hugh Fearnley-Whittingstall and religiously taking notes. 'Not as much as you think. In fact, by my reckoning, we could actually shave quite a few thousand off our annual food bill if we expanded the kitchen garden.'

Samantha appeared suitably winded. If she were the skittle she'd so evidently been designed to be, she'd be wobbling. 'And who's going to do all the work – if you don't mind my asking?'

'Oh, don't worry, I've made provisions for all that.' Cat scrolled through a file of correspondence she'd been having with Fortnum & Mason, who'd said they'd definitely be interested in looking at produce from Butely. 'If we got the garden to the point where we were more than self-sufficient and able to sell some of our produce, we could start making quite a lot of money from it. The idea,' she continued excitedly, 'is to recruit some enthusiastic young gardener to help Mimms.'

There was another snort. Samantha didn't want to seem like a pushover. 'Dunno where you think you're gonna find one of those. No one under seventy round here wants anything to do with the land. You're more likely to find them trading shares on the Internet.'

'Surely not?' said Cat, sounding artificially upbeat, even to her ears.

'What exactly are your qualifications for running this place, Cat?'

Cat could have told Samantha about the way she'd significantly overhauled the Frupps empire. She could have described the countless decisions she had to make as a single working mother trying to keep a little family afloat in Kilburn. However, the unmistakable artillery fire of Micky's football rattle summoned Samantha to the kitchen to serve lunch. Still, Cat felt they were making progress. Truculent as she was, Samantha had been there longer than anyone else on the staff and, despite all appearances, she was extremely good at her jobs – the important ones, at least. Cat would have to find someone to replace her in the dining room, but when it came to massage, aerobics and devotion to Butely, she was faultless. Dragging herself from the window, she scrolled through her recent e-mails.

catmcg@hotmail.co.uk
20 Feb

You were right about the views, Marks. And the school. Lily loves it. She hasn't stopped grinning since we arrived. Even Seamus approves of Butely. Next weekend seems like ages away. What time d'you think you'll get here?

tmarks@simms.co.uk
5 March

Have you:
1. Done *Daily Telegraph* ad yet?

2. Had words with man/woman? Not sure it's exactly image we want to present at Butely. Unless you're intending to use her as dire warning of what will happen if people don't follow programme. Better get bedroom window fixed before more havoc's caused. Good way of testing local workmanship.

Regards,
Toby Marks
PS: Figures for the new computer system attached.

By man/woman she assumed he meant Samantha. She'd been a bit taken aback by the formal leave-taking until she realised that the wording at the bottom came up automatically on all Toby's e-mails. He'd simply forgotten to reset it.

catmcg@hotmail.co.uk
5 March

Yes to telegraph ad. Will await results. Yes to installing computer system. Yes to placing ads for new gardener, new cook, new yoga teacher. Yes to establishing contact with Fortnum's. Yes to compiling list of companies who might want to block-book Butely.

PS: Just got e-mail from some TV bloke – an Orlando Vespers of Rigor Mortis Productions, if you don't mind – wanting to do a before and after docu thing on Butely. Can you imagine?
C

She felt that was quite impressive for one week's work.

tmarks@simms.co.uk
6 March

Good going, McGinty. Have you spoken to Samantha yet? Better get ads for new staff sorted. Emphatic yes to docu-soap. Must be worth at least £500,000 in free publicity.

Regards,
Toby Marks

catmcg@hotmail.co.uk

6 March

Marks, have identified following areas for immediate action.

Garden, menus, redecoration, overhaul of strategy on treatments, plumbing and heating. Gentle word in Micky's ear about not playing Queen quite so loudly when his faithful Skoda splutters up at 5.30 in the mornings. Would you prefer to eat in or out when you get here on Friday? – I could investigate some local eats . . . x C

PS: re docu-crew: have you lost your mind?

tmarks@simms.co.uk

6 March

I trust that bloody rust-bucket's not parked round the front – hardly enticing. How many building contractors have you asked to submit quotes?

At that moment Cat thought they probably stood more chance of running into Lord Lucan than a builder with a window in his Palm Pilot. She decided to wait a day before replying in order to word her response and exaggeration evenly and carefully. In the end she gave up and plumped for sarcasm.

catmcg@hotmail.co.uk

7 March

97 builders currently submitting quotes Waiting lists for start dates longer than for a table at the Ivy.

tmarks@simms.co.uk

9 March

I've attached the outline of a promotional letter I thought you could send out to all Butely's past clients, with a gap for some personal touches from you. If we could access a few thousand names we should get something out of it. How are the workmen?

If reliable tell them could be plenty more work at Butely. Get them onside now. But don't let them screw you on money front.

Regards, Toby Marks

PS: May not make Friday. Glasgow again.
PPS: Deadly serious about docu-crew.

As billets-doux went Toby's lacked a certain *je ne sais quoi*. There was a marked discrepancy between the messages he sent her with the gifts and his curt e-mails. But perhaps he was simply trying to keep business and pleasure separate. Still, she wasn't sure she liked the implication of the last e-mail. Did he think she wasn't up to dealing with the workmen? Not that it wasn't entirely academic since she had so far signally failed to find any. Samantha said it was because the entire available male workforce had been commandeered by Julian and Rupert, two ex-trolly dollies for British Airways who had taken over the Hung Drawn and Quartered, the local pub, and were, according to Samantha, in the process of turning it into a bloody dog's dinner.

Cat wished them luck in finding any customers. What no one – in particular Toby – had told her before moving to Dorset was how empty the county was. Apart from the odd scarecrow and one sighting of Jake Dowell – which could well amount to the same thing – she'd hardly seen anyone. Sometimes she wondered whether the entire county hadn't been struck down by the human equivalent of foot-and-mouth and the government had simply covered the whole thing up.

At least she had plenty to keep her occupied. The more she looked into it, the more sense it made to get rid of the monumentally hideous Long Building, which housed the treatment rooms and Sir Rodney's old garages, and incorporate them back into the main house. It would bring down costs and mean they needed fewer guests to make the place viable – around thirty to break even, she estimated, while forty would leave them with a comfortable profit. She had also decided to offer other facilities at Butely, such as art classes that didn't require fancy technology but were bound to appeal to stressed-out executive types who kept promising themselves they'd take up a hobby. Jess had already bumped into a part-time teacher at Lily's school who'd said they'd be interested in holding some seminars at Butely.

Cat got into a routine of spending the first part of her mornings wading through an endless list of queries from past patients demanding to know what she intended to do with the place. Keep it open, Cat repeatedly explained, adding politely that they were currently taking bookings for the rest of the season. It was amazing, she thought, surveying some particularly frail-looking handwriting in turquoise ink, how vehemently Butely's many friends felt about it and how opinionated they were, given that none of them had been near the place for decades. At midday she would normally have made done with a sandwich and a ciggie, but nowadays she had lunch with the patients – proper lunch, if anything by Micky could accurately be described as proper.

'How's it going?' asked Daphne, catching up with her after lunch one day on her way back to the Cottage.

'Fine.' Cat grinned. 'Just don't mention the C word.'

'Don't tell me someone else has checked in looking for a miracle cure for cancer? It's really not fair on poor old Butely's resources.'

'No. Cooking. As in Micky's.'

'I see.'

'It's not all bad news. I think I've finally made him see that reassembling food that's fallen off its plate on to the floor into a vague approximation of its previous incarnation isn't entirely in keeping with the ethics of a naturopathic clinic.'

'Ah, that would be Rodney's doing. Micky used to be rather good. He worked at the Dorchester once, you know.'

'You mean *in* Dorchester?' Somehow the idea of Micky attaining even the limited culinary heights set in Dorset's county town seemed improbable.

'No, dear. But the spirit went out of him once Rodney banned all dairy, meat, poultry and strong seasonings from the menu.'

'And I keep getting letters from old patients saying they'd love to come if we had a pool and if they could only afford it,' continued

Cat, skipping across the small stream that bubbled past the wall that separated the Cottage garden from Butely's sweeping lawns.

'That would be Rodney's doing too. He spoiled them all by accidentally on purpose forgetting to charge anyone the full fees.'

'It's a miracle it kept going as long as it did.'

'Oh, I don't think you realise just how rich he was in his day. All gone, of course, as I'm sure you know.'

'That's it,' hissed Sylvia, banging her Spar shopping trolley across the terrace. Behind her Micky stood clutching his carving knife, his apron stiff with grease. 'I cannot be expected to work with amateurs any longer.' She began unloading her drums into the back of her Morris Minor. Slamming the passenger door, she crashed the gears into first and stormed up the driveway before reversing back to announce to Cat, rather gratuitously, that she was handing in her immediate notice.

Cat watched her disappear in horror. 'That's another problem solved, then,' said Daphne cheerfully.

Cat was livid. Idiosyncratic as Sylvia Lezzard's techniques were, they constituted Butely's only form of spiritual exercise. Now all that was left to entice the modern spa guest was Samantha's aerobics.

'What on earth's been going on?' she demanded furiously.

'It wasn't Micky's fault,' said Samantha belligerently, appearing from nowhere as she always did when there was a squall brewing. 'That woman's become impossible, what with all her demands. And we all know about those bloody cassettes of hers she tries to sell completely against Buteley's rules, I might add.'

'What demands?'

'Where shall I start?'

'With Micky's Brut?' suggested Jess helpfully, who had come to see what the kerfuffle was about.

'He wears Brut?' As far as Cat was aware Micky's signature odour was a unique blend of old tofu and Benson and Hedges.

'Good a place as any.' Samantha folded her arms across her chest. 'As if pestering the poor man incessantly about making her precious car dirty with his fumes weren't enough. As if threatening

to report him to the health authorities for having the occasional –
very occasional – fag on duty, but never actually over the food, or
only that once, as if all that weren't enough, she's been making his
life a misery because she says the smell of kale has been putting her
off her strokes.'

'It's true,' said Daphne. 'Isadora hasn't been among us for
weeks.'

'It's not Micky's fault the extractor's packed up. Not that Sylvia
Lezzard's open to reason. She only goes and steals Mickey's Brut
to squirt round the room before her lessons. You can't get that stuff
any old place these days, you know.'

Cat thought Ralph-like thoughts and tried to keep the sharpness
out of her voice. 'And where do you suggest we get another exercise teacher from at such short notice?'

'I would have thought that was obvious,' said Samantha. 'You're
standing in front of her.' She nodded at Jess.

'Jess?' Cat sounded incredulous. Jess scowled.

'You keep saying Butely needs some yoga,' said Daphne.

'But Jess isn't qualified.'

'When does your correspondence course end, Jess, dear?' said
Daphne, leading Cat over to a lion and sitting her down.

'How can you do yoga by correspondence?' said Cat.

'Anything's better than Sylvia Lezzard,' said Samantha.

'Jess certainly is. My sciatica's almost cleared up since she's
shown me a few asanas,' offered Daphne.

'Well, maybe we could give it a go – as a temporary stopgap.'

'I suppose I could serve the kale *al dente*,' offered Micky, looking
conciliatory. 'That way we'd keep the smell to a minimum.'

Cat eyed them warily. They'd clearly been planning this coup
for days. But it just went to show what tremendous goodwill there
was towards Butely. At least, that was how an insane optimist
would have interpreted matters.

Once Cat had discovered the way to Micky's heart, she was on the
phone to Suzette immediately. A few days later a consignment of
Brut arrived from a warehouse on Tyneside, where Suzette – or

more likely one of her minions – had tracked down a small stock-pile. Once Cat had seen the tears in Micky's eyes when she presented him with it, she knew the battle was won. At the very least his tendency to whiff of kale would now be tempered by something slightly more palatable. And then she bought Mrs Faggot a brand-new Dyson.

tmarks@simms.co.uk
18 March

Am in process of negotiating deal with Glowbal Refinery to fit out and run gym at Butely as franchise. Could make all the difference. Just need your signature. Please supply soonest.

Regards
Toby Marks

catmcg@hotmail.co.uk
18 March

Er, hello, Marks? Have gone through previous e-mails and can see no mention of Glowbal. Who or what are they?

C

tmarks@simms.co.uk
18 March

Glowbal are fastest-growing gym chain in the country. We'd be bloody fools to turn this opportunity down.

Regards
Toby Marks

catmcg@hotmail.co.uk
18 March

Not convinced franchise is the best solution. Will Glowbal respect the heritage and ethos of Butely? Need more details. Please get them to submit a proposal. In the meantime, when are you plan-ning to come down? The Hung Drawn and Quartered's finally opened so at least there'll be somewhere decent to eat. Micky's cooking still dire but not beyond redemption, Daphne says. Also says it puts hairs on your chest.

Cat

tmarks@simms.co.uk
19 March

If you find an alternative supply of funding then we can discuss alternatives to the franchise idea. In the meantime I suggest it's your best option and that you sign before Glowbal come to their senses and go elsewhere. And find a new cook.

Regards
Toby Marks

catmcg@hotmail.co.uk
22 March

Guess what? Telegraph ad seems to have done the trick. Got a flurryette of enquiries this week, quite a few of which may even turn into solid bookings. Have spent the last few days getting acquainted with Dr Anjit. Also guess what? He's a genius. Used to work with Princess Di but he's so discreet no one knows. Got lots of ideas for Butely. Am going to investigate some of his suggestions and come up with alternative schedule of treatments.

Cat

tmarks@simms.co.uk
23 March

Keep ads running indefinitely.

Regards
Toby Marks

Even though he was so late the following Friday that they missed last orders at the Hung Drawn and Quartered, Cat's resentment evaporated the moment she saw him, arms thrust out, his lopsided grin splitting those perfect features in half, making them less imposing but more lovable. All traces of e-mail brusqueness had been erased, to be replaced by that familiar teasing warmth. She'd forgotten how his sheer presence seemed to rearrange the atoms in a room.

'There's not much in the way of food,' she said, hunting among the jars of Gentleman's Relish in the pantry. He followed her in and she felt his hands slide inside her jumper and his warm sweet breath on her neck. He pulled her against him urgently, began kissing her, tender and demanding at the same time. Tonight was definitely the night, she decided. She moved her hands inside his trousers and he moaned softly. She heard Jess clatter into the kitchen and ducked out from his clutch, chucking him a copy the *Dorset Echo* that was lying on top of a pile of tea towels while she riffled through the vegetables.

'Unread, I see,' he said, settling down to dissect it. 'That's no way to get on top of local affairs, McGinty.'

Supper was consumed far too quickly for Cat's liking. Now that the moment of sex was upon her she felt sick with nerves.

'I'm sorry I didn't have time to do a proper shop,' she said, plumping a cushion on the sagging sofa. She wanted to tell him she'd spent most of the day going through new recipes with Micky, but felt he probably wouldn't approve.

'Who needs to eat when they've got this?' He swept her into his arms. 'Jesus, Cat.' He peeled off her top jumper. 'How many layers have you got on?'

'Just the three.' She giggled, gazing at his carved features in the moonlight. He began kissing her nipples and she shivered, partly from delight and partly from nerves. 'And don't ask me to take off my beautiful cashmere socks. I'll do anything – and I mean anything, Marks – but that.'

Toby tugged at her jeans zip. 'Now there's an offer.' He licked her tummy button and began to work his way to the top of her thighs. 'I'm glad you liked the socks, though.'

'Very thoughtful.' Cat arched her neck in pleasure. 'Sleeping in them has revolutionised my nights.'

'Didn't you bring any blankets?'

'Six.' She kissed the top of his head. 'Two of them are on my bed, along with two duvets, an eiderdown and one of Sir Rodney's counterpanes.'

Toby shivered, though whether with pleasure or cold Cat couldn't yet tell. 'Christ, if it's this chilly, no wonder the guests are dropping like flies.'

'Don't worry.' Cat wriggled underneath him, kissing his chest, and wondered how the hell she was going to retrieve the condoms from upstairs without wrecking the mood. 'It's not quite this cold in the main wing.' Maybe he had some condoms with him. He was the type to be prepared. 'It's just the radiators in the Cottage that have gone on strike. Come to think of it, I should probably go and check on them. Sometimes you just need to hit them with a hammer to get them going . . .'

'In that case,' said Toby, leading her gently towards the stairs, 'allow me to warm you up.' Cat felt her heart crash against her ribcage. She prayed that Lily would stay fast asleep, that she wouldn't disappoint Toby, that the window she'd finally managed to get fixed back into its casing wouldn't drop out again. 'Come on, McGinty,' he whispered. 'It's now or never.'

She smiled at him, feeling her heart somersault. And then his mobile went off.

At eight the next morning the phone next to Cat's bed rang. It was Toby calling from Ashdown House to apologise for not returning the night before. Apparently Lady Cynthia had been so terrified by some noises she'd heard downstairs that she'd begged him not to leave her. It was strange, thought Cat, that she should hear noises the very night her son was supposed to be staying with Cat.

While Daphne, Lily and Jess were practising some new yoga positions and Toby was enjoying one of Harbury's low-fat breakfast spreads at Ashdown House, Cat poured some of the Givenchy bath oil Suzette had sent into the roll-top Victorian bath and surveyed the pile of light reading that Toby had brought down from London. Along with a pair of diamond earring studs that had taken her breath away.

'The girl in Asprey's said they were particularly comfortable. There's nothing worse than an earring that pinches,' he joked when he presented them to her.

Cat had smiled wanly. She couldn't seem to master this business of accepting presents graciously.

'For being such a rotten absentee partner,' he added, nuzzling her hair. 'Still, at least the work that's been keeping me from you has been lucrative.'

She'd put the earrings on immediately, even though a part of her wished he wouldn't keep buying her such lavish presents. It made her feel disadvantaged. Perhaps that was her failing. She was sure the kind of women who went regularly to Syrie for their Brazilians and Playboys had no problems accepting much bigger jewels than Cat's latest acquisitions. But it wasn't in her upbringing.

Normally the expansive dimensions of Sir Rodney's old bathroom, with its ancient but still splendid ocean liner fittings, were one of the great pleasures of life at Butely, even if the vagaries of the central heating meant she was normally confined to four inches of hot water. But the earrings sat heavily on her heart, if not her lobes. When she picked up the latest copy of American *Vogue*, which weighed about as much as a breeze block, and flicked disconsolately to an article Toby had highlighted entitled 'The Compelling Call of the 21st-century Spa', her heart sank farther. Toby had thoughtfully marked some of the passages with fluorescent pen.

Who can argue with the notion that these days a visit to a spa is a necessary luxury? A deep sense of foreboding seeped into Cat's bones as her big toe wrestled with the bath tap. After some melodramatic clanking the full force of Butely's lukewarm water supplies trickled on to her calves. *The modern detox destination offers a hectic schedule of scuba diving, dawn t'ai chi and electro-hydrotherapy.*

The Butely destination offers a haphazard mishmash of hunt the edible meal, afternoon bridge and one hot bath a week if you're lucky, thought Cat. And then she let her mind drift . . .

If she was honest, the call from Toby's mother the night before had come as a relief, not that she believed Lady Cynthia's story about an intruder. Sex had become a bit of an abstract concept for Cat – a bit like hang-gliding; something she was interested in but couldn't envisage herself ever actually doing. She turned back to the article in *Vogue*, where Gisele Bundchen disported herself in one of the Om's three Olympic-sized ozonic infinity pools wearing the new Gucci collection. Thoroughly deflated, she moved on to an article in *Cosmopolitan* with the word 'Controversy' stamped in red ink, like a logo, all over it. According to the author, anyone not fellating their partner three times a week was failing at the most fundamental level to create that unique bond between a man and a woman. 'You might just as well,' the piece continued bossily, 'opt out of relationships and just buy a dog.' Miserably she turned the hot tap off with her toe.

A sharp gust of wind blew through the open window on to Cat's neck as she stood up and reached for a towel. It wasn't just the facilities and the several million it would take to install anything like the gadgetry expected in the modern detox destination, she thought sourly. Butely's weather patterns left a lot to be desired too. She wrapped herself in what had become her daily uniform of tights, track pants, two T-shirts, a jumper and a cardigan, and by the time Toby got back was hard at work over the computer.

'Sorry I'm late.' He leant over and kissed her neck. 'Apparently Harbury apprehended the intruder two nights ago but Mummy's still a bit spooked. It's not like her, but perhaps that's what happens as you get older. Where's Lil?' he added.

'Playing with her new best friend, Marina. So we're completely free.'

'Mmm, that's the best thing I've heard today.' He pulled her round to face him. 'So where am I taking you tonight?'

It felt like months since Cat had been anywhere, which simply added to the pleasure of dressing up. Apart from taking Lily to school, she hadn't had much time to explore Lower Nettlescombe yet. They were only going to the Hung Drawn and Quartered, and Cat had a nasty suspicion they wouldn't be going at all if it hadn't been for a prior engagement Lady Cynthia had at a dinner party on the Wiltshire borders to which Sting and Trudie Styler were also apparently invited.

She slipped on an old pair of black trousers and one of Suzette's cast-off grey cashmere jumpers and put on the diamond earrings Toby had bought her. That would do. Glamorous enough for Toby but understated enough for the local pub – what Suzette would doubtless have called emotionally intelligent dressing.

In her mind's eye she pictured the Hung Drawn and Quartered as a riot of old horse brasses and cider mats, with the odd wood-burning stove and darts board tossed in for good measure. She imagined sleeping dogs and unhurried conversations about silage and the right to roam.

'You look wonderful,' said Toby, opening the passenger door of the Porsche for her. 'You know, I think country air really agrees with you.'

Cat smiled. She would have quite liked to have walked into Lower Nettlescombe with him, partly because it seemed romantic and picturesque, and partly because she didn't want to antagonise the locals with his flashy car. But Toby pointed out that walking back at midnight from the pub would be neither romantic nor scenic. Just cold and dark.

She needn't have worried about the Porsche. By the time they got there, the Hung Drawn and Quartered's car park was packed with BMWs and four-wheel-drive Mercedes. Toby slipped his arm round her shoulders. 'How long did you say this place has been reopened?'

'A couple of weeks,' said Cat, straining to make herself heard above the babble of voices that met them as they walked into a room that perfectly represented the ideal English pub, minus the tankards and the kitsch clutter. Cat felt momentarily overwhelmed by the crowd. So there hadn't been a micro-plague in Dorset after all. Cosy light emanated from the antique wall sconces, casting a flattering glow over everyone. Even if the food was awful – and if Samantha's dour pronouncements on the culinary skills of the whole of Dorset were anything to go by, it would be – at least the decor was pretty. 'Just as well we booked a table,' said Toby as they nudged their way past the bar. 'I'm starving.'

'Hello, hello, welcome to our humble hostelry.' A tall blond hunk with a jawline that looked as though it had been chiselled by Michelangelo and a voice that sounded as though it had been schooled by Dale Winton presented them with two handwritten menus and a huge white bowl of delicious-looking olives. In the corner, a jazz trio were tuning up their instruments. 'I see Dave Brubeck's in.' Toby winked at Cat.

'Don't think I've had the pleasure of receiving you before. I'm Julian. And over there –' their host nodded towards the bar, where a Colin Firth lookalike was mixing a Sea Breeze '– is my partner in crime Rupert. If there's anything we can do for you, please let me know.'

'Do you have any ale?' asked Toby innocently. Cat could tell he thought Julian had metropolitan pretensions above his station.

'Eight. Organic or the ordinary. They're all named after kings and princes. There's Charlie – that one's a bit bitter; Will – quite young, but strong; Prince Regent, that's full bodied, Prince Edward – just a smidgen of fruit . . .'

'What's in Henry VIII? A soupçon of syphilis?' asked Toby.

'Alas, no,' said Julian, 'we couldn't get the fresh ingredients. Here.' He handed Toby a handwritten list. 'Would you excuse me a moment? We've got the food police in.' He darted to the far corner of the dining room where a guest with a notebook proceeded to grill him for several minutes. 'Don't tell me,' said Toby as they studied the menu. 'A.A. Gill.'

Julian returned breathlessly. 'Bleeding critics. Always want detailed pedigrees of the organic beef. How do I know whether its mother was into Shirley Bassey or not?'

'Who is that?' said Cat, peering at the hunched back in the corner.

'Peter Lawson, from the *Bournemouth Echo*,' said Julian, trying – and failing – to sound blasé.

'Peter Lawson,' repeated Toby. 'Let me see. Didn't he write *How to Be a Domestic Goddess*?'

'Golly,' said Cat, worried that Toby's drolleries might seem a bit rude in comparison to the gentler ways of the Hung Drawn and Quartered. It was amazing how much of the brittle repartee she took for granted in London didn't seem to travel very well. 'How nerve-racking. Specially when you haven't been open five minutes.'

'But building up to it all our lives.' Julian put his hand to his brow in a mock melodramatic gesture. 'I can't tell you how many times we refined our business plans and reworked menus on the overnight to Bangkok.'

'One minute the mile high club, the next the Ivy,' said Toby.

'What about you?' Julian directed his question at Cat. 'What brings you to Lower Nettlescombe?'

'Butely.' Cat took a sip of her kir royale and felt herself begin to relax as it fizzed on her tongue. 'I'm hoping to revive its fortunes.'

'Ah. So you're the new lady of the manor. Good, because Rupert and I were saying only the other day that what this place is crying out for is a really good beauty spa. Meadows and fluffy livestock are all very well but man cannot live on views alone. I haven't had an oxygen facial for months.'

'I'm not sure Butely will ever be up to providing one of those.' Cat smiled. 'But then there probably aren't that many men who are as well groomed as you round here.'

'Don't you believe it,' said Julian. 'It's getting very chi-chi in this neck of the woods. Rumour has it that Mark Wainwright is planning something big in the village.'

Cat looked at him blankly. 'Mark's our local Richard Branson,' explained Julian. 'He was a hundred and thirty-three on last year's *Sunday Times* Richest Britons list. It's probably a load of old cobblers. Never believe what you read in the papers. Still, Rupert and I have just joined the rugger buggers team – honorary members,' he added proudly. 'And you can't believe what a bunch of woofters they are. Always going on and on about how there's nowhere to get a good massage, no decent yoga classes, and how you have to go for miles to find a good irrigation – and I'm not talking about watering the barley.'

'So you think people might be up for an ultra-swish gym and pool?' said Toby. 'I've been trying to persuade Cat that she needs to open one at Butely. Not just for the guests. Locals could pay an annual subscription.'

'With proper sprung floors and ozone?' asked Julian.

'Naturally.'

'In that case, where do me and Rupert sign? We're at our wits' end not having anywhere decent to work out. Oh, just a mo.' He darted back to Peter Lawson.

'What did I tell you!' exclaimed Toby before turning his attention to the menu. 'Blimey, this is a bit ambitious.'

Cat had to agree. Starters included Lebanese salad with kumquat chutney, warm octopus salad and gnocchi de chèvre. For the main course there was lime coriander lamb, Peking duck with oriental cabbage, fishcakes à la Caprice, and steamed sea bass with Thai dipping sauce. 'I bet even the pork scratchings come with treviasano tardivo,' said Toby. 'God help us – if the cooking round here's a tenth as bad as you say.'

Was it the first time, she wondered, that a challenging note had crept into his voice, or just the first time she'd noticed? Gazing around the room at a crowd that looked as though it had spent most of the day in Joseph and the rest of it in John Frieda, she suddenly felt on edge. She doubted if Micky had ever heard of treviasano tardivo. The snatches of conversation that floated above the strains of a rather good version of 'Bewitched, Bothered and Bewildered' weren't quite in the silage and combine harvester vein she'd expected either. More the stock market and property prices vein. A trio of leggy blonds, with lots of mink highlights – male and no doubt part of Julian's young farmers network – was earnestly discussing the merits of cranial osteopathy and Pilates. Cat blanched. Why should she want the food at the Hung Drawn and Quartered to be awful and pretentious? But she did.

Unfortunately it was delicious, every last morsel, down to Cat's lemongrass brûlé and Toby's vanilla panacotta with chocolate bread pudding. By the end of the meal Toby was back to his ebullient self and Cat did her best to match his repartee. She even remembered to ask after his mother. 'Perhaps it was just one of the builders snooping around – the intruder, I mean.'

'What builders?' asked Toby.

'Daphne said something about the builders being in. She said that's why Jake couldn't stay there.'

'Did she now?' asked Toby, scanning the bill efficiently and slipping his credit card on to the plate Julian had brought. 'That wasn't bad, was it? In fact, it was bloody delicious.'

'Yes.' Cat felt inexplicably stressed, and not just because of the jazz trio who, though far less self-consciously experimental than the Truelove Quartet, still conjured up distressing images of Ben. Nothing explicit had been said on either side, but somehow she had the inescapable feeling that the stakes on Butely's future had just been raised. To make matters worse, she'd just put Toby's favourite Wagner on and poured him what she hoped was a pre-coital drink when he suddenly announced he had an early meeting the following morning that would require all his concentration. Clasping her tightly and pushing his tongue into her mouth – he was the most erotic kisser she'd ever encountered – he gazed into her eyes tenderly and told her he'd have to drive back to London that night.

13

Having waved Toby off on Saturday evening, Cat settled down at the kitchen table with a glass of wine and some facts and figures he had left her in the hope of convincing her that a gym-less spa wouldn't survive a year in the current competitive environment.

'Blimey, you're living on the wild side, aren't you?' said Jess when she found Cat hunched over her laptop at eleven o'clock.

'Do you think a gym's a good idea?' said Cat, without looking up from her calculation.

'We've got to do something. Antiquated charm can only get you so far.'

Cat sighed. 'You're right, I suppose. It's a big step, though. It'd be a lot of building and disruption.'

'Not one for Ralph, then?' She sounded just a tiny bit wistful.

'Do you miss him?' asked Cat gently. She'd been so wrapped up in Butely lately she hadn't really been looking out for Jess.

'Nah, not really.' She pulled up a chair and sat down, her Doc Martens flapping over her pale bare legs.

'I don't know how you do that – run around in winter with so little on,' said Cat, half envious.

'Cold legs, warm welcome,' said Jess. 'Have you noticed how cute some of those rugger buggers in the pub are?'

'Can't say I have – yet.' Cat grinned. She was glad Jess was settling in.

'So where's Mr Cheekbones, then?'

'Had to go back to London. Urgent meeting tomorrow.'

Jess pursed her lips and gave Cat a knowing smile.

'What's that look supposed to mean?'

'When are you going to admit that you've fallen for him – and hard?'

'When we've had sex.'

Jess looked at her aghast. 'He's not part of some religious cult is he?'

Cat shook her head. 'I've thought of that.'

'But you do like him, don't you?'

'Yes, I like him.'

'Do you think he's the one?'

Cat frowned, trying to recapture the precise chemical effect Toby had on her when he was around. It wasn't easy, especially recently. Whenever he wasn't around, she kept feeling antagonized by him.

'I don't know – how do you ever know?'

'Instinct, Cat, instinct.'

Cat gazed at Jess's kohl-rimmed eyes, untroubled by any real doubts but filled with instinctive conviction, and realised with a jolt that four years learning to second-guess everyone and two years of dipping in and out of *Machiavellian Rules* had left her with no instinct at all. That was the problem – she had to try to relocate it.

Monday morning she was up bright and breezy, bustling round the Aga at 6.45, preparing Lily a nourishing snack for school, even though Lily had told her she would prefer unnourishing snacks. By ten to nine she had dropped Lil off at the school and was marching back to Butely, reflecting on the previous forty-eight hours and taking deep gulps of something that felt suspiciously like fresh air.

All things considered, it hadn't been an entirely successful weekend. Not only had she signally failed to consummate her relationship with Toby but she'd been left with the nagging feeling that somehow she was failing to show results with Butely quickly enough to impress him . . . but she'd miss him. There was no one in Lower Nettlescombe half as wittily irreverent or interesting. Not that she'd actually got to know anyone in Lower Nettlescombe apart from Mrs Potts. It was a pity there was no one to see her in her glamorous coat, but that was what you got with places of outstanding natural beauty.

In the distance she could hear the sounds of gushing water – a babbling brook probably. It certainly would be in the Thomas Hardy novels she was racing through. She'd fallen in love with Hardy's descriptions and had taken to imagining herself as one of his characters. Her favourites so far were Bathsheba Everdene, when she was feeling perky, and on gloomier days Tess of the D'Urbervilles.

Somewhere just above her shoulders hovered the dove-grey sky, as soft and moist as baby's breath. And then she felt a plop of rain. The English pastoral idyll was a very damp one – which was bad news for brickwork but, as Suzette had pointed out, good news for the skin.

She pounded on up Crab Apple Hill, which looked exactly like something out of *Under the Greenwood Tree*, her current bedside read. Halfway up, she paused to soak up the view of the little cluster of vanilla-fudge-coloured flint-and-cob cottages nestling in the valley beneath with the River Piddle coiled around them like a mossy satin ribbon. Slightly off-centre sat the church and its patch-work graveyard, and beyond that the Hung Drawn and Quartered, indigo smudges of smoke brushing against the low sky from its chimney. Beyond that, through the Butely tussocks and the ancient woodland that crowned them like a mohican, the sea glittered like a Brillo pad.

Nothing wrong with Lower Nettlescombe's scenery, she thought ruefully. In fact there was nothing much wrong at all with Lower Nettlescombe, apart from its godawful Spar. Lily seemed to be settling in nicely at the village school, which far from being a hotbed of glue-sniffing was – as Toby had forecast – a rather sensible mix of traditional and modern teaching methods.

Which in a nutshell was what she'd like Butely to be. She hoped they were doing the right thing getting in with Glowbal. Toby seemed convinced that it was their best option. They were certainly offering a slick package; all the very latest facilities for an extra-ordinarily reasonable sum. But it seemed a bit too good to be true.

She ran through the daunting list of tasks she had set herself at the weekend, including cold-calling a roster of blue-chip companies that might be interested in making corporate bookings at Butely and researching some of the treatments Dr Anjit had recommended incorporating into the timetable. And she had a mountain of correspondence to plough through. So many New Age therapists had heard of Butely's regime change and were looking for work, from Celestia Skye who took classes in animal and plant language to Aurora Blaze who used breathing to converse with the Archangel Uriel. And she'd had three letters from the karmabusters, who harnessed higher vibrational energies to release their radiance and communicate with the world. Though clearly sometimes they needed to resort to the Royal Mail as well.

One thing was sure – she was going to get on to Julian about the best way to recruit some of those young farmers to Jess's yoga class. Throwing them open to the public – on an external membership basis – would bring in some welcome income. 'Why, Mr Boldwood, far from the madding crowd, I see, what joy,' she declared to a blackbird that was busy savaging a worm. Spinning on her heels to resume her walk, she collided with Jake Dowell dressed in an antique Barbour.

'Toffee?' He held out a battered paper bag.

Cat eyed the sticky mess warily. As peace offerings went, she'd seen more appetising ones on the bottom of her wellies, but this wasn't the time to be choosy. She hadn't seen Jake since he'd been so rude following the unfortunate ditch episode. 'I don't think they're on Butely's list of approved foods – but sod it. I love processed sugar, don't you?'

'These are a bit past their prime, I'm afraid. I think they've been in the pockets of this coat for at least five years. I used to keep them for Blanche, Sir Rodney's lurcher. I haven't worn this coat since then.' He stamped his feet to get the circulation going in them.

Cat looked on with curiosity. If she hadn't had that first run-in with Jake – or run-over to be accurate – she might have been tempted to assume he was being friendly. But there had to be an agenda. Still, he seemed less stiff than on their last encounter, although that could have been because he hadn't recently dragged himself out of a ditch. He just looked as though he had. His hair was spikier than ever. It looked like a field of wheat that had been struck by lightning.

'Do you miss her?' said Cat on a hunch. 'Sir Rodney's lurcher, I mean.'

'Yes, I probably do.' He turned away. There was a small but distinct crack in his voice. She held her hand out for another toffee, in a gesture of sympathetic camaraderie.

'Food still awful at Butely, then?' he asked. She flicked her eyes towards him, checking for veiled insults, frowns and scowls. There weren't any. His skin, which was still tanned from New Zealand, was the colour of crème caramel. His eyes, a nutty colour, less obviously startling than Toby's, twinkled nonetheless. He wasn't quite as tramp-like as she'd remembered. Or perhaps she was just getting used to very low standards. Jake definitely looked more at home out of doors than behind them. Perhaps he was worried he might knock things over all the time inside. Maybe that was why he wasn't welcome at Ashdown House.

'Micky did his best with a bouillabaisse recipe but to be honest it looked like a very nasty collision between two rusty fishing trawlers.'

'Not very vegan, is it? Or are fish macrobiotic these days?' His fingers were surprisingly elegant, Cat saw. Architect's hands.

'Oh, we're just flirting with the idea of fish because of all the research about brain food. I'm a bit worried about betraying Sir Rodney, though.'

'Don't worry about that,' said Jake.

Cat watched him carefully. There was no trace of sullen resentment. More to the point, there was no trace of a limp. Not, to be fair, that there had been any official reaction to their little crash, not a single lawyer's letter. Just silence.

Encouraged, she launched into something approaching a conversation. 'The thing is, I'm just starting to realise what a challenge I've got on my hands. People are so sophisticated. Even in the country.'

'Yes, they've eased off the straw-chewing and auctioning their wives. Must be very disappointing for you.'

'That wasn't quite what I said.' Christ, he was sensitive. 'I just meant that we'll have to buck up our ideas if we're going to compete with the food at the Hung Drawn and Quartered.'

'I'm sorry we couldn't amuse you with a few ruddy-faced farmers weeping into their scrumpy over falling sheep prices. But Julian's very obliging. I'm sure if you ask he'll lay on some karaoke, shove a shrivelled chicken in the basket and maybe even arrange for a few farmhands to commit suicide.'

She bit her lip. She was damn well going to get him onside if for no other reason than to use him to track down some bloody builders.

'I was about to ask for some advice, actually. I wondered how far you thought we should modernise Butely.'

'Just do whatever you think is best.'

They walked on in silence. He had a very distinctive profile, Cat noticed. Like an eagle's. She tried again. 'I haven't seen you for . . . what is it?' She pretended to do a casual count of the weeks since she'd run him over when she knew how long it was to the day – thirty-four – on account of scanning the post anxiously every morning for a lawyer's letter. The sky turned progressively darker. Cat shivered.

'Yes, you've clearly been very busy.' Was he criticising her? she wondered. Judging her for not socialising with the villagers more?

'It has been a bit hectic. I've been keeping my head down – what with having to find two new gardeners, write a new prospectus and stop the staff knifing one another.' He gave a tight little smile, which may have been a grimace. 'But I suppose you've got your hands full too?'

'The council keep me pretty busy – with all their restorations and listing work.' He thrust his hands back into his pockets. End of conversation. A streak of lightning whipped across the sky.

'We're not about to get electrocuted, are we?' asked Cat anxiously. That would definitely liven things up but she wasn't sure death was a price worth paying.

He looked up. The sky, which had turned a muddy grey, looked as though it might split open at any moment. 'We'll survive. We've probably got ten minutes before the storm breaks properly. I'll walk you back. It's easy to get lost round here when the light's this bad.' His voice had softened, though it could have been a form of rural sarcasm.

'I wouldn't want to take you out of your way . . .' She trailed off. Taking Jake out of his way and getting him struck by lightning would suit her purposes perfectly. Especially if she got the number of some builders out of him before he went.

'You're not,' he replied briskly. 'I needed to pop in at Butely some time today and take some more measurements of the Jericho.'

Cat looked at him slyly from beneath her streaming hair. Suddenly the scarecrow seemed a man of mystery, chief of which was exactly how insane he might be.

The Jericho fixation alone made him fairly mad, which probably explained why Toby was blankly polite about Jake whenever he cropped up in the conversation. On the other hand, Lady Cynthia's appraisal of her younger son had verged on the downright hostile, which might actually be to Jake's credit.

'Sorry. I didn't mean to sound curt about your modernisation plans.' He quickened his pace. 'It's just that my father trusted you, so why shouldn't I?'

Cat could think of a million reasons why one should never agree with one's parents but instead she concentrated on keeping up with him, which wasn't easy, as the torrents of muddied water running between the ruts were turning into something that looked like sewage rapids.

'He knew you have to move with the times,' continued Jake. 'But by the end he didn't have any energy. He probably wouldn't mind about you introducing fish – as long as it's wild. And maybe you'll be able to incorporate some vegan dishes for those who still want them.'

Cat shot him a grateful smile, but since she was trailing him by some distance it was wasted. She could see that from his point of view things hadn't turned out brilliantly. He'd been done out of half his inheritance by a complete stranger. She found herself wanting to win him over. Or at least make him not hate her.

'It must seem odd, not being in New Zealand,' she began, panting after him. 'What were you doing there?'

'Housing mainly. Building low-cost solar-run pods for people on low budgets.'

'I see.'

There was a silence. What did she see? That he was a man of few words involved in typically worthy projects. It made her long for a bit of Toby's political incorrectness and witty repartee. They trudged on, Cat attempting to mask her breathlessness by turning up her collar and taking deep breaths from behind it. She began to feel faint with heat.

'Are you all right?' He turned round and looked her up and down. Another fat raindrop spattered on to her cheek. 'Quick, turn it inside out,' he commanded as the heavens opened. 'That coat doesn't look as though it was designed for rain.'

She did as he said. The coat probably cost the best part of one of Jake's pods. 'I didn't take you for a fashion expert.'

'I may not be John Galliano,' said Jake, bundling her under the shelter of his coat, 'but I know that Joseph suede and rain are not compatible.'

She was about to ask how he knew it was from Joseph, then she remembered she was now wearing the label on the outside. They reached the brow of the hill in more silence, Cat huddling under Jake's Barbour, which he held over her head like a canopy.

'Isn't country rain soft?' said Cat eventually, more to break the silence than from any real conviction. As far as she was concerned rain was rain – it all played havoc with your hair. 'In London it could strip a verruca, here it feels like milk,' she continued, as it began to beat down on them like bullets. She thought she heard a grunt, although it could have been a snort. She must stop wittering. Beneath them, on the other side of the valley, a copse of spindly ashes were fluttering gently to life, their delicate leaves unfurling in the moist, mild air.

A clap of thunder reverberated round the valley. A flock of birds streaked across the horizon. Cat jumped. 'Oh my God, what's that?'

He squinted into the sky. 'Starlings.'

Her teeth began to chatter. 'I meant that noise that sounded like a bomb.' The way the countryside swung from silence to ear-splitting shrieks in less time than it took Toby to turn his stereo on full blast was unnerving.

'Oh, that's just a shoot over at Guy Fulton's. Are you sure you're all right? We'd better get you some shelter.' He sped up as they wound down the hill towards Lower Nettlescombe. It was pelting down now. 'The Hung Drawn and Quartered?'

Cat would sooner have cut her veins and let Micky whip the blood up into one of his impenetrable gravies than spend another nanosecond with a dour schizoid.

'Fine.'

He'd better come up with some good builders.

'What can I get you, Jake – oh, hello, it's you.' Julian beamed at Cat from behind his eight real-ale pumps. A fire crackled away in the hearth. 'Kir royale, isn't it?'

'Er, is the sun over the yardarm yet?' Cat yanked off her coat and draped it over a chair to dry out by the fire.

'In Vladivostok almost certainly,' said Julian.

'In that case I'll have a large one,' she said, not wishing to be thought prissy by Jake, who obviously liked a tipple. She mountaineered up a bar stool.

'And I'll have a cappuccino,' said Jake, looking at his watch. It was 10 a.m. Great. Now he thought she was an alcoholic. 'Have you eaten here yet?' he asked.

'The other night. With Toby.' She scanned his face for a reaction. It was a perfect blank. 'It's frighteningly good.'

On cue, Julian placed a plate of tiny smoked salmon blinis in front of them. 'Here, try these. Rupert made the blinis himself. Been up since five trying out recipes. It's local salmon too – none of your farmed rubbish.' He scurried off to attend to two girls at the far end of the bar who looked as though they'd stepped straight off the pages of *Tatler*.

'Why frightening?' asked Jake.

There he went again. 'Oh, just that I'd been hoping we could keep Butely running in a low-key sort of way until we got round to raising enough money to make a few modest changes. But I'm starting to see that Toby's right – people don't want the simple things in life. Or at least they want the right kind of simple, which requires a lot of high-tech stuff to achieve.'

'I see.' His voice had taken on a gruff edge again. 'Aren't you eating these?'

'Just the salmon. I'm wheat-free.'

She saw his eyebrow flicker. 'I thought that was a celebrity thing.'

'It's a Butely thing. Actually it's an everybody thing. Toby says being wheat-free is very last year. But Dr Anjit convinced me that diet might be the way forward at Butely.'

'Did he now?'

'Blimey, not you too?' Julian glanced at the little pile of discarded blinis. 'Find that wheat-free thing works, do you?'

'Yes – and I was a real sceptic.' Cat sipped her champagne gingerly. It seemed wasteful not to drink it now Julian had poured it. But Dr Anjit probably wouldn't approve. 'Dr Anjit has been showing me some of the research that's been done in that last couple of years.'

'Madonna's macrobiotic, isn't she?' said Julian.

'Oh, well, that's conclusive, then, isn't it? Why bother with the *Lancet*?' said Jake.

Cat ignored them both. 'Dr Anjit's very up on it all. He goes to all the conferences. He even lectures at some of them. Anyway, we're in the early days of discovering just how much food affects people's mental health.'

'Gwyneth Paltrow's on it too,' said Julian, wiping a wineglass dreamily.

'I want to restore Butely to its former position at the forefront of all that,' Cat persisted. 'It's a lot cheaper than installing fancy lasers and lights that will go out of date in no time at all. And it's probably more valuable to the patients in the long run.'

'Sounds sensible to me,' said Jake.

'Does it?' She looked into his rumpled face. His eyes, now that she could see them, were a complex shade of hazel, with dark flecks that seemed by turns green and brown. 'We haven't really had a chance to discuss any of our ideas for Butely, have we?'

'Ours?' He raised one eyebrow.

'Well, mine. But I'd be happy – grateful – to listen to anything you've got to say. Anything at all. Look, why don't you come round one evening and I could talk you through some of my proposals?'

'I'm rather busy at the moment,' he mumbled into his cup.

Cat counted to ten silently. She had to persevere. At least until he'd found her some builders and filled her in with some local and architectural background.

She was about to explain exactly why he should take an interest when Rupert emerged from the kitchen with home-made oatcakes and jam.

'No wheat in that,' said Julian proudly. Cat didn't have the heart to say that according to Dr Anjit sugar ought to be blasted to kingdom come.

'How's the Jericho, then, Jake?' asked Julian.

'I was just on my way to see it when I bumped into Cat,' said Jake.

'It's not an original Thomas Crapper, is it?'

'Much more exciting than that. Crapper was nineteenth-century. Whereas according to my research Butely's might be a Sir John Harrington. Of course, the dates might not tally. There seems to be some difference in scholastic opinion as to the exact date of Sir John's death. But if we can prove it, it could be very interesting indeed – the only complete example of its kind.'

There was something disturbing about a man who got so enthusiastic about plumbing, decided Cat. She hadn't seen him this animated even when he'd been climbing out of that ditch.

'Worth a bomb, then, is it?'

'Hadn't really thought. Some American might want it in their museum, I suppose. But that's why the council's trying to list it – to stop that happening. Sometimes money's not the point, you see.'

'That's what you think.' Julian chortled. 'Bet the council would love to make some dosh if they could.'

Jake looked perplexed. 'As far as I'm aware they just want to preserve it.'

Julian winked at Cat conspiratorially. 'Such an innocent.'

'No, honestly,' Jake ploughed on. 'It's a fascinating object in its own right. Sanitation tells you an awful lot about a society. Did you know that until the 1960s, for instance, fifty-five per cent of British households still had no indoor plumbing? Yet the Victorians produced exquisite sewers . . .'

'Well, I wish the loos here had been exquisite when we took over,' said Julian. He turned to Cat. 'Place was a complete wreck. We wanted Jake to work on it. 'He's got quite a reputation round here. But he was off in New Zealand. Still, I think those two over there might have a bit of work going for a thrusting young architect.'

He nodded towards the two Tatler girls in matching black miniskirts and skinny white shirts who were chatting conspiratorially in the corner. Jake looked across at them. One of them caught his eye and held it until he looked away, blushing.

'That's Tashie and Lucy Wainwright,' announced Julian to Cat with a tinge of pride. 'Goo! Cosmetics,' he added when the reaction from Jake and Cat was more muted than he'd anticipated. A bell rang dimly in the recesses of Cat's memory vaults.

'Organic Unguents by Post. You must have heard of them.'

Cat remembered reading a piece on them somewhere last year. They'd set Goo! up three years ago when they were nineteen and twenty-one, and on the back of their Dorset Cream Hair-Pack, Portland Bill Bum Blaster and half a dozen articles in *Vogue* and various Sunday supplements, they'd turned it into a ten-million-a-year operation and were planning to float it on the stock market. She took in their endless legs, which gleamed as though the sun had melted into them. They looked about twelve.

'Rumour has it they're looking to convert a barn round here into their HQ,' said Julian. 'I'm surprised they haven't hooked their talons into you, Jake – or is there history there?' He tapped his nose conspiratorially.

'Everyone's very high achieving round here, aren't they?' Cat eyed their matching Dior handbags and felt exhausted. She helped herself to an oatcake. 'Is there anyone not listed on the stock exchange?'

'Nothing much else to do,' said Julian. 'Take me and Rupert. Thought our boat had well and truly come in when we found this place – and when someone told us Lower Nettlescombe had a spa our cup ranneth over. Didn't know our dream pub would turn out to have wet rot and that the Spar was the kind of place you went for festering veg rather than manicures. So we've had nothing else to do other than work our bollocks off.' He grinned.

'I thought you'd only been open a few weeks,' said Cat.

'The revamped version's only been open a few weeks,' explained Julian. 'But we stayed open through the building work, I'm proud to say.'

'What was that like?' asked Cat.

'Hell. Will you excuse me?'

A knot of strapping young men, handsome as Vikings, had swaggered into the Hung Drawn and Quartered.' I'd better make the rugger buggers welcome – don't want them defecting to the opposition.'

'Who is the opposition?' Cat asked Jake as Julian scampered off.

'The Royal Boar – on the A35. Also known as the Swine and Dine, on account of the rather utilitarian decor.'

'No leather armchairs or comfy sofas, you mean?'

'No seating at all – or not since the last showdown when the local skinheads and Hell's Angels used the chairs as missiles. If you want to see olde rural life, Cat, you could pop along there.'

'Where was I?' Julian bustled back, distinctly pinker of cheek than he had been.

'Keeping open,' prompted Cat.

'Oh yes, well, stands to reason, doesn't it? No business could survive closing for the duration. Not the way builders and architects dicker around – present company excepted. I don't say it wasn't hard. The day one of the baths fell through the first floor and landed on the bar was a low point. But even when we were reduced to serving from a tiny corner, we kept ticking over. How's the oatcake?'

'Delicious. Bath, you say?' said Cat thoughtfully. One way or another, all her conversations at Lower Nettlescombe came back to plumbing. Still, it was helpful taking stock from another business mind.

'Our next mission is to court middle youth,' said Julian. 'Don't knock it Jake. The four-wheel-drive brigade is where the money is. Or at least, that's what the *FT* says. Rupert calls those jeeps they all drive Towering Infernos. Packed to the gunwales, and there's usually a rank nappy or cat litter steaming away in the back somewhere. Still, it's all about diversification of assets these days. Oh, look, here comes the Rat Pack.'

'Who're they?' asked Cat as Julian skidded off to serve half a dozen or so people in fancy dress and she and Jake took their drinks over to a corner. Anyone less like Sammy Davis Jr and Frank Sinatra would have been hard to imagine.

'The Piddle Valley Mummers – our local amateur dramatics,' muttered Jake. 'I think Julian was being sardonic.'

'So now the house is worth about half a mill,' a woman screeched in a voice that was evidently used to carrying over the noise of tractors. She was wearing a sackcloth crinoline and a fake wart the size of Corfe Castle – at least, for her sake Cat hoped it was fake. 'Bloody hoot when you think what we paid for it.'

'Yes, but how much did you spend on it, Fee?' asked a badly shaven man wearing a floppy pointed hat. 'That's what people always fail to take into account.'

'Whatever are they rehearsing?' said Cat, gazing at the other mummers, who all looked as though they were in varying degrees of decomposition.

'*The Witches of Salem*. But it's not for months.'

'They're very dedicated in that case.'

'Just an excuse to bonk each other senseless, from what I can make out. They always have their rehearsals when most normal people are working.'

Cat looked at Jake in astonishment. She had him down as someone far too earnest to gossip. She found she wanted to stay in the pub a bit longer, but she should probably move on to something soft or Jake would have to toss her over his shoulder to get her home. 'Fancy another coffee?' she asked.

She went up to the bar, where Julian was arranging bowls of plump olives in front of the mummers, who were already on their second round.

'Oh, sod off, Nigel,' said Fee sharply. 'If by that you mean I'm a useless businesswoman you can piss off. I asked for a double G and T, by the way, Julian.'

'All I'm saying' – Nigel removed his hat lugubriously, and breathed in such a stentorian fashion that the hairs in his nostrils quivered like streamers – 'is that soaring property prices are all very well, but all it means is that you just end up having to spend more on the next place you buy.'

'Yes, well, when I want Norman Lamont's view of the economy I'll ask for it.'

'She seems rather cross about something,' Cat remarked to Julian.

'You know what they say about a woman scorned. Well, that's Fee.'

'With Nigel?' asked Cat, trying not to imagine them in bed together. With or without Fee's wart and Nigel's nasal hair it was a gruesome picture.

'With most of the pub. But most poignantly with Guy Fulton over there.' He nodded towards a spectacularly well-preserved man in his early sixties, with startling white hair and eyes the colour of curaçao, who was holding court among the rugger buggers. 'It ended very badly.'

'What happened?'

'Fee's husband found out about the affair and challenged Guy to a duel.'

'You're not serious,' said Cat.

'Happily I am. On Guy's shooting range.'

'Over Fee?'

'Apparently she used to be quite a looker – before the G and Ts got to her.'

'So who won?'

'Well, that's the twist, you see. Some people think that Fee put blanks in her husband's pistol so that Guy wouldn't get hurt. But another rumour has it she wanted Guy massacred. So at the last minute she got her husband's second to insist they swap revolvers.'

'Why would she want that?' asked Cat in awe.

'Because by then she'd just discovered that while she was two-timing her husband, Guy was two-timing her,' said Julian triumphantly.

'Who with?'

'Well, this is where it's even better than *Emmerdale*.' He paused for dramatic effect.

'*Who?*' asked Cat in exasperation.

Julian looked over his shoulder to make sure Jake wasn't in earshot. 'Jake's mother.'

'Lady Cynthia! You're not serious. What happened in the duel?'

'Well, they went through this big thing of swapping pistols. But once they realised the guns had been sabotaged it was called off. After that Fee went back to her husband and threw herself into buying and selling cottages. That and drinking the county dry. The whole thing went a bit quiet.'

'She's quite a goer, isn't she – Lady Cynthia, I mean. Guy must be a good few years younger than she is.'

'That depends on whether you go by her official age or not,' said Julian.

'Need any help with those?' asked Jake, sauntering over.

'That reminds me,' sat Cat guiltily. 'Any chance your customers might be interested in signing up to yoga classes at Butely, Julian?'

'You bet,' said Julian. 'Stick a notice up on the board, if you like. In the meantime I'll ask around. Glad to see you're finally opening the place up.'

'As you said, it's all about diversification of assets,' said Cat, sounding more optimistic than she felt. She had a few things she wished to discuss with Guy Fulton. But in the meantime she turned to Jake and girded her loins for a conversation about builders.

Cat had come across some smooth bastards in her time at Simms, but none smoother than Guy Fulton. There were three Mercedes in the driveway of his Queen Anne manse, one of them bearing a number plate that read 5OD U10B.

'Oh, that's my son Tybolt's,' he said, catching Cat staring at it. 'Do come in.' He closed the door behind her and she caught a whiff of pine aftershave. 'Quite witty of him. He bought it with his pay-off from the Institute of Bankers. Now he's sailing round the world. Banking never really was his thing.' He shook his head ruefully and she followed his tall, upright figure across the chequerboard hallway towards his drawing room. 'Do sit down,' he said, twinkling.

He wasn't without charm, reflected Cat, as she watched him pour them both a drink. She was shocked to find herself mentally signing him up as a potential friend. It just went to show how desperate for grown-up companionship she must be.

'I've really come about a business proposition,' she said primly, as he sat down opposite her and openly appraised her.

'Shame.' He flashed her a vulpine grin. 'I'd rather hoped this was a social call. I do apologise for not dropping round to visit you earlier, by the way. Had some business abroad – a fact-finding mission in the Czech Republic. Been following their methods of organic farming. Quite interesting.'

'You're thinking of going organic?' asked Cat hopefully. This was even better than she hoped. A rich, successful farmer with a conscience.

'Excite you, does it?' He looked amused.

Cat outlined her idea – that Guy Fulton rebrand some of the produce he farmed on the land rented from Butely with a Butely label.

'What's in it for me?' he said coolly.

'A lot of publicity and a premium-brand image. We'd pay for the packaging, of course. I've got the figures here.'

'Fine,' he said, barely glancing at the sheaf of papers in her hand. 'Where do I sign?'

'Just like that?' asked Cat, aghast. She was used to people taking months not to come to any decision. And she'd been looking forward to several evenings' worth of good-natured bartering at least.

'Sounds perfectly sensible to me.'

'Fortnum and Mason have already expressed an interest. And if they don't take the produce in the end, I've lined up plenty of others who will.'

'I'm sure you have.' There was a burbling amusement in his voice as well as his expression now.

'Well, thank you very much.' Cat stood up quickly when it became perfectly clear that Guy Fulton was mentally undressing her. 'I'd better be going now. My eleven-year-old daughter will be requiring help with her homework.' She backed out of his perfect Queen Anne drawing room all the way into the Polo, which she proceeded to thrash back to Butely. All things considered, she probably wouldn't be cultivating Guy Fulton as a friend. But, as she looked at the confident signature on the paper lying on the passenger seat next to her, she reflected that she had herself the makings of a damned good business deal.

The combined efforts of Cat's striking – if she said so herself – computer-designed poster and Julian's recommendations meant they were flooded with enquiries about the yoga classes. And when she rang the number of the builder Jake had given her and actually made contact with a human voice – not just an answering machine – and one that sounded intelligent, concerned and even interested in the work, she felt almost delirious. She arranged to meet Vic Spinoza at the end of the week. She went to tell Daphne the good news and found her peering into a packed class of rugger buggers all gawping at Jess's G-string, which was displayed to maximum advantage as she demonstrated the downward dog.

'Amazing what a little naked flesh can do, isn't it?' whispered

Daphne. 'That's one thing my years with the Bluebells did teach me, I'm glad to say.'

'It's certainly going to help with some of the running costs.'

'Are they that horrendous?' Daphne laid a freckled arm on Cat's. 'Still,' she continued, 'you wouldn't be the first.'

'What do you mean?'

'To be laid low by the whole venture.'

'Oh, I'm not laid low. In fact the whole thing's looking very encouraging.'

'Really?' Daphne sounded doubtful. 'Because in the early seventies, not long after it opened, bookings were so low Sir Rodney nearly threw it all in. It must have been around the time of the Opec crisis and no one was spending any money. Oh, Butely's had plenty of ups and downs. But it always comes through, Cat. We have every faith in you.'

'We?'

'The Friends of Butely.'

'That's nice. It's just a thought, Daphne, but where are these Friends?'

'They'll be back. Just as soon as it gets too hot to go to those health farms in Spain. As it is Veronica and the other witches have booked in again. And I really think you've won Sam and Micky round.'

'Really?' said Cat. 'Because I could have sworn I'd done something to upset Samantha. She's hardly spoken to me for days. And this morning she looked as though she'd been crying.'

'I wouldn't worry, dear. Probably had a row with Micky. They have a very volatile relationship. No, Cat, really, everyone adores you. Especially since you saw Sylvia off. And the way you've been helping Micky. At this rate we might have to include one or two of his dishes in the Butely Recipe pamphlets that are for sale in the shop. I'll help you update them if you like. Lily's been showing me how to use the Mac.' Her inquisitive mauve-orbited eyes bulged so enthusiastically that Cat didn't have the heart to tell her she was already on the case. They ambled downstairs together. 'And there's enough interest to have three of Jess's yoga classes a day,' continued

Daphne brightly. 'You should have seen her lapping up the attention at the start of the week. I wouldn't be surprised if she hadn't slept with half the class by Friday.'

'She'll be slacking if that's all she manages,' said Cat, chastising herself for being such a bitch, but it didn't seem fair somehow that Jess was winning all the popularity contests in the area. 'What amazing earrings,' she added, mesmerised by two huge chilli peppers dangling from Daphne's ears. It wasn't a complete lie. Embellished with little pods of ripe seeds on either side, they were certainly eye-catching.

'Do you like them?' Daphne beamed. 'I made them myself.'

'Really? When?'

'Last week. They're clay, glazed with enamel. It's a very rare red. I based it on Saint Laurent's surrealist collection.'

'Glazed? With enamel? Where?'

'In the kiln, of course.'

'What kiln?'

'The one I keep in the Long Building next to Sir Rodney's garage. Come.'

She led Cat across the lawns to a makeshift workroom that had been partitioned off from the main garage, now sadly depleted of Sir Rodney's vintage collection. Displayed along rough pine shelves from the ground to the ceiling were examples of Daphne's handiwork. Bowls, vases, jugs and figurines of every size, shape and colour glinted and winked in the dappled sunlight. It was like walking into the china department of Liberty's.

'You know what you said about wanting to help,' said Cat, suddenly seizing Daphne's hand. 'Well, how would you feel about helping to set up pottery classes? It would be a fantastic draw – stress-buster and all that.'

Daphne looked shocked, then thrilled, then guilty. 'You do know,' she said eventually, 'that these chilli earrings are actually male genitalia?'

'I see you're getting into the swing of things.'

Cat looked round and saw Jake striding up the hill towards her, his hair tufting up in the breeze. She felt her muscles tense. Julian's revelations about Lady Cynthia's racy past had cast Jake in an even more complex light.

'Just trying to get fit,' she gasped.

'That sounds positive. I thought you seemed a bit down the other day.'

'Really?' Perhaps he wasn't completely self-absorbed after all.

'You shouldn't let Lucy and Tashie Wainwright intimidate you. It helps having a multimillionaire entrepreneur for a father who's prepared to invest several hundred thousand in their business.'

What the hell made him suppose she was intimidated? 'I suppose you know everyone round here?' she said stiffly. She was torn between wanting to get on with her walk – she had a mountain of work waiting for her and she needed to show Mrs Faggot how the Dyson worked again – and wanting to pump Jake for local colour.

'Not everyone. But since Mark Wainwright bought the Spar, it's hard to escape him.'

'*Our* Spar?' Cat looked at him with a mixture of outrage and contempt. 'What on earth would a multimillionaire want with the Lower Nettlescombe Spar?'

'Apparently he's got plans to turn it into a blueprint for a nationwide chain of rural organic supermarkets. He's building a huge glass conservatory on to the side—'

'Designed by Norman bloody Foster, I suppose. How pretentious!' Cat fumed, feeling a surge of loyalty towards the current incarnation of the Spar, a store she had previously avoided except in extreme desperation.

'And what about poor Mrs Potts?' – a woman who had met Cat's every overture with utter indifference.

'Bound to be kept on. Mark Wainwright knows an authentic village character when he sees one.'

'Oh,' she said, somewhat deflated.

'I thought you'd be pleased. If Mark Wainwright thinks there's money to be made in promoting healthy lifestyles then there's hope for Butely.'

'Yes, but I'm trying to combine healthy lifestyles with a simple approach.'

Cat felt her good mood evaporating. Jake didn't seem to get it. He held out a hand to help her over a stile into Butely Lane. She ignored it. He shrugged. 'It's not called Hangman's Stile for nothing,' he said.

'I am capable of climbing over a gate by myself,' said Cat, as she heard the unmistakable sound of expensive suede ripping. There was a muffled choking sound from Jake. 'Thank you for recommending Vic, by the way,' she said through gritted teeth.

'You rang him, then?'

'Yes, and he's coming over on Friday to look round. He says he could start at the end of the month. Mind you, they all talk a good story—'

'Vic's a good man,' said Jake gruffly. 'If he says he'll do something, he'll do it.'

'Morning, Jake, dear.' Mrs Potts hobbled towards them while Des and Cilla scampered across her orthopaedic shoes.

'Morning, Mrs Potts. Morning, Des. Morning, Cilla. Lovely to see you. How's that left-hand serve of yours keeping?'

Cat looked at him in amazement. She'd never seen him so enthusiastic except when he was discussing the Jericho.

Mrs Potts giggled girlishly. 'Are you challenging me to a game of tennis?'

'I wouldn't dare.' Jake grinned. 'Mrs Potts used to play tennis for the county, Cat.' Cat smiled weakly. 'Got a heart of gold,' continued Jake as they walked on. 'But not to be crossed.'

Cat looked at the angles of Jake's downturned face – so much less refined than his half-brother's – in amazement. Perhaps all she had to do to win him round was wait until she was ninety and walked with a limp.

'Toby's coming down this weekend,' she said mischievously. 'Perhaps you'd like to come over?'

'I'm afraid not,' he said stiffly. 'I'm going to London. There may be a job going.'

'I thought you had a job. And I thought you hated cities. And what about the Jericho?' The words tumbled out with a force that took her by surprise. She supposed it was because arguing with Jake was better than not having anyone to talk to at all.

'It might be a really interesting job, in which case I dare say I'd survive the city. And the Jericho's not going anywhere. It all depends on whether this job's half as good as it sounds.'

And on the whereabouts of his half-brother, thought Cat. Until she'd mentioned that Toby was coming there hadn't been a word about going to London. There was something unhealthy going on between Toby and Jake. And she was determined to get to the bottom of it.

14

'Hold on to your pelvic floor,' said Suzette, dead-heading a peony on her desk with a pair of antique silver nail scissors, 'I've got the most amazing news. Remember my best friend Millie van Peterson? She's agreed to review Butely for American *Vogue*.'

'Your best friend Millie van Peterson who you haven't talked to since she questioned one of the central tenets of *Emotionally Intelligent Dressing*?' Cat stared across the lawns to where Jess and Lily were practising asanas. She was having problems seeing how having a pampered anorexic stick insect crawling over Butely's abundant cracks for the edification of two million readers constituted good news.

'Oh, that. We built bridges ages ago.'

'Well, unfortunately Butely's bridges still need a little repair work. Along with everything else.'

'How bad is it?' A flicker of doubt crept into Suzette's voice.

'Actually I'm quite pleased with the progress. The staff seem to have come round, the vegetable garden is in the process of being transformed and I think I've found a brilliant builder.'

'Yes, yes, but what about facilities? That's what Americans want. How's the gym coming on?'

'It's still a concept-in-progress,' said Cat.

'Have you thought about hiring some cranes?' said Suzette, as if she were recommending that Cat get some cheese straws in. 'Americans understand cranes. What they don't understand is idleness.'

'Better not go to a naturopathic clinic, then. Idleness tends to be the point.'

'Not at American ones. Didn't you read the schedule I e-mailed from Cal-à-Vie? And I honestly think you should stop referring to Butely as a naturopathic clinic. No one knows what you're talking about and if they do they think it's something to do with the NHS.'

'Can't you put Millie off for a couple of months?'

'Have you any idea what a coup it is to get Millie at all? She's snowed under with requests to visit the most luxurious spas in the world. Anyway, I thought you said Butely was glorious.'

Cat began to fidget with one of Sir Rodney's priceless porcelain shepherdesses. Technically speaking Butely hadn't been glorious since about 1783. For the past two hundred years, it had been coasting on its laurels, and even they had greenfly.

'Cat, everything is all right, isn't it?'

This was a marginally worse conversation than the one they would have when Cat finally got round to confessing that the pony Suzette had promised Lily had already been bought by Toby. He'd arrived on the previous Sunday afternoon for a disappointingly abbreviated visit – sometimes she wondered whether they were ever going to have sex – with a pretty little piebald called Archie. It was all a bit embarrassing really – the present was thoroughly over the top given the somewhat stilted nature of their present relationship. She didn't want to seem churlish – and Lily had been so completely thrilled – but she couldn't help feeling that Archie somehow put her under a deeper than ever obligation to Toby, a most disconcerting place to be.

It wasn't until the Monday morning after Toby's flying visit that Cat let him know about Millie van Peterson's imminent arrival, which was by then that bit more imminent. He was on the telephone from somewhere 15,000 feet above Glasgow – a location, she was beginning to realise, that never saw him at his best.

'You'll have to put her off, obviously,' he said, sounding unamused.

'Already tried that one. She's on her way. Apparently she's currently in the Maldives. Or was it the Seychelles? Either way she's incommunicado.'

'Well, have her detained at the airport. Tell her the Third World War's broken out, or there's a Botox shortage and the last dregs are being doled out in Manhattan right now.'

Cat giggled.

'I'm serious. Have you any idea how damaging this could be?'

Cat wished that Toby would remember some of the minor triumphs she had achieved at Butely lately. Like Caleb and Brian, the polite, quiet students from the local agricultural college she'd found through two of the rugger buggers, whose younger, gentler brothers they were, to help Mimms out. Already the results were little short of miraculous. It turned out that Mimms had been doing his stuff all along, planting seeds, nurturing cuttings. It was the weeding which had defeated him, and once Caleb and Brian had cleared away the debris, it was amazing how much produce there already was. At Daphne's suggestion they were going to plant an acre of lavender in one of the meadows and by the following summer they'd be selling all kinds of spin-off products.

The shop was looking a lot better too, since Cat had cleared it out and got a few new recipe books and essential oils in there. In a few months she'd have some of Butely's own produce on the shelves. In the meantime there were the letters she had personally written to all of Daphne's Friends of Butely, which had resulted in enough bookings to keep them more or less solvent over the next few months. And her cold calls had paid off as well, although most of her targets asked her to get back to them once the pool complex was up and running. Still, the human resources department at Clarence's, a small merchant bank in the City, had been so tickled by Cat's honesty that they'd booked a series of immediate packages for their senior management.

But Toby only seemed interested in how much there still was to be done.

'Whatever possessed Suzette?' he said. 'She of all people should know what demanding bitches these beauty editors are. Surely she realised we weren't anywhere near ready?'

Cat thought it best to gloss over the number of times she had evaded Suzette's questions about the true state of Butely. She shifted on to slightly safer territory. 'That e-mail you sent about getting rid of the dormies—'

'Yeah, the dormi thing makes no sense financially – they're never full, which means that one person ends up getting a vast room for peanuts. And they hardly fit in with the slick new image.' He sounded slightly bored.

'I know that so far they haven't really paid their way but that's because they haven't been marketed properly. And I agree they've been abused, but we could put a stop to that. The thing is, some people really rely on them. Sharing a room with five others is the only way they'll ever be able to afford Butely. I don't think we should lose sight of why Sir Rodney set the place up.'

At the other end of the line, and rapidly descending into Glasgow, Toby sighed. 'If we don't find some decent builders soon there won't be a place. Glowbal are keen to start on the gym and obviously we should do all the work on the house at the same time. If you can't come up with some soon, and I'm talking the end of the week,' he continued, all his former suaveness scuffed up into something a lot less winning, 'let me know, and I'll sort something out.'

She was about to try to impress him with the news that she was seeing a highly recommended builder the following day, but pride prevented her. There was a new edge to Toby's voice. One Cat didn't like. One that implied she always left him to sort things out.

Vic Spinoza turned out to be exactly the kind of builder Cat could do business with. He was kind, intelligent and he didn't scratch his head every time Cat took him into another of Butely's more shambolic rooms and ask her who had done the wiring/plastering/bungling last time round. Plus his daughter Marina was Lily's best friend.

'Least the roof is safe and sound,' he said as they stood outside surveying the dripping turrets and eaves. Cat smiled encouragingly.

'You don't know how lucky you are,' Vic got out his Biro. 'It would cost a fortune to put a new roof on a place this size – buy you a small house in London, I don't doubt. But Sir Rodney at least kept that side of things together.'

Two days after he'd done the royal tour, as he called it, Vic's estimate arrived on Cat's desk – methodically typed out and itemised down to the last new wall socket. All she needed was someone to check it over for her.

'Jake. What a surprise,' exclaimed Cat the morning after Vic's estimate arrived. She'd been lingering by Hangman's Stile for eight minutes so that she could accidentally run into him. This time she allowed him to help her over the stile, and as they approached the tussocks she manoeuvred the conversation round to Vic's estimate, trying to sound offhand. 'It looks all right to me, but then I'm just a layman. It's all terribly intimidating.' She would have fluttered her eyelashes, but Jake wasn't the type to fall for that.

'I told you – Vic's salt-of-the-earth. You can trust him with your soul,' he said, sounding more irascible than ever.

'Never mind my soul,' snapped Cat. 'It's a huge bloody bank loan we're talking about.'

Jake's imposing forehead knitted together in a frown, and then to her astonishment he laughed. By the following day he had been through Vic's entire estimate and ironed out any quibbles with Vic himself. He came round to deliver the news personally, and for the first time Cat almost thought he showed the potential to be a reasonable human being. 'I'd say you've got yourself a very good deal,' he announced excitedly, his face lighting up.

For the first time she also thought he looked almost presentable.

'Well, you'd better unmake it,' said Toby matter-of-factly down the phone later that night. 'Because I've just got the okay from Glowbal. They can start next week on the whole house.'

'Whoa, there. I thought Glowbal were just working on the gym and pool.'

'Not any more. Jesus Cat. This is going to be a triumph. Glowbal want to stuff the complex with their latest technology – some of it hasn't even gone on the market yet. They want to test it in Butely and for that they'll whack it in for half the price. And they've agreed to do any work necessary on the house.'

Cat's head was reeling. 'What about asking what I think?' She wondered whether that sounded neurotic and decided she didn't care. 'What about planning permission for this pool?'

'Shouldn't be a problem. Especially with my mother's contacts on the council.' She might have known Cynthia would be in for a eulogy somewhere. 'Christ knows,' continued Toby, 'the area needs a kick up the arse like this. In the meantime, I'm sure you'll see that it makes sense for Glowbal to do the whole job on Butely, including any alterations to the house. They can start by bulldozing those bloody dormies and tarting the place up while we're waiting for planning permission for the pool. So as you can see, we don't need Vic Spinoza.'

'But I like the idea of working with Vic Spinoza. He's got impeccable references and there's something trustworthy about him. He's doing us an incredible favour and if I blow him out now it would look bad for . . . all of us.' She had been about to say for Jake. But she didn't need to. 'He could probably charge us fifty per cent cancellation fees.'

'I doubt it,' said Toby drily.

'That's not the point,' said Cat coldly. 'Letting people down at the last minute is not the way I do business. I've more or less made it clear to Vic that he's got the job and that's that. Anyway, what do Glowbal know about restoring Grade One buildings? I thought they were just a bunch of gym anoraks.'

'Builders are builders. Crappy old partitions are crappy old partitions. It's all the same thing,' said Toby lightly. 'They've done gym roll-outs throughout Europe. I understand if you find it a bit intimidating. But you've said yourself that Butely can't really operate without a pool and this will be the mother of all pools.'

Cat's mind whirred through the business options. 'I need some time to go through their proposals.'

'I'll e-mail some details but I can tell you now that the pros are overwhelming. Anyway, we need to let them know by tomorrow.'

At the other end of the line Cat felt her whole body trembling with anger. Toby's presumptuousness was unbearable. On the other hand, if the evidence in favour of a pool was irrefutable – and knowing Toby's thoroughness it would be – she didn't want to pass on a good opportunity through stubborness. And it probably made financial sense for Glowbal's builders to do the house as well.

'I'll let you know as soon as I've thoroughly examined them,' she said.

'It's up to you, of course. But no one in their right mind could argue with the facts. If Glowbal does the whole job we'll save about fifty per cent.'

'Well, it's a pity you didn't think to share the facts several weeks ago.'

He paused. 'Look, I know Glowbal are a very slick set-up.' He made it sound as though their sickness was the reason for her uneasiness.

'I can't even begin to consider this option before I see the plans they've drawn up,' she continued.

'Okay, *meine liebchen*. Didn't know you were an expert on frontal elevations, but I'll get Glowbal to fax them over to you today.'

That note of amused condescension again. 'Fine,' she said.

It wasn't fine, though. Glowbal's proposals were undeniably – conclusively, you could say – convincing. But she felt a complete bitch letting Vic down. And though Toby was right and she wasn't an expert, Glowbal's plans for the pool complex, as it was now called, looked out of scale with the rest of Butely. Of course, she could be wrong – reading maps and plans never had been her forte – but it seemed to her that the building they were planning to erect was huge. The local council would probably blow a gasket, and rightly so.

Toby assured her that those kinds of details could all be ironed out later. The important thing was that she agreed before Glowbal changed their mind. And he acknowledged that he'd been out of line.

'I've learned my lesson. It was stupid and boorish of me to be so gung-ho,' he said carefully after she'd faxed back her signature.

'You have my permission – indeed it's a request – to beat me with a whip.'

Cat forced a tight little smile, but it vanished when she ran into Jake halfway up the tussocks.

'You decided against Vic, then, I see.' He didn't even try to slow down for her. He was obviously angry and she couldn't blame him. She began to sweat a little in the morning sun. He'd dispensed with the Barbour, she noticed, and moved into spring wear – an ancient corduroy jacket, last fashionable in 1924. But at least he wasn't perspiring. The best she could hope for was a little shade once they hit the River Piddle.

'I'm really sorry,' was all she could come up with.

'It's okay,' he said scornfully. 'I know how important it is in business decisions not to be sentimental.'

'You did say that there was plenty of work round here for good builders like him.'

'Did Vic tell you that he'd juggled another job, to do Mark Wainwright's new organic deli, so that he could take on Butely?'

'No,' said Cat quietly.

'Well, he wouldn't. But he did – and now Mark Wainwright's given the job to someone else.'

'Look, I'm sorry if it's made things awkward between you and him – but I hadn't actually signed anything.'

'Oh, well, that's all right, then, isn't it?'

He marched on grimly, like a Roman legionnaire about to conquer Gaul. There was no point even trying to keep up. Cat watched his receding figure, pin sharp in the bright spring sunshine. She didn't suppose there was much chance in the short term of getting him to check Glowbal's revised drawings.

'What do you mean by out of scale exactly?' asked Toby in a pained voice.

'Just what I say. I thought I'd made myself clear to them, but they don't seem to get it. The revised drawings still make the pool complex far bigger than it needs to be. It looks like something

Mohammed al-Fayed would dream up. . . . as a matter of fact I was thinking of asking Jake to look them over,' said Cat, taking a deep breath.

'Toilet man?' The contempt wasn't even barely concealed.

'At least he has local knowledge, which should go down with the council a lot better than a bunch of corporate bulldozers. You said yourself Glowbal have no experience of working in the country-side. Jake on the other hand knows everything there is to know about the area – and he's on good terms with just about everyone who lives round here.' Apart from me, she didn't add.

She heard Toby blowing the froth off his coffee and felt a stab of exasperation. Why did she increasingly get the impression that Butely was just one of many petty concerns on Toby's list of priorities?

'It's your decision, of course,' said Toby. 'But I really don't think it's a good idea to get another architect involved at this stage.'

There was an exasperated silence.

'Cat?' He sounded concerned.

'Yes?' She felt herself aching for some words of encouragement.

'If it's all getting a bit much—'

'It isn't,' she said hastily.

'Look, no one's saying you can't cope. You're doing brilliantly.' It was the first time he had praised her in weeks and her ego drank it in like desert rain. 'It's just that with Glowbal on the scene, the game's much bigger now. I'm really pleased you've agreed to their plans in principle and by all means get them to tone it down. But don't piss them off. What they're proposing will put Butely on the map again. And it's going to be much busier than we envisaged.'

'What are you saying?'

'Just that maybe it would be a good idea to get in a manager to help you.'

'Someone else to argue with, you mean.'

'I'm not talking about getting in someone to undermine you on the ideas front. I'm just suggesting hiring someone with experience of running a country estate, so they could take all that side of things

off your shoulders. You know, someone to look after the out-
buildings, make sure the boundary walls are in good shape, keep
an eye on Guy Fulton – all that sort of thing.' Put like that it
sounded quite attractive. 'And it would give you a bit more time
with Lily, which I always thought was one of the motivations for
this move in the first place.'

He was right. 'How much would someone like that cost?' she
asked cautiously.

'Not much. I should think you could get someone for around
thirty-five grand.'

Thirty-five grand!

'It'd be worth it in the long run. Why don't you let me put
together a short list? I've got a chum with a big place in Wiltshire
who knows all about hiring estate managers. I'll get on to him and
arrange for some candidates to come and see you.'

'All right,' she said, trying not to sound resentful. 'But I reserve
the right of veto, okay.'

'Of course, my little führer. Oh, by the way, I'm afraid I won't
be able to make it down this weekend after all. It's just till this
bloody Scottish deal is in the bag.' He sounded quite tender and,
despite mild disappointment, Cat felt herself melting like ice cream
on an Aga.

Jake stopped in his tracks, mesmerised by the small human figure
struggling across the stable yard with a shiny leather saddle. That
is to say he assumed it was human, since all he could see was a pair
of legs, as skinny as a wasp's, scuttling beneath it.

'Can I help you with that?' He smiled.

Lily squinted up at him suspiciously. She seemed to be weighing
up her options because she took a long time to answer.

'It's all right,' she said eventually. 'I'm training myself to get used
to the weight.'

'It is a bit big,' said Jake.

'So's Archie. That's my pony,' added Lily helpfully. 'But Toby
couldn't resist him. And the thing is, I'll grow into him and it's
better to have a really good pony that's a bit big than one that's

sluggish and exactly the right size. That's what Toby says anyway.' She disappeared into the stable. Jake waited outside.

Lily's voice floated through the open stable door. 'Actually, do you think you could just hold the bucket steady for a sec?'

He poked his head round the door. Lily, wobbling precariously on a rusty steel pail, was attempting to heave the saddle on to Archie while the pony tossed his mane restlessly like a petulant supermodel.

'Here.' He took the saddle from her and gently placed it on the pony's back. He stood back and watched while she fumbled with the girth.

'It's a bit stiff,' she said apologetically.

'It's a pretty impressive saddle. Did Toby buy you that as well?' he couldn't resist adding. Lily nodded. 'Don't worry, it'll ease up.'

'And the girth's been rubbing my legs.'

'You need to wear some really thick boots. That'll soften it up. Come to think of it, I've got some stuff at home that should help speed things along. I could pop it round later, if you like.'

She cocked her head to one side and looked at him thoughtfully. 'I expect they tacked horses up differently when you were a child. I'd love to see how they did things in the olden days.'

He chuckled. 'Oh, I think you'll find it wasn't so very different all those hundreds of years ago.'

She stood there awkwardly, almost as if she wanted him to go, but not quite.

'Then again,' he said, suddenly realising what she was playing at, 'you never know, you might find it interesting.' He lifted the harness off its hook and deftly finished tacking Archie up while Lily watched intently.

'I'm not actually that experienced,' confided Lily suddenly. 'I mean, I've only been doing it a year. Not even that, really.'

'No, but you'll learn. There's an excellent riding school about six miles from here.'

She grimaced. 'I'm not sure Mum's bank balance is ready for that yet.'

And obviously Toby hadn't thought to follow his gift through. Typical.

'Tell you what. How about if I gave you a few lessons – for free,' he added hastily.

Lily looked at him suspiciously. 'That would be great,' she said unconvincingly.

'Okay,' he said gently, sensing her reservations. 'You'd probably better ask your mother. And in the meantime, how about if I hunt you down a proper mounting block. I've probably got one of those lurking around at my place as well. I ought to—' He smiled ruefully. 'I'm renting it furnished from an old lady who used to breed race-horses.'

'Really?' asked Lily, her eyes snapping open.

'Really,' Jake smiled. 'I'll leave you to it, then. Let me know about the lessons.'

Lily watched as he marched towards the orchard, marvelling at the strangeness of adults. She'd thought Jake was meant to be a shit.

An hour or so later Cat found Jake pacing out the distance between the Jericho and the compost heap. Anyone that interested in water closets was either an architectural genius or a pervert.

'I've brought you some tea,' she said. 'Though it's probably a bit cold by now.'

'Thank you.' He took the mug and sipped it awkwardly.

'And some fennel seed cake.' She handed him a hunk, wrapped in clingfilm. 'It's yeast- and wheat-free but quite edible all things considered. Micky's been practising like crazy.'

'You've got very loyal staff. You're obviously good at motivating people.' He screwed his eyes up in the late morning sun, which made him look even more forbidding than usual.

Cat ploughed on regardless. 'Is that a jackdaw?' she asked, creasing her eyes in concentration. It was important to prove her commitment to the countryside, she felt.

He carried on pacing. 'A magpie.' He eyed her suspiciously. 'I didn't realise you were interested in nature.'

'Me? Oh, I always wanted to be David Attenborough when I was growing up,' she lied. She gazed across the tops of the trees, which were wrapped in a dazzling, warm pink sunshine, towards the sea, and wondered why it was Jake always made her say such idiotic things.

'God, it's beautiful.' She sighed. 'Who would ever want to alter this view?'

'Plenty of people,' he said bitterly. He took a bite of fennel cake. 'How's Lily getting on with her new pony?'

Cat looked at him in surprise. She hadn't realised he was even aware of Archie's arrival. 'She could really do with an intensive course of lessons,' said Cat, but it's a bit expensive . . .'

'I'd be happy to teach her—' He stopped, embarrassed. 'If Lily would like that.'

She looked at him slyly. He was frowning again – perhaps he already regretted offering. She decided it was probably safest to ignore his suggestion. He could always offer again if he really meant it.

'How's the Jericho coming on?'

'What do you mean?' He sounded defensive again.

'Nothing. It seems to be keeping you very busy, that's all.' She nodded at his tape measure.

'Oh, that. I was just trying to solve a discrepancy.'

'Really?'

'According to some old library records I came across the other day, there ought to be the remains of an eighteenth-century green-house here.'

'Is that significant?'

'Yes. You see, the sixth Lady Butely grew tropical lilies. All kinds. Butely was famous for them, apparently. She had vast lily beds. You'd think there'd be some trace . . .' He looked up at Cat. 'What's the matter? You look a bit distracted.'

She decided to come clean. 'I've something to ask you,' she said. 'Something serious.' She told him about the pool complex and asked whether he would check the plans for her.

'The thing is, I'm not convinced they're completely sympathetic to the surroundings.'

'Of course.' He let his tape measure snap shut with such vicious-ness that Cat jumped. 'If you're so concerned about this Glowbal lot, why are you doing business with them?'

'Because financially it makes sense. It means we get fantastic facilities at a fraction of the cost.'

'Ah, yes, silly me.'

Cat was getting heartily sick of his high-mindedness, even if part of her sympathised with it. It was about bloody time Jake Dowell learned that fourteenth-century manor houses didn't look after themselves. 'Look, Jake, in an ideal world I would have liked you to design the whole thing. But we just don't have that kind of money.'

'Do you really think that's what's troubling me?' he said in-credulously.

'Well, what, then?'

He pushed his hands through his tufts, squinted in the sun and then did something she'd never heard any man do – apologise. 'Sorry. Take no notice. I've had a bad week. If it were left to me I'd keep Butely all to ourselves – and in a year's time the bailiffs would be round. That's not very helpful, is it? If you think it's the only sensible way forward, then it probably is.'

She looked at him in amazed silence for a few moments. He appeared to be genuinely contrite. 'So will you do it?' she asked quietly. 'Check the plans, I mean.'

'I'll think about it,' he said, stalking off, leaving Cat pondering over what exactly he meant about keeping Butely to themselves – and whether that included her, and if so whether she should be pleased or appalled at the idea.

15

Cat was getting used to men exiting her life. Declan Kelly, on the other hand, was only too happy to enter it. His Golf GTi chugged through the gates of Butely one Sunday afternoon when Cat was playing Monopoly with Jess, Daphne and Lily.

'I've come about the estate manager's job,' he announced in a nasal drawl that seemed at odds with his patched tweed jacket.

'Bloody hell,' muttered Jess. 'It's Austin Powers.'

'Shut up,' hissed Cat, embarrassed. He did have rather a lot of hair. She led him into her study, where she had prepared a dossier of appropriate questions on land management. Unfortunately she was so distracted by the razor-blade medallion she spied nestling against his Adam's apple that she could barely concentrate on his answers. Lily, equally mesmerised, wandered in with a pot of tea, and hovered by the door.

'So where have you just driven from?' asked Cat conversationally. She poured some tea.

'Berkshire. Big spread – polo farm, race stud, the lot.' He fiddled with his cuffs and stretched out his jockey-thin legs.

'I see you hunt.' Cat eyed his footwear knowingly. Declan flashed her a disarming grin. 'These are polo boots. Easy mistake, though. You've probably heard of Sheikh al-Hibbah?' he continued. 'Just won the Gold Cup for the third year running. Richest family in Saudi. Amazing perks – slight downer on the alcohol front, though.'

Cat and Lily smiled wanly.

'As a matter of fact I do hunt as well. And shoot. Do you like game?'

'Monopoly's all right, I suppose,' said Lily. 'But it goes on a bit.'

'Amusing little thing, isn't she?' he volunteered. 'I was talking about pheasants – the well-hung variety, obviously.'

He uncrossed his legs, leaving Cat in no doubt as to how he was hung. Still, as far as she could make out, he certainly seemed to know his subject.

'Is that to ward off sciatica?' asked Lily, pointing at his medallion. Presumably one of the perks to which he had alluded, it was embellished with a tiny sprinkling of diamonds that didn't look remotely medical unless, like Veronica, you believed in crystal therapy.

Declan leaned towards Lily. 'How old do you think I am, young lady?'

Cat saw the oncoming disaster as if it were an articulated truck. But her reflexes were frozen. Lily looked Declan up and down. 'Would you like to see the rest of Butely?' Cat asked. Before he could demur, she stood up and opened the door, with Lily hot on her tail.

'You never answered my question,' said Declan, when they reached the Cottage again. 'How old am I?'

Lily looked him up and down again carefully, while he visibly preened. 'Sixty?' she hazarded.

'So far the only objection you've come up with is that you don't like his hairstyle,' said Toby over the phone. 'His references are impeccable.'

Cat drummed her fingers on her bureau in frustration. She was furious with herself for not being able to put her finger on her uneasiness about Declan Kelly. In the face of his references – which were indeed impeccable – it seemed pathetic to say she didn't like his manner. But she did all the same.

'He was probably taking stock.'

'Taking the piss, you mean.'

'Look, he may not have been to charm school. But he's spent seven years as a paratrooper. Got a distinction in the Gulf.'

'What for – ladykilling?'

'Do I take it from your lack of humour that he didn't try any of his ladykilling tactics on you?'

'Thankfully not,' said Cat coldly.

'Well, maybe that's your problem,' said Toby. 'Look, I've got to go. Point taken and I'll see what else I can come up with.'

Half-way through April a group of stockbrokers from Clarence's arrived the same day as the workmen from Glowbal tipped up. The former seemed to Cat to be a good omen of things to come. If she could convert more bankers to the joys of Butely she'd be able to subsidise fees for the really needy and maybe do away with them in exceptional cases.

The Glowbal builders on the other hand were ready to do serious damage – as their foreman Goran unfelicitously put it to Cat – on all the other bits of Butely that needed repairing while they waited for the council to green-light the pool. Cat had never seen so many cement diggers, hard hats and copies of the *Sun* – which was amazing since none of them apart from Goran appeared to speak any English. She began to think that having someone like Declan to deal with them on her behalf might not be such a bad idea.

'Is it really wise to get Glowbal started on the building work before we've actually got planning permission?' asked Jess one day.

'Toby's convinced the permission's a formality,' said Cat, taken aback by Jess's sudden knowledge of building strategies. 'In the meantime, there's plenty for the builders to be getting on with.'

Privately Cat had her doubts, but Toby must know what he was doing. And if she couldn't rely on him, who could she turn to?

For such a slick operation, Glowbal was remarkably dependent on what looked worryingly like a bunch of cowboys who had only the faintest acquaintance with the lingua franca. When she voiced her concerns, however, Toby told her not to be so narrow minded. 'After all, it's not as if you had hundreds of builders with received pronunciation queuing up for the job. I don't recall you having any, actually.'

'Just one,' Cat reminded him. 'A highly recommended one.' She felt Toby was deliberately missing the point about the language problems.

'Recommended by Jake. And you know what architects are like with their backhanders. Vic was probably set to give Jake a cut.'

'Oh, for God's sake—' began Cat. It was hardly her chosen role in life to defend Jake, but she was beginning to find Toby's blithe assumptions that everyone was on the make depressing.

'Having to import blue-collar workers from eastern Europe is the price this country had to pay for full employment,' he continued breezily. 'Of course, no one will ever admit that a certain degree of unemployment is desirable – far too politically incorrect. But it's the truth. Anyway, don't worry. They may not speak English, but you can be assured they're excellent with their hands, so to speak.'

'I still think it's a risk to undertake hundreds of thousands of pounds of work when final planning permission is by no means a certainty,' she said.

'First rule of business – no risk, no gain.'

'That's what Napoleon said before he marched into Russia.'

'No it isn't.'

'Well, he should have.'

'Come on, McGinty, don't let the countryside turn you into a softie.'

In years to come, Cat decided, they'd all have a good laugh about rushing into their very own Millennium Dome project just because a beauty editor from an American fashion magazine had said she might drop by. They'd all sit round the Christmas table – if there was anywhere left to put one – slapping their thighs and splitting their sides about how Cat had panicked at the sight of all those builders. How she'd fretted over the lack of planning permission. How she'd worried about the lack of any suitable land managers, as a consequence of which she'd agreed, against every squealing instinct in her body, to take Declan on – on a trial-period basis only. Because in the event Millie van Peterson forgot to turn up.

'Are you *sure* she works on American *Vogue*?' Cat asked Suzette when it was clear beyond all hope that Millie would not be gracing

Butely after all. 'It's a bit flaky, isn't it?' It was difficult following a line of forensic questioning with all the banging going on next door.

'You know how these things go,' said Suzette vaguely.

Cat didn't and said as much.

'I'm sure she'll make it up to you,' said Suzette.

A large sheath of plaster dropped on to Cat's desk, dislodged by all the banging. By the time Cat had dusted herself down Suzette had rung off. Short of drowning herself the next time she had to go and review a flotation tank and donating her life insurance to Butely's builders' fund, Cat couldn't really see how Millie could ever make it up to them.

'I'm afraid it's the Quentin Crisp approach to housework,' Cat told Declan Kelly when he'd roared up again in his Golf GTi a week later, with just two Adidas bags. The rest of his stuff was coming later, he said. She led him up to what might very loosely have been called an open-plan studio flat above Sir Rodney's old garages in the hideous Long Building. It was open-plan without the planning. She couldn't really blame Declan for not seeming impressed. He had to contend with the rising motes that floated up from Daphne's Clay Expressions workshops and the low rumblings of the treatment rooms. 'Ugly fuckers, aren't they?' he said, casting a practised eye over the line-up of yogi portraits when Cat showed him the waiting area and treatment rooms.

'I think they're distinguished looking,' said Cat stiffly, wishing the yogis' bodies were a better advertisement for their chosen specialisation. Declan's face, which was now about as sunny as the Reverend Ian Paisley's, was starting to get on her nerves. She led him back to the flat, with its rickety single bed in the corner, a rather nasty olive velveteen sofa in the middle and at the far end a row of units that might have been called a kitchenette back in the days when electric kettles seemed the last word in science fiction. The flatlet hadn't been touched since Sir Rodney's last chauffeur had died in the early nineties, and for the past few weeks Caleb and Brian had been using it for storage. Still, he could have said something nice about the view.

'Well, I'll leave you to unpack.' Cat stepped over a sack of fertiliser and tried to look as though fifty kilos of garden compost were a desirable addition to any modern living space.

'Just one thing,' he said as she backed with unseemly haste down the steep staircase. Cat paused, certain he was going to ask her where the nearest pub was. But she was wrong.

'What's the area you'd most like help with?'

She looked up and saw concern etched over his sharp features. In the half-light she couldn't make out how genuine it was. The next few weeks were going to be interesting.

'Are you sure all this work's necessary?' Cat had psyched herself into a laid-back mood and was speaking to Goran as coolly as her fury allowed. Seemingly overnight, Butely had become swagged in scaffolding.

Goran shook his head sadly and unscrewed the top of his tea flask with painful slowness.

'You can keel me, reep out my leever and suck my blood if I'm wrong,' he said earnestly. 'But the breekwork is fucked. Is wet like tears, Cat. And so I theenk big problems come. You know about dry rot, I theenk?' Cat felt a stabbing pain in her temple. Vic hadn't said anything about dry rot. 'And after we deal with the rot,' continued Goran, 'we start on the roof.'

'But the roof definitely doesn't need work,' said Cat, remembering Vic's verdict. Where was Declan the one time she needed him?

Goran looked at her as if she'd plunged a dagger into his heart. 'Why you not trust me when I offer to bite off my own arm if I'm wrong?' he asked with a wounded expression.

She looked at him thoughtfully. Poetic inspiration struck Goran. 'And mash my eyeballs.'

Cat told him to leave his arm and eyeballs where they were and called Toby.

'Did you tell Goran to start on the roof?' she asked accusingly.

'Of course not. But if he says it needs doing at some stage, then it needs doing. It wouldn't surprise me in the least. I remember that roof going on. Jake was there too. Couldn't have been more than two. It must be a good thirty-five years ago.'

'But Vic said it was perfectly all right,' Cat persisted.

'Look, Cat, we can either do this the sensible way and stick with one reputable set of builders or drive ourselves insane listening to every Tom, Dick and Harry. Which is it to be?'

She had to admit Declan *looked* busy. He had already cultivated Guy Fulton and got him to mend some fences that had blown down a few weeks earlier, and he did seem to be getting the builders under control.

Meanwhile, it turned out that all the Friends of Butely whom Daphne and Cat had feared were dead were simply waiting for a half-price deal, which in view of all the building work Cat thought only reasonable. At the end of April a flurryette of fresh bookings were confirmed. Cat went to tell Daphne the good news. She found her kneeling by a row of glistening courgettes.

'Aren't they heavenly?' Daphne stood up, dusting the gravel from her lilac leggings. 'Oh, Cat, dear, isn't it wonderful to have an alternative to kale at last? And to think some of this was here all the time. Those boys are doing a marvellous job. And so handsome too. Terribly clever of you to find them.'

Cat smiled weakly. Notwithstanding the scaffolding, things did seem to be going suspiciously well, even if some evenings she was so tired she didn't even manage to sit through the first ten minutes of Hugh Fearnley-Whittingstall without dozing off. Lily looked up from a dictionary one day and asked her what it was like to be a control freak and Cat had almost wept.

It wasn't meant to be like this. When most people dropped out of the rat race they downsized. She'd taken on a stately can of worms – and for what?

'You're doing brilliantly,' Daphne kept telling her. 'And you were right about the pottery. Those darling boys from Clarence's loved it, especially the part when I make them throw the clay on the wheel. They've all booked another week in the winter. Gerald – that's the senior stockbroker – said he was going to throw a pot every time his wife overspent on the credit cards in future. He used to go out and crash his car instead, so I feel in some small way I'm contributing to the sum of human happiness.' She beamed contentedly. 'You know, I don't think I'll ever go back to Chalfont St Giles.'

A familiar growl reverberated up the drive. Toby. Cat's heart lurched despite everything. Daphne smiled indulgently. 'Your young man.' She groped for something else to add. 'Cat, don't you think you should go out a bit more?' she said carefully. 'Integrate yourself more into village life? That way you wouldn't be so disappointed when Toby doesn't make it down.'

Cat nodded disconsolately. It was funny; in London she'd been tickled by Toby's flashy tastes, but down here the Porsche and the Vuitton and the impeccable clothes looked faintly risible. Perhaps it was because they kept having professional disagreements, but she found herself constantly re-evaluating her feelings for him – and not always for the better. It was very disconcerting, because without Toby she wasn't exactly spoiled for choice when it came to adult company.

As usual, he swept her in his arms and kissed her hungrily. He was ridiculously good looking, even though he hadn't shaved, which wasn't like him at all, and he looked hollow eyed. The workload at Simms, now that she had gone, must finally be getting to him, thought Cat, all anger replaced by waves of sympathy – and a certain gratification.

She made him a Scotch on the rocks, ran him a bath, poured half the remains of some Floris in it and soaped his back. Then she watched him unpack in her room. Tonight was definitely the night. She no longer knew how she felt about that. But maybe sex would smooth over their differences. Reaching into his Vuitton weekend bag, he pulled out a small gift-wrapped parcel.

'You're damn tricky to buy for now you have your very own stately, Mistress Cat,' he said, placing the fuchsia package in her lap. It was as if he were conscious of needing to overcome her misgivings and thought he could buy her. Nervously she untied the silver ribbon. Inside a purple velvet box was a ravishing art deco

gold bangle, inscribed with the words: *'to thine own self be true'* –
Toby.

He tilted her head towards his and kissed her lightly on the lips.
'I may give you a hard time, but I do admire what you're trying to
do,' he said.

Cat was unbelievably touched. And she suddenly felt she understood why Toby was so tough on her sometimes – the clue was in
what he'd said about her being difficult to buy for now. He was a
bit jealous after all.

They didn't go to the Hung Drawn and Quartered. Instead
Micky had saved them some wild salmon with home-made pesto
and fresh compote.

'Bloody hell, McGinty,' said Toby, pouring them both some
champagne, 'this is delicious. When did Micky learn to cook?'

'He always could. He just needed some encouragement.' She
hoped Toby got the message. She could manage Butely her own
way.

Now that the evenings were becoming balmier, they could
snuggle up on the hugh leather chesterfield in Sir Rodney's
drawing room. It was all the more blissful because Declan had
chosen to spend the weekend in London. She wrinkled her nose
when Toby asked how it was going with him.

She felt him tensing next to her. 'Give it time. You're bound to
find it difficult to adapt at first.'

Neat appropriation of blame, thought Cat, toying with the
bangle on her wrist.

'Let's face it, he's got more experience with builders than you
have.'

'So he says.'

'Okay, my little freak.' He kissed the top of her head. 'I thought
you'd be pleased to have some of the workload shifted. You've got
enough on your plate what with the shop, the kitchen and drumming up some bookings.'

'Actually the bookings are going quite well. We've had a lot of
interest – it's very encouraging.'

'She felt him stiffen again. 'Any news on the docu-crew?'

Her hand flew to her mouth. Shit – she'd forgotten to reply to the e-mail Orlando Vespers had sent her suggesting a start date. She'd never hear the end of it if it turned out she'd let all that free advertising run through her fingers. 'It's all in hand,' she lied.

They watched the fire in silence for a few moments.

'How's Lily?'

'She's fine. And she's thrilled with Archie. Jake's teaching her to ride.' He didn't reply. 'I'm still worried about the Glowbal plans,' continued Cat. 'The revised drawings they sent me seem just as overblown as the first lot.'

'Are you sure you're looking at them the right way up?'

Cat pulled a face. 'Sorry,' he said. 'Pathetic, sexist cheap shot. But you said yourself that reading maps and things isn't your strong point. Look, why don't you show them to me tomorrow and we can go through them together.'

'Fine. They're at Jake's,' she said evenly. 'I'll pop round and fetch them in the morning.'

'So you gave them to him after all. Despite our discussion.'

'Yes, I gave them to him. Because if we don't get someone sensible on the case we'll never get them past the council.' '*To thine own self be true.*'

'I've told you, my mother has brilliant contacts. The council are an irrelevancy.'

'I dare say Jake might have a different perspective on things.'

'What's the lavatory attendant got to do with it? Oh, sorry, I forgot his brilliant track record in business. Jake couldn't even organise his pocket money properly.'

'Whereas you probably had a Lloyd's syndicate going aged six.'

'How did you know?' He grinned and held out his arms in a conciliatory gesture. '*To thine own self be true.*'

'And for another—'

'Yes?' He threw her a sardonic smile. She thought of Jake's dogged belief that price wasn't the only motivating factor in life.

'Not everyone and everything can be bought.'

'Oh, please, McGinty. I suppose Toilet Man, who's never actually had to do an honest day's work in his life, told you that.'

She didn't reply.

'Is that why you're letting everyone get away with paying half their bills?' he said sharply.

'You can hardly expect them to pay the full whack with all this turmoil going on.'

'In that case, why don't you just close the place down for the duration of the building work? It would make progress a lot faster. And then you could do the thing properly when you reopened.'

She looked at him in astonishment. 'But I've just told you, we're getting more enquiries than at any time in the past few years. And there's no way we could survive financially if we closed down for a few months. Besides, there are patients relying on us to stay open.'

'But that's just it, Cat.' His voice rose slightly. 'They're not fucking patients. They're customers. And the sooner you start thinking of them like that, the better.'

'And what if I don't?' She felt the temperature in the room plummet despite the fire.

'Then the whole bloody enterprise will go down.'

'I happen to disagree. I think there's a middle way.'

'You sound like Tony Blair.' He grinned and moved towards her but she ducked away. 'Cat,' he remonstrated. 'Actually there may be yet another way. One devoid of all this stress and . . . nonsense.'

'What do you mean?' He ruffled her hair. She walked away towards the window. Toby was such a force of nature it was hard resisting his charm, but she couldn't keep letting him get away with things.

'Look,' he said eventually, 'have you ever considered that there might be other ways to make money out of Butely?'

'Like turning it into an extension of the M3, you mean.'

'No . . .' He sat down, still following her with that forensic gaze. 'I've reason to believe there's been geological exploration in the area.'

'And how would you know that?' She tried to keep her tone light. She knew she was sunk if she lost her temper.

He pressed the tip of his nose with his little finger. His eyes raked her up and down, as they had the first day she'd met him, but this time he wasn't simply undressing her, he seemed to be trying to strip the layers of her skin. 'It's hush-hush. Let's just say the Scottish project is linked to government work and—'

'Let me guess. Butely's sitting on a secret spring of the purest water in the world? As a matter of fact I have thought of it . . .'

'Have you, now?' He sounded genial again.

'And as far as I'm concerned we've got enough on our plates until we've sorted out the clinic side of things.'

'But that's what I'm saying – we might not have to. We could be sitting on a potential gold mine. I'm not saying anything for certain, but it would at least be worth checking it out, surely. Then we could knock this healing of the old biddies on the head.'

Cat looked at him in dismay. He didn't sound as though he was joking. 'But that would be a total betrayal of Sir Rodney.'

'Oh, for God's sake—'

'And of the people who depend on Butely.'

He threw back his head and snorted. 'Christ, Cat, don't tell me you actually believe this crap works?'

'Of course I believe it works. Do you think I could run this place if I didn't?'

'I thought you were just trying to be a good businesswoman.'

She wouldn't even begin to count the number of insults in that statement. Instead she'd try to score some points of her own, although she knew better than to appeal to his morality.

'Even if I wanted to dump the biddies, as you put it, I couldn't just change Butely. There's Jake, in case you'd forgotten. Like it or not, Toby, he owns half of Butely.'

'Why shouldn't I like it?' He gave a sour laugh but she could tell from his flushed cheeks that he was livid. 'Do you honestly think I'd want to be saddled with this?'

'I thought that's exactly what you wanted,' she said quietly.

He tried to rein in his anger. 'And I do. Come on, Cat.' He held out his arms again. 'Let's not fight about this.'

But something in his voice when he'd dismissed Butely a few moments earlier had Cat's self-protective radar on full alert. Her heart pounded. If he hadn't meant what he'd told her all those months ago when they'd stood in the deserted grounds of Butely and he'd persuaded her to move down here, then how could she trust anything he'd said?

'Perhaps you'd better leave me to get on with it on my own.'

'Don't be so childish, Cat –' he held out his arms again. 'I love you.' Her breath caught in her chest. She wanted to believe him. She looked at his twinkling eyes and felt her legs sway. Was this her instinct telling her to go to him? 'Anyway,' he continued jovially, 'you wouldn't be on your own. You'd have Declan.'

'I'm still not convinced he's necessary. If we didn't have to fork out for his salary then you wouldn't have to worry about some of the patients paying reduced fees.'

'We can't get rid of him. Not for at least six month anyway. I agreed to pay him up front.' He shrugged. 'It was the only way I could get anyone to agree to take the job.'

Cat looked at him aghast. 'You did what! How could you? And without consulting me?'

'You had other things on your mind. Don't worry, I borrowed the money on exceptionally favourable terms.' He smiled. Cat was livid. She'd never heard of a job offer like it. What had become of Toby's notorious hard bargaining? 'The real person you need to jettison is Samantha,' he continued blithely.

'On the grounds that she's brilliant at what she does?' said Cat coldly.

'Oh, come on, Cat, she hardly looks the part, does she?'

'She happens to be extremely dedicated. She's even talking about taking a course in iridology.'

He rolled his eyes. 'Oh, really. Well, the world's huddled, crippled masses can all breathe easier tonight in that case, can't they?' He shot her a look of withering disdain. 'And she's bloody rude. Totally lost her rag with me the other day after I wrote to give her a formal warning.'

'Did you just say what I think you said?' She was so angry she thought her fists would seize up. No wonder Samantha had been acting so strangely lately.

'Got to go through the motions of three warnings, you know that, Cat.'

'Without consulting me, once again?'

'I thought we were as one on this?'

'We don't appear to be at one on anything just at the moment,' she said, struggling to stay calm. 'At this moment I've probably got more in common with Jake's view of Butely than yours.'

'Jesus Christ, I might have known you too would be thick as thieves.'

'Hardly. He's as bloody difficult as you are. But that doesn't mean his views aren't valid. What is your problem with him?'

'I don't have a problem with him,' said Toby, his voice rising. 'But I can see you do. Don't tell me he's been shoring up your ego where Declan so clearly failed. You'd be just Jake's type, actually. If he had the balls to have a type. And you probably find him the romantic brooding sort. That would fit in with your little-girl-lost complex perfectly, wouldn't it? Not that you actually want to fuck anyone, as far as I can see.'

Cat felt the bile rising in her gorge. 'I'm not the one who has to go running every time my mother clicks her little finger. She's the one with the complex, not me.'

He slammed his glass on the table so hard it shattered.

'What's the matter, Toby? Can't you stand that he's Sir Rodney's son and not you?'

Toby looked at her with something close to hatred in his eyes. Cat knew she had gone too far. He pushed past her roughly and stomped upstairs. Moments later she heard him come down again and head for the front door. He was carrying his Vuitton case.

'Where are you going?' She tried to keep the mounting panic out of her voice.

'Good luck, Cat.'

He couldn't really be leaving. Not like this. Remorse clutched at her conscience. But she was damned if she was going to call him back. Especially when he had been so completely out of order with Samantha.

He leaned out of the Porsche window. 'Do it your way. I dare say at the eleventh hour you'll come up with one of your super slogans and save the day. How about "Can't pay, won't pay"? You'll need to keep me informed, of course. But you do at least know how to operate e-mail. We can reconvene at the next trustees' meeting in the autumn. By which time, no doubt, you'll have turned the place around.'

With that he roared off. Cat was so angry she couldn't even register shock.

An hour or so later she realised the phone had been ringing next to her for some time. As if in a dream she picked it up, hoping it was Toby from the motorway.

It was Jake. 'I've been looking at the plans and you're right – they're completely overbearing.'

She didn't answer.

'Are you all right?'

'Fine. Never better.'

'So I'm going to do some new ones.'

'Thank you, that's kind.'

'If you still think it's a good idea.' There was no response. He sounded a little put out at her lack of enthusiasm.

'I can see now that we have to have a pool and gym,' began Cat. She looked up through the mullioned windows at the sickle moon outside and tried to marshal her thoughts from the tangled mess of emotions. 'We know that lots of our former patients have been going abroad because they can get cheaper, more luxurious pack-ages. So we're obviously going to have to do something. I was naive to think otherwise.' That didn't mean she was going to fall in slavishly with Toby. 'But I can also see it needs to be done sensitively.'

'Have you discussed all this with Toby?' He sounded suspicious.

'In a manner of speaking,' said Cat wearily. 'But frankly it's up to us.'

'I abdicated any rights to veto decisions when I went to New Zealand.'

She was struck by the impact of his bitterness. She could

understand it if he hated her. She just wished he had the courage to get to know her properly.

'Jake?'

'What?'

'Nothing.' She felt angry and lonely and betrayed – and most of all humiliated by her own stupid lack of judgement. She wanted someone to comfort her. But she knew he was the wrong person to do that. She put the phone down and crawled up to bed, wondering how she could have misjudged yet another man so badly.

16

Cat had no illusions that Toby would return. She'd felt the chill winds of his anger, and something else – something that felt ominously like contempt – blast over her, and she felt more desolate than she had in a long time.

Now that he wasn't coming back she realised how lonely she was. Daphne, fond though Cat was of her, could hardly fill the emotional void in her life. And Jess's packed yoga classes had opened up a whole new network of potential friends that left almost no time for Cat.

At least Lily seemed amazingly resilient about the whole thing, but there was Archie, her pony, to think about. Toby had said he'd pay for the creature's upkeep. Now what? She could hardly apply for pony alimony.

It took her several days to win Samantha round and convince her she had never had any intention of sacking her. Naturally she couldn't sleep. She stayed up all night swotting her way through the piles of reference books Dr Anjit had lent her, or pacing around the house. When the creaking got too loud she transferred to the grounds. But it wasn't that warm outside, so she ended up dragging on the red coat that Toby had bought her, which only made her feel more miserable. Her main consolation was that while her life was going down the tubes, Lily was proving a big hit at school, thanks to a wise decision to invite her whole class to come round and groom and tack up Archie whenever they wanted.

It was just as well, Vic Spinoza explained cheerfully to Cat when he came to pick Marina up from tea with Lily one day in his Transit van. 'Otherwise the little yobs would have had a field day with her.'

'What do you mean?' asked Cat with a sense of foreboding. She was still feeling awkward about dispensing with Vic's building skills. Not that he seemed to bear her a grudge.

'Oh, you know. New city girl, with a posh London accent and everything.'

Hardly posh, reflected Cat. Then again when you had as broad a West Country twang as Vic everything probably sounded posh. He was a nice man – couldn't be more than forty. Ideal male companionship really. But – Cat closed her eyes – she couldn't ever take a man whose accent was about as sexy as a scrumpy ad seriously.

Fortunately Vic wasn't a mind-reader. 'They tied the last townie to a tree,' he continued jovially, 'and pelted him with cow pats. He got sent to a private school not long after that. After he'd had some counselling. But Lily's a survivor. Like her mum.'

Cat smiled faintly. She didn't feel much like a survivor. She added Horrible Person Who Allows Something as Superficial as a Scrumpy ad Accent Get in the Way of Friendship to her list of Personal Shortcomings. There were plenty of other gripes on that particular list. Such as the way she'd been drooping around Butely trying to look like the kind of rounded person who didn't need sixty-hour weeks in order to feel fulfilled.

Meanwhile Declan Kelly goose-stepped around the place as if he owned it. Cat watched from behind her laptop while a removal van decanted a super-king-size bed, a flat-screen television, a cappuccino maker and a huge white sheepskin rug.

'Feral,' observed Jess. 'Just look at that tasselled sofa.'

'Actually that belonged to Sir Rodney's last chauffeur. It's leaving,' shouted Cat above the drilling that had just begun above their heads. 'I think you'll find that thing that looks like an articulated cushion is Declan's seating.'

'Anyone who thinks that zodiac wall charts are suitable adult decor deserves all they get,' opined Jess. 'I bet he goes up to girls in nightclubs and tries to guess their star signs. Have you noticed how he's always feeling his balls?'

Cat still had reservations about Declan. There was something sly about him. But she couldn't sack him before he'd really started. It would be round the village within an hour and before she knew it she'd be a laughing stock. She'd have to give him the benefit of the doubt – and by extension Toby.

'It's quite funny, really,' chortled Jess as a framed poster of Elizabeth Hurley emerged from the van.

Cat was having a very hard time seeing the joke.

'When was the last time you saw Toby?' asked Daphne gently.

'Three weeks ago.' Cat looked into Daphne's lilac-orbited eyes for signs of disapproval but saw only sympathy.

'I'm being pathetic, aren't I?'

'I was distraught after one of my husbands died. Can't remember which one now. Didn't bother after that.'

'Didn't bother what?'

'Getting involved with anyone.'

'But you still remarried.'

'Financial necessity. I couldn't be a Bluebell for ever. But your generation has a choice. You can be on your own, have a child, scale the career heights . . .' It sounded brilliant the way Daphne put it. 'And you're going to make it work,' she continued. 'Now why don't we have a small Bailey's?'

She whipped out her hip flask from the inside of her tracksuit and poured them each a small warm glass. Cat knocked it back. Ever since her row with Toby she'd been surviving on a mind-bending cocktail of adrenalin, chaotic eating and the odd mercy shot from Daphne. No wonder she'd crashed into a dark depression. And on top of everything Goran and the other builders seemed to be drilling day and night until she felt her head would explode.

'At least you're proving you can manage without him professionally. The way you're juggling all those men'– Daphne cocked an eyebrow in the direction of a group of builders who were sitting outside in the sun doing their own share of juggling – with sandwiches and copies of the *Sun* – 'is marvellous. Butely's going to be a paradise when they've moved out.'

'I wish I had your optimism,' yelled Cat above the blare of

Radio 1. 'But at the moment the only people who'd find Butely a paradise would have to be profoundly deaf.'

She would have to do something about the banging, if only to prove to Declan that she too could deal with the builders. Braced by the Bailey's, she marched over to the men, whose ranks had swelled now that it was vaguely lunchtime.

Goran, the foreman, an oiled compression of lean tissue in fake Tommy Hilfiger jeans, stood up with exaggerated courtesy as she approached. By now there was a little circle of sweaty muscles in hard hats around her. It was like being at the centre of a rancid sunflower.

'Hello, everyone.' She nodded at them in a graciously assertive manner. 'Goran, I feel we need to discuss the volume levels.'

Goran's eyebrows met in one long slug of confusion. Then, as if he'd just hit on Fermat's Last Theorem, a shaft of understanding flickered in his eyes. 'Ah, yes,' he said, 'you weesh to discuss noise.' There was another pained pause. 'What is there to discuss, please?' The other builders looked up from page three.

'It's too much,' explained Cat, sensing their stares. She soldiered on. 'The guests are complaining. We're going to have to find a way of staggering the work. I've made a list.' She plucked her Palm Pilot from her pocket. 'I'd like to suggest that you confine the drilling to between two and four in the afternoon, when we get most of the patients out on a walk. At eleven, after breakfast, you can make progress on the corridors outside the library, the dining room and the drawing room. And immediately after lunch, when they're napping, you can proceed with a little light carpentry in the library and Circular Bedchamber.'

Goran scratched his head slowly. A pained expression crossed his eyes. 'I am so very sorry, Mees Cat, but if we followed thees, we would never finish. Noise,' he continued sadly, 'is what we make.' He threw his arms expansively wide to embrace his brethren in the building profession. 'We are builders.' The others nodded in sorrowful agreement. 'But I promise we weell do what we can. You can smite my head and scoop out my brains if there ees no improvement.'

Cat waited a few moments to ensure he'd finished before trudging back to her study, unsure whether she'd scored a massive victory against builders everywhere, or whether Goran would turn out to be an elaborate practical joke – a strippergram? – organised by her mother as an early birthday present.

'Do any good, does it?' Declan brought his Golf alongside Jess and eyed her breasts as if they were an interesting new breed in the *Racing Times*. 'Going for the burn, I mean?'

Jess, already inflamed by the exertions of a four-mile jog, flushed a dangerous shade of beige and ignored him. No one had gone for the burn since Jane Fonda twenty years ago.

'Bit hot, isn't it?' Declan smirked at her. If he leant any farther through the window he'd topple out. 'Just wait till we get the swimming pool finished.'

'I don't like swimming pools,' she panted primly. 'Chlorine is rank.'

'Well, this one's got ozone in it.'

Jess had never actually been in ozone. The wave pool in Kilburn was more your snot, gob and pee variety. 'What do you know about it?' she asked suspiciously.

'This and that. I keep my ears and eyes open. Like you do, Jess.'

'What do you mean?'

'Blimey, you ladies are all a bit touchy round here, aren't you? Is it something they put in the water or what? All I meant was that you seem like a bright girl to me. Got your finger on the pulse. I've seen you in the Hung Drawn and Quartered, putting it out a bit. You've got in with the locals – not like Lady La-di-da. It'll stand you in good stead. Mark my words, Jess. I think you've played a clever hand.'

'It's got nothing to do with clever,' said Jess, slowing down despite herself. 'I'd go mad if I never went out, that's all. And Cat's not la-di-da, as you put it. She's just very busy.'

'Oh, yeah. Don't get me wrong,' said Declan, lighting up an Embassy. 'I've got a lot of time for Cat.'

'Really?' Jess stopped jogging and began flexing her hamstrings. Declan's eyes raced up and down her pale, freckly legs.

'Yeah. Any lady who can keep this pile going deserves respect.'

Jess couldn't tell whether he was being facetious, but she decided to give him the benefit of the doubt.

'I don't s'pose you'd let me buy you a drink one night?'

'No thank you,' said Jess haughtily.

'Don't be like that.' His eyes slithered from her legs to her breasts again. 'No strings – not that I wouldn't like there to be. It's just that I could do with some company. It's a bit tough being the new boy round here.'

She looked up at him. He'd shaved off his sideburns and his hair didn't look quite so much like Austin Powers' any more. He sounded quite lonely.

'Jump in?' He patted the seat next to him.

She shook her head. 'Hardly worth it.'

He pulled a face and pretended to cry. She took pity on him. 'But you can buy me a drink – non-alcoholic.'

He grinned. 'Knew you'd see sense.' He put his foot down and squealed off. Jess grinned too. With repartee like that, he had to have a sense of humour.

'Cat, are you there? Cat?'

Cat sighed. Every time she picked up the phone hoping to hear Toby and found it was someone else, a bit more of her died. This time she didn't even have to wait for the person to speak to know it wasn't him. She recognised the wheezing.

'Hello, Herr Frupps. How are you?' She flopped down on the chesterfield cradling a glass of Château Margaux from under the stairs. She envisaged a long call.

'Terrible.' He shuddered. 'She doesn't understand me, Cat. I am so alone. I am having everything – and nothing. Life vith money and no love is no life at all.'

Cat sighed. He ought to try life without love *or* money. She took a swig of the Margaux. 'I understand that, Villie. Perhaps you need a new project.'

'No, no.' He was cut down by a coughing fit. 'I need love,' he wheedled, when he'd recovered. 'And Lotte needs to lose about eight of your stones. I have begged her to come to your Butely, but she is too embarrassed.'

'Oh, she shouldn't be,' began Cat, then stopped herself. It was wicked and selfish probably, but she couldn't deal with Lotte Frupps's all-enveloping gloom on top of her own.

It was forty minutes later when she finally got rid of Villie, neither of them any the happier, though Cat at least got some sleep. It was just gone midnight when she was woken, stiff and cold on the chesterfield, by the sound of Declan's Golf tearing up the gravel accompanied by a lusty roar of its exhausted exhaust pipe. She padded to the window and watched aghast as Jess and Declan fell out of the Golf, accompanied by peals of laughter and mock scuffling. Declan weaved his way to the boot, from where he pulled out a bottle of champagne, with a magician's flourish.

'For the ninetieth time, Declan,' she heard Jess drawl, 'I don't drink.'

'Who said anything about drinking?'

Cat watched Declan shake the bottle up and down before spraying it over both of them, whereupon they both collapsed in hysterical laughter.

There hadn't been a bigger betrayal since Brutus, decided Cat, absolutely livid. Nothing Jess could say or do made things better. 'It's not like I'm madly in love with him, Cat,' she pointed out the next day when Cat asked her how she could bear to let Declan anywhere near her. 'We just had a bit of a laugh. He's bloody good fun once you get to know him a bit.'

'That's what people with the clap say about syphilis – when they're completely delirious,' grumbled Cat. She was overreacting about Declan and she knew it, but she felt utterly isolated. Even Jake had left a note saying he had to go to a conference on global energy-saving for a few days. And Toby was right; he hadn't finished the pool plans on time.

'Have you considered volunteering to do something for the village fête, dear?' suggested Daphne, who had been deputed by Samantha and Micky to get Cat off their backs. 'Edna Potts is organising it, as usual. But don't let that put you off. Cynthia Dowell will take all the glory, I dare say. She usually does.'

'Do you know Cynthia well, then?' asked Cat idly.

'Known her for centuries.' How old exactly was Cynthia, wondered Cat. She couldn't be as ancient as Daphne. No plastic surgeon was that good. 'Ever since we were both Rank starlets,' continued Daphne. 'She denies it, of course. Not surprising when you consider that she slept her way through most of London – after I'd got there first, I'm glad to say. And she's still up to her old tricks. Did you notice how she suddenly started wafting around Butely once those lovely men from Clarence's were here?' Cat couldn't say she had. 'Obviously she's pretending she's recruiting for the village fête,' continued Daphne darkly. 'But Cynthia always could sniff out a healthy wallet at fifty paces. And I fear poor darling Gerald was a sitting duck. Apparently it's all round the village.'

'I thought Gerald had worked out a *modus vivendi* with his wife by throwing pots.'

'So did I,' said Daphne heatedly. 'But that's Cynthia all over. Marriage wrecker!'

'Poor Jake,' said Cat. His mother's nymphomaniac tendencies were starting to make Catherine the Great look virginal.

'Poor Jake indeed.' Daphne eyed her slyly. 'Actually, I didn't think you two had hit it off particularly.'

'Is it that obvious?'

'Whenever you talk to him you look like you're being compelled to donate a kidney.'

Cat winced. 'He is a bit . . . fierce.'

'So are you, darling. Not that I don't think it's marvellous, but you can see that someone like Jake wouldn't necessarily know what to make of it.'

'What do you mean, someone like Jake?'

'I don't know. Just that he's very special – a genetic miracle really, considering his mother. Kind, funny, generous.'

Cat felt she could justifiably take issue with all of those, but she didn't want to alienate Daphne as well. Since Cat had tackled Jess about Declan things had become very frosty between them. This morning they had hardly exchanged a word.

'I grant you he can seem a bit aloof sometimes,' continued Daphne. 'But it's shyness. And then there's the way his father died and that ridiculous will . . . oh, I'm sorry, dear. I didn't mean it like that. But you can see how it must seem to Jake.'

'Yes. I can. I do. But he's so damn prickly.' And he still hadn't got back to her with his new pool plans.

'Pots, kettles and black, darling,'muttered Daphne, pootling off towards her Clay Expressions class. 'Don't forget,' she called back, 'what I said about the fête. It's Lower Nettlescombe's millennium anniversary. It's going to be massive – bigger than Glastonbury.'

Cat stared after her small receding figure in shock. Pots, kettles and black indeed. Unlike Jake, at least she met her deadlines.

Jake's ears must have been burning. That night he called Cat to apologise for dashing away and to tell her he'd finished the plans. 'I could pop them round tonight,' he suggested. 'I want you to see them as soon as possible. I hope you don't mind but I've already dropped them off with Barry Dean. An acquaintance of mine on the council. There didn't seem much point in presenting Glowbal with a new set of plans if they didn't stand a reasonably strong chance of being approved by the council. Of course, anything you want to change we can,' he added hastily. 'But getting them on board early is crucial.'

'And what does Barry Dean think of them?' asked Cat. She was bemused by Jake's sudden burst of initiative.

'These things are never a foregone conclusion. But I'm reasonably confident. So shall I bring them round?'

Cat looked down at the unravelling hem of her tracksuit and felt exhausted. She certainly didn't feel up to providing the hospitality that Jake was entitled to expect if he dropped in with some plans that had taken him days to work on. 'That's very kind. But could it wait till tomorrow morning? I could meet you by Hangman's Stile on the way back from school.'

'Okay.' Did she imagine it or did he sound just a touch deflated? 'Hangman's Stile it is.'

'Oh, look at that.' Cat pointed at a flotilla of small white sails scudding out on a blazing blue sea towards the horizon and squinted up at Jake. His hair had grown a bit, and now that it was brushed behind his ears he somehow looked less volcanic and more tractable. 'On days like this, I wouldn't trade that view for anything.'

'Unfortunately not everyone agrees.'

'Look how beautiful those oaks are.'

'Beeches. Listen, shall we look at these over a coffee in the Hung Drawn and Quartered? Or kir royale if you prefer.'

'Coffee will be fine, thank you. I thought you'd never ask.'

Strolling up Butely Lane next to Jake gave Cat a fresh perspective on village life. He knew everyone and everyone seemed to have a friendly word to say. 'Morning, Jake. Have you signed up?' shouted Mrs Potts.

'What for?' muttered Cat.

'I'm not entirely sure,' said Jake. 'But I'd put money on it having something to do with Lower Nettlescombe's millennium anniversary.'

'Fête worse than death, then?'

He rolled his eyes at her feeble joke, but at least he didn't actively snarl. He may even have twinkled a bit.

'What do you suggest, Mrs P?'

'Pony rides.' She unlocked the door to the Spar before sweeping her eyes over Cat as if seeing her for the first time. 'That's what you usually do.'

'Fair enough.' He took Cat's arm and led her into the Spar

behind Mrs Potts, who flicked on the fluorescent lighting and groped around the counter for her clipboard.

'Here it is,' she said eventually. 'Just fill your name in there, Jake.' She turned to Cat. 'Now, Miss, er . . . Can I help you?'

'Yes,' said Cat, seized with inspiration. 'I'd like to volunteer for something.'

'Really.' Mrs Potts peered at her lugubriously.

'How about face painting?' suggested Cat, thinking of her flake ad.

'Not much call for that round here, whatever *that* is when it's at home. But if you think it's a good idea, dear . . .' She shoved the clipboard towards Cat.

'When's the work starting, Mrs P?' asked Jake.

'Any minute,' said Mrs Potts disapprovingly. 'Though why Mark Wainwright wants to chuck his money away when the place is perfectly fine as it is beats me.'

They simultaneously cast their eyes round the relentlessly dismal cheer of the Spar. There was a silence in which Cat could have sworn she saw Jake smile.

'I'm sure it will all be worth it, Mrs P,' said Jake as he opened the door for Cat.

'It's like living in Docklands,' muttered Cat, 'the amount of building and upwardly mobile shuffling that's going on right now.'

'I see you've finally whipped off those baggy cords, Jake,' purred Lucy Wainwright, as they emerged from the shop. 'Summer must be coming. Long may it reign.'

'Isn't it idyllic?' exclaimed Cat, running her eye along the higgledy-piggledy thatched cottages lining the lane and stopping on the little bridge that spanned the River Piddle. 'Smell these lupins – heaven.'

'Foxgloves,' corrected Jake.

She braced herself for a lecture. But he was grinning. She realised she knew remarkably little about Jake's interior life. She'd more or less decided he didn't have one. But he must have. Everyone did.

*

'I've volunteered to do the face painting at the village fête,' said Cat proudly when she ran into Daphne, who was just on her way to Clay Expressions.

'Is that wise, dear?'

'Of course it is. I used to be quite good at art.'

'I don't mean that, dear. But have you met some of the children round here?'

'No. I don't know their parents either, apart from Vic. And that's precisely why I want to take part in the thousandth anniversary of Lower Nettlescombe. There's going to be jousting, minstrels, a falconry display. I thought you'd be pleased. You're the one who said I should throw myself into the community.'

'Little shits, some of them,' said Daphne, throwing the entire featherweight of her frame against the door to the workshop, which was warped and difficult to open.

'Aren't you taking part, then?'

'I shall be fortune-telling as usual. But I don't know why I bother. It's all for the greater good of Queen Cynthia, as far as I can see.'

'What's the matter, Daphne? You were all for it yesterday.'

'That's before I knew things had got serious with Gerald.'

'Gerald?'

'The stockbroker from Clarence's. He's threatening to leave his wife for Cynthia. Not that she'll want that. It's all about the chase with her. She's like a praying mantis.'

'I see. Oh dear. Do you think I should resign from doing the face painting in protest against her low morals?'

'Certainly not. If you like I could try and get you on the rota for the bring-and-buy. Most of it comes from Cynthia, and those helping out on the stall get first dibs. I got a brand-new Dior skirt last year for five pounds.'

A large lorry drew up outside the Long Building just as Declan emerged from his shag-pad to supervise its parking. Intrigued, Cat and Daphne watched as two dozen propane heaters and two dozen multi-storey cages were unloaded into the deserted garage next to Daphne's workshop.

Cat marched over to Declan. 'What's going on?'

'Just a new hobby of mine,' said Declan chirpily. 'I'm going to be breeding pheasants.'

'Is gassing the new polo, then?'

Declan looked hurt. 'These heaters are to keep them at the right temperature. I reckon this could be a nice earner. It proved very profitable when I did it in Berkshire. A lot more profitable than organic veg, anyway.'

'That's very interesting, Declan. The only problem is that I don't recall us ever having had a conversation about this.'

'I didn't want to bother you, Toby said there was no need to pester you about estate matters.'

Cat wondered how long he'd been having discussions with Toby behind her back. 'Not bother me?' she repeated incredulously.

'That's right.'

'Are you a complete moron?' she fulminated. 'In case you'd forgotten, I'm in charge here – and I pay your wages, by the way. Of course you have to consult me on everything.'

Declan rolled his shoulders and jutted his jaw. When his voice finally emerged it was an outraged sliver of its former self. 'I'm not used to being talked to like that, Cat. I won't pretend I'm not shocked. But I don't hold with hitting birds, so if you'll excuse me I'll just go and calm down.'

'Just twisting their necks,' called Cat as he strode towards his Golf. 'Which is the only way you're ever going to pull one,' she continued under her breath.

Declan turned round with an air of martyred sanctity. 'You're a very difficult lady, Cat.'

'And you're an idiot,' she yelled as he reversed past her. 'Breeding pheasants and organising shoots is just about the worst idea since someone on the *Titanic* suggested going the scenic route past some icebergs.'

Something inside her had snapped. And something or someone seemed to be tapping on her shoulder. Either that or a bird had just shat on her. She swung round angrily, ready to do battle with the pheasant deliverers, or Jess or Goran or any of the other people sent to try her patience. She found herself eyeballing an earnest-looking face in thick black NHS glasses that may or may not have been a post-modern parody.

'Sorry to bother you, but I'm looking for Cat McGinty.'

Her first instinct was to lie, but Declan was already smirking through the windscreen.

'You've found her,' said Cat, attempting to sound serene and in control. 'And you are?'

'Orlando Vespers.' He held out a trembling hand. 'Rigor Mortis Productions.'

Cat looked at him blankly and he backed away a little, towards a car containing three other equally earnest-looking people, at least two of whom were also wearing thick spectacles.

'The docu-crew?' continued Orlando helpfully. 'You did say the fourteenth, didn't you?'

Four days after Orlando's arrival, she heard the phone ringing downstairs in her study. She had no idea what time it was. She was aware only that there was almost a full moon and that a stillness had fallen over the whole of Butely. At first she thought it was Villie again. Then she thought it might be Toby, desperate for a reconciliation. Then, as the old-fashioned ringing tone persisted, echoing round the Cottage like something out of an amateur production of *Dial M for Murder*, she decided it must be a wrong number, and turned over to ignore it. But it continued. Eventually she shrugged on a dressing gown – even in May, internally Butely operated its own chilly micro-climate – and tiptoed downstairs. There was no need for a light – the moon was bright enough. Slowly she picked up the receiver, watching the fir trees dance gently in the breeze outside and hoping whoever was calling would have lost patience by the time she said hello.

'Bitch!'

Cat took a deep breath. Something was wrong here. Wasn't she the one meant to be furious at being woken at – she glanced at the silver engraved carriage clock – 3.30 in the morning?

'Your plans for Butely are making you a lot of enemies.' The voice was muffled, probably by a handkerchief. It sounded male.

Or possibly female. 'You think you can get away with messing around with our heritage and ruining our future? But you can't.'

Cat wanted to point out that the two didn't necessarily go hand in hand, but she didn't have a chance. At the very least she felt entitled to know which plans in particular her caller objected to. Whoever it was needed to be more specific. On the other hand, telling them this might look like encouragement. 'What plans?'

'What plans?' the voice echoed bitterly. 'You're wrecking the fabric of our village. Not to mention the balance of the environment.'

An eco-warrior, then. Probably a fifth-former from the local comp. 'Oh, don't be so melodramatic. I'm just taking down a few useless walls and tidying up the facilities . . .'

Bad choice, facilities. It smacked of town planning euphemisms. It was like talking about improving traffic flows when you were secretly planning a sixteen-lane motorway, or referring to pee-drenched subways as atmospheric catacombs. But she was still half asleep.

'Don't fuck with us, Cat McGinty.' It didn't sound like a fifth-former now. 'We know where you live. We know your routine. So back off and there won't be any problems.'

She put the phone down shakily and went back to bed, where she tossed and turned until morning.

17

'Okay, what we need, Cat, is for you all to look as natural as possible.'

This *is* natural.' Jess poked her head round one of the sheets hanging from the washing line over the Aga.

'Yes,' Orlando explained patiently, 'but the thing is we can't actually see any of you behind the sheets.'

'So you want us to take them down?'

'That would be helpful, yes.'

'But they're not dry. And anyway, if we take them down it won't look natural.'

'It's true. We always have sheets drying,' said Lily. 'In London they didn't exactly dry, though, because the heating usually wasn't working. But that was because of Ralph.'

Orlando looked at Cat for support. She shrugged helplessly. '*Cinéma-vérité*, Orlando. That's what it's all about.' She hadn't wanted this damn TV crew in the first place.

'Ah, yes, exactly, Cat. I'm glad you brought up the cinema aspect because, as you know, truth is a relative term, particularly cinematic truth.' He pushed his glasses, which were in danger of sliding off, up his nose.

'Cinematic truth is a downright lie, then, in other words?' said Jess.

'Do you think that when you see documentaries on the royal family and film stars they've edited out sheets and underwear, then?' asked Lily.

'You did say this could all be carried out with the minimum of disturbance,' said Cat.

'Yeah,' said Jess, wondering why she was agreeing with Cat. She was mortally offended by the way Cat had had the temerity to complain about her going on a date with Declan – especially in view of the pitiful way Cat conducted her own love life. But it was too late to change tack now. Anyway, since Orlando hadn't flirted with her once since his arrival she wasn't predisposed to be obliging on his behalf. 'I don't suppose Steven Spielberg would find a sheet an insurmountable obstacle.'

'I think you'll find Steven Spielberg's scouts would have removed all sheets to begin with,' said Cat, enjoying Orlando's discomfort. Two days after the abusive phone call she was still feeling shaky and she seized the chance to get back on good terms with Jess, who had been distinctly aloof lately. She needed all the moral support she could muster. Orlando blinked. 'But then I don't suppose you have any delusions about being on the same level as Spielberg, do you, Orlando?'

'Well, I don't think we should be aiding and abetting the endless lies we see on television. It's corrupting,' said Jess. 'I mean, women up and down the country will look at this documentary and feel inadequate because we haven't got sheets drying in our kitchen and they have.'

'The thing is, Jess . . .' Orlando was speaking very slowly and calmly, which, as Cat knew because it was a tone she had often adopted herself, meant he was close to throwing a hand grenade at someone. '. . . sometimes by manipulating an image you can actually portray a more fundamental truth.'

Cat looked at her watch: 8.15. At this rate they'd never get to school. She stood up and removed the sheet, wincing inwardly at the look Jess was directing at her.

As usual the car park behind the Hung Drawn and Quartered was chock-a-block when Daphne and Cat made their way through it on foot the following evening. Jake was already seated in a corner when they arrived.

'How lovely to see you, Jake. Isn't it lovely to see him, Cat?' Daphne squirrelled her way on to the window seat beside him, before Cat had a chance to demur.

Jake mumbled something – Cat thought it might have been a hello – and ambled off to get them some drinks. Daphne winked at Cat. 'So handsome, don't you think?'

But Cat was scanning the packed room, wondering who, if any of them, was her mystery caller. She had to pull herself together and stop being so suspicious. At this rate she'd never make any friends in the village.

'Ahem.' Lady Cynthia's strangulated tones floated over from the inglenook. 'I welcome you all—' She cast an imperious eyebrow around the room. '—to the first general meeting of the annual village fête.'

There was a polite shuffling. 'About as popular as Mira Milošević,' whispered Daphne. 'But not nearly as much fun.'

'As, of course, you all know, this is a very special fête,' continued Lady Cynthia.

'Pure RSP – Rank Starlet Pronunciation,' muttered Daphne. 'She used to talk like a navvie before her agent sent her to charm school. Not that it did her much good. Never got beyond understudying poor dear Glenda Jackson in *Hair*. Or was it *Elizabeth R*?'

'Because, as we're all aware, it's Lower Nettlescombe's one thousandth anniversary.' There was a general flurry of tooth-sucking and similarly impressed gestures. 'Some of us, of course, have been part of the community almost as long. While others—' She paused and looked pointedly in Cat's direction. '—haven't.'

Cat was too distracted by the arrival of Declan and Jess – who practically fell into the packed room, arm in arm and giggling – to register the jibe.

'What this all means,' Lady Cynthia enunciated with scrupulous clarity for the brain-challenged among her audience, 'is that we want to mount a really splendid fête this year, with more stalls than ever.'

There was general nodding and agreement.

'Be about the only thing she hasn't mounted,' whispered Daphne. 'You ought—'

At that moment Lucy and Tashie Wainwright launched into the room, hair and Dior bags sending wineglasses and beer mats flying.

There was some appreciative whistling from the rugger buggers.

'Hi, everyone,' Tashie beamed, smiling at the open mouths of the men. She looked sweetly at Lady Cynthia and waved. Cat was thrilled to see she was wearing a T-shirt with 'It Makes You Think' emblazoned across the front in *diamanté*. Perhaps the Wainwright girls weren't so awful after all. 'Don't let us interrupt, guys,' said Tashie.

Cynthia scowled. Lucy, who had just bought herself a miniature chihuahua, plucked it out of her bag and placed it on a leopard-print throw that was draped over the arm of Veronica's chair, where it promptly laid a miniature poo.

'For heaven's sake!' Veronica batted a doughy arm in front of her nose in disgust. 'That's Dolce e Gabbana.'

'Sorry.' Lucy gazed around the room helplessly for something to mop up the chihuahua's latest *œuvre*. 'There, there, darling.' She kissed the chihuahua's puzzled face. 'Did the lady frighten you?' She turned to Veronica with an air of pained patience. 'Poor Lady Godiva – she keeps doing that on poo-coloured things. I think they confuse her.' She picked up a packed of Rizlas and began dabbing at Veronica's shawl with them.

'Thank you very much,' snapped Samantha. She snatched her Rizlas from Lucy's talons.

'I thought she'd given up,' said Cat to Daphne.

'Roll-ups don't count, apparently,' said Daphne.

'If we may proceed,' said Lady Cynthia in a strained voice, tapping the side of her glass with her diamond ring. Cowed by its vast proportions, the babble subsided. 'Of course, we shall all be keeping in mind Lower Nettlescombe's reputation for family fun and good taste. And, as I was saying, what this all signifies is that we shall need more volunteers for the steering committee, now that some of our former members have dropped out.'

'What does that mean?' whispered Cat.

'Dropped dead,' said Daphne. 'Any nibbles on the bar?'

'So do I have any volunteers?' The room went ominously quiet and the entire population of the Hung Drawn and Quartered suddenly lost the ability to raise their arms. 'None at all?' Lady

Cynthia's voice grew shriller. Shortly, thought Cat, she would turn into Margaret Thatcher. 'I see.' There was a hint of menace in her voice.

There followed an embarrassed silence. 'I don't know why she's looking so put out,' scoffed Daphne. '*She* doesn't go to the steering committee meeting.'

'Why not?'

'It's obvious, isn't it? The steering committee's the one that does all the work. Cynthia presides over the honorary committee.'

Slowly, almost without realising she was doing it, Cat levitated her arm, gingerly at first, like a paparazzo raising his lens above a hedge, then, as Lady Cynthia appeared to lose the ability to turn to Cat's corner of the room, more forcefully.

'Well, if you change your minds please come and see me,' said Lady Cynthia in a voice she had pitched more in sorrow than anger. Despite her irritation at having her gesture ignored, Cat had to admit that Cynthia's thespian skills were more impressive than Daphne had led her to believe. 'And now without further ado, I shall hand over to Mrs Potts, our resident fête dynamo.'

'Well, she went down like a bowl of vomit.' Daphne beamed. 'The most popular beheading since Marie-Antoinette, I'd say. Oh, hello, Jake, darling.'

Jake had finally returned with the drinks and settled down next to Daphne.

Lady Cynthia graciously passed the microphone to Mrs Potts, who made several attempts to heave herself out of an armchair before two of the rugger buggers took pity and hoisted her up. If she was a dynamo, thought Cat, her mechanism had rusted over decades ago. Once she was vertical, Mrs Potts slid her watery eyes over Lady Cynthia, leaving the entire pub in no doubt as to her opinion of her. Suddenly Cat felt herself warming to Edna Potts, even if she proceeded to read the list of forthcoming attractions for the fête in a monotonous, flinty voice that could have made the script for *The Sopranos* sound boring.

'Ferret racing, the Ages of History procession, pony rides, the crowning of Lower Nettlescombe's very own Dairy Queen, guess the cake weight, tug o' war, fortune-telling . . .' Cat waited expectantly for face painting. '. . . guess the age of old Mr Hugh's cockerel –'

'And guess the age of old Mrs Hugh's toy boy,' called out one of the young rugger buggers by the bar.

Fortunately Mrs Potts appeared heckle-proof. 'Deaf as a post,' whispered Daphne. 'Looks like one too.'

'– line dancing –' droned on Mrs Potts.

'Not just any old line dancing, Mrs P,' called out Julian. 'We're putting on a country and western medley of Rodgers and Hart.' He beamed triumphantly at the packed room. 'Rupert's idea.'

'Well, I hope it doesn't overlap with *The Wisshes of Ssshalem*' said Fee haughtily from a corner.

'I don't really see what *The Witches of Salem* has to do with Lower Nettlescombe's history,' began Cynthia.

'It's an allegory, ishn't it?' drawled Fee.

'– pin the tail on the donkey –'

There was ribald guffawing from the bar again. 'Actually, Mrs P,' said the ruddiest rugger bugger, 'we thought this year it might be more fun to pin the nipple on Jordan.'

'Oh, really,' exclaimed Lady Cynthia.

'– and of course there's the fancy dress,' continued Mrs Potts unabated. 'With a prize for the best costume.'

'That'll go to you-know-who, then,' Daphne sniffed.

'Oh, I know about this,' whispered Cat. 'Lily's class have got to dress up as the Knights of the Round Table. She's rechristened Archie Sir Galahad.'

'And Guy Fulton has once again generously agreed to install a miniaturised shooting range on the green,' Mrs Potts' voice became animated for the first time and she looked at Guy Fulton adoringly, while Fee and Cynthia shot him withering glances. 'And of course there'll be nude fishing . . .' Mrs Potts returned to her drone. The audience stopped dozing.

'Things are looking up, boys.' Declan sniggered, cupping his hands round Jess's breasts.

'Yes, very droll,' said Lady Cynthia as Mrs Potts began rifling through her notes. 'What Mrs Potts meant to say was newt fishing.'

There was a chorus of groans from the rugger buggers.

'Didn't you, Mrs Potts, dear?'

'Didn't I what?' Mrs Potts looked up from her notes malevolently.

'Mean to say newt fishing?' Lady Cynthia said slowly and loudly.

'That is what I said. And there's no need to shout. I'm not deaf.' She shuffled her papers again. 'Flower arranging –'

'That's all very well,' said the chief rugger bugger. 'But shouldn't the fête be offering something a bit more up to date? Like having massages from Lower Nettlescombe's Dairy Queen?'

There were more cheers and whistles from the bar.

Cat raised her hand again. This time all eyes turned towards her. 'I can't promise any massages. But I can offer to set up a little tent with acupuncture and reiki sessions and perhaps some nutritional advice.'

Lady Cynthia stood up and eyed Cat with the friendliness of a killer shark. 'Thank you, Ms McGinty . . . but I think you'll find, once you've actually been to one of our fêtes, that that sort of New Age thing doesn't fit in with the ambience.'

Cat felt herself flushing. 'Don't take any notice,' said Daphne *sotto voce*. 'She hasn't been the same since the Change.'

'– and last but not least the bring-and-buy,' wittered Mrs Potts. 'So bring along your smart old frocks, everyone. And, er, buy. And don't leave it all to Lady Cynthia's generosity.' She blinked myopically at Lady Cynthia. 'I 'spect these fêtes have cleaned you right out of all your lovely M & S clothes, haven't they?'

Lady Cynthia directed an even more putrid look at Mrs Potts. 'Thank you all again for coming,' she said graciously. 'And all volunteers do please remember to leave your names at the bar with Julian.'

Cat was desperate to get swept along in the festive speculation. Even Julian and Rupert were getting into the mood by planning a lavish banquet for the night of the fête, featuring a millennium's worth of typical Dorset fayre, from roast swan to salsified cod. 'Of course, if we were being really authentic we'd offer chicken tikka and Budweiser,' said Julian when Cat went up to buy a round. 'What's your contribution, by the way?'

'I'm supposed to be face painting, but there's not a lot of preparation you can do for that.'

Cat cast a jaundiced eye over Orlando and his docu-cronies in the far corner. She wished they'd take some time off. It was hard enough blending into the local fauna without having a camera crew permanently in tow. Besides, having her every move trailed by Orlando's docu-crew just highlighted her loneliness. The artificial partitioning of her life into handy ad-break-friendly portions had thrown its aridity into even starker relief.

'Well, if you need anyone to practise your Britney Spears look on, there's always Rupes and me.'

'I was thinking more along the lines of painting the children like animals and pixies.'

Julian looked at her with a mixture of curiosity and amusement. 'Look, I know Lady C can be a bit grand – and God knows dealing with one highly strung queen is hard enough work.' He rolled his eyes in Rupert's direction. 'But I think you should persist in your ideas. If you ask me the fête committee could do with more young blood. Why don't I nominate you as treasurer? Could you make the next steering committee meeting on Thursday?'

'Let me see,' said Cat. 'It would mean putting off Guy and Madonna again, but what the hell?'

'Great. Seven-thirty, chez Mrs Potts.'

'I knew there was a catch.'

'She's not that bad.'

Not wanting to be seen as the village malcontent, Cat changed the subject. 'How come there isn't a treasurer already?'

'There is. Mr Rocomb. Terrible Alzheimer's. No one's got the heart to get rid of him but I figure he won't remember anything about it. Should be a good party – the fête, I mean. Mark Wainwright's planning a massive firework display to launch his new organic super-deli.'

'Don't tell me it's going to be finished by then?' Cat was

appalled. How come Mark bloody Wainwright could get a team of builders to complete on time when hers were constantly going AWOL?

'So he says. Got an army of builders starting on Monday.'

'D'you think Mark Wainwright will get his organic supermarket finished in time for the village fête?' she asked Vic Spinoza at the school gate the next day. She tried not to sound desperate, or overly interested.

'Search me,' Vic stooped down to examine Marina's computerised drawing of what looked like a post-apocalyptic lunar landscape. 'What's this, darling?'

'The world after GM crops have been planted everywhere,' Marina said matter-of-factly, before stuffing the work of art into her rucksack and pulling out a Fruit Winder.

Cat was about to point out that as yet no one had come up with conclusive proof that GM crops were necessarily a bad thing when she caught sight of the tears at the corner of Vic's eyes – pride presumably – and thought better of it. 'It's very imaginative,' she said instead.

'So's the school's head. I'd be amazed if Mark Wainwright does get it ready. But I dare say he'll get what he wants. Money always does. I expect you had a fair few of those City dealer types round where you lived before.'

'Surrounded,' said Cat, thinking of Stig and Sadie's feverish dealing in number 19.

'Always thought I'd like a spell in London,' said Vic wistfully. 'How's your building work going, by the way?'

'Oh, you know.' Cat hoped this would satisfy him. 'It's going.' She briefly considered confiding in Vic about her caller but decided against it. He didn't look as though he needed any more burdens.

'Like that, then, is it?' He bundled Marina into the Transit van. 'Hope they're not giving the rest of us builders a bad name.'

Cat laughed a carefree sort of laugh. Vic looked crestfallen. 'Are you all right?' she asked gently.

'I'm fine. It's just that it's three years ago this week that Marina's mum died . . . it keeps hitting me.' He broke off.

'I'm so sorry.' Cat felt humbled. 'If there's anything I can do . . .'

'Introduce me to one of your glamorous London friends?' He smiled ruefully. 'All the nice women are taken round here.' He paused pointedly. 'Not that I'm quite ready for romance.' He gave an embarrassed chuckle that was more like a cough. 'She was a hard act to follow. Mustn't complain, though. I've got a beautiful daughter. Still, it gets a bit lonely sometimes, if you know what I mean.'

Cat nodded. Poor man. She knew exactly what he meant.

'Are you really going to be treasurer of the Lower Nettlescombe Fête committee?' asked Lily as they walked arm in arm up Butely Lane.

'If they'll take me,' said Cat, catching herself thinking how convenient it would be if Vic and she were to fall in love. She must be hormonal.

'Don't you think you've got enough on your plate?'

Cat eyed her daughter in wonder. Sometimes it was impossible to believe Lily wasn't twenty-five. In London treating your daughter like your sister seemed the only option. Now Cat wondered whether she hadn't somehow robbed Lily of some of her childhood. But she didn't know how else to talk to her.

'You know what they say. If you need anything doing—'

'—ask a control freak.'

'Lily! I think that's uncalled for.'

'I think Lily's on to something,' Orlando piped up timidly from the ditch where he was trailing her with the rest of his crew.

She threw him a wounded look. 'Orlando, it's hard for me to pretend you're not there when you keep interrupting . . .'

Orlando's face turned the colour of the poppies speckling the verges.

'Sorry, Cat.'

'Does he have to follow us everywhere?' Lily grimaced.

'He says it'll give a more rounded picture than if he just shoots me at work,' said Cat.

'In that case he'll have to wait till you drop dead.'

'What do you mean?'

'You're even busier than when we were in London.'

'So are you.' Cat sounded hurt. 'When you're not round at Marina's you're out with Sir Galahad.'

'I could report you to the NSPCC for child neglect.'

'Lily!' This time it was Orlando's turn to remonstrate.

'God, can't I get any privacy round here?'

Orlando wandered off, ostensibly to conduct an artistic discussion with the rest of the crew.

'He's just doing his job.'

Lily rolled her eyes. 'Oh, please. It's obvious, isn't it?'

'What is?'

'He fancies you,' she mouthed.

'Lily, will you stop trying to matchmake?'

It was Lily's turn to look affronted.

'Look,' reasoned Cat, 'we're happy as we are, aren't we?'

'We're happi*er*,' began Lily.

'You said it was tons better here than London.'

'That was when I thought you were cutting your hours.'

'It's the builders, isn't it? Are they distracting you from your homework? I've already told them once to keep the noise down. I'll have to speak to them again.'

'I quite like Goran . . .'

'No,' said Cat sternly. 'Don't even think about pairing me off with that Neanderthal.'

'All right.' Lily plucked at some wild roses tangled in the hedgerow. 'But I'm still missing a father figure. That's what Daphne says, anyway.'

'Does she, now?'

'Have you considered Marina's father?' Lily bent down casually to tie up a shoelace.

'As a matter of fact I have.' Cat's heart tightened when she saw

the look on Lily's face. 'And it's not going to work.' She shrugged.
'Lily, I'm sorry but I just don't fancy him.'

'What about Jake, then?'

Cat groaned. 'Mr Ray of Light?'

'What do you mean?'

'Well, he's a bit grumpy, isn't he?'

'No he isn't. I think he's nice. He's a great riding teacher.'

So he had been giving her lessons. Why was she only just discovering this? She must be the world's worst mother. She decided not to say anything.

'He knows loads about nature.' Lily eyed Cat slyly. 'And he's very handsome.'

Cat snorted. 'If you go for the *Horse Whisperer* act.'

'Who?'

'You must have seen Robert Redford!' chipped in Orlando. '*The Sting, The Great Gatsby, The Way We Were* . . . That's Myfanwy's favourite film of all time.'

'Myfanwy?' asked Cat and Lily in unison.

Orlando blushed. 'My girlfriend.' He hesitated. 'She works on *Woman's Hour*. She's a bit of a film buff. She gave me an NFT membership last Christmas. That's how I know all the classics. He began humming 'Raindrops Keep Falling on My Head.' 'Now Redford *is* incredibly handsome, if you don't mind warts—'

'Jake,' said Lily staunchly, 'is handsomer. And he doesn't have warts.'

As was increasingly the case, Goran and his coherts had downed tools for the day by the time Cat, Lily and the docu-crew meandered up the driveway, even though it was only five past four. It was hopeless: Goran seemed to know only two speeds of working – full throttle and not there. Meanwhile Butely was beginning to look more and more of a shambles. Not content with smothering the façade with rackety scaffolding which sounded like a brass band every time a stiff breeze blew, they had dismantled the floorboards in one of the dormies, throwing the bookings into chaos – and had removed all the hideous old fire doors only to find that the new ones they'd ordered didn't fit.

Declan ought to be dealing with it but he was too wrapped up in his pheasants. It all left Cat with a major headache to sort out. In the meantime she had to make Lily's supper, because Jess, as usual, had disappeared. Through the kitchen window, Cat could see Declan's polo boots sticking out from beneath his Golf GTi. He'd been tinkering around underneath it for hours. It didn't help her mood when she noticed Jess's Doc Marten's poking out next to him, but she didn't want to give Declan the satisfaction of making a scene with Jess. She would address the situation later in private.

In the meantime, while the pasta was simmering, she went into her study and sifted through her e-mails. There were half a dozen from the personnel departments of some large companies asking whether she was prepared to negotiate on rates. A begging note from a charity suggested Cat might like to donate a week at Butely for one of their raffle prizes. And an e-mail from the classified department of the *Daily Telegraph* asked whether she was sure she wanted to stop running her weekly adverts, reminding her there was a standard cancellation fee.

Puzzled, Cat scrolled back through her file of correspondence with the *Daily Telegraph*, searching for anything she could have written that might have been construed as a cancellation. There was nothing as far as she could see. So how had they got the wrong end of the stick? Along with Daphne's list of old Friends of Butely, the *Telegraph* ad had proved a lifeline. Incensed, Cat marched over to Declan's Golf and thrust a print-out of the *Daily Telegraph* e-mail at the fender. 'Do you know anything about this?'

An oil-spattered face appeared from beneath the chassis and squinted at the letter. 'Nothing to do with me,' said Declan breezily.

Cat, who was spoiling for a fight, felt the wind squelching from her sails.

'What is it?' asked Jess, her chilli-coloured pigtails merging from beneath the bumper. Miraculously, she had caught the sun, Cat noticed, and she was wearing a new bikini top that showed off her cleavage to full effect. A large glob of black oil was making its way slowly but confidently towards the tip of her left breast.

'It's a letter asking why we wanted to cancel the one thing that has kept clients coming to Butely over the past months. And I'm asking myself the same question.'

'So am I, Cat.' Declan sprang to his feet and scratched his head indignantly. 'They've obviously cocked up. Bloody newspapers. Can't get anything right. Don't you worry, I'll sort this out.' Cat looked at the black specks that had worked their way into the sweaty cracks of his face. Confronted by such monumentally irritating support, she had little choice but to retreat. Fortunately the phone in the main house started to ring. Cat sprinted across the lawns to pick it up.

'Hello. Hello. Can you hear me?' said a brittle voice.

'Butely Clinic. How may I help you?'

'I didn't expect to get a human, I must say.' Whoever it was sounded mildly affronted. 'That is Butely? In Dorset-England?'

Cat confirmed that indeed it was.

'This is Barbara Cass,' the voice continued with the kind of authority that indicated Cat should know who Barbara Cass was. 'Personal assistant to Sister Slammer.' It sounded impatient now as well as brittle. 'We'd like the penthouse suite, obviously.'

'We don't really have one of those,' said Cat carefully. She could put Sister Slammer in a dormie, she supposed – at least they were spacious. Outside Declan was pretending to spank Jess with a spanner. 'Actually we don't have that much of a house,' said Cat ruefully. There was a puzzled silence.

'So what do you have? Is it like caves?'

'No, we have rooms, dating back to the fourteenth century. But some of them don't have floors.'

'Is that to do with Eastern philosophy?' The voice sounded suspicious now.

Cat felt honour bound to paint an honest picture of Butely. 'It's not really Eastern philosophy, more to do with Grade One building regs really.' There was another perplexed silence.

'Have I got the right number?'

'This is Butely,' said Cat.

'Butely Naturopathic Clinic. Dorset-England? The place we read about in the *New York Times* column?'

Cat began to find the conversation alarming. God knows what Suzette had written about the place. If she was in guilt mode about the Millie débâcle she'd probably made Butely sound like a cross between Nirvana and the Four Seasons.

'We're having a bit of building work done at the moment. It's a bit noisy at certain times of the day.' Though not many times, thought Cat sourly, now that Goran and his gang appeared to have adopted a part-time approach to their Butely obligations.

'That's okay. Miss Slammer gets tinnitus anyway.'

'And we're a bit rough around the edges. Did the article say that?'

'Butely is where you find yourself, through humour, old-fashioned walks in idyllic countryside, fad-free wholesome food and a character-building sense of history,' repeated Barbara Cass, reading Suzette's column. 'Miss Slammer loves history.'

'Anyway, we've reduced our rates, to make up for any inconveniences.'

There was another silence while Barbara Cass ingested this, by far the most mystifying comment so far of the entire conversation.

'Is that like a special price, because of who Sister Slammer is?'

'Not really.' Cat was about to explain that, *au contraire*, Butely was means tested, but thought better of it. 'We'd love to see her. Shall I make that a firm reservation?'

> *'I'm a messed-up bitch with a life full of pain*
> *My man slept around and ran off with the cocaine*
> *Did a lot of shit – it ain't nothin' to boast*
> *Then he sold my life story to the* New York Post.'

'They're autobiographical,' said Lily when Cat, armed with some of Sister Slammer's lyrics she had found on the Internet, finally tracked her down in Sir Galahad's stable. 'They explained it all on Trevor MacDonald.'

'I see,' Cat scanned the words again, desperately seeking the germ of Shakespearian grandeur that one of the reviewers on amazon.com had alluded to.

Lily gazed up at Cat with a worn-out worldliness. She had been brushing Sir Galahad for the past forty minutes, trying out different plaiting techniques on his mane, and now she had a pile of home-work waiting for her. 'She's about to go into the *Guinness Book of Records* for having the three fastest-selling consecutive rap CDs in history. You must have heard of her.'

'Of course I have,' said Cat hurriedly. 'I just wondered if that was her real name.' She swept her gaze over Sir Galahad's spotless accommodation. The discrepancy between what Lily deemed an acceptable level of hygiene in her pony's stable and what passed for cleanliness in her bedroom never failed to amaze.

'She used to be called Slap Bitch. She changed it when her boyfriend got put in prison.'

'What's he in for?' asked Cat with mounting foreboding.

'Drive-by shooting and attempted rape.' Lily started polishing Sir Galahad's hoofs with a tin of Nivea Daphne had given her. 'But he didn't mean to. He was high.'

'Oh.' Cat wondered whether Barbara Cass would believe her if she rang back and told her that Butely had been blown up.

'Why?'

'She might be coming to stay.' Having a celebrity at Butely would certainly signal to all her detractors that she had no inten-tion of giving up.

'Really?' Lily stopped polishing for a split second. 'That figures.'

'Why?'

'She's totally pilled out.' She returned to the hoofs. 'Mum?'

'Yes?'

'Are you okay?'

'What do you mean?'

'Toby's not coming back, is he?'

Lily was still wearing her riding hat. With her spindly legs she looked like one of the cuter insects from *A Bug's Life*. Cat stared into her daughter's eyes. Even in the twilight of the stables she could make out a kind of resigned acceptance on Lily's face that nearly broke her heart.

'No, darling, that didn't work out. But it's fine. I'm really happy about it, actually.'

Lily looked unconvinced, which made Cat feel even worse, because funnily enough, much as she missed Toby's company, she knew herself well enough to understand that whatever she'd felt for him hadn't been love. But right now she didn't know whether she could explain this to Lily without sounding callous.

Lily turned her attention back to Sir Galahad's mane. 'Jesus – men,' was all she said.

'We'll have to redecorate the dormi immediately – starting with putting the floors back in,' said Cat frantically over the noise of Daphne's pottery wheel. 'We need to make a good impression on Sister Slammer. If only Goran hadn't gone AWOL. Oh God, why did I ever agree to this booking? What time is it in LA? Maybe I can call and cancel.'

'Two in the morning, dear,' said Daphne. 'Stop worrying. I'm sure this Slammer person has been in far less salubrious places than Butely.'

'That's another thing. We're not exactly equipped to deal with a pilled-out sociopath.'

'At least give it a whirl,' said Daphne. She sounded distracted. 'You said yourself that diet can work wonders. Just get Dr Anjit to do one of his print-outs on aggressive foods.'

'I don't think you've quite grasped the concept of Sister Slammer,' said Cat in exasperation. 'She's hardly in the Family Von Trapp mould.'

'I never could bear that film. Dreadful acting.'

Cat stared disconsolately at Daphne's face, paler than usual beneath a thin grey film of clay dust that had settled on her cheeks, and realised with a start how much she'd come to rely on her for moral support. 'What's really worrying me is the building. It doesn't seem to be making any progress lately.'

'You don't suppose they could be moonlighting?' said Daphne.

'I've thought of that. But where? Surely Declan would be on their case. Anyway, you'd think Glowbal would want to get this job finished as quickly as we do.'

'Mark Wainwright seems to be making uncannily fast progress on the Spar,' said Daphne thoughtfully.

'Does he? I've been so wrapped up here I've hardly been into the village lately.'

'Well, there you are.'

'You're not suggesting Goran's lot are working on it?'

Daphne shrugged.

'That's disgusting. The bastards.'

'It's just a thought. We don't have actual proof.'

'I'll get some, then.'

'Cat?'

'Yes?'

'You will be careful, dear, won't you?'

The more Cat saw Declan's thin lips pressed against his mobile whenever he thought she was nowhere near (she wasn't, she had found an old pair of Sir Rodney's binoculars) the more she was convinced he was talking to Toby. But she had nothing concrete to go on. There was nothing to be gained by confronting him over the *Telegraph* ads again, however. Instead she borrowed some more money from the bank and bought Declan his own laptop, organised an e-mail address and told him that no woman could resist a technically literate man. Fortunately he was far too ignorant about computers to realise she'd set it up so that everything he received bounced on to her address as well. If she couldn't catch him plotting on the phone, she was sure that sooner or later she'd nail him on the computer.

He seemed to fall for her sudden flattery. At any rate his chest had puffed with pride when she'd told him that, having realised how busy he was, she hoped the computer would help him with his pheasant accounting. Men were amazingly simple, really. It beat her why she messed up with them as much as she did.

*

It was hard to determine who was more shell-shocked by the next steering committee meeting, which took place in Mrs Potts' cottage – the dusty cast of characters who had been attending similar meetings for centuries, or Cat. Either way it was a clash of cultures. Cat was appalled at their indolence – they seemed to have no sense of urgency whatsoever; anyone would think they were planning a fête to celebrate Lower Nettlescombe's next-but-one millennium – and the committee members were dazed to the point of concussion by Cat's all-bludgeoning energetic enthusiasm.

They were so stunned, in fact, that she ended up walking away with responsibility for the treasury and sponsorship (a new concept) as well as promising to investigate a host of novel new ideas.

'That went brilliantly in the circumstances, didn't it?' She beamed as she walked back along the high street afterwards with Julian and Jake.

'What circumstances would those be?' asked Julian.

Cat looked bemused.

'You don't think you came on a teeny bit strong?' asked Jake carefully.

'What do you mean?' asked Cat in astonishment. 'What does he mean, Julian?'

'Search me.' Julian pushed his hands into his jean pockets and winked at Jake.

'I mean some people might think your suggestions about booking a sheep shearer, hiring a dunking stool, some human cannonballs, a motorised sofa for kiddie rides, a jazz band and a Bob the Builder train were a bit much, coming as they did in a glut. But that would presumably be before they heard you go on to recommend that the committee talk to some spiritual healers and introduce an organic food section.'

'Nobody objected at the time.'

'Too shell-shocked.'

'Mrs Potts even told me to make some preliminary investigations.'

'Only because she doesn't believe anyone would have the energy or the telephone numbers to take her up on it.'

'She's in for a bit of a surprise, then, isn't she?' said Cat, feeling strangely invigorated. 'You know what they say. If you want something doing—'

'—ask a control freak,' said Julian.

That was the third time in as many weeks someone had used the phrase to describe her. 'Is that how I come across?' she asked defensively.

Julian chuckled.

'Is it?'

Jake threw her one of his rueful grins. 'A little. Maybe,' he said.

Exasperated, she walked on in silence, wondering what it would take to get anyone in the village to appreciate her just a little.

At the risk of playing to everyone's prejudices about her so-called control freakery, Cat had a hunch that if she drove to Mark Wainwright's deli-in-progress that night, certain hitherto inexplicable events would fall into place.

To be on the safe side she packed a torch, the Polaroid camera Suzette had bought Lily the last time she'd been in London and Lily's riding crop. Then she parked the car at the end of the village, just past the bridge, and walked the rest of the way, crouching nervously whenever something black flew overhead. She heard the evidence she'd been expecting from halfway down the street – a muffled babble of Croatian voices and the subdued but unmistakable sound of heavy objects being carted around. She walked on a bit further, to get a better view and take some photographs. She'd already decided to keep out of sight. It would be insane to tackle a bunch of burly builders under cover of darkness. Anyway, all she needed was some pictorial proof and she had Goran – and Declan, because she was convinced he was implicated – dangling by the goolies. She found a perfect position behind the phone box – she noticed that even in Lower Nettlescombe they reeked of pee – and hoped her pounding heart wouldn't give her away. God knew what they'd do if they discovered her. There was a lull in the conversation – presumably they were on one of their infernal breaks and otherwise occupied with eating or drinking. Then someone – it sounded like Goran – made a joke and they all laughed. Well, there was a lot to find amusing – how they were taking her for a ride, for instance.

'You bastards,' she muttered from behind the phone box.

Goran looked out into the dark. For a moment she caught his eyes in the lamplight, haunted and afraid. A bastard, but a poor one, she thought. He probably had a huge family back home who relied on every penny he could scrape together to survive. Then she thought of how she and Lily stood every chance of being homeless if things continued as they were.

She snapped away with the camera, and as Goran stepped out into the lane she ran back to the Polo, which, for once, started first go, and sped back to Butely, not knowing whether to be appalled at the risk she had just taken, or jubilant that at last she had speared Declan.

She waited as long as she reasonably could before bearding Declan at 7.30 the next morning in the shag-pad.

'Morning to you too.' He sat up in bed. There was no evidence of Jess, thank God. Cat couldn't help noticing the fuzz on his chest, which seemed to extend all the way down his body. It was hard to know where his scalp ended and his pubic hair began. No wonder he slept naked, apart from the razor-blade medallion.

'I thought you'd like to see these.' She place the incriminating Polaroids on his duvet. She stood back, folded her arms and waited for him to wriggle out of this.

Which he did with exceptional ease. 'That lying, thieving bastard,' he thundered. To Cat's horror he leapt out of bed and threw on his clothes, racing past her down the stairs and out into the driveway, where he stood sentinel until Goran and the other builders turned up. At which point Declan treated them all to a ferocious tongue-lashing and landed a few well-placed punches on Goran's bemused face.

At least the builders were making headway again – the dormi even had its floorboards back. A world-famous celebrity was checking in shortly. And work on Mark Wainwright's Spar had ground to a halt. That a wealthy businessman should experience some of her own difficulties was somehow wholly satisfying to Cat. All she needed was for the planning permission for the pool to come through – an event she was certain was imminent, given Jake's involvement – and for Jess to start talking to her again for life to be perfect. And for whoever her mystery caller was to see the error of their ways. Because although she hardly liked to admit it to herself, Cat was more rattled by that than by everything else put together.

Jess, meanwhile, had her own problems, chief among which was her suspicion that she was starting to get quite fond of Declan. She knew it was absurd. She knew *he* was absurd, though she'd got him to flatten his hair a little. But he was bloody good fun. He took her on elaborate mystery tours that ended up with go-karting and candy-floss. He whizzed her off to Lulworth Cove at midnight. He balanced buckets of water on the tops of doors so she got drenched – you probably had to be Australian to appreciate that one, she explained to Lily. She had no illusions that he would be particularly faithful, but that suited her too. She wanted a summer of mucking about, after a serious spring – and Declan was someone who looked as though they'd graduated summa cum laude in mucking about.

And he made phone calls – all the time, when he thought she wasn't around. Which was where Jess's problems began. Because once or twice she was sure she'd caught him talking to Toby, which even to Jess's skewed way of looking at things didn't seem quite right. If Declan had queries about the estate, shouldn't he be discussing them with Jake – or Cat? She wished she could talk to Cat about it. But Cat was so distracted and aloof at the moment, Jess didn't feel like it. In any case, by the time Cat got back from one of her steering committees, or lecturing the builders, Jess had usually forgotten why she'd felt anxious in the first place.

18

'You'll never guess who's here.' Declan poked his head out of the Golf window as Lily and Cat walked along Butely's drive after school.

'God?' suggested Lily.

'Ha ha. Guess again,' said Declan. Losing interest, Lily picked up speed in anticipation of some of Micky's wheat-free scones, which she and Cat had taken to dining on every afternoon after school.

'Ann Boleyn?' called Cat from the front door. She didn't want to hate Declan. Hating him was just so obvious. But hate him she did.

'I said you'd never guess,' Declan crowed.

'Shouldn't you have your hands round the neck of some pheasant?' asked Cat sweetly.

'Sister Slammer,' he announced triumphantly.

'She's not supposed to arrive until next week.' Cat didn't know why she was so aghast. A week, a month, wasn't going to make much difference to Butely's condition.

'Well, she has,' he gloated. 'Don't worry – Jess dealt with it all. And Samantha gave her this great spiel about boot camp and handed her a mop. That should impress the busybodies in the village. I s'pose you've noticed that the peasants are revolting. Maybe having a real live celebrity about the place will help get them back on our side a little.'

Even Declan had noticed a certain *froideur* between her and the villagers, then. And how was it that whenever Cat was reaching the conclusion that he was an out-and-out slimy bastard, he somehow always managed to wrong-foot her with his supportive cheeriness? 'Where is she now?' asked Cat, trying to sound businesslike and aloof.

'Micky's got her scrubbing the kitchen floor. Like they do at those Montessori schools. Just think what this will do for bookings when word leaks out to the media that we've got the world's most successful female gangsta rapper.'

'But it's not going to, is it?'

'If you say so. Personally I would say it was just the sort of publicity Butely was crying out for.'

Cat eyed him suspiciously. It was there again: the impression that beneath the cheerleading nothing gave Declan more pleasure that the prospect of Butely going under. 'We're not desperate.' she said.

'Okay. Just bumped into Sir Christopher Wren by that old toilet. Strange bloke, isn't he?'

'I'm sorry?'

'Jake. Tricky bugger.'

'I wouldn't say that,' lied Cat. There was power in numbers and she wanted Declan to perceive her and Jake as a united front.

Declan ploughed on. 'Obvious he's got a soft spot for you, though. And I don't blame him.' Cat felt her stomach churn at Declan's ludicrously ill-judged admiration. 'Pity.' He pulled out his cigarettes and offered her one.

'I don't smoke,' said Cat haughtily.

'About Jake, I mean,' muttered Declan, striding off. 'Someone ought to point out that lusting after your brother's ex is off limits – even in the country.'

Silhouetted in the doorway of Micky's kitchen, where Samantha so often blocked the light, loomed all six feet of Sister Slammer, next to the outline of a broomstick. Her sinewy arms were clamped in a variety of leather amulets. Her muscular legs were strapped into gold Dior snakeskin boots and a pair of low-slung jeans that looked as though they'd been attacked with a machete – her version of dressing down, Cat supposed. She was swaying gracefully to Judas

Priest's *Greatest Hits*, her eyes fixed on the remains of a Worcestershire sauce label that stood aloft on a pile of floor sweepings, as proudly as the first flag planted on Antarctica.

'Now Micky, you are not going to tell me this Worcestershire shit's organic.'

'It's for Bloody Marys,' said Micky, glancing at his leek soufflés rising nicely in the oven. 'For me and Sam off duty – and for you, if you behave.' He winked demonically, his lined face cracking like old parchment, until he caught sight of Cat.

'Oh, hello, Cat, didn't see you there.'

'I'm off that shit,' announced Sister Slammer, seemingly oblivious to Cat. Apparently she was so used to being surrounded by endless hangers-on she no longer bothered to question who anyone was. 'Yeah.' She warmed to her theme. 'Since I came off the methadone and the booze and the pills and stuff, I feel, like, really weirded out. It's like being cleansed, or reborn or something. I can't explain it, but it's like being . . . oh hell, what's the word?'

'Sober?' suggested Micky.

'Sober?' Sister Slammer turned the full beam of her dark, soulful eyes on Micky's grizzly apron. 'Yeah, maybe that's it. You know, Micky, you're amazing.'

Micky gave a little embarrassed cough. 'Rosie, allow me to introduce you to Cat McGinty. She runs Butely.'

Sister Slammer swivelled round, her peroxided extensions lashing Cat. One of her eyebrows had been speared by a diamond pin that was shaped like a thunderbolt.

'Oh my God, I love this house,' she gushed. Cat tried not to stare at her glossy skin, which looked as though someone had gone over it with Brasso. In view of its owners heroic substance abuse, it was far more gorgeously smooth than it had a right to be. 'I'm going to do my house just like this. I love the paint effect.' She ran her nails, which were constellated with more stars than the Great Bear, along the skirting board. 'What is it?'

'Dry rot,' said Micky.

'Dry rot,' repeated Sister Slammer. 'Do they sell it in Laura Ashley? I'm crazy about this English look. I was going to do my house like the Petit Trianon. But I'm scrapping it. That architect's dead meat.'

'It's very nice to have you,' said Cat. 'I hope Micky's not working you too hard.'

Sister Slammer looked momentarily confused before emitting a dry little laugh. 'Yeah, well. The Jungian module can seem a bit arduous sometimes.'

Cat coughed. 'Micky, could I have a word with you in a minute?'

Micky looked at her innocently across his soufflés. 'No problem, Cat. Would you like Sam to be there too?'

'Micky's a genius.' Sister Slammer looked at Cat pointedly. 'I can't get over the fact he can cook as well.'

'As well as what?' asked Cat uneasily.

'All that analysis shit.' She sashayed towards a window and gazed out at the ha-ha. 'They didn't teach cooking at home,' she said wistfully.

'I'm crap as well,' said Cat in a sisterly voice. 'I like to blame it on my mother.'

'I didn't have a mother,' said Sister Slammer.

Cat made a note to look up some psychiatrists with more in the way of official qualifications than Micky had to offer. 'I love your tattoo,' she said.

'Which one?'

'There, just above your torso.' Once again Cat found her gaze sucked towards a blue shadow seeping out beneath Sister Slammer's Lurex halter neck.

'That's a bruise.'

'I see.' There was an agonising pause. 'You ought to see Doctor Anjit,' said Cat eventually. 'He could give you some arnica.'

Sister Slammer laughed bitterly. 'Take more than that, girl.'

'Acupuncture, then? He's one of the best in the country.'

Sister Slammer looked pained.

'Rosie's not really doing needles any more,' said Micky.

Cat considered asking how she got the bruise and decided she didn't have time to listen to the answer. She had a mountain of administration to sort out for the fête.

★

'She's quite sweet really, don't you think?' Lily glanced up from her vichyssoise – since Jess had been too busy to cook and they'd switched to Micky's leftovers things had been looking up on the culinary front. 'Once you get over the bullet wound.'

Cat flicked a J-cloth in the vague direction of a fly. 'Do you happen to know how she got it?' she asked casually.

'Her boyfriend shot her. Is there any more soup?'

Not for the first time since Sister Slammer had descended on Butely, Cat felt a twinge of guilt that perhaps they weren't as equipped to deal with her emotional problems as they might be. The only profile they'd built up of her had been made of pottery, in one of Daphne's workshops, and that had shattered in the kiln. Even Daphne was now far too preoccupied helping Edna Potts with the bring-and-buy stall and recruiting new pupils for Clay Expressions to give Sister Slammer her full attention. In any case, she was of the old school of thinking that no problem was too knotty not to be happily treated with either a spin on the pottery wheel or a glass of Bailey's.

'She's not clinically depressed,' Lily stared into the soup thoughtfully. 'Just an aggressive-dependent. She says being with Jake is good therapy.'

'Jake?' Cat ladled some more soup into Lily's bowl.

'He's been teaching her about sparrows and stuff. They've been on a few walks together. And she wants him to draw up new plans for her English country manor in Bel Air.'

'I hope she isn't bothering him,' said Cat crossly. 'He's got a lot on his plate.'

'He doesn't seem to mind. She's asked him to design floorboards that creak, like Butely's. Her real name's Rosacea, you know.'

'Why doesn't that surprise me?' For reasons she wasn't quite ready to acknowledge, it seemed somehow fitting that Sister Slammer should be named after a type of acne.

'She said I could borrow some of her stage props to wear on the float.'

'Like what?'

'Just some chains and stuff.' Lily turned uncharacteristically vague. 'You know, it's really great having you around more.'

Cat was fully aware that Lily was changing the subject, albeit to one that was close to her heart. 'You said the other day I was a control freak.'

'I was tired.'

For a while they worked side by side on the kitchen table – Lily on her geometry, Cat on another revised building schedule for Goran. This was how it was meant to be, thought Cat, gazing at the top of Lily's head. Life at Butely had its downsides – she didn't even want to start thinking about the JCBs on the lawn outside, the phone calls or any of her other pressing problems, numerous as they were. Essentially country life was turning out to be a gratifyingly satisfying existence. She hoped Lily appreciated this. A loud clap echoed outside, like gunshot. She went to the kitchen window.

Through the arch in the wall that divided the Cottage garden from the main grounds, Cat could see Declan pointing a pistol above his head while Jess knelt by an imaginary starting line, with her pert bottom poised in the air like a bunny girl's tail. He fired it in the air and Jess bolted down the drive, giggling like a tipsy hyena. It didn't take long for Declan to catch her up, just as it didn't take long for them both to end up in the fountain. Brimming with indignation, Cat dragged her eyes from Jess's pigtails, now sopping wet, but not before she saw Declan straddle her in the water and Jess wrestle him on to a sleeping lion.

It was odd, Jess thought, as the Golf bumped its way up a deeply rutted track on Guy Fulton's estate towards the clay pigeon range. Superficially, at least, Declan was pretty feral, and yet she'd grown quite fond of him in the last few days. At first she'd only agreed to go for a drink with him because she'd been intrigued. And she'd gone on a second date because she was seething with resentment at the way Cat seemed to think she had the right to dictate who Jess went out with. But somehow one thing had led to another. He was very generous – always splashing out in the pub. And against all expectations, he had turned out to be a laugh. Not a very sophisticated one – more like the men she'd hung out with during her year on a sheep-shearing farm outside Wadonga. He liked rugby-tackling her and firing his airgun in moments of excitement, and a lot of his humour revolved around wind that wasn't strictly of the meteorological variety. But he reminded her of home. And he had a car.

'Are you sure Guy won't mind us crashing?'

''Course not,' Declan stroked her knee. 'You heard him the other night. He practically invited the whole pub to drop by any time.'

'That was 'cos one of his horses had just come in at forty to one and he was pissed.'

'*In vino veritas*, darlin'.' Great tsunamis of Hugo Boss for Men wafted towards Jess from the driving seat of the Golf. She was so clean living these days that it almost knocked her senseless.

'All right, then.' She giggled and stuck her feet up on the dashboard.

'Careful, darlin'.' Declan flicked her toes with a chamois leather. 'That's real walnut veneer, that is.'

Guy Fulton wasn't expecting them, of course. He wasn't even there. But that didn't stop Jess and Declan tagging on to a party of stockbrokers down from London for the day.

'You can be my PA,' said Declan generously.

'We'll never get away with it.' Jess giggled nervously. 'They're not going to believe we're bankers.'

'Watch this, darlin'.' Declan swaggered over to the party. 'Hi, guys, sorry we're late.'

The stockbrokers watched in perplexed amusement as Declan attempted to pass himself off as a City slicker. Since the only information he had on this particular life form was from *Wall Street*, his performance stretched credibility to a criminal degree. But he was an excellent shot, and Jess's shorts were very tight, so the real stockbrokers let it pass, even if Declan wound them all up towards the end by repeatedly shouting out 'Greed is good' every time he hit a target.

It was gone ten o'clock when they stumbled into the Hung

Drawn and Quartered and the pub was heaving. The rugger buggers broke into a good-natured chorus of 'Do You Think I'm Sexy' as Declan and Jess squeezed their way past them to the bar. Declan grinned and waved. 'Am I in the wrong pub or is this the monthly meeting of Mensa?' He tugged Jess over towards a table occupied by the mummers. 'Mind if we join you?' He pulled up a chair that had been temporarily vacated by Fee and grabbed Jess. 'Right, my round. What's everyone having?'

Thirty-six pints of Prince Will, three apple juices and three double G and Ts later, he had most of the pub eating out of his palm, thanks to a series of outrageously disloyal stories about his former employer, the sheikh.

'Did he really have four wives?' asked Jess, light headed on apple juice and lack of food. It was almost midnight, and she'd drunk so much juice she was starting to experience a nauseating sugar rush. She went outside for some fresh air, hoping Declan would take the hint and whisk her home. But he was in full throttle about the sheikh's marital arrangements.

'To marry one wife is unfortunate,' said Julian, clearing some of the glasses. 'To marry four looks like advanced masochism to me. But then I'm biased. My wife's in a bad mood tonight.' He threw an ominous look towards the kitchen. 'Can't get the ballotine of suckling right. This is the second attempt as well. He's determined to serve it at the fête. I told him everyone would be just as happy with organic burgers. But he won't listen.'

'Must seem a bit tame nowadays, over at Butely,' drawled Fee, who had returned to the circle several rounds earlier and was moving in on Declan now that Jess had popped outside.

'Don't you believe it, darlin'. There's all sorts of hanky-panky going on up there.' The circle instantly snapped to attention at the promise of fresh scandal.

'Really?' said Julian, trying to sound nonchalant.

'Don't tell me you didn't know about the *ménage à troize*.'

'*Trois*,' slurred Fee. 'It's a silent S.'

'Cat and the Dowell brothers.' Declan ignored her, relishing the rapt expressions of the hushed crowd.

'Toby isn't a Dowell,' piped up Fiona. 'Cynthia was married to someone else when she had him. Can't recall who. She never could keep them for long.'

'You're not saying they're at it simultaneously?' asked Julian in delight. He couldn't believe that of all the villages in England, he and Rupes had lucked out in a den of iniquity. 'Jake's such a decent chap.'

Declan snorted. 'Toby, you mean. Jake's putty in her hands. It was Toby who ended it. Especially when he found out what she was planning to do.'

'Not . . . orgies?' asked Julian excitedly.

'No, you berk. I'm not talking about sex—' An anti-climactic depression descended on the pub as the rugger buggers looked at their watches and contemplated how late it had got suddenly. 'I'm talking about something that turns Cat on far more,' said Declan hastily. 'Money. Success. She'd do anything if she thought it would make her a packet. Frankly it's only a matter of time before she takes Butely by the goolies and flogs it off to the highest bidder.'

'That's not what she told me,' said Julian. 'She more or less stated she wanted to keep Butely as it is.'

The door opened a fraction and Jess came back in. She was about to make her way past the throng at the bar towards Declan when she stopped in her tracks. At first she thought she'd misheard him. 'You didn't believe that, did you, mate?' He was addressing Julian. 'She's planning to turn it into a lifestyle theme park – with a multiplex cinema tagged on and a bunch of poxy shops and one of those girly wine bars. If she can get permission, that is. Which with Jake on board, she probably will.' He shook his head in apparent disbelief at their willingness to be taken in by a pretty woman.

If there was one thing Julian and the rugger buggers had in common it was a horror of being thought naive. Within nano-seconds they'd leapt on Declan's gossip, claimed it as their own and embellished it.

'I s'pose that would explain a lot,' said Julian. 'I never did under-stand how she could make it work as it is.' He shook his head sorrowfully at the perfidy of women. 'She was adamant about not changing anything.'

'Keep it as it is?' snorted Declan, unaware that Jess had returned. 'Keep it as it is?' he repeated. 'Do me a favour. She'd nuke it if she thought there was money to be made. You've got to understand what you're dealing with. Her sort are ruthless, however cute they might look on the outside. Any chance of one last round, Rupert?' He caught sight of Jess standing at the back of a crowd. 'Oh, hi, darlin'. You took your time. Been shopping? Come over here.' He patted his lap.

Jess froze. She had no idea what lay behind Declan's outburst against Cat – whether a genuine misunderstanding or some more malicious motive. She willed herself to walk over to him as if she hadn't heard a thing and wriggled back on to his knee, removing Fee's hand from it in the process.

'Have I missed anything?' she asked the flushed faces gathered round Declan. She had the distinct impression that the atmosphere had changed, that a hostility that hadn't been there before had crept in.

Fee leant towards her tipsily. Jess felt Declan tense beneath her. 'Is it true,' – Fee's pupils had dilated into black holes – 'that that rap singer dyes her pubes blonde?'

Declan let out a sigh of relief.

'I wouldn't know,' said Jess haughtily, flicking some cigarette ash from her beer mat on to Fee's pashmina.

'You've missed absolutely nothing, darlin'.' Declan kissed Jess's ear and stood up suddenly. 'But we've missed you. Scrap that round, Julian. Come on, sweetheart.' He bundled Jess towards the door. 'You look a bit pale. Let's get you home.'

Cat was up late again, poring over an old map of Butely, trying to work out the likeliest spot for a mineral water spring to be. It must have been midnight when the phone rang. Her blood froze. She knew instinctively it was her mystery caller and yet reflexively she still picked up the phone. There was a moment's silence and then the abuse started. The whole call couldn't have lasted more than a couple of minutes but the menacing taunts seemed to go on for ever. Whoever was on the other end sounded so calm and rational that at first it was hard to believe the malevolence of what they were saying. But as the menacing drone went on – threats against her and Lily – Cat began to shake.

She put the phone down, and then she dialled 1471. But whoever was calling wasn't stupid enough to allow themselves to be traced. By now she was too spooked to wonder why all the silver linings in her life came with sooty black mushroom clouds attached. She couldn't think of anything. Who hated her this much – not Toby surely? Shivering and with a dry mouth she went into the kitchen and put the kettle on.

The Golf lurched round the bends back to Butely, making Jess feel queasier than ever. It was all she could do to stop herself being sick, let alone think of a subtle way to get to the bottom of Declan's behaviour.

'Did I hear you say something about Cat's plans for Butely back in the pub?' she asked innocently.

His hands gripped the steering wheel tightly. 'Don't think so, darlin'. Must have been hallucinating. I keep telling you all that healthy-living stuff is bad for you.'

'So you don't know anything about the long-term strategy?'

Declan couldn't resist the bait. 'Yeah, Cat takes me into her confidence, of course, but I'm sure she tells you everything as well.' He eyed her slyly.

'Hardly,' said Jess. Her instincts told her her best policy was to play as dumb as possible with Declan. 'We're barely communicating at all at the moment.' That part at least was true.

He seemed surprised – which only proved how little attention he normally paid to her. 'Yeah, well, you know, it's all highly confidential stuff.' He paused importantly. 'But I don't s'pose there's any harm in telling you. After all, it affects your future so it's only fair to tell you.'

'Tell me what?'

'That's she's hell-bent on developing it into a business centre or a theme park or something and selling it on.'

'But what about the pool complex?'

He laughed cynically. 'Just a cover for what she's really doing. Blimey, Jess, don't look like that. You're as naive as that lot in the pub. You didn't honestly believe all that stuff about wanting to keep the place intact as some leaky refuge for clapped-out old biddies, did you?'

'No,' said Jess. 'You're right, I'm sure. But tell me, how did you find out?'

'She showed me the plans herself. Talked me through the whole thing.'

'No!' Jess wondered how far Declan would go with his elaborate lies. She had no doubt that that was what they were. She might not be talking to Cat at the moment, but she knew her well enough to know she'd never betray Butely.

'Don't sound so surprised.' He pretended to be affronted.

'It's just that you two don't always see eye to eye.'

'Oh, that's just our banter. I reckon she's got a bit of a soft spot for me, actually. Anyway, some people always need to show off how clever they are. She couldn't resist explaining how much money she was going to make. Gagging for it, she was.'

'And what about Jake? Doesn't he own the land?'

'Oh, she thought of that too,' said Declan hastily. 'Got it all wrapped up. She's going to present it to him as a fate accompliss. Poor bloke doesn't stand a chance.'

'I suppose this is top secret?' said Jess.

'Totally.' He drew a finger across his throat. 'Pain of death.' Then he winked. 'On the other hand, maybe we owe it to the locals to make them aware of what's going on. After all, it's their heritage that's at risk too.'

Cat was still nursing her tea when the Golf squealed up the drive. She went to the window and watched while Declan almost fell out of the driver's seat and with elaborate chivalry opened the door for

Jess, who looked the worse for wear. So much for abstinence.

'C'm'on, darlin',' Declan's voice floated on the still air. 'I'm dying for a slash.' At least romance wasn't dead, thought Cat.

'You've just had one,' said Jess. She stumbled out of the car, still feeling sick.

'Just a tick.' Declan unzipped his jeans and peed into the fountain.

'Declan!' Jess giggled nervously. 'You're a bloody Neanderthal.'

'Wanna see my cave?' He sniggered lasciviously.

'Not tonight.' Jess pushed him away and teetered towards the Cottage. She needed to think in peace. 'I've got a headache.' She clattered into the hallway, leaving Declan staring forlornly at the lions. At the foot of the stairs Jess noticed the light in the kitchen. She bent over unsteadily to remove her shoes and sent Lily's rucksack flying, which in turn knocked over the coat-stand.

'Shit! . . . Sorry, Cat,' she said sheepishly as Cat appeared in the kitchen doorway.

'It's a bit late in the day for consideration,' said Cat, 'given that most of the county must be awake by now.'

'Yeah, sorry about that,' Jess whispered. The last thing she wanted was a lecture. It was almost one in the morning, she still felt queasy, and all she wanted was to collapse into bed and make some sense of this evening before she laid the evidence before Cat.

Seeing Jess skulking in the moonlight made all Cat's forbearance evaporate. She was sick of being the boring one always stuck at home with work – and she hated the hectoring tone her voice took on these days whenever she had a quarrel with Jess.

'You want to watch it,' she said, her frustration getting the better of her. 'You'll end up as the village joke.'

'What do you mean?'

'For God's sake, look at your behaviour. You're making an idiot of yourself.'

'And you're making yourself into a tedious martyr. You're like that bossy, virgin politician. What's her name – Ann Widdewell.'

'Combe,' said Cat, outraged. 'Someone's got to act like an adult round here.'

'Oh, here we go.' Jess's voice was rising shakily.

'What's that supposed to mean?'

'You want to let yourself go a little, Cat, otherwise you're going to lose the few friends you have around here.'

'Unlike you, I suppose.'

'I see flirting with Jake's done nothing to improve your mood.'

'I do not flirt with Jake.' Why did everyone keep getting the wrong end of the stick?

'Well, maybe that's your problem. You're going to end up a dried-up old witch if you're not careful.'

'And you're going to end up with a reputation. If you haven't got one already.'

'I don't need lectures from you on how to live life, thank you.'

'Yes, well, it would take more than a lecture, I suspect,' said Cat coldly.

'Well, at least not everyone hates me.'

'They don't hate me either,' said Cat, berating herself for such a lame response.

'Yeah, right.'

'What are you talking about?'

'Look, just stop making me feel I've done a gigantic shit on the precious flagstones when all I've done is go for a date or two,' Jess snapped.

A light shone in their faces. Lily was at the top of the stairs with her torch. She rubbed her eyes ruefully. 'What's going on?' she asked sleepily, flashing the beam at each of them in turn.

'Now look what you've done,' said Cat.

'I suppose you're going to fire me,' said Jess quietly the next morning when Lily was upstairs cleaning her teeth. She was secretly hoping for an apology. In view of the way she was batting for Cat it was the least she deserved.

Cat had already played this scenario through in her head. Jess's yoga classes were far too popular for Cat to get rid of her. 'I wouldn't be so childish,' she said haughtily.

Was this a ham-fisted attempt at an apology? 'Very well,' said Jess with as much dignity as she could muster in a pair of Ralph's old bathers.

'But I think from now on we should keep things on a strictly professional basis.'

'No worries,' said Jess. 'I was thinking the same. Shall I draw the lines down the fridge or will you?'

'There's no need for sarcasm.' No apology, then.

'Fine.'

'I honestly think it's better this way. No hard feelings?'

'None.' It was unbloodybelievable.

'Good,' said Cat brightly.

'Bitch,' said Jess under her breath.

The next general meeting to discuss Lower Nettlescombe's fête was at the Hung Drawn and Quartered five days later at six o'clock on a gorgeous July evening. The sun, which barely minutes earlier had been kissing the tops of the chestnut trees, turning them fuzzy, was sailing across a sky the colour of forget-me-nots. Cat, who was meeting Daphne there, strolled briskly down the high street, trying to take in the picturesque scene, as any normal, rounded person would, while also trying to push several thousand problems to the back of her mind.

She was so deep in thought that she almost collided with Jake as he stepped out of his front door. He was even more tanned than usual, which made his eyes seem more alive. For a moment she could detect a flash of Toby's spirit, which startled her.

'I didn't expect to see you,' she said, slightly winded.

He cocked his head. 'I live here,' he said. He squinted at the sun and seemed to sniff the air. Another local custom, no doubt. He could probably forecast the weather for the coming year just by smelling the breeze. 'The house special keeps getting better and better,' he said.

The tantalising aroma of Rupert's ballotine of suckling pig floated down the street.

'Mind if I join you?'

'I'm only going as far as the pub,' she said shyly. 'It's the fête meeting.'

'I know. So am I.'

They strolled along the lane together. By the time they reached the Hung Drawn and Quartered it was already standing room only. Julian was holding forth on some new pop sensation that had just been signed up for a five-million-pound two-album deal. 'Eight years old, for Christ's sake. It's immoral.' He wiped some scrumpy off his pale cherry-wood bar sorrowfully.

'Yeah, I mean, if he'd been seventeen they'd have had to pay him at least ten million,' said Rupert, peering out from the kitchen. 'It's almost child abuse. I don't know why they don't just shove them up chimneys and have done with it.'

'Very funny.' Julian scowled.

'Rupes has a point, Jules,' piped Lucy Wainwright. 'I mean, if a kid gets the chance to make a mint before he's ten, what's the big problemo?'

'A pint of Prince William and a tomato juice, please, Julian,' said Cat.

'Bloody awful music, that's the problemo,' called one of the rugger buggers from the far end of the bar.

'You're missing the point.' Julian sighed. 'I have no objection to children fulfilling their potential, but this is exploitation.'

'You don't have to buy their records.' Fee lit a cigarette.

'Who's the tall stranger, Fee?' asked Julian, smiling at a gawky boy moping behind Fee in a kaftan and goatee.

'My son Douglas.' She tossed her pashmina and bag at Douglas. 'Go and find us a table, there's a good boy.' Douglas slunk off on what was clearly a hopeless expedition. 'Just back from his year off,' she said to Julian.

'Doesn't have much of a sense of direction, does he?' joked Julian, as Douglas circled the Wainwrights longingly.

'Doesn't have much of anything. Least of all gumption.' Fee stuck a cigarillo in to a lipstick-smeared tortoiseshell filter. 'I thought he'd spend his year off whoring his way round the Far

East. Instead he appears to have spent most of it helping to set up a fair trade thingie in India.'

'Sounds worthwhile.'

'Bloody dullsville, you mean. Honestly, I don't know what's wrong with today's youth.'

'In your own time, Julian,' said Cat under her breath as Julian failed to notice her standing at the bar again. 'He's a bit distracted,' she whispered to Jake, who had sidled up behind her to see how she was getting on with the order.

'Right.' Julian rapped on a beer glass with a knife. 'I hereby declare this meeting open. Now as you all know, tonight has been designed so that the steering committee can keep the honorary committee abreast of what's been happening. To avoid boring you all, I think the best thing – if it's okay with you, Lady C – is if we go round each of the steering committee members and get a brief update on what's been going on.'

Despite her irritation at being temporarily usurped as the committee's mouthpiece, Cynthia managed a gracious nod in Julian's direction and the next forty minutes passed uneventfully enough with various tedious updates.

'In other words,' Jake whispered to Cat, during one of Mrs Potts' monologues, 'nothing's moved on much since the last meeting.' Eventually Mrs Potts appeared to be coming to the end of her speech.

'Well, if that's everything—' began Julian hopefully.

'Not quite,' said Cat, aware that the audience was about to stumble into a coma.

'Really?' said Julian. Cat wondered whether she had imagined it, or whether he was being curt. He was probably stressed out by Rupert's increasingly ambitious plans for the fête banquet. 'Perhaps you could keep it as brief as possible,' continued Julian. 'Since treasury reports tend to be of a rather dry nature. We don't want to kill everyone off.'

'Oh, it's not financial,' said Cat. 'You remember at the last meeting you said that if I wanted to follow up some of my suggestions I should?'

Julian looked at her powerlessly.

'Well, I have.'

'What suggestions might those be?' barked Fee. 'What exactly does one have to do to get a drink round here, by the way?'

'I'll be very brief,' persevered Cat. 'But if you recall, some of the ideas mooted to pep things up a bit included a dunking stool, stocks, a flight simulator, sheep shearing, human cannonballs, motorised sofa rides for the children, a jazz a cappella band, reike, spiritual healing, light energy and a Bob the Builder train.'

She looked up from her notes. Lady Cynthia who was holding court *sotto voce* on the other side of the bar, had talked all through her speech. Cat did her best to engage the rest of the room with a dazzling smile. 'I'm pleased to inform you that, without exception, they've all been provisionally booked. The sheep shearing was a bit tricky, but they juggled some dates and they're on. Plus we're going to have Indian head message and a nutritionist on hand, courtesy of Dr Anjit.' From the other side of the bar, Lady Cynthia's voice grew louder. 'And while I was ringing round,' continued Cat valiantly, 'I found some fire-eaters, if anyone's interested.'

She sat down to thunderous silence.

'I have a question?' Fee's son Douglas raised his hand eventually.

'Yes,' said Cat gratefully.

'Will there be trading without money?'

'Cat, have you done anything to upset Julian?' asked Jake as they walked down Butely Lane towards Hangman's Stile.

'Me?' Cat sounded wounded. 'I'd say half the pub had upset him.'

She felt him looking at her. She experienced a sudden longing to tell him about the midnight caller, but she wanted to hear him out first.

'He seemed a bit put out,' said Jake gently. 'Didn't you notice?'

'The whole bloody village is a bit put out, if you ask me. Must be something to do with fête nerves.'

'Not to worry.' She felt him suddenly squeeze her shoulder. 'Cat, there's something I have to tell you. Look, I've got an appointment now in Dorchester, but if you could get a babysitter tomorrow night, would you like to come to supper?'

Having found herself swept along in a complex rip tide of negotiations to organise sponsorship and thrilling new attractions, Cat barely noticed a creeping frostiness in her dealings with the other villagers. When Mrs Potts snubbed her in the makeshift extension to the Spar, she put it down to deafness. When Caleb and Brian made awkward excuses not to come into the Cottage kitchen for their usual dose of tea and fennel seed cake, she attributed it to busyness. But when half a dozen of the rugger buggers feigned not to recognise her when she bumped into them in a café in Dorchester – despite the fact that she'd spent a lot of time recently discussing the running order of the marathon tug o' war they were planning – she began to see a pattern emerging. But she put it down to jealousy – and pique. When they saw what a success the fête was going to be, they'd all come round.

Number 6 High Street couldn't have been more different from the blinding white perfection of Ashdown House or the impressive modernism of Toby's Clerkenwell penthouse. A cosy lair of dark colours, old furniture and interesting books, it rambled back from the street, bigger, but only just, than its tiny façade; Butely in miniature but without the builders. In the little bay, beneath the mullioned windows, was a polished oak table, laid for two and decorated with an azure jug of peonies and sweet peas. Cat was touched by its homeliness. Jake's cottage was everything, more or less, that she had always imagined Candida St John Green's abode to be.

Jake immediately poured them both a drink. 'That bad, is it?' said Cat lightly. She sat down in a faded striped armchair and picked absent-mindedly at the old horse blanket draped over its back. There was a reassuringly equestrian smell about the place that contrasted pleasantly with Lady Cynthia's candles and Toby's rampant testosterone. But for some reason she was nervous.

'I might as well get the bad news over with,' Jake began tentatively. 'I, er, like your shoes, by the way.'

She looked up at him encouragingly. He had on a faded green pullover that matched his eyes. Now Cat thought about it, he didn't look so bad himself, even if he seemed about three times too big for the room.

He walked over to the bureau, pulled out a letter from one of its cubby-holes and handed it to Cat. 'I got this from Barry two days ago. I'm sorry, Cat. I should have shown you immediately but I've been trying to do what I can to salvage the situation. I was hoping I'd be able to sort it all out without you having to know anything.'

'What is it?' she asked, alarmed.

'The council.' He stared at the floor. 'They're going to refuse permission for the pool complex.'

'Oh,' said Cat. She took another sip of vodka. 'Isn't that the norm? Don't they always refuse just so that they can spend a bit more time debating it? Keep the work flow steady?'

He smiled ruefully. 'Sometimes. The thing is, these protests can delay things indefinitely. Barry thinks it's an open-ended campaign. He says he's never seen anything so professional.'

She scanned the letter. 'He also says he admires your work and will do everything he can to help you in the long run. Does that mean it might go through eventually if we keep appealing?'

'Impossible to say,' said Jake glumly. 'Meanwhile the big question is what to do about the builders. There's not much point in paying them to continue working if there's no guarantee that you'll get permission to have the pool complex.'

'I take your point.' She finished reading the letter. 'Oh dear, the protesters do seem to be foaming at the mouth a bit. Who's behind it . . . ah, I see.'

Jake bustled into the tiny kitchen and returned with a delicious-looking fish pie which he placed next to the little jug of sweet peas and peonies.

'Poor you,' said Cat softly.

He sat down opposite her, the knees of his old moleskin trousers brushing against hers. He looked thoroughly miserable.

'No, it's not very supportive of my mother, is it?' he said. 'On the other hand I prefer to view this latest behaviour as a token of her enormous love for Toby rather than a manifestation of the contempt she holds me in.' There was an unmistakable tinge of bitterness in his voice, despite the attempt at levity.

'So you think she's been beavering away on this campaign ever since Toby and I had our row?'

'In her misguided way I think she feels he needs avenging for being left out of the will. She couldn't understand why he agreed to help you in the first place, since he wasn't benefiting directly.'

'That might explain the phone calls,' said Cat pensively.

'What do you mean?'

'Nothing, really. It's just that ever since Toby stopped coming down I've been having the occasional late-night conversation with someone who clearly doesn't like me being at Butely.'

Jake looked mortified. 'My mother?'

'Oh, I'm not suggesting she's making the phone calls herself.' Cat felt another surge of sympathy for him. 'It doesn't even sound like her.'

'She was an actress, don't forget.'

Not a very good one, according to Daphne, thought Cat. 'What I meant was that it could be one of the people who signed her petition. Whoever it is seems to think I'm hell-bent on destroying Butely.'

'How horrible for you,' said Jake. He sounded angry now. 'Why didn't you tell me earlier?'

'Oh, we had far worse in London,' said Cat jauntily. Now that she had finally told someone about them, the calls seemed less menacing. 'Stig once tried to throw a brick through our window. Admittedly he thought it was his own window – he'd had a row with his girlfriend. But it was quite scary at the time. Fortunately he was too stoned to get it over the hedge.'

He was looking at her with an unfamiliar gleam in his eye. If Cat didn't know him better she would have said it was tinged with admiration. She was pretty impressed herself by her sang-froid. Anyway, if the calls really were connected with Cynthia she didn't have anything to worry about.

'The thing is, Cat, my mother wields a lot of influence round here. She could delay the building indefinitely.'

'She made her aversion to doddery old people spoiling her views clear the first time I met her.' Cat grimaced. She couldn't bring herself to believe that Toby could ever have sanctioned the phone calls. Cynthia had obviously taken the law into her own hands.

They sat in silence for a few moments. 'I think it might be a good idea if you didn't set too much store by the pool complex idea. What about your original idea of running Butely pretty much as it is now?'

'It's a non-starter. I didn't know much about the business then. Even Daphne's crowd expect sprung floors and ozonic hydrotherapies.' Cat helped herself to some more fish pie. 'There's nothing for it. I'm going to have to swallow my pride and implore Toby to sort Cynthia out. I'm sure he wouldn't actually want to see us destitute. More wine?'

Jake went to fetch another bottle from the kitchen.

'Let me help you.' She stood up and accidently crashed into him. An electric shock passed between them. 'Oh my God, I've turned into a cattle prod,' she said, attempting to diffuse a potentially embarrassing situation.

'Apple crumble?' he asked quickly.

'Yes, please. I didn't know you could cook. You are a dark horse.' She smiled and for a moment their eyes locked.

'They taught us at the curiously enlightened school my mother sent me to.' He lowered his eyes.

'Toby's more of a takeout man.'

'Different schools.'

'Tell me to mind my own business, but what is it between you two?'

He placed a steaming bowl of apple crumble in front of her.

'Cream?'

'You haven't answered my question.'

He passed her a jug of double cream. 'We don't get on because we're completely different. Which isn't that surprising. We have different fathers.'

Cat let it drop. But something had subtly changed between them. Whether it was that stray electric spark or Cat's allusion to Toby's relationship with his half-brother, the molecular make-up of the room was charged. True, it had taken them months to arrive at a point where they could spend several consecutive hours together in an atmosphere of sweetness and light, but now they'd achieved it she had a feeling that in time – another fifty years, say – they might become inseparable friends.

19

The British Midland jet hovered over Glasgow, awaiting permission to land. Toby gave a cursory glance out of the window at the rows of Victorian buildings below, glittering in the brilliant early morning sun, before directing his attention back to the stewardess, whose head had been level with his groin for several minutes as she grappled with his seat belt, which had inexplicably jammed open.

'Yes, it is a magnificent city,' he said in a deliberately bored voice to the middle-aged American tourist next to him. He'd been ignoring her the entire flight, keeping his eyes closed as far as an adequate view of the stewardess's legs permitted. But now that they were about to land she'd raised her voice to such an extent he couldn't escape her.

'Is it Georgian or Victorian, do you know?' she asked, encouraged, as he had feared she would be, by his grudging politeness.

'I think you'll find it's neo-Princess Diana, with a bit of Olde Spice Girl cropping up in the suburbs,' he said rudely. She looked at him with a puzzled expression and he closed his eyes again. He was sick of the sight of Glasgow. These trips to Scotland had become increasingly frequent over the last few months – and increasingly time consuming. But Felix insisted on face-to-face contact. He couldn't be doing with fuckin' poncy Southern technology – telephones and e-mail, for instance – he said. Nothing beat seeing Toby in person, he said – apart, possibly, from beating him in person. But since that was a bit risky, even for Felix, he made do with thumping the desk, smashing his whisky tumblers and smacking his fist against his palm whenever he felt his instructions required extra emphasis. Which in Toby's opinion they never did. There wasn't much room for misinterpretation when someone told you to pull your fuckin' finger out otherwise they'd mush you and your reputation into the ground. And he was pretty sure he understood what Felix meant when he told Toby that he was a cretinous moron who couldn't be trusted to run a fuckin' bath.

He slid wearily into the back seat of the taxi and took a wee dram of the miniature bottle of Teacher's the stewardess had slipped into his pocket. When in Rome . . .

When Edna Potts went down with a nasty bout of summer flu – not, of course, that she admitted to having flu *per se*, any more than she ever confessed to being anything other than in exceptionally rude health – it was only a matter of time before Cat stepped into the breach. It was Daphne who organised the *putsch*, nominating Cat to take over the running of the bring-and-buy, leaving Jake to second her. It was a mixed blessing as far as Cat could see and, thanks to Mrs Potts' advanced years, one that was in a state of near-impenetrable chaos. Notable among the eccentric methods Mrs Potts had always employed with the clothes stall was snipping out the labels before putting the items out on trestle tables.

'Surely people would pay more if they realised how good some of the clothes are,' Cat said as she and Daphne sat up late one night sorting bags of donations. 'That looks awfully like a Prada kilt that was in Selfridges last year for four hundred pounds.'

'Don't be silly, dear,' said Daphne, holding it up for inspection before slipping it into her basket and placing £2.50 in the plaster pig Lily had lent them. 'Half the villagers wouldn't know Prada from Pinky and Perky. It would just intimidate them.'

'I'm not so sure,' began Cat. 'It seems to me that some of them are more clued up about labels than Joan Rivers on Oscar night.'

'Besides, it really winds up Cynthia. Oh, I say, Cat, do look at this pink Dior jacket. It would look marvellous on you. Oh, and see, here's the black taffeta skirt to go with. Very New Look.' She laid the outfit across Cat's knees and Cat ran her hands across the filmy layers. It was months since she'd had an excuse to really dress up – not since Toby had whisked her off to Hermione's ball, she thought wistfully. She popped the skirt on over her jeans and did up the hooks and eyes one by one, savouring the faint scent of Calèche that wafted out of the silk. Daphne clapped her hands. 'Oh, it's got your name on it, Cat. You have to have it. You need to make a bit more of yourself, you know.'

'Perhaps I could reserve it,' said Cat.

'You must have it now. Otherwise some pig farmer will buy it to insulate one of his sties.'

Cat shook her head wistfully. 'I couldn't.'

'Whyever not? There's masses here. We haven't even started on those bags Sister Slammer donated.'

'I've got a nasty feeling those are full of hot pants and chains. She had them sent over from LA. She's decided they don't go with the beautiful wardrobes Jake's designed for her.'

'You really should have it, dear. It's either you or those Wainwright sisters and they can afford to buy new.'

'I'd have to pay a fair price – a hundred pounds, say. It must be worth thousands.' She shook her head sadly. 'No, I can't afford it.'

'Well, what about this, then?' Daphne plucked a multi-coloured artist's smock from another bin liner. 'The label's already been snipped so you can't have any qualms on that score. And it's just the thing to wear to the fête in your role as Lower Nettlescombe's artist in residence.'

'All right then.' Cat, who hadn't been brought up by a fashion editor for nothing, slipped on the smock, which felt suspiciously light and delicate to be worth £2.50. 'This is couture! Are you sure Lady C doesn't want it?'

'I did think some of the bags looked as though they might have been intended for the dry cleaner's. But Edna swore they were all meant for the stall.' Daphne yawned. 'It's a bit late now. Anyway, Cynthia's a tad young for that sort of thing, if you ask me. You'd be doing her a favour if you took it off her hands.'

'Morning, Toby,' simpered one of Felix's bevy of secretaries. 'Isn't it a lovely one?'

'Glorious,' said Toby wanly. Anyone would think these people never saw the sun at all. 'How is his master's voice today?'

'Booming.'

'Glad to hear it.' He winced.

She darted from behind her desk and blocked his way.

'But you can't go in yet. Felix isn't ready.'

'Sorry.' Toby glanced at his Rolex and strolled past her. 'I don't
do delays.'

Felix was pacing round his desk screaming abuse at the squawk
box on it. Toby couldn't help feeling glad he wasn't on the
receiving end of this particular tirade. 'I don't care what the fuck it
takes, you shitty little ponce. What the fuck do you think I'm paying
you for?'

He flicked his finger in the direction of the secretary, who had
scurried in after Toby. 'You – out.' She flinched. 'And take Mr
Marks with you. I'm not ready for him yet.'

Toby ignored Felix, sitting down opposite him with a great deal
more bravura than he felt. The secretary threw him one last
desperate silent plea before scuttling out the door.

'I said out,' roared Felix. Toby held his ground. He knew he was
sunk if he gave into Felix's bullying. 'Felix,' he began calmly, 'we've
got a lot to get through today. I think you've made your point with
whichever unfortunate is on the other end of that line. Can I make
mine now?'

It was a calculated gamble. Normally he could almost make Felix
smile with his unruffled refusal to be cowed. But he saw immediately that he'd misread things. Felix shot him a malevolent look
before grinding his fist down on the phone with such force that it
shattered.

'You make me sick, you useless wanker,' he snarled. 'For
months you've been coming up here with your fuckin' designer
briefcase and your fuckin' designer spreadsheets and what have we
got to show for it? Sweet FA. And after all your noncey promises
that bitch is still hanging in there.'

'Only just.' Toby adjusted himself nervously in his chair. He
was sure Felix ordered them extra small just to humiliate his
opposition.

'Only just is just too much. You told me she'd have crawled back to that shit-hole in London by now.'

'Yes, well, she's had a bit of luck on her side. No one could have guessed that a gangsta rapper would book in. And she's got some daffy old bird living there who keeps finding just enough of her old muckers to come and stay to give the illusion that the place has got a future. It hasn't, of course, as they'll find out come winter.'

'It was up to you to make sure she didn't have luck on her side,' roared Felix.

'I've done my best. But she's more resilient than I thought.'

'You said she was an idiot.'

'I didn't mean it literally. For Christ's sake, Felix, she worked at Simms for four years. Something must have rubbed off.'

'I'm starting to think she might not be the dickhead of the story.'

'No, the real dickheads so far are those builders of yours.' Toby was panicking slightly. 'A kindergarten could have discovered what they were up to. Still, the planning on the pool complex has all but hit the rocks. I think you owe my mother dinner, by the way. All I had to do was hint to her that Cat had changed her mind about running it as a retreat for the rich and successful and planned to turn it into a multi-media conference centre instead, complete with a mall and a multiplex, and she was off, bombarding the council with petitions and rallying the great and the good for miles around against Cat. And if there's one thing that pathetic bunch at the council hate, it's controversy. I didn't even have to bribe them.'

'Well, maybe you should have,' thundered Felix. 'Because that brother of yours has been making a right bloody nuisance of himself. He's like a dog with a fuckin' bone.'

'Yes, well, I don't think we need to tremble on that front. He's hardly Norman Foster. He won't even have a clue who's behind the campaign. So he's not going to know who to schmooze, is he?'

Felix tossed an envelope at Toby's face. It just grazed the corner of his eye. Inside was a copy of the letter Barry Dean had given to Jake, telling him about Cynthia's pivotal role in the campaign against Cat.

'I think you'll find he knows exactly who to hold responsible. And it won't take a genius to make the link between Lady Cynthia and you!'

'Fortunately Jake's not a genius.' Toby sounded calmer than he felt.

'That fuckin' councillor doesn't seem to think your brother's hopeless. And I'd like to point out, Toby, that there's no guarantee that bloody council won't give them the go-ahead on the pool if they appeal enough times.'

'Oh, come on, Felix. You were the one who said every man has his price. I'm sure if you offer them enough pieces of silver they'll come round to your way of thinking. Cat will never get planning permission.'

'Yes, well, Barry fuckin' Dean appears not to have a price, so far.'

'Well, the protestors can go on blocking Cat's plans indefinitely. And sooner or later Cat will run out of money.'

'No sign of that so far, however,' stormed Felix. 'And if I might remind you, Toby, we don't have till "eventually".'

'How did you get hold of this?' asked Toby, feeling markedly less confident than he had five minutes earlier. His eyes were still watering from where the paper had struck his cornea.

'Declan, of course,' snarled Felix. 'That airhead au pair stumbled across it and he got her to show it to him.'

'Au pairs! Felix, really. MI5 must be quaking in their boots.'

'It tells us more than you did.' He marched over to the window. 'And your brother better fuckin' watch it or he might just find himself falling off a piece of scaffolding.'

'I don't think you'll need to go that far,' said Toby.

Felix shot him a vicious look. 'You know, sometimes, Toby, I'm not sure you've got what it takes to see this through.'

Toby attempted a dry laugh, which came out more like a strangled sob. 'Come on, Felix. You know me. Always save the best till last. By the time I've finished she'll be begging us to take the place off her hands.'

'We'll see.' Felix's face has assumed an icy calmness now, which was much more deadly than his chaotic rages. He flipped over the calendar on his desk. 'Frankly I'm getting a bit bored. You've got six more weeks. After that I'm pulling you off this. The deal will be null and void. Oh, and I'll take every bit of business I've got out of Simms as well. And I'll make sure they know who's to blame.'

It was Toby's turn to storm out of Felix's headquarters. Until now he'd always maintained his cool – it was his only weapon against Felix's billion-pound might. But he was furious. There was no reason at all for Felix to pull out of the Butely deal. It was a brilliant scheme and he knew it. He sat in taciturn silence on the flight back to London, too angry even to flirt with the stewardesses.

He was in shock. Ever since he'd first been loaned out as a consultant to Golden Fields PLC eight years ago, Toby had had the unmistakable feeling that Felix Hark had singled him out for advancement. He guessed that beneath the bluster and the foul language, Felix had a sneaking regard for him, and this had been confirmed when Felix had come to see him in New York, just before he got called back to the London office, with a plan to buy Butely.

'It belongs to your family anyway, doesn't it?' Felix had asked, in uncharacteristically laid-back mood one evening when they were relaxing over drinks in the Four Seasons.

'In a roundabout way,' Toby had said wryly.

'What the fuck does that mean?' said Felix, scooping a handful of peanuts into his mouth.

'It's my ex-stepfather's. Though why it should concern you I don't know. It's a tip. Can't be worth more than half a million in its current state. And it would probably cost twice that to make it properly habitable. If you're looking for a country seat I could find you a dozen better ones.'

'I'm not looking for a country seat, you fuckin' poof,' said Felix, sounding almost good natured. 'What if I told you Butely has oil? Lots and lots of it.'

'I'd say someone had been leading you up the garden path.' Toby snorted. 'There isn't lots of oil anywhere in Dorset. Just the occasional spurt.'

'Well, that's where you're wrong, arsehole. I've got the documents to prove it.' And he'd shoved half a hundredweight of paper into Toby's lap. 'All kosher – from Golden Explorations.'

Toby looked momentarily confused.

'A mineral and mining subsidiary of mine. It's completely above board. They've been doing work for the government in the area on something completely different, as it happens. Stumbling across this little discovery was a complete – and completely pleasant – fluke.'

Toby had taken the documents back to his SoHo loft and stayed up most of the night devouring them. Not that he'd needed to. By page four he'd read enough facts and figures to assure himself that they were sitting on a potential gold mine – or something that was even better. He'd called Felix at the crack of dawn.

'Okay, you've convinced me about the oil,' he'd said, trying to sound blasé. 'But in an area of outstanding natural beauty . . . you'll never get permission to drill.'

'You fuckin' poof – what do you think I've got friends in high places for?'

'I'm impressed.'

'So you fuckin' should be. This could well turn out to be one of the biggest onshore drilling projects this country's ever seen.'

'What do you want me to do?' said Toby. He was so excited that for the first time in years he thought the asthma he always used to get when the weather turned hot was about to come back.

'Persuade the old boy to sell.'

'Easy,' said Toby, overlooking, in his initial thrill, the number of times Sir Rodney had said he would never part with Butely.

'Good, because after that there's the small matter of smoothing things over with those wankers on the council.'

'Nothing that a few backhanders won't sort out, I'm sure. It'll be like taking candy from a baby,' said Toby, taking his cue from Felix.

'It better be,' said Felix tersely. 'It's worth ten per cent of all we find if you manage it.'

★

It was ironic, thought Toby, pouring himself another British Midland whisky. At first everything had gone so well. The gods had really seemed to be on his side. From being an improbable outside bet, the old boy had finally done the decent thing and kicked the bucket, leaving Butely to some clueless control freak who wouldn't last one chilly spring there, let alone a whole year.

Admittedly he'd been taken aback about the will. In fact, hearing that Rodney had left the place to Cat – a woman he barely knew – and Jake – a useless dreamer – had felt like rape. Especially when he, Toby, had put so much time and effort into schmoozing the old boy in the last few years. All those visits when he'd got back from New York, not to mention the endless solicitous notes he'd written him while he was there and the trips he'd made to Dean & Delucca to get Rodney his favourite brand of maple syrup.

Yet in another way, knowing that Rodney had been so smitten by Cat – the old goat – had validated his own feelings for her. And Toby had been very taken by Cat, almost from the first.

Well, perhaps not quite the first. She'd seemed a bit of a neurotic liability – a typically sloppy Londoner – after all those slick Manhattan women. Though to give her credit, her shoes had always been unimpeachable. And as he'd got to spend more time with her he'd come to appreciate her energy, her wit, her brain – her bloody endless legs. And yes, perhaps his feelings for her had become that bit more intense once she inherited Butely. But that didn't negate what he'd felt for her in the first place. The galling thing was, it could have worked. If Cat had been the soulmate he'd been looking for, he could have explained about the whole Felix set-up and somehow got her to help him convince Jake as well. He'd fantasised about cutting her in on the deal quite a lot, as it happened. He'd nearly told her everything that last night they were together. But she'd made it clear pretty early on that she was just another idealistic loser. Pity. He'd been quite keen on Lily too. It had all looked so good on paper. With a kid practically at senior school, Cat would probably have been quite happy not to have any more babies, unlike most of the other women who'd tried to get him up the aisle in New York.

It hadn't helped having Felix get hysterical about the deal so early on. If he'd given Toby more time he could definitely have won Cat round to his way of thinking. As it was he'd had to make some decisions that had alienated her. But even after that monumental row he'd still hoped she might come begging for his help. Fat chance. He should have screwed her once or twice when he'd had the chance. God knows, she'd practically laid herself out on a plate. If he had he might have flushed her out of his system a lot quicker. But oh no. He'd decided to play the so-called chivalrous card. He'd wanted to make her think he was really serious about her – and in his experience, the best way to convince women your intentions were serious was not to shag them till they were gagging for it. At least, that was how it was in New York, thanks to *The* bloody *Rules*. He ought to sue the authors of that crap for wrecking his life.

All right, so not shagging his dates had in the main suited him very well – he couldn't cope with the histrionics that normally followed the deed the next day. He'd rather keep the whole thing light and, as they seemed to see it, romantic. And satisfy his physical urges with a professional who wasn't going to have a nervous breakdown because he didn't call her afterwards.

But Cat had been different – more enigmatic, less needy somehow. It was probably just having the kid. Her biological clock wasn't on red alert. But even watching her flailing around from afar – via Declan – had been a lot less fun than he'd anticipated.

Part of the problem was that Cat hadn't been nearly as clueless or incapable of delegating as he needed her to be. Sometimes he imagined he missed her. Then Jake had ambled in on everything with his galumphing size elevens, as he always had done, and – to paraphase Felix – truly gone and fucked things up.

Sometimes Jess got the distinct impression that Declan though she was an idiot. At first she'd been entertained by his references to birds, tits and love nests – it was a bit like talking to an ornithologist. She wasn't offended by his liberal use of politically incorrect phrases because she'd developed the hide of a rhinoceros on the sheep-shearing station. Half the time she wasn't even aware they were incorrect. But gradually, the way he placed his hands over her ears and said 'Not in front of the children' whenever anyone talked about something remotely intelligent began to pall. She didn't like the way his mobile was always ringing either. The first time it had happened he'd been tweaking her nipple. Reaching into his back pocket for his phone with his spare hand, he'd prodded her with his keys. And she could hear Toby loud and clear.

'Oh, it's you,' he said, suddenly pulling himself off Jess and wedging himself back behind the steering wheel. 'Yeah, I'm alone.' Declan eyed Jess and grinned. 'Don't worry. Everything's under control.' He slid his hand down the waistband of Jess's cut-offs and began a finger dance. 'What do you mean?' The tone of Declan's voice changed. He sounded probing and defensive at the same time. His finger dance became more staccato. She squirmed and tried to prise his fingers away. 'I'm not sure that's going to be possible,' he said, sounding more tense than ever. He pulled his hand away from Jess roughly. She winced. 'Look, I said no one's here. It was just one of the pheasants.' He shot a warning glance at Jess.

There were some muffled comments down the line. Leave it with me,' said Declan petulantly, before tossing the phone in the glove compartment next to him. Jess said nothing.

He gripped the steering wheel. After a while he seemed to remember Jess was still in the car. 'Come here, darlin'.' But Jess didn't want to go anywhere with Declan. In the space of a phone call her remaining affection for him had all but vapourised. Instinctively she felt something was badly wrong. She needed time to think. 'Sorry.' She scrabbled out of the car. 'Don't feel very well. Got to go.'

'What's the matter, love?' Declan leaned out of the window. 'Got the decorators in?'

Jess looked at him uncomprehendingly. 'They're always in these days,' she said. 'Goran's finally toeing the line.' She fled across the moonlit drive towards the Cottage, wondering how to articulate the extent of her anxiety to Cat when she had so little in the way of concrete evidence.

*

'What the hell do you mean by leaking Sister Slammer's stay here to the press?' Cat had stormed straight up to the shag-pad and caught Declan in bed again.

'Come on, darlin' – it was bound to leak out eventually.' He stretched his arms behind his head and yawned. There was so much hair under his pits it looked as though a litter of old English sheepdogs were nestling there.

'Only because there's a slimy little runt on the loose. How much did the papers pay you?'

Declan looked hurt. He flicked the duvet away to give Cat a full-frontal. 'Not that little. And what makes you think it was me?'

'The fact that you're one of the most unprincipled, amoral, self-interested, selfish people I've ever met.'

'In that case, darlin'.' He swaggered past her towards the door. 'You need to get out more.'

The morning of the fête dawned with conflicting omens. The sun shone bright and blameless. Fluffy little clouds scudded gently overhead, just quickly enough to suggest a welcome breeze. Under foot, meanwhile, the unmistakable dust ruts of an old Mercedes' rapidly retreating tyre tracks told Cat that Weezie, Veronica and Joanna had done a runner.

' Ain't right.' Sister Slammer fiddled with the diamond pin in her eyebrow sadly as she examined the disturbed gravel with Cat. 'If you need any financial help, I would be honoured to help you out. No strings—'

'That's very kind.' It was the first time in months that anyone apart from Jake had offered her something for nothing.

Daphne trotted up in her Prada skirt. 'Don't worry, they'll be back. Just as soon as they've wangled another load of dosh out of their publisher.'

'Is that what your crystal ball says?' snapped Cat. With the fête looming she felt she'd done quite enough for charity.

'No, it's what they always do. I think it's some sort of literary superstition. They'll pay you back just as soon as the royalties start flooding in. I have to give them credit where it's due. They're not mean.'

Cat didn't think they were due any credit – especially from her.

Sister Slammer adjusted her hot pants and suddenly froze.

'What is it?' said Cat.

Sister Slammer raised her head and sniffed the air. 'Paparazzi. I can smell them. Look.'

Cat followed her gaze to a copse of trees near Butely's gates where the unmistakable glint of sun bounced off long-range lenses. She was going to murder Declan.

'I'm so—' she began.

But Sister Slammer was already rolling up her minuscule T-shirt. 'Thank Christ,' she said, sauntering across the lawns. 'I was beginning to think no one cared.'

Cat had only just put the phone down when it rang again. It was Daphne, calling from the village green.

'Don't panic,' she began importantly, 'Lower Nettlescombe's WI have arrived. They're just setting up stall as we speak.'

'How lovely.' Cat sighed, picturing pink-cheeked WI ladies and fluffy yellow Victoria sponges and fairy cakes and remembering with a shudder the sushi stalls and fusion barbecue from Lady Eleanor's fund-raisers. She looked at her watch. 'They're a bit late, aren't they?'

'Nothing to worry about, dear. Just a bit of a rumpus earlier. The rugger buggers got a bit excited about the motorised four-poster. They insisted on trying it out – all fifteen of them. I'm afraid they upended it into the cake stand.'

Cat's hands went clammy. Although she wasn't the only member of the steering committee, having put so much into its organisation she felt uniquely responsible for the outcome of the day. 'Just how ballistic are the WI ladies?' she asked. All her earlier optimism began to evaporate like two-day-old perfume.

'Fairly,' said Daphne in an attempt at casual gaiety. 'But I think they're coming round to the idea of having a trifle stand.'

'Does this mean the rugger buggers won't be fit to kick things off with the tug o' war?' said Cat, her heart sinking.

'Only one of them had to be actually *hospitalised*,' said Daphne carefully. 'I think it was shock more than anything.'

'So we'd better start with the Lower Nettlescombe Mummers instead?' Cat ran a finger down her endlessly revised schedule.

'Not an ideal solution – they're still waiting for their costumes to dry off.' Daphne raised her voice in an attempt to make herself heard above the roars of two of the rugger buggers, who were now taking it in turns to immerse one another in the pond using the ducking stool. 'Apparently they had a dress rehearsal upstairs at the pub last night and things got a bit out of hand.'

Across Butely's lawns there came an ear-piercing screech. Cat ran outside. Lily had been ambushed by a dozen or so of Declan's pheasants on her way to Sir Galahad's stables and was being chased across the lawns.

Cat flew towards her, waving her arms around wildly. 'How dare you!' she screamed at the pair nipping at Lily's heels.

'It's okay, Mum,' said Lily. 'They're not hurting me. They just shocked me.'

'You look terrible. You're the colour of putty.'

'That's 'cos I'm nervous about today. Sir Galahad's being a bit temperamental.'

'I'm not surprised,' retorted Cat, 'with all the racket those birds are making.' She was livid. Having Declan torture dumb animals and contravene the entire spirit of all Butely's conventions was bad enough, but if he was going to turn the poor traumatised beasts loose so that they terrorised them all, she was going to have to put her foot down, literally. 'Scram, *scram*.' She kicked out at them. The birds struck up a chorus of indignant squawks and began eyeing Lily up proprietorially.

'Please don't have another row with Declan,' pleaded Lily.

'They're not rows so much as reprimands.'

'Right,' said Lily. 'And he is a complete git. But every time you lose your rag with him something bad happens, haven't you noticed?'

Cat would have liked to have quizzed Lily more forensically but one of the birds began pecking at her boots. 'Bugger off!' she shouted, shaking her arm violently.

'Dear oh dear,' Declan rolled up alongside them in the Golf. 'Not very in keeping with Butely ethics, is it, Cat, to go around beating up poor defenceless pheasants? Next thing you know we'll have the RSPCA round.'

Cat stuck her head through his open car window, partly to see whether Jess was with him. 'This is completely unacceptable, Declan. I'm going to insist that you put them back in their cages. They've just attacked Lily. She's scared to death.'

'All right, all right, keep your bra on.' Declan raked his eyes over Lily, who, even Cat had to admit, didn't look anywhere near death, just a bit shaken. 'Let me explain something about farming, love. They wouldn't exactly be free range if we put them back in their cages, now, would they?'

Cat drew herself up to her full height. She was not going to have any more conversations leaning through Declan's car window, even if it meant directing her comments from now on at his aerial. 'That's not my problem, I'm afraid. I demand you put them away.'

'Yes, well, we'll see what Toby has to say about that. He's very keen on this little pheasant project. He reckons if all else fails we could turn Butely into a hunting, shooting and fishing gaff. You do realise, don't you, Cat, that since Elle Macpherson got into it, it's become very big business?' He flicked some cigarette ash over her feet. 'It's the new rock and roll, babe. In the meantime' – he glanced at Cat's jogging pants – 'hadn't you better get ready for the Party in the Park? Catch you later, girls.' He put his polo boot down on the accelerator and skidded off, leaving a squall of dust in his wake.

'See what I mean, Mum? Now you'll just be upset all day.' Lily shook her head wistfully and trudged towards Sir Galahad's stable.

The village green was clotted with stalls and an early crowd, waiting impatiently for things to get going. At the far end, beneath an awning tricked out with bunting, Jake was saddling up the last of the ponies. Cat waved shyly, but he didn't see her. 'Thank heavens,' panted Daphne, her gypsy hoop earrings spinning as she hurtled up to Lily and Cat. 'I thought something terrible must have happened to you both.' She turned to look at the feverish activity. Dr Anjit had been brilliant at rounding up all his colleagues, thought Cat, with a stab of affection. There was already a queue forming outside the alternative health marquee, where last-minute touches were being made to the Indian head massage, internal Alchemy, light energy, and reflexology stalls.

Douglas, wearing a frayed Kurt Cobain T-shirt, love beads and Birkenstocks, eyed Cat lugubriously. She flicked her eyes over the programme and looked at her watch nervously. Norman Biggleswaite, 'heart-throb to the short sighted and the insane', should have been performing a cappella on the bandstand by now.

'Stop worrying,' soothed Daphne. 'As you can see, those vultures from the WI have already raided the jewellery stall.' Cat looked at the WI ladies' Viyella dresses, now so studded with brooches they could have picked up a hundred and sixty satellite stations between them, even with Lower Nettlescombe's notoriously poor reception.

'Oh, hello, Douglas,' said Daphne. 'I thought you were still in Uttar Pradesh. Did you have a lovely time? I hope you looked up darling Rofi. His palace is quite something, isn't it?'

'I was too busy setting up a system of sustainable cash crops to hobnob with a fascist regime of maharajas,' mumbled Douglas.

'That's nice,' said Daphne. 'Now you couldn't find Julian and ask him when he's actually going to start the fête? I'm counting on him and Rupert to spend, spend, spend on the bring-and-buy. The vicar usually shows a keen interest too.'

Douglas slouched off, muttering something about the curse of global consumerism.

Cat eyed a queue of small, sullen-looking girls that had formed by her paintbox. 'Your audience awaits,' announced Daphne. 'A lot of them really wanted to have their hair braided.' She nodded towards the Wainwright sisters, who were setting up an elaborate beauty stall opposite Cat's. 'But I told the mothers they could leave the little minxes at our stall as long as they liked. You could turn out to be the most popular attraction of all. Now remember, it's a pound for the face, two pounds for body work. Look, I've got you a pint of Prince William and some of Nettlescombe Primary's home-made toffees to get you going. *Courage.*'

Out of the corner of her eye, Cat could just see Lady Cynthia, cool as a Ralph Lauren ad, being ushered on to the podium in front of the real-ale tents. With a sinking heart, she set out her face paints. A thunderous crack from Julian's pistol rent the sky asunder and two medieval jousters emerged on horseback from a striped marquee in suits of armour that Cat recognised from Ashdown House. There was a chaotic flurry of wind noises from the jousters' trumpets – and a barrage of sniggers from the rugger buggers.

With practised timing, Lady Cynthia waited for the cackles to subside before summoning her vowels into something resembling modern English. 'The past few months have seen our traditions and way of life in Lower Nettlescombe come under greater threat than ever,' she began. There was a nerve-grating squawk of feedback from the microphone. Cat felt the eyes of the village upon her. 'But Lower Nettlescombe has not been invaded since 1066, and it will not be invaded now.' Vigorous applause and cheers broke out.

With as much dignity as she could, Cat began mixing her paints, mentally running through the repertoire of animals and flowers she could recreate. At least the day couldn't get any worse. Lorna Cuthbertson, a ginger-haired girl with a runny nose and a belligerent expression, was second in the queue by Cat's paint kit. She tugged on Cat's skirt and shoved a crumpled magazine under her nose.

' 'Ere, can you do me like Kylie?' Cat looked at her with something close to hysteria and a certainty that at least the day couldn't get any worse. But that was before she saw the placards.

20

It must have been nerves combined with the gnawing knowledge that even after all her work on the fête the villagers hadn't entirely taken her to their hearts, but for several horrible moments Cat thought the placard-wavers were aiming their discontent with the world directly at her. Slightly apart from the fray, she could see Douglas waving a peace banner and chanting.

> *'One, two, three, four,*
> *Capitalism rapes the poor.*
> *Three, four, five, six,*
> *globalism stinks'.*

Whatever else he'd learnt at the Uttar Pradesh collective, it wasn't scansion, thought Cat. Instinctively she looked round for Lily, who was miles away, grooming Sir Galahad for the hundredth time in anticipation of his starring role in the Ages of History procession at 4 p.m.

Cat's life flashed before her. She was surfing on a lethal cocktail of adrenalin and half a pint of Prince William. In reality, the mob was a desultory half-dozen of Douglas's acne-spattered chums, whose anger wasn't so much specifically aimed at Cat as the entire litter of Lower Nettlescombe fat cats. And then suddenly the two protesters who seemed to be taking most of the initiative laid down their banners and pushed past her, swooping down on Lorna Cuthbertson. It seemed that while Cat had been busy making the small boy at the head of the queue look like Spiderman, Lorna had decided to sample one of Cat's toffees and was in the process of choking. It was Vic Spinoza who came to the rescue, rushing over from the coconut shy he was manning to give Lorna the Heimlich manoeuvre. Orlando and his docu-crew were in seventh heaven.

After the St John Ambulance crew had ascertained that there was nothing much wrong with Lorna, the heat seemed to go out of the protesters' fervour. Julian, invigorated from crowning Jess the Lower Nettlescombe Dairy Queen, invited everyone over to the real-ale tent for a half-price pint.

At half past three, Jake handed charge of the pony rides to Caleb and Brian and ambled over to Cat's for a break. 'Are you all right?' He watched her applying blue eyeshadow to her fifth Britney. 'You look a bit pale.'

'I'm fine. Actually I know this is going to sound silly. But earlier – that incident with Douglas and his friends – well, for one mad moment I thought they'd come to get me.' She peered at him over mini Britney's head. He wasn't laughing, or frowning. In fact he looked almost concerned.

'Oh, Cat . . .'

'What?' she said hurriedly.

'No one hates you. They're just a bit suspicious, that's all. Why don't you invite them over to Butely later in the week so that you can show them exactly what's going on?'

'Do you think that would make any difference?' she asked glumly, casting around for her tube of gold glitter.

'All the difference. Honestly, Cat—' He broke off.

'What?'

'Ow!'

'Sorry!' Cat dabbed the child's cheeks, now streaked with black tears, apologetically.

'For someone so good at management you're not very good at managing your own PR.'

With Jake at her side, Cat moved through the real-ale tent dispensing casual-sounding invitations to drinks to everyone she met.

'Would that be on the house, dear?' piped up Mrs Potts from

behind a display of sulphuric yellow dahlias which had taken first prize in the Grown from Seed competition. 'Gone to seed more like,' muttered Daphne to Cat's elbow. 'Ghastly common colour. Some people have no idea.'

'Of course,' said Cat. 'And there'll be a buffet of organic Butely nibbles too,' she added rashly, 'so that you can test the Butely philosophy for yourselves.'

The rest of the afternoon passed in a more or less contented blur of ferret racing, rabbit weighing, motorised bed riding and crystal ball gazing. Lily and Sir Galahad came third in the fancy dress competition. Cat made £51, Rupert took a turn to be dunked in the village pond by Julian, then insisted on having a go at dunking Julian, after which Julian dunked Rupert for even longer, after which they had a fight. By seven o'clock there were only a few stragglers left on the green, and they were inebriated rugger buggers who had been drowning their sorrows in Prince William and Prince Harry after coming second against the Royal Boars' first eleven in the tug o' war.

At 7.30 Cat wearily set about the daunting task of helping the local scouts clear up the mountain of litter that was strewn like dandruff across the green's once pristine sward. Daphne came to tell her that although the counting wasn't quite complete, Butely's one thousandth fête looked like being its most financially successful to date. 'Mainly thanks to you and me, my dear, though I say it myself.'

Might as well, thought Cat. No one else would. Out of the corner of her eye she saw the remaining rugger buggers doing a moonie as a gleaming black Jaguar swept past the green. Harbury sat in the driver's seat, and behind him, waving imperiously, was Lady Cynthia, on her way, no doubt, to dinner with Sting and Trudie.

The At Home went as well as could possibly be expected given that the guests had to pick their way past a tower of scaffolding, two cement mixers, two dozen bags of cement mix and several miles of dust sheet.

'Big job, is it, dear?' enquired old Mrs Potts with startling insight.

It was a gloriously mild September evening, the sort that casts long gold and black shadows on the grass and bathes everything in a soft pink light. Cat had decided to begin the tour by plying everyone with vats of an excellent organic elderflower wine that Micky had made. This was followed by sizzling heaps of Guy Fulton's locally made lamb sausages, and tiny wild salmon and egg tarts. By half past seven, there were quite a few soft pink faces.

Micky had come up trumps – which was just as well because news of the free booze and food had spread and forty-seven people turned up. The day before, Cat had asked Vic Spinoza – not because he'd ever given any sign of objecting to what she was doing at Butely, but because she felt she needed some moral support and because she liked him. Julian, who, as part of his settlement following the pond ducking incident, had managed to persuade Rupert to take over the running of the pub for half an evening, appeared on the dot of 6.30. Naturally the same couldn't be said of Lady Cynthia. She hadn't even proffered the excuse of dinner with Stella McCartney. Instead she'd got Harbury to call on the afternoon to say she was indisposed.

'I thought Butely was supposed to be macrowhateveryoucallit,' mumbled Mrs Potts, stuffing another miniature quiche in her mouth.

'Macrobiotic,' Cat smiled patiently. 'It still is, for those who want that discipline. But we've decided to broaden our appeal. The emphasis from now on is going to be on fresh organic local produce. Those are Butely's very own sausages,' she explained, as another disappeared into Mrs Potts' mouth. 'We won't be using anything that has to be flown halfway round the world or degrades the soil or animals in any way. What we've looking for in every-thing we do here is a sustainable realistic alternative to bad habits. And that's exactly why' – she paused, taking a leaf from Lady Cynthia's book of oratorical skills – 'we would never do anything that would jeopardise the land around Butely . . .'

'So you're not planning to flatten the place and turn it into a multiplex, then?' asked Douglas in a voice that fluctuated between outraged gruffness and a squawk.

'Of course not. And even if we wanted to, we'd never get planning consent. Butely is Grade One listed. That means we can't do anything serious without permission. That's one of the reasons we're pulling down that old fifties block. It should never have been put up in the first place.'

'So you're not turning the place into a celebrity wedding hotel?' said Tashie Wainwright, sounding crestfallen.

'Absolutely not.'

'And no All Bar One?' demanded Julian from the back. So that was the reason for his recent frostiness. Cat rolled her eyes in mock horror. Where had they been getting all this negative propaganda from?

'Not in a million years.'

'So why does that young man seem to think that you are – the one with all the jewellery?' Mrs Potts narrowed her eyes suspiciously before narrowing her mouth round yet another sausage.

Cat's breathing became a shallow rap. So Declan had been betraying her, after all. She didn't know which emotion to yield to first – indignation or relief that her hunch had been right all along. Indignation won, combined with shock that he could really have been so callous. 'He's got the wrong end of the stick, that's all,' she said hurriedly. She lowered her voice conspiratorially. 'He's a bit simple, I'm afraid. We've got him on a scheme that works with minor offenders to release them back into the community.'

The guests looked awestruck.

'Will you have collagen implants?' asked Fee, brightening at the prospect.

Cat shook her head. 'No, but Dr Anjit's found some very interesting herbal and vitamin treatments that have proven to be very effective in dealing with wrinkles.'

'Oxygen facials?' asked Julian.

'Not really. Though we will have ayurvedic massages that work on the face.'

'So you reckon you can make money out of Butely the way it is?' Julian looked sceptical. He was gutted about the facials.

'Not quite the way it is. As you can see, we're modernising. But in other ways we're going back to basics – what Butely does best.'

There was a ripple of disappointment as the prospect of an almighty village feud receded. Cat's face settled into a rictus of bright amiability. 'What we are doing – or hoping to, as some of you know – is building a new pool with all the latest technology—'

'Whatever do you want one of those for in England?' said Mrs Potts querulously.

'Well, for one thing it will be indoors,' explained Cat, 'and for another, Dr Anjit here assures me that water can help enormously in the treatment of certain rheumatic and arthritic complaints.'

'All right for millionaires, isn't it?' grumbled Mrs Potts.

'And we'll be offering very favourable prices to villagers. In fact' – she thought of Toby and felt a small curl of satisfaction – 'we'll be continuing Sir Rodney's policy of means testing. No one will ever be turned away from Butely for financial reasons.'

'Can't see you lasting more than five minutes, then. But good luck,' shouted Lucy Wainwright, who felt a bit iffy about sharing a pool with *hoi polloi*.

'If you don't mind my saying,' offered Vic, 'it does sound a bit naive.'

'Not once we've signed up a raft of corporate members to subsidise it all,' said Cat. 'There are hundreds of companies out there looking for exactly this kind of place to keep their employees in healthy working order.'

'You mean some companies actually pay for their workforce to lie around in towelling robes all day long?' asked Mrs Potts, eyeing up the tiny pavlovas.

'That's not all they'll be doing here. They'll be learning how to incorporate exercise into their daily lives – not just by going to the gym, but by using the park more often, taking up a bit of gardening. But to answer your point, basically the answer's yes. Companies will pay. They see it as a bit like booking their staff in for an MOT.'

This was greeted with incredulous, but not actively hostile, looks.

'Now in a moment,' Cat continued, 'I hope you'll join me on a gentle ramble round Butely. We'll start with the herb garden, where I hope you'll see how we're working to help people lead healthier lives.'

She stopped, fearing she might have come across as unbearably smug. There was a silence – and then suddenly Douglas began clapping. Soon everyone joined in. Cat felt her eyes misting over. Jake had been right all along. All the villagers had required was some human contact. They made their way to the kitchen garden, now looking as lush as a bishop's robes, thanks to Caleb and Brian. By 9.30 Cat had shown them as much of the inside of Butely as she could, without supplying them with hard hats and safety harnesses, but there was no sign of anyone flagging. Irrigated with copious amounts of elderflower wine, they seemed to have taken root on the lawns. Cat could hardly stop grinning all night as one by one they came up to compliment her on the food. One or two even wished her luck. Only Orlando looked downcast.

'What's up?' She wandered over to him with a plate of baked figs. 'You've barely taken any footage tonight. That's not like you.'

'I thought you'd be pleased.' He fumbled with his mobile and kicked out at one of the stone lions. It was the closest she'd ever seen to him losing his temper. 'It's Myfanwy,' he said mournfully. 'She wants to put Sister Slammer on bloody *Woman's Hour*.'

'Is that a problem?'

He adjusted his glasses, which had slid down his nose, and sighed. 'She can't let me have anything for myself. She's so bloody competitive.'

'I doubt if Sister Slammer wants any more publicity at the moment,' said Cat.

'Really?' He brightened.

'She's been splashed over all the papers the past fortnight. Didn't you notice any long-lens cameras?'

'I've been a bit wrapped up.' He leant against a lion.

'I ought to kill Declan for leaking the fact she was here, but I have to admit we've been flooded with enquiries ever since.'

'Usually the others read all the papers and précis them for me,' he added, so that Cat wouldn't think he was hopelessly out of touch.

They sat in silence, ruminating on fate's strange twists, their peace punctured only by Mrs Potts asking Jess whether they would be supplying sausages to Walls. Roused from his grief, Orlando ambled off to demolish the last few canapés.

Cat finished her wine and sat back to watch as the pink flames of the sun embraced the sycamores and oaks in a warm, late summer sunset and the undulating lawns soaked up the light. Some late yellow roses scrambled over a nearby wall, sending out gusts of heady scent. She was starting to know every inch of Butely and beginning to love it as much as she had ever loved anything.

Gradually the guests wandered off, some of them too tipsy to head in the right direction. By 10.30 the light had gone, and so had all but a handful of rugger buggers.

'Congratulations.' Jake loped over and sat next to her. 'That was a brilliant performance.'

'I meant it,' she said defensively.

'I didn't mean to imply—' He scrunched his face up in his hands. 'Me and my eloquent ways. What I meant to say was I really, genuinely thought you did a wonderful job. And I don't just mean the pep talk . . .' He traced an arc in the fountain with his forefinger. 'I may not always have shown it, but I have nothing but admiration for you . . .'

'Why, thank you, sir,' said Cat hastily, sensing his acute embarrassment. Admiration wasn't necessarily the first emotion she would have hoped to arouse in Jake, who, she was starting to see, was probably the most appealing man for miles around. But it was better than nothing.

'It's true. Your spirit is what they always describe in novels as indomitable. I was never quite sure what it meant before I met you.'

She looked into his speckled eyes for a moment and felt her heart contract.

'Looking back, I can see I haven't always seemed as supportive as I might.'

'I didn't exactly make it easy for you—' She felt his leg brush against her thigh. Her heart began to thud. After months of chafing against his inscrutability, she felt nervous at the prospect of him opening up.

'No worries,' she said in a bad Australian accent. 'It may all just work out anyway. At least the natives don't want to boil me alive any more. Do you know, I've even just had quite a fruitful conversation with Mark Wainwright about supplying his shop with a range of specially designed Butely products. And it looks as though Fortnum's are going to take the sausages. I was thinking that eventually we could even market some of the treatment oils Dr Anjit's been working on. I thought you might like to design the packaging?'

'The thing is, Cat,' – he tapped his foot nervously – 'I've been asked back to Auckland. The grant's come through and they want to start building fifty solar-powered pods immediately.'

Cat felt hot and sick and dizzy and as though she'd been kicked in the stomach and hit on the head simultaneously.

'It's a bit short notice, isn't it?' The yellow roses had gone blurry.

'I know. Typical. But I can't say no. And it's only for a few weeks.'

That wasn't quite so terrible. But still pretty bad.

'What about the planning permission?' she said pathetically.

'I've redrawn the plans and filled out all the forms. There's nothing more we can do for the moment.'

'What about Lily's riding lessons?' She fumbled around for straws.

'I've already spoken to Caleb, who said he'd love to stand in for a few weeks.'

'But how much experience does he have? Is he British Equestrian Society approved?' She really was desperate.

'He's not quite Olympic standard, but I think he'll just about do.'

She looked across and saw he was smiling. It changed his whole face. She loved the way it made him look like an enthusiastic little boy.

'That's all right, then,' she said brightly.

He leant towards her until he was so close she could feel his breath on her neck, and cupped her cheek. She closed her eyes expectantly.

'Got it,' he said, opening his fist a little for her to see. 'Didn't you feel it?'

She gazed at the fluttering creature nestling in his hands. 'A Yellow Admiral?' she hazarded.

'A moth. At least they're both insects. You're improving.'

Jess prided herself on not being finicky about men – unlike some she could name. But she was starting to go off Declan. And now that she'd been watching his behaviour without the filter of lust-tinted spectacles, she was starting to question everything he did, including the numerous calls to Toby. The night after Cat had entertained half the village at Butely, Declan had spent the best part of their date jabbering on his mobile. Jess pretended to be deeply preoccupied changing a tape in the Golf while Declan lowered his voice and start talking in code. What really infuriated her was that he obviously thought she was too stupid to realise what he was up to.

But when she'd questioned him about the precise nature of his relationship with Toby, he'd started to get narky. 'What are you,' he'd said with discernible menace one night as they were getting out of the Golf, 'the Gestapo?'

That really rankled. Sketchy as Jess's political knowledge was, she knew the Gestapo had been shits. By the time he deposited her in the drive she was itching to slap him, but he grabbed her round the waist and slid his hand down her shorts. Against her better judgement, Jess felt herself giving into the rhythmic motion of his fingers. Arching her back, she wrapped one leg around his waist in a vague approximation of the Standing Tree pose and slid her hands down Declan's sinewy back to his taut, lean bottom. He began breathing in staccato bursts as he attempted to rub his face into her breasts, which were pushing over the top of her sports bra like perfect Delia Smith soufflés.

Jess wriggled closer to him, clamped a hand over his balls and tickled his buttocks with her toe. He groaned, tore off his belt and let his trousers drops round his ankles.

'I'd better go now,' whispered Jess, opening one eye and casting it across the top of the Golf's roof.

'Bugger that,' gasped Declan, pulling at her shorts. He wrapped his mouth round her nipple and began blowing on it. Jess felt his penis slapping between her thighs with all the subtlety of a twenty-one-gun salute as it searched for entry. 'Jesus, Dec,' she said, 'it's like being assaulted by a battering ram.'

'Show me to your castle,' he moaned.

'Certainly not,' said Jess with as much dignity as she could muster. 'Stop that right now. What if Lily sees us?'

'Birds and the bees, isn't it?' panted Declan, pumping away.

Jess lowered one leg and tried to ease the other down.

'What are you doing?' groaned Declan.

She pushed against his shoulders. 'I'm pulling up the draw-bridge.'

'Too late now.' He pinioned her against the garden wall between his arms. 'Come on,' he pleaded. He pushed his tongue into her mouth so hard she thought he was going to give her a tonsillectomy. She could hardly breathe. She could feel him writhing in frustration as he tried to locate her portcullis. Slowly she drew up her leg again and kneed him in the stomach. He wrenched her head round towards him. 'Like it rough, do you, darlin'?'

'Get off!' She lowered her other leg and tried to push him off.

'Oh no you don't.' He still had her trapped between his arms. He was much stronger than his wiry frame suggested. She started to feel frightened. He pressed against her, crushing her into the wall. The flintstones dug into her shoulder blades. Taking a deep breath, she raised her leg again and this time kneed him in the groin. While he was doubled up, she scurried to the safety of the Cottage, leaving Declan in excruciating pain and mystified as to why women always put him through this charade.

Twelve thousand miles away in Auckland, Jake missed Cat more than he had ever imagined. He kept telling himself it was a waste of time. At the very best, he couldn't see them ever being more than good friends. It simply wasn't possible that someone who'd been in love with Toby could fall in love with him. They were too different. He tried to tell himself that he could probably live with being friends with Cat, even though he'd almost let his passions run away with him when she'd come round for supper. That was why he'd jumped at the job in Auckland. But it hadn't stopped him thinking about her practically all the time.

Everything reminded him of Cat. When he looked at the sea he remembered the way Cat had climbed up a tree on one of her walks to get a better view of Lulworth Cove. The sky at night reminded him of teaching Lily about the Milky Way. When the sun shone he thought of Cat hunched over her bureau all through the summer – the way she almost wrapped herself round her computer in concentraton. When it rained, he thought of the first time he'd bumped into her on that walk in that ridiculously impractical coat of hers, with the wind beating at her hair, and the way her nose crinkled up when she thought she wasn't getting through to him.

It was useless. He'd hoped his feelings might cool, but instead he thought about her all the time. And now he was standing in a second-hand bookshop in a dusty backstreet away from the harbour, because he'd seen a small watercolour in the back of the window that reminded him of Butely.

The peculiar thing was that it *was* Butely. It turned out to have been painted in 1905 by the ninth Countess of Butely. And so of course he'd had to buy it as a present for Cat. And the studious young man hunched over an old copy of the *Literary Times Supplement* at the till had told him there was more on Butely. That was when he'd disappeared up a ladder on to a tiny rickety mezzanine, only to emerge a few minutes later with a chaotic pile of papers, from which eventually he'd extracted some lovely old plans of Butely as it had been between the wars.

It would have been churlish not to buy them. But it was only a few days later, on a rare evening when he got home from work before ten, that he had time to study them in any detail and realise quite what he'd stumbled on.

*

'You were right about Declan,' Jess said cautiously to Cat the next morning.

'Which particular bit?' asked Cat warily.

Jess stretched her arms out on the table and rested her head on top of them. 'All of it,' she said vaguely. 'I finally realised when I watched you standing up for those poor pheasants.'

Only Jess could construe someone wanting to put birds under lock and key as somehow standing up for them, thought Cat.

'Perhaps I overreacted a bit.' Sensing a major victory, Cat felt she could afford to be generous.

'And to think I believed Declan when he told me he was just rearing them for ambience.'

'Easily done,' said Cat. 'I'm not gloating, believe me. Look what a shit Toby turned out to be.'

'They're both shits. I caught Declan red handed reading *Pheasant World.* It was open on a page listing reliable abattoirs. And he still denied he was planning to breed them for profit.'

'I must admit, he does make Ronnie Biggs look like a pillar of the community,' said Cat. Jess looked crushed. 'So have you ended it?' Cat tried not to sound too hopeful.

'Not officially.' Jess sounded sheepish. 'I've wanted to for weeks. Ever since I realised all that stuff he's been telling everyone in the Hung Drawn and Quartered wasn't true.'

'About me wanting to bulldoze Butely or turn it into a multiplex at the very least, you mean?'

'So you know about all that?'

'I only found out two days ago when the villagers came round. Mrs Potts let it out.'

Jess pulled a face. 'He was so convincing. He always looked depressed when he said it. As if he'd tried really hard to persuade you to keep Butely as it is. At one point I thought he'd become your business confidant. I was a bit jealous, to be honest.'

'But I was jealous of you! You always seem to be having such a good time here – and it was meant to be my rural idyll.'

'We're a right pair, aren't we?'

Cat nodded. 'When did you realise what he was up to?'

Jess looked mildly sheepish. 'I first suspected something the night we had that row about me getting back so late. I'd been in the pub with Declan and when he thought I was outside he started holding forth to everyone about how you were going hell for leather to change Butely into some big money-spinner. I was going to talk to you about it the next day . . .'

'We've both been complete idiots, haven't we?'

Jess nodded, staring at the tea dregs in a Meissen cup. 'I'm really sorry I didn't tell you earlier,' she said.

Cat shrugged. 'My fault as much as yours. I've been so wrapped up in my own bubble.'

Jess smiled, grateful for the way Cat was taking everything. 'How are things with Jake, by the way?'

'Fine. He's been a huge help with the plans.'

'That's not what I meant. Are you two an item?'

Cat looked shocked. 'Whatever gave you that idea?'

'The way you look at each other, for a start.'

'Would that be the disgusted look or the simply exasperated one?' said Cat. 'I grant you things have improved lately, but he still flinches every time I go near him.' She remembered the electric shocks she'd felt every time their knees had touched that evening at his cottage and felt a flutter of desire in her stomach.

'Well, it's obvious, isn't it?'

'Is it?'

'He thinks you slept with his half-brother.'

A fog of misunderstanding cleared. For all her natural pessimism, Cat knew Jess was right. If only they hadn't stopped talking to one another she could have cleared this up weeks ago. 'It hardly matters now,' she said.

'You miss him, don't you?' said Jess quietly.

'Yes.' Cat suddenly felt exhausted.

'I'm sorry,' said Jess. 'He's really nice. And you need friends.'

'Thanks.'

'That's okay.' They sat there in convivial silence, each reflecting on how much they'd missed one another. 'Is there anything I can do to help?' asked Jess.

Cat shook her head, then changed her mind. 'Actually, there is.' Jess looked across the table expectantly.

'Could you bear not to give Declan the boot just yet? I've a feeling he needs to be watched.'

Jess convinced herself that pumping Declan for more information while not arousing his suspicions put her in the same league as MI5. As a master spy, naturally she needed to invest in new underwear. She raided an Ann Summers catalogue and gritted her teeth the next time he leaned over in the Golf and fumbled with her jeans zip.

'Come here, my lovely,' he said thickly, looming towards her left breast. She darted out of the car and sprinted towards his front door. 'Come and get me if you want me.' She threw him a come-hither look. She deserved an Oscar, though she said so herself.

Declan didn't need asking twice. He'd been waiting weeks for this. Snorting like a pig on the trail of white truffles, he fumbled with the door key and bundled Jess up the rickety staircase to his shag-pad. Inside, the flat was so untidy it looked like a breaker's yard. Declan headed towards the unmade futon, kicking piles of laundry out of his way and plucking off his clothes as he went before collapsing in a heap.

Biting her lip, Jess perched at the foot of his futon and peeled off her belt and jeans. By the time she got down to the crotchless knickers, Declan's eyes were out on bargepoles. She allowed herself a small pout of satisfaction and narrowed her eyes in her best Charlotte Rampling style. This Mata Hari business was quite a laugh.

'Come here, you minx.'

Jess held up a finger. 'Wait there, you naughty boy.' She took off her T-shirt to reveal a black lacy half-bra. She ran her hands up and down her flat belly, moving them gently down her thighs and up towards the little bush that poked out of her crotchless panties. Declan attempted to focus his eyes before lunging towards her and getting tangled in a pair of Y-fronts.

She let him snuffle away for a bit, listening to his breathing grow more stentorian. 'My, my, Declan.' She shifted in the bed a little in an attempt to rescue her bra from Declan's dribble. 'What a big boy you are.'

'All the better to eat you,' said Declan, nestling snugly between her breasts.

'Shit!' he exclaimed suddenly and sat bolt upright.

'What is it?' she asked, mildly concerned in case somehow Declan had seen through her.

'Need a slash.' He toddled off to the bathroom, tossing her a lascivious grin before he disappeared. 'Don't go away now, darling'.'

When he returned after the longest, loudest slash Jess had ever had the misfortune to be privy to, she had arranged her limbs expertly so she looked just like something out of a poster for *Chicago*.

'Oi, wait for me.' His eyes were now practically dangling from their sockets in his excitement. He frantically undid his studded belt, half kicked off his jeans and staggered towards the futon, toppling on to Jess and ramming his tongue into her throat. 'Oh, babe,' he shouted. 'Oh, babe.'

Oh God, thought Jess. Oh God. He must have been listening because before too much more damage was done, Declan passed out.

Cat was making her own sacrifices. She was up most of the night tapping away on her computer. She'd managed to get into Declan's files, but typically it turned out he wasn't the type to use e-mail. No wonder he was always on his mobile. There was, however, one from Toby addressed to him, still unopened, but he'd obviously given up on sending any more as soon as he realised Declan didn't deign to read them. She was still scrolling through the programmes, searching vainly for any last clues, when the phone next to her rang. It was Jake. Her heart jumped.

'Where are you?' she asked, rubbing her eyes and trying to keep the excitement out of her voice.

'Rag—' There was a crackle on the line.

'Where?'

'Raglan.' There was an almighty hiss. 'How are you? How's Lily? How's the building going?'

'It's all fine. They've almost finished the alterations in the main house. You wouldn't recognise Goran. He's become quite the responsible foreman.'

'I knew you'd do it.' He sounded pleased.

'Didn't you get my e-mail?'

'It's been a bit tricky the last few days. Something to do with the storms we've had here. The electricity's been down.'

That figures, thought Cat. Hence the need for solar power.

'I've got some great news,' Jake's voice echoed from the other side of the world. 'It's the Jericho,' he continued.

He couldn't have run her up to talk about the Jericho, surely – unless it was an ancient Dowell form of courtship.

'The original plans I looked at for Butely were incomplete, which meant that I couldn't corroborate my suspicions.'

'What suspicions?'

'You see, I knew that back in the eighteenth century there had been a whole row of Jerichos at Butely. The fourth Lady Butely was obsessed with water closets. It became something of a family tradition. Between them they commissioned quite a collection to go alongside the original one. Apparently the family would spend entire mornings sitting on the loo next to each other discussing the previous evening's gambling losses. The fourth Earl fell through the planks of one and drowned in a deep pit of excrement.'

'I see.'

'Which necessitated a complete overhaul, as you can imagine. Technically, some of them were incredibly advanced. One even had a primitive system of running water. God, I wish they were still standing.'

'That's absolutely fascinating, Jake—'

'No, wait, I'm not explaining this very well.' The line went dead and for a few moments all she could hear were waves of empty energy. She wanted to cry. And then Jake's voice came back again. 'Can you hear me? Good. Look, I'm going to speed up. They pulled them down, you see – the Victorians. All except the original Jericho – even they could see the value of that. They replaced them all with vast water-lily beds – the land, as you can imagine, being somewhat well fertilised. I always suspected that was the case but I didn't have any proof because that bit of the plans wasn't there. And then incredibly – ridiculously – I found them.'

'What do you mean?' She was hopelessly lost as to the relevance of this conversation by now, but it was nice hearing his voice.

'In a funny little shop in Raglan selling old architectural prints. I came across the missing plans showing the lily beds.' He'd been looking for a present for Cat, but was too shy to mention it. 'An amazing coincidence, don't you think?'

Cat was lost for words.

'The lily beds went to rack and ruin in the wars, of course. But owing to some curious local by-law, long since forgotten, but not defunct, those lily beds mean that a similar water feature could be re-established on the site—' He broke off to read from the spidery, archaic-looking architectural notes in front of him. 'Provided that structure should not dominate the landscape or the main house.'

'Oh my God,' said Cat slowly. 'You mean we don't need planning permission to build the pool complex after all—'

'Because we've already got it,' finished Jake triumphantly.

'But does this still hold?' Cat frowned uncertainly.

'Absolutely. I've looked through all the documents and I called Barry Dean to double-check. This by-law was passed in 1910, around the time they brought planning in. To the best of my knowledge, there's been nothing since to supersede it.'

'And even the council didn't know about the lily beds?'

'Clearly not. The plans must have gone missing without anyone noticing.'

'But this changes everything.'

'S'pose so.' He sounded casual but she could tell he was very pleased with himself.

'You're amazing,' she said at last. She wanted to propel herself twelve thousand miles and hug him. 'So what next?'

'I've been thinking about that—' There was a whistling sound, as if an Exocet were hurtling down the line towards her.

'Jake? Can you hear me?'

He couldn't. And this time the line really had gone for good. But Cat already knew what to do, starting with an e-mail to Glowbal.

Three days later Suzette called from Rio to let them know it was 97 degrees in Ipanema.

'I hope you've got sunblock on.' Cat leaned out of the kitchen window and looked up at the Dorset sky, which was the colour of charcoal and about to be streaked with hailstones.

'Better than that,' exclaimed Suzette, who was actually swaddled in bandages following a teensy face-lift – a present from Eduardo which it would have been churlish to refuse. And – at her age – bloody stupid.

'What could possibly be better?' asked Cat, wondering whether her mother had rung purely to compare weather patterns.

Suzette padded out on to the balcony of Eduardo's beachside penthouse and winced in the blinding sunlight. None of the articles she'd read had prepared her for the killing headaches. She retreated back inside.

'Have you thought any more about that e-mail Eduardo sent you?'

'The one offering to head up a plastic surgery department here, you mean?'

'There's no need to be disparaging.'

'Sorry. But I thought you'd realise it wasn't Butely's thing.'

'Some of us are more open to new ideas than others.'

'If this is your way of telling me you've backtracked on three decades of columns against going under the knife—'

'No, no,' said Suzette hastily. She'd just have to hope that by the time Cat saw her again she would have forgotten what she looked like before the face-lift.

'It's very kind of Eduardo to offer. But it's really not the way I want to take Butely. I don't think Sir Rodney would have wanted it.'

Sir Bloody Rodney hadn't been a woman with sagging eyebrows, thought Suzette bitterly. 'I'm worried you'll miss out on valuable revenue if you don't offer anything. Having surgery is just like having a facial these days. Except that no one in New York bothers with facials any more. They prefer to have it all peeled off and resurfaced—'

'Lovely. Look, I'd better be getting on.'

'There is one thing—' said Suzette hesitantly.

'Yes?'

'I'm married.'

It was three days since her encounter with Declan's futon and Jess was still thanking her lucky stars that he'd been so drunk he'd passed out before he'd been able to complete the task. But she still didn't have anything to nail him with. With a heavy heart and a vague plan, she went with him to the Hung Drawn and Quartered, where she kept buying him pints of Prince Charles before bowing to the inevitable.

And bowing was what she'd decided to do, as well as kneeling, twisting and stretching. 'The thing about this position,' said Jess, as she eased Declan into the Eagle, 'is that it really intensifies the sensations in your internal organs. When you come it's incredible.'

'Yeah, *when*,' he grunted.

She tweaked his nipples and massaged his balls until he'd worked up a nice sweat. And then at the crucial moment, just as she'd hoped, he collapsed on top of her with chronic cramp.

She dozed next to him for a while, not wanting to leave. The call came through at a quarter to one in the morning and woke her instantly, which was more than could be said for Declan. Sensing it must be from Toby at this time in the morning, Jess, who in her sleep had worked her way to the very farthest edge of the bed, rolled back towards Declan, kneading his balls, and when that didn't work gently kneeing him in the groin. Still half asleep he reached for his mobile.

'Cocks R Us,' he mumbled.

Toby's voice fulminated loudly from the other end. Jess felt

Declan's buttocks tense. Instinctively she sensed him eyeing her.
She turned over and groaned softly, hoping Declan would assume
she was reliving last night's ecstasy.

'What's up?' said Declan, clearing his throat in a futile attempt
to sound *compos mentis*.

Jess rolled a little closer to him to try to hear what Toby was
saying. Declan put his hand over the mouthpiece. 'I'm a bit tied up
at the moment.' He looked down at his feet, which had been lassoed
together by Jess. There was more cursing at the other end of the
line. 'Yeah, well, it's not my fault if she's gone and found a way
round the planning permission. I had Glowbal on the line earlier
asking what the fuck they should do.' He looked at Jess again and
shuffled with the phone towards the bathroom, locking the door
behind him.

Shit. Jess waited a few seconds and followed, pressing her ear
against the door. All she could hear was Declan taking another pee.
Fortunately it was a heated conversation and Declan's voice rose
above the gushing waterfall

'So what you're saying is we're gonna have to do something
drastic.'

There was silence while Toby presumably elucidated.

'And how am I supposed to get her to agree to sell?'

Whatever the plan was, it must be sketchy, Jess thought, because
it didn't take long to outline. 'All right, all right. Yeah, I get the
message, Toby,' said Declan insolently. 'Time's running out.'

There was a pause while Toby presumably reread Declan the
Riot Act.

'Yes, I realise that's the point, mate. Yeah, I am reading you,
Toby. Loud and clear. I'll see what I can do, okay, but I'm not
prepared to go to prison for this, no matter how much money you
chuck at it. Do you understand?'

Jess heard him turn the key and, her heart battering so loudly she
thought it would shatter her ribcage, she scrambled back into bed.

21

Jess lay next to Declan for hours, drifting in and out of sleep, terrified in case she woke him. Her brain spooled through the fragments of conversation she'd overheard. They didn't amount to anything very much – other than an overwhelming conviction that he and Toby were planning something disastrous. She scrambled back to the Cottage as soon as she could, without arousing Declan's suspicion.

'Where's Lily? she said, clattering into the kitchen at half past seven. Her bra straps were twisted in knots and her cheeks were spotlit by two small glistening smudges of coral.

'Mucking out Sir Galahad.' Cat glanced at the kitchen clock and shoved some bacon in the Aga. 'I'd better go and call her in a sec if we're not going to be late for school.'

'I need to talk to you first,' said Jess quietly. She hadn't had time to shower and she could smell her sweat from last night – mingled with Declan's. She stood up suddenly and took a tea towel from the dresser, holding it under the cold tap before dabbing it on her forehead and under her arms.

'Whatever's the matter?' Cat put the kettle on.

'I heard them talking on the phone last night. Cat, I think they're mixed up in some kind of deal to force you to sell Butely—'

'What do you mean?'

Jess pressed the tea towel against her cheeks. 'Toby and Declan. They're up to something.' She looked at Cat exultantly. 'Something really bad.'

Cat ran the milk frother under the tap while Jess explained about the conversation she's overheard. 'Is that it?' said Cat, trying not to sound disappointed. 'Not that I doubt your word,' she added hastily. 'But we need something a little more . . . substantial to go on.'

'I know, I know,' said Jess, slightly piqued. Being a master spy wasn't as easy as she'd thought.

'Does Declan know you suspect anything?' Cat asked suddenly.

'No. Yes. Maybe. Oh, I don't know. Either way I'm not sure this was such a good idea. He's not as thick as he looks.'

'I've a good mind to post this through Declan's letter box!" Lily burst into the kitchen carrying an old newspaper with two huge pheasant droppings on it. 'Look what his birds left outside Sir Galahad's stable. They must have escaped again. It's disgusting.' She paused, taking in the sombre expressions around the table. 'What's the matter with you two?'

'Nothing's the matter,' said Cat brightly. She took the newspaper from Lily and put it by the recycling bin before getting the bacon out of the oven. 'Now eat up. Jess, let's talk when I get back.'

'Aren't you pleased about Sukes?' said Lily as they waded through a sea of slushy black leaves on the way to school.

Cat gave the question due thought. Over the years she'd mentally prepared for her mother becoming a lesbian, adopting a Chinese baby or popping up as a *Playboy* centrefold. But marriage had never been on the cards. She knew that she ought to be thrilled for her.

'I'm thrilled,' she said unconvincingly.

'Why are you walking so fast, then? You only walk this fast when you're annoyed.'

Cat slowed down. 'I'm walking this fast because it's cold.' She wrapped her arms round her chest and shivered.

'That's because it's practically autumn.' Lily surveyed the sky solemnly. 'Looks like it's going to be a chilly one.'

'Oh really.' Cat smiled wanly. 'And how do you know that, Mr McCaskill?'

'Look at all the birds.' They stopped and peered up at the steel sky that arced over them. 'Great flocks of them all getting out of

England as fast as possible. Jake says that's a sure sign it's going to be a harsh winter.'

'Does he, now?'

'Yes. Are you missing him?' Lily asked casually.

'Haven't really thought about it,' lied Cat. She was completely taken aback by how much she missed Jake. He didn't always say much, but she had come to value how what he did say always made sense. Having worked at Simms, where even the mail boy had been in love with the sound of his own voice, she found Jake's reticence particularly endearing. And she'd feel a lot better equipped to deal with whatever trouble was heading her way with him by her side. She hugged Lily and shivered again. She and Jess were probably being paranoid. Toby was ruthless but she couldn't believe he was evil. And yet she couldn't escape a sickening sense that something calamitous was about to happen.

Petula placed the carrier bag of shirts from Toby's favourite Savile Row tailor on his desk, hoping he'd like the colours she'd chosen.

'Pomegranate,' exclaimed Toby, extracting the first one. 'Nice one.'

'Yes, well, I knew you didn't have one in that colour.'

'Oh, and pistachio.'

'Although you've got almost all the shades they do now. You'll have to get on to Richard James to do some different ones.'

'And lavender.'

'Good with your skin tone.' She blushed. It was almost like old times.

'Three! Aren't I the lucky one.'

'You did say you were going to be gone three days this time.'

He grimaced.

'What's the matter?' she asked, perching daintily on the edge of his desk and crossing her legs. 'Glasgow wearing a bit thin?'

'You could say that. If I have to put up with one more pan-seared tuna . . . The cooking, like everything else up there, is about three years out of date.'

'So what's really bugging you?'

He narrowed his eyes and looked at her as though he were weighing something up.

'C'm'on, Toby. I haven't worked for you all this time without knowing when something's wrong. I've never seen you this stressed by anything. And you're so secretive.' She leaned back on one elbow and looked at him conspiratorially. 'You never used to be.'

He swivelled his chair away from her gaze towards the window and stared across the square for a few moments. When he spun back towards her his hands were clenched round his face. He looked like a small, tormented boy. Petula's heart twisted.

'What would persuade you to sell your home?' he said eventually.

'The offer of a bigger, better, nicer one,' she replied immediately.

'What if you already had a very big, very nice house?'

'Then whoever was trying to get me out would have to do something to make it less nice.'

He scrutinised her thoughtfully.

'You've been looking a bit peaky lately, Toby. Are you sure there's nothing wrong? You're working all the hours God sends. It's not like you,' she added archly. 'I'm starting to worry about you.'

'Bless you.' His hand brushed her knee as he put down his pen. Her heart lurched.

'Listen, why don't I pop out to Pronto Pasta and get us some lunch? At least that way you can eat while you work.'

'Sod Pronto Pasta.' He stood up suddenly and reached for his coat. 'I'm taking you to the Ivy.'

Cat went over and over the events of the past few months, trying to make sense of the disparate obstacles that had fallen – or been deliberately placed – across her path. Of course, it was unlikely that Cynthia Dowell had waged her campaign against Butely without Toby's knowledge, but that on its own didn't constitute a crime.

She scrolled through Declan's file again to see whether anything had come in from Toby – there was nothing. Of course there wasn't. Toby would have known that Cat would be suspicious by now so would be avoiding any traceable contact with Declan. And that was why none of this made sense. He wasn't an idiot. That was why all those decisions he'd taken – threatening to sack Samantha, suggesting they close down altogether during the building, hiring Declan – must have been deliberate mistakes, designed to sabotage everything. But why? Even if she accepted that he hated her enough to want to wreck her life, why would be jeopardise his own reputation? He was still the executor of the will and a trustee. If Butely went belly up it wouldn't reflect well on him professionally. And he wasn't the type to let his emotions get the better of him. He might loathe her, but he wouldn't let it cloud his judgement in business unless he stood to gain more from Butely's demise than he would lose.

Increasingly Cat became convinced that Glowbal was somehow the key to understanding all this. But when she quizzed Goran it was obvious he didn't know any more than she did. Glowbal, despite being an international fitness company, hired builders on an ad hoc basis. He was paid in cash, promptly, at the end of each week. And as he explained, 'That ees all I need to know. Where I come from, asking questions' – he cast his eyes wildly about her study – 'leads to death and deestruction. I have money for food and shelter, Cat, and so I am satisfied.'

Cat, however, was anything but.

It was like old times again, thought Petula, as she let Toby spoon crème brûlée into her small pink mouth.

'I am right, aren't I, about you being stressed?'

He looked at her and sighed.

'C'm'on.' She flicked out a cream-tipped tongue and ran it slowly round her bow-shaped lips. 'You can tell me. And you should tell me. It's obvious you need some help on this.'

He poured some more wine. She noticed his hand was shaking. She stretched out her finger, the one sporting the engagement ring, and ran it up and down the back of his palm, to steady it. 'Here, let me.'

'The thing is' – he took a gulp of the claret – 'it's not entirely orthodox, in that it's not strictly speaking part of my Simms brief.'

'I figured that much.' She leant across the table to remove a hair from his lapel, brushing her hand against his cheek as she did so.

'Obviously it's nothing illegal,' he said hurriedly.

'Just immoral?' said Petula. She closed her eyes as he popped another spoon of pudding in her mouth.

'It is of a very delicate nature,' he continued.

'I'd be disappointed if it wasn't.' Some cream trickled down her chin and into her cleavage. Petula affected not to notice.

Toby leant over to dab it with his napkin. 'Can't have you ruining that fetching little shirt, can we?' He smiled at her with such sweetness that at that moment Petula would have done anything he asked, immoral, amoral or downright punishable by imprisonment.

He must have been worried about things, thought Petula, to have taken her back to his flat after lunch. It was the only place, he said, where they could be sure of being completely private.

It had taken him a year to invite her, she thought, stepping through the front door and surveying the view from his windows, but it was worth the wait.

'Stunning.' She gazed round the room admiringly. 'I bet your friends are gobsmacked when they first walk in.'

'Hmm,' said Toby neuturally. He went to the kitchen to make them some coffee. Petula followed him in, cooing over the reclaimed aluminium table. 'So,' she said, lifting herself on to the zinc counter, 'this is all connected with Felix Hark, I take it.'

'How did you know that?' He handed her an espresso cup.

'Oh, come on. I've put enough of his calls through to you. And I also know that the amount of time you're spending in Glasgow isn't warranted by the fees you're charging him on Simms's account.' She sipped her coffee delicately. 'So obviously I figured that you were engaged in extra-curricular activities. Which, from the expression on your face, are about to intensify.'

For a moment he looked utterly bereft.

'Don't worry,' she said. 'I'll cover for you.'

She followed him back into the living room. 'Petula,' he said suddenly. 'How would you like to make twenty-five grand tax free?'

Petula raised a manicured eyebrow. 'That much overtime?'

'If you reach certain incentive targets,' he said coyly, 'you could make yourself another twenty-five.'

She draped herself over the Precious O'Down sofa. 'My, we are going to be busy.'

'Indeed. And we're on a deadline. Felix has given me two more weeks to sort everything out, or the deal's off.'

'Really.' She reached into her bag for a notebook, kicked off her shoes and curled up on the sofa again. 'Come here' – she patted the noduled expanse next to her – 'and tell me all about it.'

So he did.

She might have known Cat would be at the bottom of everything. Still, revenge would be sweet.

'She's had a lot of luck on her side,' said Toby, reaching for the whisky.

'Obviously,' said Petula, stretching a leg out. 'It's not her innate business skills that have kept it going.'

'The thing is, Felix is panicking. He's owed about three hundred million in China – and he's unlikely to see any of it this side of 2050. The share price of Golden Fields is plummeting and he's allowing himself to be bullied by those tossers in the City.'

'So he's desperate to get his hands on the oil.'

'More than desperate. He's already leaked word of it in the city. If he doesn't come up with something soon he'll be a laughing stock as well as broke.'

'And you really believe Butely can save him?' Trust bloody Cat to get her hands on an oil well *and* a manor house.

'Probably not three hundred million's worth. But enough to keep faith in the City.'

'And Cat's the only thing standing in his way.'

'Yup. I'm almost starting to feel sorry for him. Felix is shitting himself and he's a ruthless man. I wouldn't put it past him to try and kill her.'

'Oh, I wouldn't feel sorry for her,' said Petula. 'I'm sure we can find a slightly less harsh alternative to murder.'

★

While Toby was in Glasgow, Petula called in sick and spent her time surfing the Internet or in the library, digging up everything she could on Dorset. By the second day she'd found what she needed. She called Toby jubilantly.

'Have you any idea how lethal asbestos is?' she asked, her voice almost breathless with excitement.

'I'm no expert but I've seen sufficient *Panorama*s to know it kills people quite effectively. What are you getting at?'

'There's a local school for young offenders not far from Butely that's been closed down permanently because of asbestos.'

'I see.'

'Had its roof replaced in 1974, the same year Butely's was done. By the same contractors, as it happens.'

'You're brilliant.'

'It's tragic,' she purred. 'Because one it's disturbed the whole place becomes a no-go area. Takes months, sometimes longer, to clear it. No business – especially one as precarious as Butely – could survive. Especially if it didn't have insurance for such an eventuality. You did cancel the insurance, didn't you?'

'Not yet. The thing is, it would require Cat's signature – something I've a feeling she wouldn't be too keen to give, just at the moment.'

'Then fake it,' said Petula firmly. 'And get those Glowbal people of yours to open up that roof pronto.'

Toby put the phone down shakily. When he'd joked about getting involved with the Scottish play, he hadn't actually envisioned becoming closely acquainted with Lady Macbeth as well.

'Fuckin' great, that is,' roared Felix. 'Fuckin' masterful. Asfuckin'bestos. What's that supposed to do, choke her?'

'In a manner of speaking, yes,' said Toby.

'Yes, well, normally that process takes about thirty fuckin' years, whereas you have eleven fuckin' days.'

'Oh, for God's sake, Felix, be realistic,' said Toby. For the first time ever in Glasgow, he was starting to feel hot.

'Don't come the vicar with me,' said Felix. 'I've got those wankers from the City baying for blood. I need this fucking deal to go through now.' He brought his fist down on his desk so violently the walnut looked as though it had just been in an earthquake. 'If you won't take the necessary action, I will. What's the telephone number of that twat you've got working there?'

'Declan?'

'Yeah. Ex-SAS, isn't he?'

'Not exactly. He was in the Gulf War, though.'

'Then he knows what it takes to survive.'

'What do you mean?' said Toby, pulling at his collar, which suddenly felt tight. Petula must have got his size wrong.

'Just give me his fuckin' number.'

Toby handed it to him and listened, motionless, while Felix dialled.

'Declan, is that you? Well, this is Felix Hark. Yeah, that Felix Hark. Listen, I've got a little proposition for you. Yeah, Toby knows all about it. We need to turn the heat up at Butely a bit. Literally. Yeah, that's right, a fuckin' fire would be just the ticket. Naturally we'd renegotiate your fuckin' contract. I assume you do know how to light a match? Perfect. I'll leave it with you.' He slammed the phone down. 'What's the matter, Toby – run out of fuckin' wisecracks? Listen, you know what they say about getting out of the kitchen. But remember, if this deal goes down, you're going with it.'

Toby went straight to the airport. By the time he got on the plane he was wet with perspiration. The stewardess eyed him with distaste. 'Can I get you a flannel, sir?' she asked as he boarded.

'Just a seat with a phone,' he said tersely.

He sat down heavily. He was about to experience the biggest ironic twist in his life yet, apart from the one that had seen him fall for Cat in the first place. He keyed in Goran's number. From using the asbestos ploy to destroy Cat financially, he was now about to call on it to save her life. He had to get her and Lily as far away from Butely as possible.

'Goran, can you hear me?' He gulped some water. 'Thank Christ. Now listen carefully.'

Towards the end of the same day, Goran knocked on Cat's study door and announced in a broken voice that he had some terrible news.

'It's the roof,' he began, fiddling with his yellow helmet. His huge square jaw trembled. For a moment Cat thought he was about to cry. 'We opened up the ceiling in the end dormitory – the one where the damp is worst – and we found—' He paused, rubbing his dusty forehead with an equally grimy hand. '—some asbestos. Not even white asbestos, but bluish brown.'

Cat felt her mouth go dry. She knew asbestos was deadly – and that blue asbestos was the deadliest of all. Grimly she followed Goran up to the dormitory while he threatened to tear out his own kidneys and pop them in the microwave if it turned out he was wrong. Cat held a scarf over her face as she stared up at the mountain of grimy-looking granules in horror. Thank God Lily was on a sleepover at Marina's.

She was on the phone to Vic Spinoza within seconds of getting back to her study. It was a bit cheeky, she knew, but she didn't know who else to turn to.

'Are you sure it's blue?' asked Vic.

'Positive.'

'In that case once the inspectors verify it you're going to have to evacuate the place.'

'That's what Goran said. He told me we had to clear the grounds completely.'

'I don't know about that. You shouldn't go near the main house, certainly. Once asbestos is disturbed it's pretty lethal.'

'Lily . . . oh my God.'

'Don't worry about Lily,' said Vic gently. 'She can stay here as long as you like. But you'll need to sort somewhere for yourself, Cat. Once it's disturbed you can't just seal it back up again. The whole roof will have to be excavated. It could take weeks.'

Cat's shoulders sagged. 'What do I do next?' she asked bleakly.

'You'd better report it to the health and safety authority first thing tomorrow. They'll send some inspectors round, I expect, and after that it will have to be dealt with as quickly as possible.'

Cat blinked back the tears. If they had to close now, there was no way Butely could survive. The bank had made it perfectly clear it wouldn't lend any more money.

'I'm so sorry,' said Vic. 'Look, if you and Jess need somewhere to stay you're more than welcome here with me and Marina. It's not very elegant . . .' He trailed off and coughed. 'I don't know why this business with the asbestos happened. That roof was as right as rain. There was no need for anyone to go tampering with it.'

Cat had a pretty good idea how it might have happened. What she didn't have was proof, and given the dismal failure of her plan to intercept Declan's e-mails she couldn't think how she would ever get any.

'You're early,' said Petula, looking up from her laptop. Toby had given her the key to his flat so that she could work there during the day and Alan, her profoundly dull but reliable fiancé, wouldn't get suspicious about her not going into the office.

'We sorted things earlier than expected,' said Toby grimly. He tossed his Vuitton briefcase on to the sofa.

Petula jumped up and helped him with his coat. 'Let me make you some lunch. You look exhausted.'

She rustled up a veal cutlet and some potato dauphinoise she'd been planning to surprise him with that evening.

'Delicious,' he said, looking more like his old self. 'Is there anything you can't do?' He ran his eyes up her legs admiringly.

'If so, no one's told me.' She bent down to load the dishwasher, allowing Toby a lingering glimpse of her thighs. To her frustration, he wandered out of the room and picked up the phone.

'Goran, is that you? Did you open the roof like I said? And it was there? Blue? Thank Christ.'

Relieved, he put the phone down. Petula handed him another glass of bergundy. He smiled his dazzling smile.

'That's better,' she said, running her hands across his shoulders. 'God, you're tense.'

She began to massage his neck with firm strokes. He moaned softly. She pushed him gently towards the sofa. 'Not that bloody thing,' he remonstrated, leading her towards the bedroom. 'You don't want to cripple me.'

'It would be better without your shirt.' She sounded plausibly businesslike.

'Fair enough.'

Petula watched him unbutton it, barely able to breathe. As she'd always suspected, he had perfectly defined muscles – not like Alan's flabby ones. She fetched a bottle from her handbag. 'Be prepared.' She grinned and slid on to the bed next to him. She smoothed some oil into the hollow of his back and moved her hands up and down. 'You're very knotted on your right side.' She slipped her legs either side of his back and knelt on the base of his spine, feeling her way with her fingers inside his trousers. He moaned again and turned over. 'And now for a little vertical integration,' she murmured. Gripping her hair, Toby pulled her towards him. He unzipped her jacket and worked her breasts out of their balconette bra, kissing them just a little roughly. Squealing with pleasure, Petula edged back down his body, her skirt up round her waist. She had on the tiniest G-string Selfridges could offer. It showed off her heart-shaped pubic hair to perfection. Toby groaned more urgently, reaching up to kiss the little heart. Petula pushed him away gently and began to fondle the outside of his trousers. She'd waited five years for this and she didn't intend to rush it.

It was Declan's suggestion that they move into the rooms next to his shag-pad. As usual, he was full of synthetic emotions, dripping sympathy, which made Cat's flesh crawl. But it was better than inposing on Vic.

She spent a few frazzled few days seeing all the staff and guests off, amid tearful farewells and promises that they'd all be reunited in a few weeks. She sent letters to everyone who had booked in for the next couple of months, explaining the situation as best she could. It wasn't easy because, as Vic explained, there was no knowing exactly how long it would take to put everything right, but he reckoned they should be ready to reopen by the end of January at the latest.

'I can't believe that after everything I've done Butely's still closing down,' said Cat shakily.

'It's only temporary,' said Daphne. They were waiting in the hall for the taxi to take Daphne to the train station. Daphne squeezed her arm, not daring to say anything in case she broke down. Cat had put on such a brave performance for everyone else, the least Daphne could do was keep up appearances as well. 'Without you Butely would have closed its doors months ago. You're doing a splendid job. And you're going to do even more when it reopens.' She hugged Cat to her bony, frail body, sweeping her eyes up the beautiful carved staircase, trying to dispel the gloomy conviction that she was seeing it for the last time.

It took a day and a half for Cat and Jess to scrub out the rooms next to Declan's shag-pad, which hadn't been used in more than thirty years, and make them fit for female habitation. And even then they couldn't quite expunge the whiff of Declan's pheasants which seeped up through the floorboards – or his Huge Boss aftershave.

She watched Lily and Jess wheel their small suitcases across to the Long Building and felt the tears pricking. For the first time it struck her that Butely might not ever reopen. Already it had the air of a forlorn sleeping beauty that had been deserted. There was such a strong sense of melancholy hanging over everything that Cat could almost taste it. Maybe it was the smell of winter, she thought, but that night it had the horrible tang of defeat.

It wasn't even a proper flat, more of a bedsit with a galley kitchen and two featureless boxes off it. Lily and Cat shared the larger of the two. The previous incumbents – Sir Rodney's first chauffeur, who'd moved into it with his wife when he retired, leaving the bigger flat for his replacement – had decorated it with ornate wall lights from Argos and pine-panelling-effect wallpaper that couldn't disguise how flimsy the walls were. They could hear Declan zipping and unzipping his flies. And it was cold. Outside, autumn turned wintry. Inside, the electric radiators would barely heat a cupboard. The pheasants were probably snugger than they were. No wonder Lily refused to invite anyone over to play after school.

Two days later Cat was woken in the middle of the night again by her mobile going off. Filled with dread, she picked it up. There was a monumental spitting down the line which made her heart soar. Jake!

'Where are you?' She was suddenly worried. He was meant to be coming home soon, but from the sounds of things he was back up a mountain.

'Outside the Cottage. Where are you?'

It was typical, thought Cat, that Jake should return the night she was wearing her most unattractive pyjamas. She scrabbled about in the wash basket for something more alluring and then decided her best bet was the red sheepskin and a hat. Fortunately, it was almost pitch black outside, apart from a sliver of moon, white as opal. As her torch guided her across the lawns to the Cottage, she heard an owl hoot and smiled. At least she wasn't terrified every time she heard an animal cry out any more – at least not as terrified as she was of seeing Jake after all this time.

She heard him breathing, softly, before she saw him. 'Ill met by moonlight, proud Titania.'

She was glad he'd spoken first – and touched that his first thought, even jokingly, had been of *A Midsummer Night's Dream*. She had to admit that standing in the long black shadows of Butely's oak trees, their nearly naked branches silhouetted against the silent shuttered house, was quite Shakespearian, even if she looked more like a Fool than one of his Arden heroines. 'It would be even worse met by floodlight,' she said. 'But fortunately you can't see what I'm wearing.'

'I hope it's warm, whatever it is.' He stamped his feet. 'It's absolutely freezing. Winter's come early.'

She badly wanted him to hug her. 'It's not that bad. Or perhaps I've just got used to the cold. The heating's even less efficient in the Long Building than it is everywhere else.'

'What on earth are you doing there?'

She told him about the asbestos.

'Jesus Christ,' he said eventually. 'So that's why Toby was so insistent about the roof.'

'You think he wanted it to be disturbed?' She still needed confirmation that she wasn't being paranoid.

'There was no other reason for that roof to be meddled with. It was perfectly sound.'

Then he said there was no way she and Lily and Jess could continue living in that rat-hole above the garage.

'It's not that bad,' she protested weakly.

'Yes it is, I've seen it.'

An owl swooped overhead and she winced involuntarily. He pulled her towards him and wrapped her in his coat. She could feel his heart beating.

'You can put up with my doll's house for a few weeks.'

'We couldn't possibly.'

'What's the matter, not grand enough?'

She looked at him and saw he was smiling. 'You know what I mean. We couldn't impose.'

'And I couldn't possibly let you sleep another night in that fire trap. The entire block is a jerry-built disgrace.'

'We'll have to sleep there tonight – or at least what's left of it.'

'All right,' he said, and walked her back to the Long Building. They stood outside for a few moments. Cat snuggled against him. 'You're so warm.' She leant her head against his shoulder and felt his hand stroke her cheek.

'Come on. Let's get some sleep. I'll be round first thing in the morning.'

'It would probably be better if you came in the afternoon,' said Cat, reluctantly letting go of him. 'Five o'clock? That would give us a bit more time to pack.' And make it harder for Declan to see what they were up to, since he would probably be out on one of his mystery errands at that time.

Jake watched her walk up the stairs before setting off down the drive and along the lane to Lower Nettlescombe.

He arrived at five on the dot and helped them load their luggage into the Polo. Cat had forgotten quite how attractive he was. His hair was longer and after the summer and a month in New Zealand it was almost blond. His cheeks were sunburned, which made his eyes twinkle more than ever. Next to their strained, pale faces he looked as though he'd come from another planet.

'Are you sure about this?' said Cat, as they roared off down the drive. Seamus stiffened in his cage on Lily's lap.

'Bit late now, isn't it?' said Jess.

Cat certainly hoped so.

''Course I'm sure,' said Jake. 'Can't have you freezing to death.'

'The funny thing is it's been really warm today in the flat,' said Jess. 'Maybe the heating's finally working.'

'It's still a poo-hole,' said Lily. Seamus miaowed his agreement.

'I can't promise you a palace,' said Jake.

'Mum says it's adorable,' said Lily. Cat drew her hand in a slitting movement across her throat.

'I don't know about that,' said Jake. 'But I'm quite fond of it.'

'Where will we sleep?'

'Well, there's a sofa bed downstairs – I'll have that . . .'

Cat noticed him looking anxiously in his wing mirror. 'What's the matter?' she said, suddenly full of foreboding.

'I'm not sure,' he said quietly. 'But something seems to be on fire.'

'D'you want me to pull over?' she asked.

'No,' said Jake quickly. He glanced at Lily's anxious face in the mirror. No need to alarm her. 'Keep driving. It's probably someone still celebrating Guy Fawkes.' He looked in the mirror again. The sky behind them was streaked with blue-and-yellow flames. 'Nothing to worry about,' he said evenly.

It was an hour later, after they'd unpacked and organised their sleeping arrangements – Jake downstairs, Lily and Cat in Jake's room and Jess in a tiny study downstairs off the kitchen – that Cat heard an almighty explosion, almost like thunder. Jess was in Jake's study meditating and Lily was in the sitting room doing her homework.

'What was that?' she said, putting down her wineglass.

Jake walked over and put his arm round her. 'I'm pretty sure,' he said slowly, 'that was the Long Building.'

22

Cat insisted on going back with Jake. She couldn't let him face the conflagration, if that's what it was, on his own. The sky itself was eerily still. It was only as they rounded the bend to Butely that it seemed to burst into life – which was ironic, reflected Cat later, because the smoke billowing into the dark velvet night was deathly.

It had been easy enough to maintain a calm façade until they'd left Jess and Lily behind, both blissfully unaware of what was happening, and set off in the Polo. They saw the tips of the crimson and blood-orange flames lapping at the sky, like serpents' tongues, long before they reached the approach to the drive. Cat felt Jake look at her. She wanted to hear him say something comforting but he didn't say anything and nor did she. Her mouth had gone dry and her palms clammy. Her heart was somewhere near her throat, suffocating her.

Once they turned into the drive, the trees obscured the flames. But they could hear the fire. She had always known about the colours, but this was an inferno of noise – a behemoth that was crackling its way to hell. She was still searching for her voice when Jake pulled over and stopped the car suddenly. Two fire engines had got there before them and the top of the drive was already cordoned off with tape. The heat was so intense it was like standing on the lip of a volcano. For once the cocooning canopy of oaks felt claustrophobic.

'It's coming from the pheasants' quarters,' said Jake. Silently they ducked under the tape and scuttled along the terrace, Butely's dark, empty turrets lit like the set of *Gone with the Wind*.

'Thank God,' exclaimed Cat, as it became clear that the main house was, as yet, unharmed. They watched from the kitchen garden as arcs of water blasted the flames enveloping the Long Building. 'Oh my God—' A new thought struck her. 'Declan.'

'It's all right,' said Jake tersely. 'His car's not there. I don't suppose the pheasants were so lucky, though.'

Cat's hand flew to her mouth. She and Jake uttered the next words in unison. 'Sir Galahad.'

They raced over to the stables, but apart from whinnying indignantly at the noise, he seemed unscathed. Fortunately the stables were quite a way from the Long Building and safe from the flames. 'I'll take him to Guy Fulton's in the morning,' said Jake.

Cat had no idea how long they stayed in the grounds, offering silent prayers that the flames wouldn't spread to the main house. As the red-and-orange-streaked sky turned from black to navy and then to a leaden grey, and the fire finally seemed to be wearing itself out, she and Jake crept back to the car and drove to the doll's house, where Jess and Lily were sleeping like babies.

They broke the news to Dr Anjit, Samantha and Micky first thing in the morning, and were touched by their offers to help in any way they could. And then they told Lily and Jess.

'Oh my God, what about Sir Galahad?' cried Lily.

'Don't worry, he's safe,' Cat reassured her.

'What about the pheasants?' asked Lily, forcing down some of the porridge Jess had made.

'We're not sure yet,' said Cat gently. 'But we think they probably died.'

'Oh well,' said Lily brightly. 'And Declan?'

'Lily!'

Later in the morning, Jake took Sir Galahad to Guy Fulton's. Jess and Cat dropped Lily off at school. They watched her bound across the playground to tell the rest of 6B about the latest instalment of life in a quiet backwater. And then they drove to Butely.

They left the Polo at the bottom of the drive and walked the rest of the way, hunched against the sharp wind. Jake was waiting for them, having already settled Sir Galahad at Guy's.

'That's one way to redecorate,' said Jess in a low voice when they rounded the bend. Her face looked grey as she took in the charred rump of the Long Building and the forlorn skeleton of Daphne's kiln.

'No visitors beyond this point.' A policeman bustled in front of the tape and blocked their way as if they were a bunch of football hooligans.

'We're not visitors,' said Jess. 'We live here. Or we did – oh, it's you, Jim.'

'Oh, hi, Jess. Sorry, didn't recognise you with all those layers on.'

'Cat, Jake, this is Jim, one of my star pupils,' said Jess. 'He could do the lotus before anyone else.' Jim beamed at them proudly.

'Is it still dangerous?' asked Cat.

'Put it this way, you wouldn't want to touch any of those walls, unless you were into char-grilled pheasant flesh.' He shook his head. 'Terrible business.'

'There wasn't anyone in there, was there?' she said tentatively.

'Only those birds. Poor things. Were you hoping to look round? Because if so I'm afraid you won't find anything much. As you can see, it's a bit of a mess.'

They looked helplessly at the blackened building, which had now lost its roof and most of its windows as well as the doors into the downstairs area where the pheasants had been, so that it looked like a toothless, cinderised Hallowe'en pumpkin. Thinking how close they'd come to being wiped out along with the pheasants, Cat looked at Jake for reassurance. He had turned as white as the Mother's Pride sandwiches Jim had in his lunch box.

'And in any case,' Jim continued, 'you won't be allowed near the place until we've made a thorough check.'

'Is that routine?' asked Cat bleakly.

'That's right.' Jim scratched his head slowly. 'Though in this case who knows what they'll find?'

'What do you mean?' asked Jake.

'It doesn't quite add up, you see. Big fire like this is usually caused by a gas leak, but the only gas in the garage comes from those propane heaters, right?'

They nodded mutely, the stench of burnt rubber and metal stinging their nostrils and working its way down until it wrapped itself like an iron rope round their lungs.

'Thought so,' Jim said sagely. There was a crackle from his walkie-talkie. 'That's right, sir,' he said into his breast pocket. 'Right away, then, sir. Excuse me.' He looked at them apologetically. 'If you want to pop down to the police station they'll make you some nice hot tea. I'd offer you some myself – nothing better when you've had a nasty shock. Except perhaps a malt whisky.' He chuckled to himself. 'Only the missus forgot to make me any. Tea, that is. I could murder a cup of Darjeeling. But the missus doesn't hold with it. Says it tastes like mouldy bacon.'

While Jim elaborated to Jake on his missus's shortcomings in the comestibles department, Cat and Jess trudged back across the gravel to the car. 'What did he mean about the propane heaters?' said Jess. 'I don't get it. Even if Declan didn't give a shit about us, he kind of loved those birds.'

Cat was dealing with her profound sense of shock. If Declan was behind this, then Toby must be behind Declan. The notion that he hated her so much that he might want to kill her and Lily made her despair. She began to sob silently, vowing to bring him to justice if it were the last thing she did. Then Jake caught up with her and took her hand.

It took the loss adjusters just under a week to complete a detailed assessment of the Long Building and come to their regrettable conclusion that the propane heaters had been turned to dangerously high levels for as long as twenty-four hours before the explosion occurred. Consequently, much as they would have liked to reimburse Cat and Jake fully for the damage caused, they said, they were unable to hand over a penny.

Meanwhile, Glowbal's builders had gone missing. And so had Declan. Cat logged into his e-mail again to see whether by any chance he was using the account. It was futile, as she had known it would be, but she also knew she wouldn't be able to sleep until he and Toby had been caught.

★

Eight days after the fire, Cat got a call on her mobile from Goran. He was in a phone box. It was a terrible line, not helped by his shaky delivery, but she managed to establish that he was in Folkestone.

'I am so sorry, Cat, to leave you like thees,' he said. 'You know I would suck my brains before I leave a job unfinished. But the money, she no come, for two weeks. Ees no good. It destroys trust and without trust the heart ees like pulp, Cat. And now I go home. I have family to feed.'

'Where did the money come from?' asked Cat urgently, in case he ran out of change before she'd got to the bottom of things.

'I told you. I never ask questions. Ees way to keep out of trouble. I just collect from post office in the Spar, along with the others.'

Petula liked to think of herself as something of a cynic. So she was completely taken aback by the depth of her feelings for Toby. She had lusted after him ever since he'd employed her. And even though after years of unrequited lust she'd reconciled herself to the knowledge that she might also be *in love* with him, she had never imagined herself suffering from any idiotic delusions if they were ever to get it together. She knew his reputation. She also knew hers. She had always assumed that any relationship would be strictly based on sex and that it certainly wouldn't interfere with her relationship with Alan.

The first few days of carnal intimacies with Toby had certainly been businesslike. She had made him come repeatedly, with formidable and – she liked to think – imaginative efficiency, as he had her. But then she caught herself mooning over him in the office, doodling his name on her notepad, imagining them together, with roses round the door and even, God forbid, children. She'd never felt anything like it.

But then she'd never known anyone like Toby. What a bloody idiot Cat had been. She deserved all the asbestos that came her way. He was the last of the great romantics, showering her with flowers, compliments and expensive, erotic underwear. After two weeks of this she really was in love. She would have done anything for him, including burn in hell. Once or twice she thought she'd even caught Toby on the verge of telling her he loved her. She would have to tell Alan, of course. She could hardly wait.

It was Jake who managed to coax Mrs Potts into revealing that the money had been drawn each week from the account of a small company called Silvermine Ltd. It took another couple of days for Cat to get a company search done on Silvermine. Not that it got her very far. But at least one of the director's names was familiar. Toby Marks. The other turned out to be a Vicky Taggart, who, when Cat did a search on her, turned out to have been married to a Felix Hark, who ran Golden Fields. Initially she couldn't make the connection until she remembered a phone conversation Toby had had in the car the first time he'd driven her to Butely. With someone called Felix. It seemed like a lifetime ago.

After this it was inevitable she would begin following Golden Fields obsessively in the papers. And there was a lot to follow. Golden Fields was making headlines in the business pages on a daily basis, thanks to its share price, which was fluctuating in increasingly manic swings. 'Can Hark the Shark swim his way out of this?' asked the *Daily Mail*. 'Golden Fields' future looking tarnished,' announced the *Sunday Times*. 'Up against the Great Wall of China,' crowed the *Guardian*. And then there was 'Hark set to confound his critics with new investment' in *The Times*.

It was fascinating, but she still needed the missing link that connected it all to Butely.

The police were making even less progress tracking Declan. 'You'd think he'd be traceable by aftershave if not by DNA,' grumbled Cat. The health authorities told them they wouldn't be able to start work on the asbestos until after Christmas, which was academic since they didn't have any builders. Meanwhile, in the run-up to the festive holidays, Golden Fields' share price started to go through the roof, 'in anticipation', reported the *Financial Times* 'of some unexpected good news relating to one of its investments'.

★

Ten days before Christmas Cat received a call out of the blue from a lawyer claiming to act on behalf of a reclusive billionaire who wanted to buy Butely.

'Have they seen it lately?' said Cat morosely. 'It's looking a bit the worse for wear.'

'Its current condition is irrelevant,' said the voice neutrally. 'My client is in love with its architecture and position.' He paused delicately. 'And fortunately my client is in a financial position to be able to spend whatever it takes to restore it to its previous glory.'

Cat couldn't deny that she was temporarily tempted. A client that rich and besotted might be the kindest fate for Butely. It might be a bit tricky to win Jake round – but lately, given his current bonhomie . . . who knew? They could buy somewhere else more manageable – somewhere that would be much more compatible with running a modern, fully equipped naturopath clinic.

'Eight and a half million, say?' continued the voice smoothly, 'including the land, obviously.' Cat's dreams were shattered instantly. This was so much more than Butely was worth in its current – or any other state – that the offer couldn't be genuine.

'Who is your client?' she asked suspiciously.

'I am not at liberty to say,' replied the lawyer. 'But I do urge you to consider this offer. I doubt you'll receive a better one.'

That was probably the most honest thing the lawyer had said in their entire conversation – as Cat and Jake both agreed later when Cat reran the dialogue.

'It doesn't make sense,' said Cat, as she helped Jake clear up the kitchen after supper. 'I know Butely's an architectural gem, but this offer is ridiculously high.'

'You think it's somehow linked to Toby and Declan?'

'Yes. But I think there's something bigger still, connecting everything together. All the bad luck with the asbestos, the builders not being paid, the fire . . . it's not coincidence.' She shook her head grimly. 'There's been too much bad luck, too many instances of Toby – a man who, though it pains me to admit it, is extremely bright – making lousy decisions, to be plausible. I can't shake off the feeling that Silvermine is part of this. Or

Golden Fields. Their shares have rocketed recently. Apparently they're expecting some good news any minute from one of their "investments".'

'And you think that investment is Butely.' Jake looked at her quizzically.

'I know it's ridiculous,' Cat shrugged helplessly. However worrying the situation was, having Jake to share things with made everything seem less threatening. 'It doesn't make sense. What can Butely possibly have to offer that would make it so appealing to a huge company like Golden Fields? But at the moment I can't think of anything else.'

Jake ran his hands under the tap and stared out of the window thoughtfully. 'In that case,' he said eventually, 'you should string this lawyer along for a few days and then let him down – and see what happens to Golden Fields' share prices.'

Cat did exactly that for four days – partly hoping that at some point the purchaser would become involved. But the lawyer made it clear the deal depended on his client remaining anonymous. Golden Fields' share price continued to soar, until the day after Cat informed the lawyer, somewhat shakily, that she was unable to sell after all. Astonished, the lawyer repeatedly asked her whether she was sure. Firmly Cat told him it was her final decision.

'Do you really think that's wise?' asked the lawyer, all trace of neutrality expunged.

'Time will tell,' said Cat solemnly, 'but I would never forgive myself if I gave up on Butely now. And nor would my daughter. It's her heritage, after all.'

'I see.' There was an intimidating silence. 'Well, it's very important to look after daughters, isn't it?' he said eventually. 'They are so vulnerable.'

'It was horrible,' said Cat shakily to Jake. 'Maybe I'm being neurotic, but there seemed to be some kind of implicit threat in what he was saying.'

'You're not being neurotic.' He put his arms round her. 'But let's not get this out of proportion. If the worst comes to the worst, we can always go away for a bit, but I'm sure it won't be necessary,' he added hastily. 'Not with Jim hanging around every day.'

'That's true. Thank God his missus doesn't hold with Darjeeling. I'm sure that's what keeps him popping up so much.'

'In the meantime, let's keep tracking the share price—'

Cat smiled wanly. 'I never thought I'd see you taking such a keen interest in the financial pages.'

'The things we do for love—' He checked himself.

It was just a turn of phrase, Cat told herself, but her heart flipped all the same. It flipped again the following morning, but for a different reason. Golden Fields' share price had dipped dramatically.

'The stupid, stupid bitch.' Toby slammed down the phone, oblivious to the curious stares outside his glass office.

Petula glided towards his desk and discreetly brushed against his legs. 'There, there, has that nasty Felix been bullying you again?'

Toby shot her a look of such venomous force she stopped in her tracks. 'You don't get it, do you?' She could see the skin above his eyebrows throbbing as he attempted to master his emotions. When he spoke again it was in a low voice, dredged up from the depths of his contempt and coated in bile. 'Felix is history. Or rather we are. Cat refuses to sell and so Felix has kicked me off the job. Out, finished. And he'll be withdrawing the legitimate parts of his business from Simms this afternoon – complete with a formal complaint about me.'

Beneath her perfectly applied mask, Petula turned white. 'There'll be other deals,' she said eventually. She pulled up a chair next to him and took his hands gently in hers. They were trembling. 'Between us we're quite a team. You said it yourself.'

'I'm trying to tell you that after this I'm not sure if Simms will even want to keep me on.'

'So?' Petula crossed her endless legs. The sight of her underwear never failed to cheer Toby up, except this time. 'We'll go somewhere else,' she persisted. 'Who could resist us?'

He stared at her blankly. When he finally spoke it was with a

Lisa Armstrong

painfully calm clarity that made his words all the more lethal. 'I'm also trying to tell you that there is no us. Never has been, never could be, never will be, except over my dead body possibly. But even you couldn't fancy necrophilia.' He got up and walked to the door, tossing his Prada jacket over his shoulders.

Petula remained stationary for so long that the consultant who had taken Cat's place eventually poked his head round the door of Toby's office to ask whether she was all right.

She wasn't, but she couldn't articulate why because she had never suffered from a breaking heart and a crumbling sense of order before. It took her a day or two before she could even brush her hair or eat anything. But gradually, her survival instinct returned, along with an overwhelming urge for revenge. She was so numb it didn't even shock her when she found out from work that Toby had taken leave and disappeared. She was going to pay him back – tenfold. She couldn't bring herself to speak directly to Cat, but that didn't mean she couldn't ring Jake and share one or two insider secrets with him.

At first Jake thought he'd underestimated Toby. The concierge of the old rococo building adorning the sea front in Beaulieu-sur-mer vehemently denied seeing anybody coming or going from Lady Cynthia's apartment – and he would know, he repeatedly pointed out. But when pressed with two-hundred-euros and a bottle of crème de menthe he confessed to having just got back from a fort-night's holiday in Chamonix with his son and daughter-in-law. 'It's not often I get a holiday,' he told Jake importantly. 'And never in the summer, of course. I must be here for the residents. But Lady Cynthia, she did not come this year.' He shook his head in disappointment. 'It is not good for the apartment to be empty for so long. Even her son has not been for some years. And he used to love our little town so much. It is him you are looking for?'

Jake nodded.

'You are an old friend of Lady Cynthia?' The concierge eyed him slyly.

'You could say that.'

The concierge shrugged lugubriously. 'Ah, monsieur, you have had a wasted journey.'

'It must have a wonderful view,' said Jake carefully. 'The fourth floor, isn't it?'

'The seventh,' said the concierge sharply. He eyed Jake again. 'It is the penthouse, of course.'

A hunch – and not wanting to admit defeat – led Jake to a pretty little bench under a palm tree across the road from his mother's apartment, from where he could look out towards Africa, as well as keep an eye on the block of flats. He sat down and looked out across the limpid coastline, edged with its silver beaches, soaring cliffs and a sea that was still the colour of cornflowers, even in early December. A few yachts tacked across the bay while the elderly but obviously affluent denizens of Beaulieu trotted along the croisette. He could see why his mother was so attracted to the place. It was elegant, demure and reeked of money. She had bought the apartment at least twenty years earlier – with some of Sir Rodney's money – and had often spent Easters and most of the summer there. Not that she'd ever invited Sir Rodney – or Jake for that matter. He found he no longer minded. Beaulieu was lovely but it wasn't his kind of place. It beat him why Toby had always had such a soft spot for it – all the women looked at least forty years too old for him.

For the millionth time he wondered what Cat had ever seen in Toby. It was the one flaw in her wonderful character. But perhaps he was being too harsh. Growing up, he'd learned from just about every female within a hundred-mile radius of Butely that his half-brother was utterly irresistible – handsome, charming and witty. Not that it had particularly bothered Jake at the time. He had a crowd of friends of his own – less numerous and flashy than Toby's set, who always seemed to be jetting off somewhere glamorous *en masse* – but he liked them. And he'd learned to make allowances for Toby – at least he had after his father had explained certain things to him about Toby's early childhood. He was pretty sure he'd never actually been jealous of Toby. It was just that he'd somehow expected more from Cat. He watched two fishermen tie their boats up on the jetty, listening to the throaty chug of their engines.

Still, if Cat could be taken in by Toby, she probably wasn't really his type. If only he could get past the magnificent way she'd confronted all the hurdles at Butely, or the way she wagged her eyebrows when she was teasing Lily, or fiddled with her hair when she was agitated, twisting it into more and more startling shapes, or the two adorable freckles on her inside left wrist, he'd see they weren't compatible at all.

A convertible Mercedes pulled up across the street. A tall, dark figure jumped out and strode confidently into the building. Toby!

Jake remained frozen on the bench, watching the lights being turned on in a bank of French windows flanking a balcony on the top floor. He wanted to leave Toby time to unwind, hoping to startle him even more. Eventually he crossed the street. The concierge was nowhere to be seen. Judging from the smells emanating from his flat, he was cooking supper.

Jake climbed the curving steps of the sweeping stone staircase two at a time. There were three doors on the seventh floor. A blast of Wagner told him he'd find what he was looking for behind the one directly opposite him. He rang the bell and waited. He was about to press it again when the door swung open – and for a moment Jake wondered what the hell had possessed him to come and find Toby like this.

Toby had a glass of kir royale in one hand, and for a moment Jake thought it would smash to the floor. He had to hand it to him – he regained his composure extraordinarily fast.

'To what do I owe this pleasure, Jake?' Toby's eyes darted over Jake's rumpled jacket with a look of exaggerated amusement. 'You weren't just passing, I take it?' His words were faintly slurred. The kir clearly wasn't his first drink of the evening.

'I came expressly to see you.'

'Bit of a risk, in that case. How on earth did you know I'd be here?'

'A guess. I'd like to come in, if you don't mind.'

'Can't think of anything that would please me more.' Toby led him into a room with exquisite views out to the bay. It had been decorated according to some interior designer's idea of simple Provençal style – with plenty of expensive, distressed painted furniture and enormous earthenware lamps about the place.

'Drink?' said Toby, opening the doors on to the balcony. Jake followed him out.

'No, thank you.'

'Oh, Jake, always so earnest.' Toby sat down on a cushioned wooden armchair. 'At least sit down.'

He stretched out his legs, which were bare and tanned and casually dressed in linen trousers and loafers. 'I take it you haven't come to compare cocktail notes?'

'Actually I've come to compare arson notes.'

'What the hell are you talking about?'

'The Long Building burnt down three weeks ago – in the unlikely event you didn't already know. The insurance company won't pay because they suspect foul play.'

Toby barely missed a beat. 'Bloody good job, if you ask me. The place was an eyesore.'

'There were four people living there at the time, for Christ's sake. Cat, Lily and Jess moved in there after the asbestos was discovered.'

It was Toby's turn to be wrong-footed. He had been convinced that the asbestos would ensure Cat was safely removed from Butely by the time Declan torched it. It had never occurred to him she'd move into the Long Building. If he'd ever even known about the rooms next to Declan's flat he'd long since forgotten they existed.

Only a slight ripple as the skin tightened across his cheekbones betrayed any emotion at all. 'Really.' He adopted a vague tone of voice. 'Oh yes, the asbestos. I suppose the insurance people are blaming it on the propane heaters. Naturally we'll fight it.'

'I doubt it would get "us" anywhere.' Jake's astonishment at Toby's apparent nonchalance was almost as strong as his fury. He bit it back. 'The police seem to think the evidence is pretty incriminating. But the money's not really the point.'

'No, it never is with you, is it, Jake?' Toby got up and mixed himself another kir royale. 'So what is the point?'

'That's what I'm here to find out.'

'Oh, for God's sake. She is all right, isn't she?'

'No thanks to you.'

'Forgive me, then, Jake. I don't quite see why you had to make this dramatic journey like one of the seven headless horsemen of the Apocalypse. Unless it's some kind of hopeless gesture to impress Cat.'

Jake was determined not to give in to the anger that was rising in his gorge like lava. He told himself that if Toby was resorting to personal gibes this early in the game he must be feeling vulnerable.

'I made this dramatic journey, as you put it, because the police are involved. So pretty shortly you can expect a visit from some horsemen a lot more apocalyptic than me.'

Toby drained his glass and deposited it shakily on the table between them. 'What makes you think I've got anything to do with it?'

'Please, Toby. Spare me the innocent act. I have it chapter and verse from your office.'

Petula!

'She even told me how you recommended to those bosses at Simms that they didn't give Cat the rise they'd been planning to.' Jake looked unflinchingly as the blood drained from Toby's face.

'A woman scorned! Jesus, Jake, surely even you know what unreliable witnesses they make at the best of times.'

'Please, Toby,' said Jake. 'She said she'd even be prepared to go to court.'

It was then he turned white. 'For God's sake, you must know I didn't have anything to do with this fire,' he said eventually.

Jake said nothing.

'Jesus, Jake, I'm not a murderer.' Toby slumped visibly. In those few seconds Jake realised that whatever else Toby was guilty of, he wasn't capable of burning an occupied house down. 'For Christ's sake, why did you come – if you knew everything already?' Toby ran his hand through his hair. Jake saw it was shaking.

'I wanted to find out why,' he said evenly. 'I don't get it, Toby. Why do you hate us so much? What have I done to earn your undying contempt?'

Toby shook his head angrily. 'You always were a prim little git,' he said at last.

'And you were always resentful,' said Jake. 'Though God knows why.'

'Even you can't be that thick,' snarled Toby. 'Jesus, what do you think it was like playing second string to Little Lord Fauntleroy?'

'I think my father always tried to be even handed.'

'He couldn't disguise his distaste for me, though, could he?' Toby drained his glass. 'Though Christ knows I worked for his approval. I got better A-levels than you. Went to a better university than you. I was a better sportsman. But nothing I ever did was ever enough, was it? And even though I was around more than you, and always made sure I went to see him whenever I was in Dorset, he left me with nothing. Just the insult of an annual fee. As though I wasn't part of the family. Which technically, of course, I'm not.'

Jake looked out over the bay, where the sun was slowly setting, turning the sea into a blaze of pink and mauve. 'Are you honestly saying that you were prepared to destroy Butely over some petty jealousy?'

'You still don't get it, do you?' The drink made him sound increasingly menacing and out of control. 'I wasn't trying to destroy Butely. I'm not a bloody vandal. I wanted to have it and maximise its potential, not piss around with it the way you two were. That would have been the ultimate revenge, don't you think, for all those years of exclusion?'

'What are you talking about?' Jake asked. There was a pitying inquisitiveness to his voice that drove Toby mad.

'Do you know how much I stood to make from Butely's oil?' Toby laughed mirthlessly. 'At least ten million. Hardly the action of a loser, was it?' The taunting braggadocio returned to his voice.

'Only now you're out of the deal. And probably out of a job.'

'Really? And what would you know?' Toby got up heavily and opened another bottle of champagne.

'Haven't you been reading the papers?' asked Jake. 'The financial press are having a field day with Golden Fields and Felix Hark has issued a statement laying some of the blame for his problems with Simms.'

They sat in silence for what seemed an age, listening to Wagner's *Ring* cycle crashing through the night air.

'Why didn't your father leave me anything, then?' said Toby, finally breaking the silence. He sounded like a plaintive little boy.

'He didn't think he needed to. He knew I was never going to make any money of my own. And he took pity on Cat – a single mother and all that. You know what a soft touch he could be.' Jake thought that putting it like that would appeal to Toby's sense of vanity, and he was right.

'I would never have hurt Cat, you know. That business with the asbestos was to make sure she got the hell out of Butely . . . where she could be safe.' There was a wheedling undercurrent to his voice now that infuriated Jake.

'Well, one way or another you were almost responsible for killing her, and Lily and Jess,' said Jake. His voice sounded lethally calm.

Trembling, Toby picked up his glass. 'Look, Jake, what do you want from me? Why the hell are you here?'

'It's very simple. In decreasing order of importance, I want your immediate resignation as a trustee of Butely; your solemn undertaking to help the police track down Declan; and your full co-operation in handing everything you've got on Felix Hark over to the police.'

There was an audible intake of breath. 'Fine on the other two. No problem, Jake. But Felix – he's pretty ruthless, you know. Wouldn't want to cross him.'

'Cat already has,' said Jake. 'And not that you probably give a shit, but he got one of his heavies to make threatening noises about Lily if she didn't sell Butely. Did you know that about your precious client, Toby?'

It was this last piece of information, delivered unemotionally, by Jake, that conclusively shattered through Toby's veneer. After that, he had no choice but to comply with Jake's demands. He may have been a ruthless monster, but unfortunately for him he was a ruthless monster with a strong sense of shame.

23

No one was very shocked when the health authorities informed Cat that they wouldn't be able to clear the asbestos for another month. With a similar situation at nearby East Scraggerton there was a bit of a backlog, the man from the council told Cat apologetically. Now that Goran was back in Croatia, Jake has smoothed things over with Vic, who was happy to take on the remaining work, as soon as he could find a window in his schedule.

In the meantime, Cat went to visit Butely every day as if it were a sick friend in hospital, taking care to check all its nooks and crannies. If Butely was beautiful in the summer, with all the roses and honeysuckle in bloom, it was even more magical in the depths of winter, when the lawns were capped with a light dusting of snow and the trees dripped with stalactites that glittered like diamonds in the stark light. A thick frost had bedded itself into the surrounding countryside, like fine icing sinking into a soggy fruit cake. Despite being on top of one another in Jake's cottage, Cat found herself looking forward to Christmas there. Although Jake was out most of the time, frantically trying to finish some plans he'd been working on to restore Dorchester's Corn Exchange, or checking up on Sir Galahad with Lily, he always made it back in time to have supper. They took it in turns to cook, although Jake's meals were the best by far. It was almost like being a conventional nuclear family, thought Cat wistfully. Sometimes after supper they'd put one of Jake's jazz records on – he had a vast collection that even included some of Cat's beloved musical scores. One night she came down from her shower to find Jake twirling Lily round the room to 'I've Got You Under My Skin'. She watched from the doorway, kicking herself for ever thinking he was bad tempered when most of the time he had simply been wryly deprecating. She wished he'd take her in his arms and dance with her. But even when she told him that 'Bewitched' was one of her favourite songs ever, he didn't take the hint.

It was Jake's idea to invite Vic and Marina Spinoza over for Christmas Day. Cat was touched by how moved Vic was when he rang the next day to accept.

'We normally go to my sister,' he said, thanking Cat profusely.

'Won't she mind if you don't turn up this year?' Cat asked.

'I think she'll be relieved. Don't get me wrong. She's been kindness itself ever since Lesley died, but she'll be pleased that we've got somewhere else to go. When you're a widower,' he added sadly, 'people tend not to want you around at Christmas. It's almost as though you're toxic waste and they're scared you might somehow contaminate their happiness.'

Jim, the policeman, popped in on Christmas Eve to keep them fully apprised, in his slow, methodical way, of police progress on hunting down Declan.

'We're getting closer to apprehending Mr Kelly every day.' He pulled a chair up to the kitchen table and eyed the tea caddy on the dresser longingly, before launching into a laborious account that made it painfully clear the police were in fact making little headway.

Despite everything, it was one of Cat and Lily's best Christmases. Cat thought back to Toby's lavish gifts of the year before. She wouldn't be seduced by knights in shining Armani ever again.

Since all of them, apart from Vic, were broke, Cat ruled that they should all make their presents. Jess gave them all revolting homemade flapjacks with wheatgrass and Lily knitted them all scarves which she wrapped with the needles still attached because she hadn't got the hang of casting off. Vic, who was exempt, splashed out and bought them all lavish gift sets of Chanel Number 5, Opium and Mitsouko, chosen by Marina. Cat gave Lily the untouched laptop she'd bought for Declan and Jake a tiny lurcher puppy that Guy Fulton had sold her for next to nothing as a thank-you for introducing his lamb to Fortnum's. Jake gave Cat a series of sepia elevations he'd drawn of Butely. Then he blindfolded Lily and drove them all to Butely, where he'd built her a tree house over-looking the sea. It even had a solar panel he'd found in a junkyard. Lily and Jess scrambled up the ladder, followed closely by Marina. Jake watched them, fondling the baby lurcher's ears, which were poking out of the pocket of his Barbour.

'You can have a joint house-warming when you move back,' he said, rubbing Cat's hands to get the circulation going.

She was so touched by his faith that the tears stung her eyes. She forced them back. 'So you think we will move in one day, then?' she asked as brightly as she could. 'I was starting to wonder.'

'Of course you will.' He pulled her towards him tenderly. Vic tactfully strolled off to examine a fascinating foxhole he'd just discovered. Cat looked up at Jake adoringly and closed her eyes.

'So this is why we haven't seen much of you lately,' called Jess, ramming her head through the tree-house window.

'I couldn't have done it without Vic,' admitted Jake.

'You must both have worked like the clappers to get this finished,' said Jess admiringly. Thanks to the Opium and the tree house she could see she was going to have to start viewing Vic in a new light. 'Isn't it about time Butely went solar?'

'I've been thinking along those lines too,' said Jake. 'The problem is that Butely's listed. You can't do a thing to change the outside, but we can certainly have panels in the pool complex. That should make the whole thing a lot more eco-friendly.'

And cheaper, thought Cat gratefully. 'What are you going to call the puppy?' she asked.

'Guinevere,' said Jake. 'It goes with Galahad and I want them to be friends.'

Lunch was a raucous affair – and a culinary triumph, thanks to Jake. Jess sprinkled artistic swirls of sunflower seeds on the white tablecloth in the hope that people would nibble them between courses, rather than reaching for the Belgian chocolates Vic had brought. After they'd pulled every last cracker they played forfeits. Jake smiled at Cat as she tried to mime *Tomb Raider*, and if Lily hadn't snuggled up to him she was pretty sure he would have put his arm round her instead.

January the second brought them down to earth with a resounding thump. With Glowbal now entirely discredited and off the job and Vic back in the picture, Cat could see how ridiculously low Glowbal's quote for the job had been.

Jess peered over her shoulder at Vic's estimate. 'Blimey. It's almost enough to make you wish we hadn't discovered what a bunch of crooks Glowbal was. I can see Vic's cut his quote down to the bare bones, but it's still way more than Glowbal's. It's all that fancy equipment, I suppose – the stuff Glowbal was going to provide for nothing.'

'But Glowbal never had any intention of finishing the job,' explained Cat patiently. 'At least, not properly. And if they had done we'd have been in hock to Golden Fields and Felix Hark for ever.' She shuddered. 'It makes my blood run cold to think about it.'

Unfortunately Vic's estimates made Tim Bonnington's blood run even colder. The bank manager put his foot down and to Cat's fury refused to sanction the loan. Yet if there was one thing Toby had been right about, it was the necessity of having a pool. Every single enquiry that had failed to materialise into a solid booking confirmed it. She sat up late into the night poring over the figures on Jake's kitchen table, trying to make them add up. By the third night she was almost in despair. To have come this close to making a success of things and have it all implode in front of her eyes was almost unbearable. She heard Jake creep up behind her. He placed a hand on her shoulder, sending ridiculous shudders down her spine that rippled all the way to her groin.

'I thought you'd gone to bed,' she whispered.

'It's a bit distracting, with you just next door,' he said sheepishly. Did he mean the whirr of the computer was keeping him awake, or some other electrical force? With huge self-control she returned to her sums.

'Is it the bank loan?' he asked sympathetically.

She nodded desolately.

'There is a solution, you know.' He sat down opposite her. 'Butely's probably got enough oil to ensure we never have to worry about money again.'

'You really believe that's all true, then?' A flicker of hope lit Cat's eyes.

'Completely. There're spots of oil all over Dorset. I wouldn't be surprised if that wasn't why the Tenth Earl let those lily beds go to rack and ruin. I think he'd begun to suspect something in the 1930s – around the time the Butely family were running out of cash, coincidentally. That would certainly explain all the excavation that went on around there.'

'Then the war happened so they couldn't go ahead,' said Cat excitedly.

'And the tenth Earl was killed, before he had time to pass on the secret.'

'Would that account for the marshy patches?' said Cat, suddenly recalling what Sir Rodney had told her about blockages in the Butely soil, the first time they'd met.

'Possibly. I don't know.'

They ruminated in silence for a while, each lost in their own thoughts. A whole new spectrum of possibilities opened up in front of Cat, one in which she could turn Butely into a leading research centre where profits and bottoms lines were irrelevant.

'I'll make some tea.' Jake stood up. 'And then you can redo your sums.'

Almost hyperventilating with the thrill of her new vision, Cat looked up at the columns on her screen and began to adjust the figures based on a hypothetical estimate of Butely's oil revenues. Over the top of her screen she could see Jake filling the kettle, staring out of the little mullioned kitchen window into the velvet blackness. It was below freezing outside and the night had a magical clarity Cat had learned was only to be found in the countryside, with each star piercing the darkness like a tiny shard of crystal bursting through a silk tent.

She switched off her laptop and walked over to him. 'I couldn't,' she said, sliding her hands round his waist and leaning against his back. 'Oil money really is filthy lucre. It would destroy all the things we love about living here. I'm going to make Butely work on its own, if it's the last thing I do.'

He held her hands and they stood without saying anything for ages. A small part of Cat wished Jake had put up more of a fight. You couldn't take all the materialism out of a material girl, and she would have quite liked to have rolled in filthy lucre. But by far the biggest part of her knew she was doing the right thing, and to her surprise just knowing it felt ridiculously good.

There was only one thing left to do. The next morning, her stomach curdled with nerves and her fingers itching for the first time in months to hold a cigarette, she picked up the phone and dialled Villie Frupps's number.

'So have they caught him yet?' Suzette methodically flicked the Chantilly cream off her Green & Black hot chocolate into a gilt leaf saucer and looked daggers at the waitress in her pert black-and-white dress. Idiotic girl – if she'd asked for the lo-fat version once she'd demanded it a thousand times.

'Who? Having been interrupted halfway through her latest masterpiece for the Butely monthly newsletter, Cat was only half listening.

'Declan.'

'Not yet,' said Cat, shifting some paragraphs around on the Mac.

'Why doesn't that surprise me? I dare say they're far too busy chasing loyal British subjects for so-called outstanding tax bills to catch any real criminals.' Suzette gazed peevishly out of the café window on to the snow-clogged street outside. It was very galling to think that Rodney had been right all along about his stepson.

'How's Verbier?' asked Cat.

'Very white.'

Early in their courtship, when Eduardo had told her how much he adored skiing, she couldn't grasp how serious he was. So she'd told him she loved it too, more out of politeness than anything else. And now she was paying the price. While Eduardo thought she was having private lessons in *langlauf* she was tucked away with the pert waitress in a backstreet in Verbier consuming her weight in hot chocolate.

'The good news,' bubbled Cat, 'is that my old client Wilhelm Frupps has decided to invest in Butely.'

'The pornographer?'

Cat ignored her. 'He believes that Butely is a very interesting business project.' Actually it was Cat who'd pointed out its money-making potential. Villie had simply seen it as a way of keeping Frau Frupps's health club bills down.

'Well, it's all nudity, I suppose.'

'The building on the pool and the new gym started last week. I must say, it seems to be a lot easier to build something new than restore something old.'

She could say that again, thought Suzette, catching sight of what looked suspiciously like the beginning of a liver spot on her hand. 'Any romance in the air?' she asked hopefully.

'Perhaps,' said Cat coyly. She was torn between desperately wanting to talk about Jake at every opportunity and not wanting to jinx whatever there was between them. 'I have actually. He's kind, considerate and steady.'

Suzette thought he sounded deathly.

'And what does he do?'

Cat racked her brains for the kind of man least likely to appeal to Suzette as a future son-in-law and thought of the lugubrious Jim. 'He's a policeman,' she said happily.

In the middle of February they moved back into the Cottage and Orlando's docu-drama hit the screen. With their hearts bungee-jumping, Cat, Lily, Jess and Jake piled into Sir Rodney's old drawing room to watch it.

'I can't look,' moaned Cat as the titles flashed up against the sound-track of 'Keep Young and Beautiful'. 'It's too horrible. They're just going to send the whole thing up.' The cameras cut to a particularly poorly executed portrait of one of the yogis – the one with the most protuberant belly.

'Look, it's Veronica,' heckled Jess.

'Not unless she's had Lipo,' said Cat. She hadn't forgiven the three witches who still owed Butely for their last stay.

'*Deep in the wilds of Dorset lies a sleeping beauty,*' crooned a honey-toned voice-over. The cameras switched to a view of Samantha taking forty winks on the bench outside Micky's kitchen.

'She told me she'd given up smoking,' said Jess indignantly. 'Look!'

Cat prized her fingers away from her face. There in Samantha's left hand, dangling dangerously close to Seamus's backside, were the dying embers of a cigarette with three inches of ash attached to it.

'At least she hadn't smoked much of it, by the looks of things,' said Jake. He smiled up at Cat from where he was stretched out on the floor by her feet.

'That little shit,' fumed Cat.

'Give him a chance,' said Jess. 'It'll probably get better as it warms up.'

'I'll warm him up. If this proves slanderous—'

'Calm down. It's going to be fine. I know it is.' A close-up of Jess's G-string rising above her waistband as she performed Downward Dog flashed up on the screen.

'The bastard,' yelled Jess.

'Calm down,' said Cat.

There were a few more minutes of predictable Benny Hill-style footage and patronising voice-over and then, miraculously, the whole timbre of the programme improved dramatically. '*So much for the received wisdom about health farms,*' the voice-over continued.

'Perhaps they recorded this bit after Orlando and Myfanwy made up,' suggested Lily.

'It doesn't work that way,' snapped Jess. 'They record the whole thing at the end.' She tossed her plaits. 'I doubt if they're even together any more.'

'. . . *but at Butely they do things differently,*' the voice pressed on silkily. '*Or at least they're starting to. Under the new management of thirty-six-year-old Cat McGinty*—'

'Can they get anything right?' snapped Cat. She wasn't even thirty-five for a month.

'Shhh.' Jake grinned at her. 'I think you're about to hear something to your advantage.'

The rest of the programme couldn't have panned out better if they'd paid Orlando to do an ad for them. Butely had never looked more ravishing – fortunately dust and cracks don't reproduce well on TV. Cat came across as focused, principled and enterprising. 'Amazing how telly distorts, isn't it?' said Jess.

Perhaps because there had been so many genuine dramas and crises during Orlando's sojourn there, he hadn't needed to create any scandals or misrepresent them. The upshot, the programme concluded, was that the world was a better place for having somewhere like Butely. '*At the end of the day,*' drawled the voice-over, '*this is an institution that values well-being more than wealth, whose owners are more interested in making a fair profit than a fortune. Can it survive in the twenty-first century? Who knows? But if Cat McGinty can't succeed, who can?*'

'Told you it would be positive,' crowed Jess as the closing credits rolled.

'How come you were so sure?' asked Cat.

Jess winked back.

Cat felt marginally deflated. She'd been convinced that Orlando's hagiography was down to her irresistible aura of authority – not the fact that he and Jess had been going at it like rabbits behind his girlfriend's back.

'What about poor Myfanwy?' asked Cat crossly.

'She should be grateful, the shrivelled-up cow. He left me a far more experienced lover than he found me.'

'I think it's time to turn in, Lily,' said Jake hastily. 'And I should be going, so we can leave the adults to their philosophy.'

After the docu-drama went out the number of people calling to find out about Butely went stratospheric. Not even Sister Slammer singing Butely's praises on *Woman's Hour* could match the power of TV exposure. Cat's newsletters were paying off too, and the number of companies enquiring about tailor-made packages to offer their employees as incentive bonuses quadrupled – though the lack of a completed pool and modern gym facilities still put some people off booking.

'It's weird,' said Cat, her cheeks flayed by the biting winter wind, 'even people who have never been on an exercise machine in their life don't want to go anywhere unless it has enough equipment to challenge an Olympic squad.'

'Veronica Beddowes does.' Jake blew on his fingers. As usual, Cat had come out without her gloves and borrowed his. It was a bitterly cold morning. The kind when the air if almost crisp with frozen fog and the world seems enveloped in a uniform opacity. 'I heard her on the phone to Samantha this morning.'

'Frankly Veronica Beddowes doesn't fall into the category of needy people I want to reach.'

'No. I'm afraid the only falling she's been doing lately is in the gutter and out of dresses,' said Jake, scooping Guinevere out of a puddle.

Cat pulled her coat tighter. She was wearing her old jeans and Jake's faded, celadon cashmere jumper, the one with two darns over the elbows.

'She went on one of those celebrity reality shows. The one where they sent eight vaguely famous people up in a huge balloon and made them vote each other out.'

Cat looked mystified.

'I can't believe you didn't want any of them. Lily was hooked. Anyway, Veronica won. And now she'd got her own TV show. *Trouble and Strife*. The idea is that they get wives who've been bosses around by their husbands for years to turn the tables. It's a ratings smash.'

'Bit low-brow for you, isn't it?'

He grinned. 'The point is that at least she'll be able to pay her bills now. She's loaded. And she certainly qualifies as needy. The success has gone completely to her head.'

'How do you know all this?'

'It's the talk of the Hung Drawn and Quartered. *You* need to relax. You've been working like a maniac these past few weeks.'

'Why don't you ask me out, then?' The words tumbled from her mouth before she had a chance to think them through. She blushed crimson and was about to recant when she heard him say he'd be delighted and what was she doing that night.

She was ridiculously excited to be going out, given that she saw Jake practically every day on some pretext or other and that they were only going to the Hung Drawn and Quartered. She began getting ready at five o'clock, starting with a few of the breathing and stretching exercises Jess had shown them and moving on to a long hot bath, which, now that Vic had got one of his plumbers to tinker with the system, was no longer an oxymoron. She poured in three capfuls of Mitsouko perfume, washed her hair and told herself not to be so silly. She hung her head over the lip of the bath and practised some visualising techniques, but all she could see was Jake's gentle smile getting closer and closer until his lips were pressed against her and his hands were running up and down her wet skin, making ripples in the water and causing havoc in her body. Horrified, she opened her eyes and began scrubbing her arms with a loofah.

Her skin was still slightly damp from the steamy bath when Jake arrived at seven on the dot. He was back in his old moleskin jacket. His still-tanned face looked lean and amused. Her heart almost stopped. They decided to walk to the pub because Jake agreed with Cat that it would be picturesque. She was wearing a pale blue cashmere polo neck and an old dark grey velvet skirt. Her newly washed hair swung round her shoulders and for the first time in months she'd put on some make-up.

'You look nice,' said Jake as they wandered along under the canopy of oaks and sycamores that lined the drive like Giacometti sculptures. The wind rustled through the branches as they chatted easily about the events of the day and swapped affectionate anecdotes about Lily. Cat marvelled at the transformation in their relationship. She'd gone from writing him off as a cold bastard to discussing Lily with him as if he were a surrogate father, or at least an uncle.

Julian had reserved the most secluded table in the house for them, the one in the nook opposite the fireplace, and sent over glass after glass of kir royale on the house. Cat ordered oysters, on Julian's recommendation, and insisted on sharing them. If it hadn't been Jake sitting opposite her in the flickering candlelight, it would have been ridiculously romantic. As it was, Cat was beginning to think the situation was hopeless. She would have had to be blind not to notice the way he stared at her sometimes, as if she were an ancient archaeological dig just waiting to be brought back to life. But he never acted on it.

She remembered what Jess had said. Somehow she had to let Jake know that she and Toby had never actually got round to consummating their relationship. The chatter in the restaurant was discreetly low key – half the county seemed to be using the place for romantic trysts, quite a few of them with people they weren't meant to be with. But it did mean that everyone looked glamorous and animated. Then 'I've Got You Under My Skin' started playing, which Cat decided to take as a sign – after all, it was practically their song. She flirted outrageously with Jake, but it all seemed to float above his unruly head. In desperation, she strained her knees as far as they would go under the table so that they brushed against his. Just once, when they both reached for the bottle of wine, their hands touched, by accident, and she felt a thousand jolts. It was practically the most erotic thing that had ever happened to her. Julian smiled at them beatifically from the bar.

On the walk back, her cheeks flushed from the wine and the fire, Cat threaded her arm through Jake's and rested her head on his shoulders. She could have sworn his lips brushed against her hair but it was such a fleeting sensation it could have been a falling leaf. When they got to her door he refused all invitations in, turning on his heels, leaving Cat quivering with desire. If Jake didn't do something soon, she'd have to take matters into her own hands.

24

Thanks to Villie's generous intervention, Vic's reliability and the fact that they no longer had to replace the roof, Butely's restorations cracked on at a gallop. Which was more than could be said for police progress in catching Declan. Felix, being a much bigger fish, was easier to net and was currently on bail, while Golden Fields, the conglomerate he had ruthlessly built up over three decades, went spectacularly down the tubes in less than three months, leaving a lot of journalists and investors red faced.

At the beginning of March, Toby received an e-mail from all seven of the Vices informing him that his services were no longer required. Even if his involvement with the disgraced Golden Fields hadn't damned him, his ruthless pursuit of every attractive woman in the building, including some of the Vices' mistresses, hadn't won him any friends. By the end of the month he had also accumulated letters of rejection from every major and not so major consultancy firm in London and New York.

Eventually he managed to find a role in an up-and-coming company in Singapore. Torn between his insane ambition and the exigencies of his heat rash, he chose the former. He consoled himself with the thought that at least the air conditioning in Singapore would be ferocious, keeping the worst symptoms of his rash at bay. And he would always have Petula, although he had noticed a certain frostiness in her manner lately. It was a measure of the self-delusion that he had wrapped himself in ever since he had been fired that he still had no idea how much she loathed him after he had humiliated her. And it was a measure of Petula's taste for revenge that not even telling Jake everything about Toby had sated it.

'We could have quite an amusing time of things in Singapore,' he said one morning, leaning back in his swivel chair. He had been banished from Simms House but had sneaked back in to collect some suits Petula had picked up for him from the dry cleaner's.

'Sorry, Toby,' said Petula, tipping the contents of her desk into some plastic Muji boxes and pointedly discarding a file of printed e-mails that Toby had sent her over the years. 'Alan would never, ever agree to uprooting to Singapore.'

'But it's a terrific step for your career and the money's phenomenal,' he wheedled.

She continued packing. 'Where are you going?' he asked in mock horror. He went down on one knee and clasped his hands to his heart. 'Not forsaking me, fair Mistress Petula?' He waited for the inevitable reassurance that of course she wasn't.

'I've been promoted to the eleventh floor.' He mouth was set in petulant victory. She would never forgive Toby for devoting so much time to Cat when she'd offered herself on a plate or for missing her wedding when she'd been counting on him to make it a day to remember. 'One of the Vices needs a new PA and he specifically asked for me.' He watched the back of her long legs, slick with moisturiser, as she bent down to pick up another crate. 'Don't worry,' she continued blithely. 'I'll make sure your new company engages the best PA in Singapore and I'll brief her on your every last little desire, if you like.'

Marginally consoled, he ambled down the corridor to see whether anyone was free to have lunch with him in the Ivy but the swotty gits were all too busy. He felt miserable – and furious suddenly with Declan for getting off apparently scot-free while he was being banished to bloody Singapore.

It was during his third Bloody Mary on his own in the bar of the Ivy that he suddenly remembered a conversation with Declan about a girlfriend in Jersey. 'My bolt-hole,' he'd called her. 'In more ways than one.' Cursing himself for not remembering earlier, he left the Ivy without eating, thereby ensuring he wouldn't be getting a table there again for some time, and called Jim at Dorchester police station.

Later that afternoon, Petula rang the latest recruitment agency in Singapore and asked for details of their best PAs. 'They must be over fifty and very serious,' she specified. Over the following days she received details of half a dozen that sounded suitable. She picked the ugliest and via a satellite conference told the woman, who had a mouth like a rat-trap and eyes that were sunk so deep into the folds of her face they were like currants that had dropped to the bottom of a cake, how much Toby liked being left to his own devices all day. 'Don't interrupt him with coffee, or waste time on niceties,' instructed Petula sternly. 'He's driven and reclusive – almost a hermit.' She remembered his heat rash. 'Oh, and he hates air conditioning. Whatever you do, make sure the office is kept at a constant thirty degrees.'

The work on Butely finished bang on time, at the end of May. With the Long Building out of the way and Caleb and Brian working like beavers to reclaim the land it had stood on for vegetables, Vic's teams of builders had been able to concentrate on the pool complex and redecorating the interior of the house.

'You've done an amazing job,' said Samantha, not even trying to keep the admiration out of her voice.

'I hardly recognised the place,' said Micky, taking in the new pool, the gorgeous limestone showers, sprung floors and separate saunas for men and women.

'It's not so different,' replied Cat hastily. 'You'll still be able to give your Scottish douches, Sam. And all we've done in the main house is spruced things up a bit. Some of the rooms still haven't had their final coat of paint, but at least the wet and dry rot have been sorted out. It's the complex that really makes a dramatic improvement.'

She gazed at the pool, flooded with light from the glass roof which extended all the way into the gym and the new treatment rooms. Jake had also tacked on two workshops, one for Daphne's Clay Expressions and another, with a sprung floor, for Jess's yoga classes. Cat had spent hours discussing treatments and exercise programmes with Dr Anjit, and in the end she felt they'd achieved an almost perfect balance between tried-and-tested solutions and more experimental ones. With Caleb and Brian offering gardening courses as well, and Micky's increasing interest in preparing lots of delicious organic food, Butely was on its way to living up to Cat's original vision.

All they needed now was some patients.

'It'll be just like old times,' gushed Veronica down the phone to Cat. 'I could squidge into one of the dormies with Weezie.'

Cat wasn't falling for that again. 'I'm afraid the dormies are full, but I've got a lovely little single left. The light's marvellous in the mornings and you have wonderful views of the orchard.'

Veronica's disgruntlement was palpable from Soho, which is where she was between takes of her new series of *Trouble and Strife.*

'How little?' she asked.

'Big enough to swing a TV award in and very cosy.'

'Warm?' barked Veronica.

'As toast. Oh, and Veronica. You will bring some valid means of payment this time, won't you? Only under the new system we can't activate your key until your credit card's been swiped.'

Cat half expected Veronica not to turn up after that. But she hadn't reckoned on Veronica's excitement when she'd heard a rumour that Cherie Blair might be checking into Butely.

But even if Veronica hadn't turned up, Weezie would have. Having decided that writing was too much like work, she'd become a lifestyle consultant, coaching other people in the art of spending their money – a hefty chunk of which went on her fees. Her latest client was Tiffany Miller, the beleaguered wife of a footballing sensation who'd been caught by the paparazzi in a three-in-a-bed romp. Tiffany had tearfully taken her husband back, after extracting a huge amount of money out of him, part of which, under Weezie's expert guidance, she was spending on a stay at Butely, to get in shape, as Weezie said, for the next stage of their shopping marathon.

★

At the beginning of May Jake asked Cat what she wanted for her birthday. 'To forget about it,' she grumbled. Secretly she was thrilled that he'd remembered. '*Urgh*, thirty-five.' Surely she ought to have attained some kind of spiritual enlightenment by now. But she was as driven as ever. Only the other day Jake had teased her about turning everything, even napping, into a competitive field sport. That was probably why he didn't want to get romantically involved with her.

'At least you've achieved something.' She was sitting on the floor while he sat on the sofa and massaged her shoulders. She twisted round to look up at him.

'So have you.'

'Butely, you mean? Wouldn't have done any of it without you. And I certainly don't have a family, which you appear to have achieved all on your own.' He picked up one of Lily's pony books, which she'd stuffed down beside one of the cushions, and wistfully replaced the bookmark.

Cat wanted to tell him that if he wasn't so stubbornly blind he could have an instant family. That what she really wanted for her birthday was for him to whisk her off somewhere – anywhere – so that they could be alone together. But somehow she couldn't find the words.

Jake couldn't remember when he'd first got the idea of a surprise birthday party. But he felt that if he could organise one he would impress Cat, and in moments of heightened optimism he even hoped that somehow together they might lay to rest the ghost of her relationship with Toby.

He spent the next fortnight on the phone organising the party – just a smallish one for the people he knew Cat had grown fond of since arriving in Butely, and of course her mother, whose number he got from Jess. That, as it turned out, was his biggest mistake. Once Jess was involved there wasn't much chance of the party remaining small. By the time Jess had invited the rugger buggers and the young farmers it was pretty obvious that all Butely's patients would have to be invited as well. There was no need to invite the Piddle Valley Mummers, because when they heard about it from the rugger buggers they invited themselves. Then Julian said you couldn't have a party without a band, so he got on to the Wessex Salsa Five.

When Sister Slammer, who was in Britain on the first leg of her comeback tour, heard what Jake was planning, she said she wanted to sing a few numbers as well. At which point Jake decided he had to break the news to Cat about the party. After all, she'd probably want to buy a new outfit.

The day of the party dawned. Spruced up and drained of damp by Vic, Butely's red brickwork shimmered in the sunshine like a giant conker, nestling in an undulating idyll of lawns and meadows. The lilac that looked like skeletal ghosts in the depths of winter had just unfurled the first of their petals and the sharp, sweet scent wafted in through the open french doors of the library and dining room.

As usual Suzette had arrived just late enough in the day not to have to get involved in any of the preparations yet still with enough time to hog most of the hot water, loosen half a bottle of Fracas into the atmosphere and spend several hours getting ready.

'My God, you two look fantastic.' She swept approving eyes over Lily, still in her jodhpurs, and Cat, who, like Butely, had never looked more beautiful. The last eighteen months at Butely had brought a glow to her skin and sharpened the contours of her body. Now that she'd got used to Butely's draughts – which had been considerably improved by Vic – she no longer required multiple layers of insulation and got by quite happily most days in a pair of old corduroy trousers and a single jumper. Country life suited her, thought Suzette. Either that or she'd been having dermabrasion.

'Eduardo.' She beamed proudly. 'Meet my family.'

A tall, distinguished man with mossy-looking eyebrows and a nose like a camel's hump stepped forward and flashed a grin so dazzling Cat felt she'd been caught in a storm of paparazzi lenses. Feeling awkward and very Anglo-Saxon, she held out her hand and then bit her lip as Eduardo bent down and kissed it.

'Let me show you round.' She led them through the flagstoned hall of the Cottage and upstairs, which now that Mrs Faggot had finally got to grips with the Dyson was a picture of rural prettiness.

'What a charming room,' purred Suzette, taking in the burnished antiques, the wonky whitewashed walls and deep window seat, framed by Colefax and Fowler's rambling roses. Rodney's choice, she presumed. Unless Cat had orchestrated all this, which she very much doubted.

Jess and Daphne watched in stunned awe as Suzette swept Cat and Lily upstairs with Eduardo. 'I don't think I've even seen anyone so immaculate,' muttered Jess. 'He makes Toby look like Swampy. And that tan. Do you think if comes off on the sheets?'

'Along with the toupee,' said Daphne. She was still stinging from the news that Lady Cynthia was sunning herself in the Bahamas with Gerald.

Despite the long flight, Suzette was desperate to see the rest of Butely. While Eduardo trailed after her like a weary conquistador, Suzette explored every corner, secretly imagining what her life would have been like if she had become Lady Dowell. Certainly she would have kept the study less cluttered than Cat chose to.

Still, all in all it looked lovely. Even Cat was hard pushed to find fault. Under Caleb and Brian's loving solicitations, the gardens were sprinkled with roses and lilies. Inside, Butely's wood panelling gleamed in the soft sunlight and its flagstones sparkled like uncut diamonds. 'Rodney had excellent taste,' said Suzette, eyeing the casual huddles of antiques as they traipsed through the main house. 'I'll give him that.'

'And who are these?' enquired Eduardo, eyeing the patrician noses and chinless features of some of the ancestors with professional relish.

'Butelys, mainly,' said Cat, leading them up the carved staircase, where to her eternal satisfaction Mrs Faggot had clearly been busy with the beeswax.

'Someone obviously didn't cleanse, tone and moisturise,' said Suzette, examining the fourth Countess. 'And just look at the ears on the fifth Earl. You would have made a fortune, Ed—' She broke off suddenly as she reached the portrait of a still-lovely blonde woman in her late forties. She was wearing a pale grey silk shawl-collared dress – Balenciaga, Suzette decided. And she was dripping in rubies.

'Who's this?' she asked in a strained voice.

'Edwina Dowell,' said Cat, gratified to see that someone had arranged a huge vase of peonies on the oak chest beneath the arched window at the top of the stairs. 'Sir Rodney's mother.'

Eduardo peered at the painting appreciatively. 'Excellent jawline,' he pronounced.

Suzette looked at Cat and then at the portrait. 'If you don't mind, both of you, I think I'll go and lie down. I'm suddenly feeling the effects of the flight.'

Cat was still fastening up her dress when the first guests crunched up the drive, past the flaming torches that Micky had posted along the terrace – under the strictest instructions from Daphne to monitor them closely all night, as they were all still suffering from post-traumatic flame disorder.

'Goodness, Jake,' Daphne said, contriving to bump into him as he arrived from his quick change back at his cottage. 'I barely recognised you. I don't think I've ever seen you looking so smart.' With his hair combed and his taut, long limbs offset by his dark suit, his charms were obvious to everyone. 'You look marvellous. And so does Butely,' she added. 'Your father would have been so impressed.'

'With Cat – yes, hugely. And so he should be. She's worked miracles,' he said proudly.

'And so have you – in a different way. You make a magnificent team.' She let the words hover over them, and folded her arms expectantly. 'Well?'

'Well what?' Jake grinned.

'Daphne,' gasped Weezie, plucking a glass of champagne from a passing tray. 'What a simply amazing frock. And so clever of you to wear it back to front. Now you must let me introduce you both to my new best friend, Tiffany Miller.'

A human skunk with a shock of streaked hair that looked as though it had been dragged through a very expensive Mayfair salon backwards bobbed up behind Weezie's left shoulder and thrust out a set of white-tipped claws. Gingerly Jake shook her hand. Impressed by his no-nonsense grip, Tiffany wedged herself between Weezie and Jake and eyed him acquisitively.

'Tiffany's married to Ferdie Miller, Manchester's new striker,' simpered Weezie.

'Forward,' corrected Tiffany.

'She used to be a model.'

'I always fancied being one of those,' said Fee, spilling out of her dress. She looked across the room to where Guy Fulton was holding Tashie and Lucy Wainwright in thrall.

'You see, girls, there are seven magic lessons in life—'

'Not including boob jobs and abortions, you mean?' Tashie giggled.

'If you'll just excuse me,' said Jake, eager to escape Tiffany, who was rubbing up against him like a Siamese cat.

'Tiffany and Ferdie have just moved back from AC Madrid,' continued Weezie breezily.

'Milan,' snapped Tiffany.

'Great party,' said Jess to Jake, as she headed with Vic to the dance floor, where Rupert and Julian were making the most of both having the night off and Marina and Lily were dancing with the rugger buggers. 'Oh, hi, Orlando, I didn't expect to see you here,' said Jess, raking her eyes over a stoop-backed girl in serious-looking glasses and miles of Accessorize hippie beads. If she thought they would brighten up her truly horrendous frock, she was sorely mistaken, thought Jess happily. 'You must be Myfanwy.' She beamed, as Myfanwy turned round properly and she saw full on how deeply plain she was. 'I'm Jess.' She pumped Myfanwy's claw-like hand. 'And I'm really, really happy to meet you.'

Upstairs, the sultry strains of the Wessex Salsa Five floated across the warm still evening and through the windows of Cat's bedroom as she stared at herself anxiously in the speckled mirror on her dressing table. She was having second thoughts about the strapless black silk dress she'd bought in Dorchester and about her hair, which was either sexily abandoned or a complete mess, depending on one's familiarity with catwalk trends. As she rose to the challenge of finding a wrap, she heard a gentle tapping.

It was Jake. He poked his head round the door. Her heart jolted as she saw his reflection. For one moment their eyes locked in the mirror before he wrenched his away.

'It's my party and I'll have a style crisis if I want to.' She grimaced.

'You look wonderful.' He walked into the room, dodging the puddles of discarded clothes. She stood up and turned to face him, hoping he would move closer. But they both remained stubbornly where they were.

'So do you.' It was as if the air between them had sprouted nettles – she might as well be Sleeping Beauty trapped permanently in her poky, God-forsaken turret.

'Daphne almost didn't recognise me.' He grinned. 'Come on. You're missing a great party.'

There was a minor kerfuffle outside as a gold Bentley barrelled up outside Butely's front door. Cat looked out of the window and saw Villie Frupps's chauffeur helping Mrs Frupps, in baby pink elephant taffeta, out of the passenger seat.

'Hurry up, please,' said Villie imperiously. 'I have a speech to make.'

'Oh no,' groaned Cat, 'a message from our sponsor.' She laid her head on the dressing table in mock horror and to her delight felt Jake's eyes boring into her back.

'Then you'd definitely better come down – and stop him.'

A sudden gust blew the casement window open and hurled a vase of roses off the table. Jake reached forward to catch it just as Cat stood up. For a second their eyes and lips were level. Cat closed her eyes. It was now or never, she thought. She knew Jake wanted to kiss her as much as she did him. Suddenly his hands were in the small of her back, pulling her up towards him. Her lips pursed like a closed flower and she felt a swooning sensation as Jake's face came closer. She could feel his breath on her cheeks now. Oh God, she'd wanted this for so long and now it was finally happening. The sweet, heady smell of nicotiana and honeysuckle floated in through the windows. Outside, the Wessex Salsa Five were singing 'They Can't Take That Away from Me'. She clasped his adorable face and pulled it towards hers.

'Oh, Cat, darling . . .' Suzette swept into the room like the bad fairy in Sleeping frigging Beauty, wanting to know whether Cat had any straightening irons. Jake sprang back to the other side of the room, quick as a fox, while Suzette twittered on apparently regardless. 'This damp climate's playing havoc with my hair and I've only got American plugs . . .' She trailed off. 'Am I interrupting anything?'

'I'll go down and stall Villie,' mumbled Jake, stalking out of the room.

'Anyone I should know about?' Suzette asked chirpily.

'No,' snapped Cat, who was beginning to have *déjà vu*. She eyed her mother's immaculate locks suspiciously.

'Actually I came to see you about something else.'

'You amaze me.'

'Don't get waspish. It really doesn't suit you. You look absolutely wonderful, by the way. Country life seems to agree with you.'

'You look nice too,' said Cat grudgingly, taking in her mother's very expensive dress.

'Saint Laurent.' Suzette preened. 'Everyone said it would go off after poor darling Yves retired, but you know I think Tom Ford's almost better. Of course, he can't compare with Yves in his heyday but—'

'Is this a conversation you need me for?' Cat grabbed a pale pink shawl and tossed it over her shoulders. 'Only I'd better get down before I miss my party altogether.'

'Yes, you better had. And you deserve it.' Suzette fumbled in her clutch bag for some Neal's Yard calming spray. 'I just wanted to say that I'm very, very proud of you, Cat. I know how much you've achieved here already – and I know I haven't always been there for you—'

It was the first time Suzette had ever alluded to her shortcomings in the maternal department and in that moment any bitterness, any rebellious grudges Cat had ever nursed against her mother, evaporated.

'You're not so bad,' she mumbled.

Suzette sat down on the edge of Cat's bed and patted the eiderdown next to her. 'Come and sit down. You're making me even more nervous.'

Cat's heart began thumping again. Surely her mother wasn't going to tell her she'd had IVF and was expecting quintuplets? She sat down queasily and allowed her mother to stroke her hand.

'A long time ago I did some very foolish things,' began Suzette. 'And with the wrong people, or so I thought at the time. But I want you to know that I never regretted having you for one minute, my darling.'

A lump formed in Cat's throat.

'Got any ciggies?' Suzette cast her eyes round the room.

'I don't smoke.'

'You used to.'

'You were saying.'

Suzette decided the best way to take the next few fences was at a Grand National gallop. 'Yes, well, your father wasn't really dead when I said he was. I did it to protect you really. I'd seen friends tear their children apart when their marriages failed and I thought we'd be happier in our own little unit. Which is why I never told you about Rodney.'

'Rodney?' said Cat, momentarily bewildered.

'Sir Rodney.'

'You mean he's—'

'Your father. 'Fraid so. I would have told you earlier, but it was all so awkward.'

'For you, you mean.'

'Don't be like that. I can see I was terribly, terribly wrong. But it didn't really hit me until this afternoon, when I saw that portrait of Evelyn Dowell. She's the dead spit of you, Cat. I can't believe you didn't spot it. She's even got the diamond and ruby bracelet

Rodney gave me all those years ago. Look—' She fished a glittering strand out of her bag and placed it round Cat's trembling wrist. 'It's yours,' she said, her lip quivering. 'I want you to have it. It's now where it rightfully belongs. Suits you too, darling. Which is lucky, because I'd never have thought rubies were your colour.'

But Cat wasn't listening, because all she could take on board was the fact that Jake was her half-brother. She buried her head in her hands and let out a pitiful sob. Just her luck. She'd finally found her father, only to lose the man she loved.

25

Cat floated down the staircase to her party as if she were in a dream
– mute, passive, completely unable to control events.

The torches lining the terrace and the drive only added to the air
of make-believe. Butely looked wonderful. *She* looked wonderful.
At least according to anyone who stopped to speak to her she did
– and that was just about everyone. And they all seemed to be
enjoying themselves.

She was dimly aware of the Wessex Salsa Five playing 'I've Got
You Under My Skin' as she skimmed through the crowd looking
for Jake. By now, all the downstairs rooms were filled to overflowing. It seemed that the villagers had taken it upon themselves
to share Cat's big day with her, whether or not they'd been officially
invited.

It took ages to find Jake and then, as she was about to give up
and retreat to the bar, he suddenly swung round from a cluster
standing in the hallway and disarmed her all over again with that
unexpectedly dazzling smile of his. Cat took his hand and followed
him as he led her to where the Wessex Salsa Five were playing and
allowed herself one precious dance.

But of course one dance led to three and then Cat found herself
seriously wondering whether she might get away with not breaking
the news to Jake at all. After all, no one was saying they had to have
children. Then reality bit like a vituperative alligator. She asked
whether they could go outside. Hand in hand they strolled past little
animated groups on the terrace who all seemed to be smiling
benignly at them. If only they knew, thought Cat bitterly. She
shivered and quickened her pace until they'd left everyone behind.

Beyond them a three-quarter moon hung suspended over the sea like a giant rose petal.

'I'm sorry about my mother interrupting like that,' began Cat, wondering how many more times in her life she'd have to apologise for Suzette.

He smiled and pulled Cat towards him to keep her warm. He had never been so playfully intimate. She could smell his skin and feel his heart beating. 'She's quite a character, isn't she?' He took her hands in his and kissed the freckles inside her left wrist.

'I suppose she's been telling you about all the marches she used to go on with Julie Christie? Or the letters Jane Fonda sent her?'

'She did mention something about them. What's the matter?' he asked, looking at her tenderly. 'You're acting like a ghost. Are you regretting sharing your intimate thirty-fifth with all these people?'

It was now or never.

'Nothing's the matter.' Even to Cat, her brightness sounded implausibly hollow. 'Look, an owl.'

'It's a squirrel.'

'Oh.'

He leant towards her and kissed her lips gently before pulling away. Cat tilted her chin up towards him. And suddenly they were kissing again, much more urgently. Eventually Jake pulled away and gazed at her so tenderly she almost decided not to tell him anything. 'I can't tell you how much I've wanted to do that almost from the first day I met you.' He smiled and drew her against him again.

A gust of wind rustled through the trees and she brushed the hair out of her eyes. All of a sudden, Jake seized her right wrist. 'What's this?' he asked, fingering the ruby and diamond bracelet. Even in the moonlight, Cat could see the blood leaching from his face. Toby, she couldn't help thinking, would have noticed the bracelet long before he'd have realised anything was wrong with her. He'd probably have given her a rough estimate of its value too.

When Jake finally coaxed her into delivering her bombshell, she almost wished he was Toby. But only because Toby would have made a joke about keeping things in the family as well as convincing her that marrying a half-sibling would probably drum up some valuable publicity for Butely.

They talked through everything, reaching the conclusion that Jake would have to go away – probably to New Zealand, probably indefinitely. Indescribable though the pain of separation would be, it was nothing compared with the pain of seeing each other every day, knowing they could never be together. And then they talked it through again. They even discussed what would happen to Guinevere. Jake was keen for Lily to have her while he was away, but Cat thought it would be too upsetting for them all to be constantly reminded of Jake, so in the end it was decided they'd ask Barry Dean whether his family would have her. Throughout their conversations, neither of them broached exactly how long Jake was planning to go for – or even whether he was ever planning to come back.

Telling Lily was heartbreaking. They tried to do it casually and present the news that they were all related as a wondrous twist of events. But Lily was far too savvy to be fobbed off. She had watched Cat and Jake becoming closer and closer – and had mapped out a cosy life for the three of them, just as Cat had.

She hardly ever cried, and when she finally crawled into bed after she'd made them repeatedly explain things to her – as if hearing them again and again would help her to discover the flaw in their argument that would prove they'd got everything wrong – she felt so exhausted she almost thought she'd never cry again. But when Jake dropped round two days after the party to say goodbye to Lily, she realised just how wrong she'd been.

Cat did a lot of brooding over past relationships in the weeks after Jake left Lower Nettlescombe. She now realised that Toby and Ben, in their diametrically different ways, had both represented a rebellion against Suzette. Whereas everything she had felt for Jake had come from the heart. They were meant for one another. He was her perfect other half – perfect, that was, apart from that small detail about incest. Who in hell's idea had it been to get so damn picky about that?

For the first fortnight she mooched around Butely like a particularly badly dressed tramp, barely changing out of her tracksuit – and when she did it was only to climb into a similar one. She couldn't get animated about anything, not even when Daphne rushed in breathlessly one morning to tell her their first crop of lavender was almost ready for harvesting. It was Lily who eventually took her to task.

'For heaven's sake stop dripping around the place feeling sorry for yourself. I miss him too, you know.'

Cat looked at her daughter aghast. Lily had been so stoical on the face of things that Cat, sunk in her own misery, had assumed her daughter was coping brilliantly.

'It's just our luck. We find out we're related to a knight – and then we find out the man who could have been my stepfather is my uncle. Bloody typical.'

'Lily!'

'Well, it's true.' She slammed the fridge door open and searched vainly for some decent food. Jess had been too busy lately to raid Micky's freezer, and Cat kept forgetting to eat. Gloomily Lily went to the pantry for some cornflakes. Cat blew her nose loudly on a hankie and slumped even further over the mug of coffee she seemed to have been nursing for the past two weeks.

Lily swept her eyes disdainfully over her mother's faded tracksuit trousers and the darned green jumper of Jake's she'd been wearing for weeks. 'You know, I think I preferred you when you weren't interested in men. Couldn't you at least go back to being a workaholic?'

As ever, it was work which saved her. Fortunately, there was plenty to do. Now that Butely had such a glamorous state-of-the-art pool, all the enquiries they'd had in the past were turning into firm reservations, and Cat rapidly found herself in the surreal position of having to open a waiting list for bookings. The shop began to take on a life of its own too, as patients clamoured to buy bottles of the treatments Dr Anjit had administered to them during their stay.

At the end of June Fortnum and Mason confirmed a huge order for Guy Fulton's sausages, as well as agreeing to take all of Caleb, Brian and Mimms's salad vegetables. They also expressed what they called a 'warm interest' in seeing the winter crop when it came in. Better still, Mark Wainwright, who'd been downright sullen towards Cat ever since she'd put an end to Goran's moonlighting on his Spar, made laboured overtures to woo her into supplying vegetables for Millhouse Foods, as he'd rechristened the Spar. He even sent her a bunch of all her favourite flowers, with a note imploring her to fix a business lunch with him since her carrots and lamb's lettuce were the best in the county. Even this couldn't arouse Cat to anything more energetic than a mild level of apathy.

They'd been open four weeks when Millie van Peterson from American *Vogue* turned up. Swallowing her bitterness over the way Millie had let them down last time, Cat cannily placed her in a vast double overlooking the tussocks and the sea. It also happened to be next to a suite in which Nick Wilde, a handsome Oscar-winning actor, was staying while he lost some weight for his next role as a Bosnian soldier. Cat knew she ought to be thrilled by these visitations. Frau Frupps certainly was when she heard about them.

Millie wrote an ecstatic review. 'Who needs porcelain sands and azure seas,' she wrote, 'when you can have the loamy soil and lambent coastline of Cornwall? This is just the place for communing with nature, feeling at one with the county's best-loved author, Sir Oscar Wilde, and working on some inner body conflicts all at the same time.'

Fortunately the subs at American *Vogue* were used to Millie's ramblings and corrected her gibberish just in time. But Cat couldn't be bothered to get thrilled about anything much at the moment. She even contemplated moving back to London – anything to get away from the memories of Jake. Everything reminded her of him. Each time she looked out of the window across the moonlit lawns on one of her many sleepless nights, she thought of the way he'd held her on their last evening together and the thrilling intimacy of that first dance. When she shuffled round the grounds she thought of all their walks, of that sleepy but graceful loping stride of his. And when she curled up on the chesterfield in the sitting room at night she remembered the countless times she'd plotted their future together. It was hopeless. She couldn't turn on a light switch, chuck a piece of coal on the fire or pass the pool house without thinking of the scores of kindnesses he'd done them and the well of good sense and decency that had prompted them.

It wasn't really as if she had anything more to prove at Butely. But one look at Lily's reproachful eyes, the single time she floated the idea of going back to London, sent her scuttling back to her mug of coffee. Besides, Demelza had sent them one of her hand-crafted cards, made out of sequins and bits of Sahri fabric, telling them how happy she was in Makesbury Road and how much work she still felt she had to do there. Preston, the estate agent at Fiend & Duffer, told Cat that Stig the pot-head had moved out of number 19 and was having an affair with Demelza.

Gradually, life returned to normal – or a semblance of normality. It was true that Cat didn't feel as though she'd ever be able to listen to Frank Sinatra or Ella Fitzgerald or Billie Holiday or *South Pacific* ever again. And it was equally true that she often found herself singing the words to 'Why Do the Birds Go on Singing?' But for Lily's sake she pulled herself together. At the end of the first fortnight, she put all her tracksuits in the dustbin. As Lily said – and she was after all Suzette's granddaughter – self-respect began with self-presentation. So Cat washed her hair, put on some nice clothes, went back to her computer and slowly but surely began to feel like a human being again. A broken-hearted one, perhaps, but at least she could *feel*. And although she didn't always consider this to be an improvement on numbness, she knew that in the long run it was healthier.

★

She thought about taking up jam-making and other therapeutic rural pursuits, but settled for tidying the house when she couldn't sleep and going for walks again. The first walk felt very peculiar – knowing that she wasn't going to bump into Jake by Hangman's Stile. Each blade of grass, each tree, each wild flower seemed to bear traces of him. But she kept going and gradually she started to feel a bit better, physically at least. She never felt like any of Thomas Hardy's more cheerful heroines any more though – only a very miserable Tess.

She didn't know what exactly inspired her to give yoga another try – apart from a vague suspicion that if she could learn to take life a bit less seriously, it might stop trying to have a laugh at her expense. What was it Ralph had said about the seventh wave, whatever that was? Something inane. She'd been thinking about Ralph and his philosophies quite a lot recently.

Jess turned out to be a gifted instructor. She didn't encourage her pupils to cry in class or tell them their sweat was God's flowers. And to Cat's astonishment, she wasn't more interested in looking at herself in the mirror than helping everyone else improve their techniques. She darted round the studio like quicksilver, easing people into positions they never imagined they'd achieve, laying her hands lightly on their bodies and paying as much attention to the older students as to the rugger buggers. She even got Marina and Lily to join in sometimes. Cat didn't expect to find redemption through yoga. But her muscles got stronger and she started sleeping better.

'You're an amazing teacher,' Cat told Jess after her fifth class in as many days.

'Thanks – I think.'

'I mean it.' After she'd stretched, breathed, twisted and crawled her way inside every position, Cat was finally beginning to see the point of it. Perhaps it was something to do with seeing the world upside down – it changed your perspective. 'I can't believe how good you are.'

Jess looked at Cat archly. 'I suppose you're going to get competitive about yoga now, are you?'

'I don't know what you mean.' Cat sounded injured. 'It's not as if I'm going to be coming regularly.'

'No, obviously. That would mean opening your mind.'

'Perish the thought. But I may drop in occasionally, just to monitor things.'

In July Jim dropped in to the Cottage's gleaming kitchen to tell them with ill-concealed pomp and circumstance that Declan had finally been apprehended in Málaga.

'Nice cuppa, by the way,' he said, eyeing the teapot hopefully. 'Lapsang?'

'Possibly,' said Cat. 'And possibly not.' The tap dripped balefully. 'What was he doing there? I thought the last we'd heard he'd disappeared into the ether somewhere over Jersey.'

Jim leaned forward conspiratorially. 'Between you and me, I never did rate my colleagues in Jersey. I shouldn't say this, but ever since *Bergerac* they've sort of rested on their laurels.' He straightened up. 'But we at the Dorset Constabulary are made of sterner stuff. Turns out our friend Mr Kelly had hooked up with that sheikh of his again and was engaged in some shifty horse-trading. They'd been doing a lot of deals in Málaga.'

'Did he admit to starting the fire?' she asked nervously. She had thought her happiness depended on seeing Declan brought to justice and placed somewhere he couldn't harm her or Lily for so long that she could hardly bear the thought of following the progress of whatever trial might unfold.

'More or less. Shouldn't be a problem to prove it now we've established that he was the only person who knew how to work those heaters. And that verdict from the insurance company that the heaters had been tampered with will probably turn out to be a blessing in disguise. And there's always Mr Marks's evidence, which makes a fairly watertight case against him.'

'What about the phone calls?'

'Ah, well, that's the funny thing, see. He seems genuinely not to know anything about those.'

'I see.' Cat sounded crestfallen. So they must be somehow connected with Cynthia, or Toby. What a pair . . . poor Jake.

'Probably just one of the locals,' said Jim. 'Still, at least they've stopped now, haven't they?'

Cat nodded.

'And the main thing is we've got Declan Kelly by the goolies. Trouble is' – he reached for the teapot sorrowfully – 'you can't ever tell with judges these days. They'll probably let him off with a light caution and a round-the-world holiday.'

Cat nodded. Declan's capture and – hopefully – imprisonment, which had preoccupied her so much at one point, barely impinged on her thoughts at all. She realised now that happiness didn't depend on it, because she was sure she was never going to feel happy again.

At the beginning of September the annual Butely fête was set up on the village green again. Pleading work commitments, Cat kept her involvement to a minimum, to the secret relief of everyone, even though they all had to admit that the previous year's fête had broken all fund-raising and attendance records. But still, with Cat in charge it had been a bit too much like hard work.

Taking a break from manning Butely's fresh produce stall, she nipped over to Daphne's gypsy caravan for some fortune-telling. Daphne peered intently into her crystal ball and told her that the next three months would contain three life-changing events.

The winter of her discontent, thought Cat. That was all she needed.

But Daphne was right. The first life-changing event was when Lily and Marina moved to Dorchester High in the second week of September. The second came in October, when Jess, who had been acting in a strange, jittery manner for days, finally plucked up courage to tell Cat that Vic had asked her to marry him.

'And I've accepted,' she added hastily, before Cat said something incriminating.

'I wasn't going to say anything. I think Vic's wonderful. I just . . .' She looked at the happiness etched all over Jess's face. 'Well, I envy your certainty about things to do with the heart, that's all.'

Jess looked at her with a puzzled expression. 'Nothing's ever certain, Cat. But in the end, you have to trust your instinct. It's the only thing any of us have to go on. Oh, and don't worry. I don't have to move out just yet,' she continued hurriedly. 'Not while you're still . . . not quite yourself.'

Cat was touched by Jess's concern – and by the idea of her and Vic together. And she was gratified to find she didn't resent their happiness. In a crazy way, they made a perfect couple. Perhaps she would never quite get back to being her old self after all. And maybe that wasn't such a bad thing. She brooded over what Jess had told her about instinct. Ralph had pretty much said the same thing, and so, in her way, had her mother – over and over again. Maybe they were right. If she'd gone with her instinct, instead of always trying to rationalise everything the way Simms had drummed it into her to do, she would never have got involved with Toby in the first place. She wouldn't have been so stubbornly opposed to Jake . . . It was a hopeless line of thought. But one she couldn't resist following.

What she dreaded most was Christmas without Jake. Last year's had been so perfect. She wondered whether she was destined to mark every future Christmas in the same way – her sixteenth without Jake; her fortieth . . . It was an unbearably bleak prospect, especially when Jess tried to cheer her up by offering to cook them all Christmas lunch over at Vic's.

'Are you sure you're all right?' she asked Cat one night over a hastily assembled supper of Micky's leftovers.

'What do you mean?' asked Cat defensively. She'd been making a monumental effort to be cheerful lately for Lily's benefit.

'It's just that you seem so calm these days, you almost appear not to be noticing anything.'

'Give me strength. You spend five years telling me not to get so het up. Then you moan about me being laid back.'

Jess leant back in her chair and surveyed the slightly too tidy kitchen thoughtfully. 'It doesn't suit you quite as much as I thought it would . . .'

There was a scramble in the hall and the sound of someone tripping over some rollerblades.

'Cat?' Daphne burst into the kitchen, her face a crumpled tangle of lines and wrinkles. Cat had never seen her look so old.

'What's the matter?' said Cat in alarm, expecting to hear that Lily had had a bad fall from Sir Galahad.

'It's Jake,' said Daphne. 'There's been a terrible accident. The hospital telephoned Ashdown House from Auckland. Lord knows why they bothered. Cynthia's sunning herself in Barbados again, of course. But at least Harbury had the sense to let us know.' She shook her head tearfully. 'I always said that bike was a terrible idea.'

The only details Cat gleaned from the nurse on duty when she called was that there had been a horrendous collision with a school bus and a lorry on a steep bend outside the city. As usual, from what she could gather, Jake had been trying to do the right thing. 'He was trying to warn the oncoming bus about the lorry. He tried to turn back, but the lorry didn't see him and ran him down. He's very brave, Mrs—'

'McGinty,' said Cat automatically.

'Are you related?' asked the nurse suddenly.

'Yes,' said Cat sadly.

It took every last atom of Machiavellian wiliness Cat had ever learned at Simms to find a flight to New Zealand three days before Christmas. In the end it was Villie who lent her enough for the only available seat – in first class.

'I am admiring you for going, though frankly, my dear, if it's as bad as you say, maybe you should save your money,' he wheezed from his country estate in The Royal Berkshire.

It wasn't the ideal Christmas, sitting next to Jake in intensive care, watching his heart monitor peak and dip like a wordless Shakespearian tragedy. But even though all she could do was squeeze his hand, at least she felt she was doing something.

Squeezing, hoping, trying not to cry. And watching her lovely, soulful half-brother. It was all that was left for the moment.

It was a tiny hospital, and within a few days all the staff knew about Cat and Jake and were rooting for his recovery. 'He must be a very special brother,' said the sister, 'for you to have flown all this way. Though why he hasn't got a wife beats me.' She swept her eyes appreciatively over his motionless body. Then she looked at Cat's lifeless face and left her to her vigil.

'What's the matter?' asked Cat in a terrified voice as a doctor and two nurses bustled into the room with an exaggerated calm she had come to recognise as trouble.

'He needs more blood. He's lost a hell of a lot,' said the doctor curtly. He was a locum Cat hadn't seen before. 'We're running low.' His shoulders were set doggedly. 'It's Christmas and everyone's playing silly buggers on the roads.'

'Take some of mine, then, for God's sake.' Cat pulled at her sleeve savagely.

The two nurses eyed the doctor. 'She's his sister,' explained the dark-haired one. 'So it could just work.'

'What do you mean, my blood's no good?' stormed Cat. Jake needed a transfusion and suddenly they were niggling about details.

'It's not that it's no good,' explained the nurse again. 'It's just incompatible. Lots of brothers and sisters don't share the same blood group. Look.' She showed Cat Jake's notes. There were some hieroglyphics that looked like –D-/-D-. 'It's extremely rare,' continued the nurse with discernible pride in her voice.

Cat swallowed. This didn't seem the moment to celebrate Jake's medical exclusivity. 'So do you have any that matches?'

'Nope,' said the nurse serenely. 'But don't worry, it's not a big deal.'

'Of course it's a big deal,' thundered Cat. 'Where are you going to get some extremely rare blood in New Zealand when the rest of the world has closed down for Christmas and all you've got to call on is ten million sheep?'

The nurse smiled at her pityingly. 'We may be smaller than your big smart London hospitals, but we're not completely primitive. We'll find some blood – and you'll be amazed how quickly too. The first thing is to contact his mother.'

'She's on holiday,' said Cat automatically. It was true. The whole of Lower Nettlescombe had been agog at the number of times Cynthia had been to Barbados that year.

The nurse crinkled her nose. 'I hear phones have been invented.'

'What's the likelihood of her blood matching?' said Cat, growing hysterical.

'About one in a thousand,' said the nurse chirpily. 'But it's worth a shot.'

For the first time in years, Cat found herself praying.

A glimmer of a frown rippled across the locum's brow. Things must be dire. It had been six hours since the hospital had sent out an alert for blood – and still no sign of Cynthia. Harbury had obliged with the telephone number of her hotel but it was the middle of the evening when the hospital called and she was out at dinner with friends somewhere. Typical, thought Cat bitterly. Even in the middle of the Caribbean Cynthia managed to have a jam-packed social diary.

She turned back to look at Jake. He seemed so still and pale and unbelievably fragile, her heart twisted in anguish. She didn't know what was worse, watching the life ebb out of him or seeing the sympathetic expressions of the nurses when they poked their heads round the door.

At some point – Cat had lost track of time long ago – the nurse who had exasperated her so much over the matter of blood came in with a mug of hot tea. She placed it on the table next to Cat. Then, just as she was about to leave, she came over and hugged Cat.

Cat didn't let go of Jake's hand once. She talked and talked – partly to keep herself rooted in the room. She told him what they would do once he was better. How he'd come back and help her run

Butely. How they'd make everything work out. How having him there as her brother was better than not having him at all. But she didn't know whether she believed any of it.

At a quarter to two in the morning Barbados time Cynthia Dowell was scrupulously removing her make-up when the phone rang. For several rings she ignored it. Wiping off the day's traces was one of her unmissable rituals, one of the reasons, probably, why she still looked, according to Toby, not a day over thirty-nine.

But the tone was persistent. Probably Gerald calling to apologise for his appalling drunken behaviour earlier. Ever since his wife had filed for divorce he'd been impossible.

'Yes?' she said loftily.

'Lady Cynthia Dowell?' said the voice from Auckland. 'Thank God we've finally tracked you down. This is Doctor Mayes. I'm afraid your son has been involved in a serious accident.'

Visions of Toby on a respirator flashed up before Cynthia. The cloud of cotton wool she was holding fluttered to the floor and she almost dropped the phone. 'Is he—?'

'He's lost a lot of blood. And it's a rare group, Lady Cynthia. That's why we're calling you. We need to give him a hell of a transfusion, and fast.'

The breath was trapped in her chest and she struggled to speak. 'But I'm in Barbados – it's going to be hours before I can get to Singapore—' Tears streamed down her cheeks, freckling her silk dressing gown.

'Don't worry about that. We can have the blood flown out. We're not in Singapore, by the way. We're in New Zealand.'

It took a moment for her to process the information. Then relief flooded through her. 'You mean it's Jake that's had the accident?' Her breathing began to steady.

'Yes.' Dr Mayes sounded confused at the change in her tone. 'Lady Dowell, would you happen to know off the top of your head what blood group you are?'

'Of course,' she said crisply. What sort of idiot did he take her for.

Dr Mayes' heart sank as she told him. 'I take it, from your response, that that's no help,' she said curtly.

'No,' said Dr Mayes despondently. 'It isn't.'

'So pointless me coming, then?' She scooped up the cotton wool from the floor.

'What about his father?' said Dr Mayes quickly. 'Could you tell us where we could find him?'

Her heart began to pound again. She said nothing for what seemed a long time, while her conscience did battle with her common sense. 'How ill did you say Jake was?' she asked eventually.

'Jesus, that Lady Dowell's a bit of a cold fish, isn't she?' said Dr Mayes when he went in to update Cat.

'You could say that. Still, at least her blood comes ready frozen.'

'It's the wrong type, Cat,' he said as gently as his brusque manner allowed.

She looked at him with hollow eyes.

'But the nurse is trying his father now. Don't give up.' He squeezed her hand awkwardly.

'What is the nurse, then?' said Cat. 'A medium?'

Dr Mayes frowned.

'Our father's dead, for God's sake.'

'He sounded remarkably perky for a corpse,' said the nurse, bustling into the room. 'And what do you know? He's a bloody –D-/-D – excuse the pun. As miracles go that's almost up there with the virgin birth. Happy Christmas, everyone.'

26

'I always knew everything would work out in the end,' said Suzette.

Cat grinned at Jake and nuzzled her cheek against his hand, which was resting on her shoulder.

'More lemon and ginger zinger anyone?' Lily set the big glass jug down on the garden table. It was a beautiful, balmy evening, and they were taking advantage of the weather to eat out.

'It is rather good,' said Suzette. 'Micky's?'

'Yes, and he's put me in charge of marketing it,' said Lily proudly.

'Has he, now?' said Suzette approvingly.

'Yes. Mum and Jake think it will be a good outlet for my entrepreneurial flair. I'm placing it in Butely's shop and Mark Wainwright's to begin with. But after that the sky's the limit.' She turned on her heels, her long colt-like legs bolting across the lawns in search of Eduardo, who was in the pool house.

'Quite the perfect family, aren't you?' said Suzette contentedly. Cat looked into Jake's eyes – those eyes whose colour she'd never quite been able to determine – and pulled a face. 'I'd like to think that was partly down to my example,' continued Suzette. 'Though it would have been nice to have been present at your wedding. I would have been, of course, if you had given more than two hours' notice.'

'Like you gave me?' said Cat. Not that she was cross. Far from it. Lately she'd been seeing Suzette's good points more clearly than her bad ones. Come to think of it, lately she'd been seeing everyone in their best light. Perhaps that was what they meant by happiness. And she was happier than she'd ever imagined. At first all she'd wanted was for Jake to get better. Then he had and she'd just wanted to enjoy not being his half-sister. And then, out of the blue, he'd asked her to marry him as he was helping her over Hangman's Stile. And out of the blue, she'd said yes. Instinct was a wonderful thing.

'Anyway, if you and Eduardo stay on a few more days you'll be able to come to Jess and Vic's wedding. You always were such a fan.'

'As it happens I have come round to her way of thinking a little.'

'Since she told you she'd help you with that yoga book, you mean?'

'Eduardo's got another two hundred lengths to do,' said Lily, returning with the jug. 'Can I show you the packaging I've designed, Sukes?'

'I do hope you're going to make sure she doesn't get exploited?' Suzette sighed, as Lily went to fetch her computer print-outs.

'Not much chance of that,' said Jake. 'Mark Wainwright said dealing with Lily made negotiating with the CBI look like a piece of cake.'

'Good,' said Suzette. They watched the sun skim the tops of the trees, its rays bouncing off the sea in the distance. 'Why do you think your mother was so keen to claim Sir Rodney as your father, Jake?'

'When you were so keen to disown him, you mean?' said Cat.

'You must admit it's a bit ironic. And Guy Fulton's terribly attractive. Frankly, if he'd fathered one of my children I don't think I'd have been able to keep quiet about it.'

'I suppose she liked the idea of me being heir to all this,' said Jake. 'And she was furious with Guy at the time for dallying with Fee. And don't forget, she was married to Rodney when she conceived me, so I don't suppose it would have been particularly convenient having to admit that Guy Fulton was my father.'

'She wasn't at your wedding, I assume?'

'No,' said Jake quietly.

'Luckily for us she was abroad when we got married,' said Cat. 'And I must say when it was confirmed that she had been behind those horrible phone calls we weren't entirely sorry she couldn't be with us.'

'How did you find out about that? Don't tell me that ridiculous policeman got to the bottom of it.'

'Actually it was Edna Potts who gave it away. She mentioned to Jake one day that she'd seen Harbury sneaking out of a phone box in the middle of the night. She'd been up with indigestion and heard a noise across the village green. Naturally she *never* gets indigestion, so she was able to remember the exact night. Anyway, Jake confronted Harbury, who was so cross at the way Cynthia had just upped and gone to live in Barbados, leaving him out of a job, that he confessed everything.

'With that rich banker?' Suzette asked casually.

'Sadly,' said Cat sweetly, 'he dumped her in the end and went back to his wife. Said no amount of broken china could be costlier than running Cynthia. Still, she's not totally evil. She did come clean about Guy Fulton in the end. And if it weren't for her "Rural Idyll" columns I'd never have been interested in moving to the country in the first place and . . . well, the rest is history.'

'I still find it extraordinary that a national newspaper could commission a weekly column from such a complete amateur,' said Suzette disdainfully. 'Still, I suppose that's British journalism for you. And where did she get that ridiculous name?'

'Candida St Green, or Lady Cynthia?' said Jake.

'Point taken. Anyway, now it *all* belongs to you, Cat,' said Suzette dreamily.

'Technically,' said Cat.

'So it's down to you to decide what to do about the oil?'

'I'm not going to do anything with it,' said Cat sleepily.

'But it could give you financial security for the next ten centuries,' said Suzette. 'And I'm sure you could rearrange the land afterwards just as Capability would have wished.'

'That may be.' Cat yawned. 'But we can get by just fine without the oil. So we've decided to do just that. At least for the foreseeable future. And who knows, in years to come we'll probably let a much more serious business mind than either of us decide.'

'Who?' asked Suzette. 'Not Toby, surely?'

'Hardly.' Cat smiled and nodded to Lily, who had come back to the table and was running her eye down a spreadsheet forecasting next year's profits for Micky's ginger and lemon zinger.